CW00706308

DON'T YOU WANT ME?

Richard Easter

This edition first published in Great Britain in 2020 by The Vivid Press.
thevividpress.co.uk

© The Vivid Press/Richard Easter, 2020

Richard Easter has asserted his rights under the Copyright, Design and Patents Act, 1988, to be identified as the author of this work.
This paperback ISBN; 978-1-9162169-4-5

All rights reserved. No part of this publication may be reproduced, stored in a retrieval system, or transmitted, in any form or by any means without the prior written permission of the publisher, nor be otherwise circulated in any form of binding or cover other than that in which it is published and without a similar condition being imposed on the subsequent purchaser.

AUTHOR'S NOTE

Some of the locations and most of the characters in this book are fictitious. But to the best of my knowledge and research, everything else is factually correct for the time period, April - July 1981. Also the story reflects the standards, attitudes, and language of its time.

So to those who were there and those for whom this is their first time, welcome to 1981. It was a hell of a year.

Richard Easter, August 2020

/ An end, a beginning.

Everyone's life begins and ends with a single heartbeat, and Jeanette West had reached her last. But as her breathing slowed and became shallow sighs, at least she was warm, her surroundings familiar and much loved.No dreams flickered behind closed eyes, no final thoughts nor memories of a life lived well.

West's mind had faded and body would soon follow, but she wasn't alone. Someone stood at the end of her bed and smiled as she died.

Jeanette was only the first.

1 / 29th July, 1981. London.

Beep beep. T-Bom-Bom. Tikitatikatatikatatikata. Ki-Bom-Bom.

Anna Leeding's clock radio sounded at 7:15 a.m. and DJ Mike Read was on the air. "A brand new sound from a brand new band!" He seemed inordinately thrilled by the idea. "Climbing the chart, it's Soft Cell with "Tainted Love" on 275/285, National Radio One."

"Please God, no," Anna moaned as her hand grasped for the off button. Soft Cell, whoever the hell *they* were, bleeped on relentlessly.

Beep beep. T-Bom-Bom. Tikitatikatatikatatikata. Ki-Bom-Bom.

Oh. Oh, here I am. She managed to think. *Good God, my head feels like it's full of lighter fluid.*

She opened her eyes and stared at the ceiling. Anna's mind vibrated with low level humming, a slightly queasy sensation as if her brain sloshed about untethered, so she let the music *ki-bom-bom* to its conclusion, too drained to care.

The DJ blasted back through the fadeout. "I think that could be a future number one, what about you? But there's no "Tainted Love" today, that's for sure, ha. Today's a celebration and Kool And The Gang have just the song! Is it too early for a party? No!"

Yes, for the love of God, it is. I don't want Kool or any *of his gang right now.*

Anna slammed down the OFF button before Kool's backing vocals had *whoo-whooed* their first *whoo-whoo*.

Silence, at last.

Oh. Last night. Oh.

She closed her eyes again and tried to remember details but nothing focussed at first. Anna remembered the general arc of the evening, occasional phrases, images, a drunken stumble up Great Portland Street. They'd started at the Yorkshire Grey near the BBC, then the Crown & Sceptre, then...*a lot was said, wasn't it? My God, yes. Too much? No. Yes. Everything changed. Agh, with all this going on,. I can't afford a hangover.*

As she gingerly swung out of bed the liquid rolling returned, so Anna grabbed her temples with both hands and risked a glance in the wardrobe mirror.

Amazing.I've aged five years in one night, forty-three already, no TARDIS required. She pulled at the bags under her eyes.*Oh Jesus.*

She turned her head this way and that, studied the wreckage that had been a blonde bob yesterday, then ran her fingers through it. Anna had kept almost the same style since the sixties since, like herself, it needed little maintenance and fitted virtually every social situation.The bob fell into place as required, her dried out brain protested and she managed to creak to her feet.

*

Anna had a brief wrestling match with a dressing gown before she managed to pull it into submission, then padded out into the hallway. Her ground floor flat was just off Tottenham Court Road, so she could walk to work in less than ten minutes. That was a blessing and a curse; blessing, since she could lie in until the very last moment, curse, because she was often dragged in with very little notice.

A scrap of paper with a smudged phone number sat on her hallway table. Anna looked at it thoughtfully then gave a little smile.

Unexpected, Jesus, so *unexpected but very welcome.I'll think about that later. Coffee.My head needs coffee. My* life *needs coffee.*

She walked into her tiny kitchen, flicked on the kettle then dragged herself into the boxy living room.

The television screen regarded her blankly and just as impassively, she stared right back. It was an eighteen inch Ferguson which rarely saw action, but was all she needed. Anna certainly wasn't going to buy a video recorder any time soon, since she had no reason to save any TV shows for posterity.

Today's viewing, however, was different.

She glanced up at the clock. 7:50 a.m. Generally at this time, BBC1 broadcast the last few minutes of the Open University, followed by the test card then programmes for schools. The same went for ITV and BBC2, but not this morning.

Anna sat down and marvelled at *actual* TV on so early, because today Prince Charles and Lady Diana Spencer were to marry. After they'd announced their engagement in February, Royal Wedding fever had infected Britain and now the main attraction was finally here; The Charles & Di Show. So in a breathless break with normal scheduling, both BBC and ITV were to cover the entire event. Anna knew the streets around St Paul's were already mobbed, since some keen royalists had bagged their places days ago to get the best view. The cameras panned over their tired but excited faces.

1981. She watched the reds, whites and blues. *God, look at it. I can't keep up, it's crazy. I've seen so many police getting pelted I can't even tell where in the country the riots are happening any more, or why. Who knows, or cares? These happy people don't. Ah, never mind, have a cup of tea and a bourbon, there's a wedding on.*

There were two versions of Britain this year, both with hundreds of people on the streets, either royalists or rioters, cheering or protesting. Which country you belonged to depended on where you got out of bed; Brixton or Buxton, Toxteth or Totnes. So while some places might have petrol bombs today, most would enjoy fireworks. For the majority, the riots weren't just geographically distant but mentally, too. The flag wavers on TV just slid past the headlines and looked for the latest shots of Diana.

Here we go again, running away from facts and into fairytales. Mind you, nothing new there, she thought.

It wasn't just the older generation, either. Teens and early twenties were also taking refuge from 1981, but in music and fashion rather than pomp and circumstance. Every youth cult since the '50s was back on the streets; Teds, Skins, Mods, Rockers, Rude Boys, Soul Boys, Rockabillies, Punks, and now, just in time for the 1980s, the New Romantics.

The New Romantics looked like they were at a fancy dress party with no theme. Anna had seen them on the streets; pirates, highwaymen, aristocrats with frills and floppy hair. Even Lady Di sported a blonde fringe and frilly blouse, so occasionally the princess to be looked like a singer on Top Of The Pops.

The New Romantics escape reality by dressing up out of it, but their motive is the same as those cheering crowds; whatever it takes, whatever fantasy works, get me out of this. Get me out of 1981. Anna stared at the TV. *What fun this year's turning out to be. All the R's. Reagan, riots, royals, Romantics and Rippers.*

Since the mid 1970s, the north of England had been terrorised by a multiple murderer who preyed on women using a ball-pein hammer.

He seemed to have an uncanny ability to elude capture by moments then fade into darkness, so the newspapers had predictably dubbed him the Yorkshire Ripper. For years, he'd attacked and killed women across Greater Manchester and Yorkshire, but after each assault he'd simply dropped off the face of the earth. Like his nineteenth century namesake, the Ripper had become a folk devil and the subject of countless theories. But unlike his Victorian progenitor, he was eventually pulled into the light. Last January, a routine number plate check turned up some highly incriminating evidence in the car of one Peter Sutcliffe, who confessed almost immediately. The man who'd murdered thirteen women and attempted to kill another seven had finally been caught by complete accident. Once the trial started in May it became obvious that Sutcliffe's crimes were enabled by luck on his part and incompetence on that of the West Yorkshire Police. Chief Constable George Oldfield had put much store on a taunting letter and cassette tape which claimed to be from the killer, but these turned out to be hoaxes which had sent the police down many dead ends. At the trial, although Sutcliffe pled manslaughter through diminished responsibility, the jury sent him down for life many times over.

Anna often wondered if she could have caught the Ripper any quicker. It was impossible to know, a futile exercise in *what if*, but as a woman she might have approached the case from a different angle. Then again, perhaps being female was neither here nor there. Sometimes you had to ignore what was in the mirror and become who you needed to be. She'd done it a lot over the last few years.

Anna supposed she wasn't far removed from the beaming crowds, waving royals, screaming rioters and pouting Romantics. You did what it took, *became* what it took to get through 1981.

The kettle indignantly hissed from the kitchen, so she slouched back, poured herself a cup of coffee then returned to the TV.

BBC1 was busy telling the whole story of the fairytale romance again, complete with now familiar clips; Diana and her engagement ring, Diana racing from reporters in a Mini Metro, and nursery teacher Diana with the sun streaming through a thin skirt to reveal her legs.

Ah, Di, Anna tapped out her first cigarette of the day. *It doesn't matter if you're about to become royalty, when there's a bloke behind the lens, watch out. And they haven't even started with you yet. They haven't even* started.

Anna was well aware of what the press could do if they really put their minds to it. She hung the cigarette from her lips like Bogart and scanned the crowd.

You? Is it you? Maybe you? You? Are you there? Where are you? Who are you?

All those people and not one of them knew what was happening in their city.

Peter Sutcliffe, like the tool of his ghastly trade, had been a very blunt instrument, allowed to destroy lives through luck and incompetence.

The person Anna sought was of a different order.

If Sutcliffe was a hammer, then this person was a scalpel, so sharp, you couldn't see the cuts until the thinnest sliver of blood appeared. Unlike the Ripper, *this* killer didn't act on impulse or blind fury, since it seemed every step had been worked out to the smallest detail. For the last three months Anna had tried to follow a complex dance but was left spinning as she tried to keep up.

While Sutcliffe had played out his terrible act in the spotlight, this person stayed backstage. Nobody outside Anna's orbit even knew about this particular drama, which was so authentic it looked like real life. People had even seen the spectacle happen but just walked on by.

There was a serial killer working in plain sight and nobody had seen their crimes. Nobody except Anna, and now it appeared she was supposed to.

The crowds wore plastic Union Jack bowler hats, waved flags and home made signs. Leeding saw Romantics and royalists, but willed herself to see a Ripper.

You? You? Is it you? Are you there, or backstage again, ready to cue the next act, feed us our lines? Is it you? Is it you? Or you?

As Anna watched, her head tick-tocked left-to-right, right-to-left, left-to-right, then she blinked five times in quick succession but didn't seem to notice the movement. For a moment her expression was blank, but then she raised the cigarette to her lips, inhaled, scanned the crowd and thought.

And so it was on the morning Detective Inspector Anna Leeding died.

2/ 6th April 1981, London.

Three months earlier, D.I. Leeding had stood on the doorstep of number ten Selly Mews, West One.

*

Hidden behind Harley Street, Selly Mews was invisible to most passers by, exactly how the wealthy residents liked it. Their places were often second homes worth fifty-thousand pounds or more. Last time Anna checked, her poky flat was worth maybe four, maybe five thousand, if anyone would have even considered buying it.

But Selly Mews was different. The street was cobbled, flowers hung from baskets and little china orphans watched from windowsills. It had a quaint chocolate box quality out of keeping with the exhausted city around it. The surrounding buildings reduced traffic noise to a barely audible hum and that stillness was surprising because London's busiest point, Oxford Circus, was barely two minutes away.

Anna scanned the Mews and saw a police Rover SD1 was parked unobtrusively at one end. *Good*, she thought. *No point coming in with the federals spinning. Softly, softly, as that old TV show said.*

The weather had been unseasonably cold this April. Some parts of Britain had already seen dense snowfall, which was predicted for London, too. She rubbed her hands together and knocked on the door of number ten.

It opened just a little and a WPC looked through the gap. Anna held up her warrant card.

"Oh, ma'am, it's you," said the WPC, who opened the door, automatically stood to attention and looked a little surprised.

"Uh huh, it's me, morning." Anna stepped into the hallway.

"Morning, er, ma'am." The WPC seemed uncomfortable.

New girl, thought Leeding. *Getting her first dose of reality.*

OK, first impressions.

Perfume. Not mine, certainly not the WPC's, so, the owner's?

Thick cream carpet, gold painted (maybe even leafed) dado rail.

Glass, flower shaped lamp shade, also with gold trim.

Clean. Maybe obsessively so.

Female owner, then, almost certainly, or theatrical. Creative. Likes to project class. Concerned with appearance.

And, oh, I see. A broken wine glass on the carpet. No stain in that expensive shagpile,though, so it was white wine.

Anna looked at the shards of broken glass then glanced up a stairway to her left.

Fell from up there, did it? Or dropped down here?

These first impressions took just a couple of seconds and were non binding. Generally Anna was right on her initial sweeps of a scene but never assumed so until the facts were in. She looked back at the WPC and extended a hand.

"We haven't met yet. New, aren't you? D.I. Leeding."

The WPC wasn't sure whether to salute or shake hands, so went to perform the former before she turned it into the latter.

"WPC Lisa Fisher, ma'am."

"Hm, good name for someone on the force. Fisher, I mean."

"Yes, it's been said."

Anna took in the officer. *Probably about twenty-five, which means she's come to the force later than most. At twenty-five, she should have been a WPS by now. Perhaps she's just not very good at her job and promotion had passed her by,* but Anna didn't think so. Fisher gave off an air of efficiency and intelligence and still looked fresh and optimistic, which suggested she hadn't been too blasted by the experience as yet. The WPC couldn't stop staring, which Leeding found a little off putting.

She's a little out of her depth. I remember the feeling.

"So why am I here, Fisher? All I was told was suicide."

"Inspector Walker didn't want to go on the radio with too much detail. The, er, subject is high profile, you see. He was keen to avoid press,er, scuttling and skittering all over the place."

"Scuttling and skittering?"

"His words not mine."

"Yes, I guessed. High profile? High profile how?"

Fisher cocked her head at the stairway. Up its length was a constellation of framed photographs which all featured the same woman. Anna mounted the stairs, then gasped.

"Jeanette West? It's *Jeanette West?*"

"Yes ma'am."

At the tail end of the '60s, after Twiggy and The Shrimp had kicked open the door, a second wave of It Girls had flooded through, including Jeanette West. First spotted on the King's Road in a bikini top and mini skirt (she'd known exactly what she was doing and where she was doing it) "Westie" was quickly scooped up by The Swinging Set, partied with Stones and Beatles at the most exclusive hangouts, and crucially appeared in all the right magazines.

In 1974 she married businessman Clive St. Austenne, who'd become both her lover and manager. Born in the East End as Clive Tripp, he'd changed his name to St. Austenne to project the image of a jet-setter. Jeanette West, however, kept the maiden name she'd become famous with.

Anna recognised some of the photographs from '68, '69, which gave her a curious sense of sadness. Leeding was on her way up the ranks back then, but West lived in another world. In those days, while Anna walked the beat in flat shoes and starched shirt, Westie stalked the catwalks in mini skirt and Quant.

I used to wonder what it might be like to meet you, she thought. *And now I'm going to, in a way neither of us could have imagined.*

There was Westie opening champagne with Simon Dee, Westie arm in arm with Clive St. Austenne and Keith Richards, Westie in a trucker's wet dream line up of Veruschka, Penelope Tree and Pattie Boyd. Then, right in the middle of the stairway in pride of place, the iconic David Bailey shot of Jeanette naked on a Hyde Park swing.

"I used to have a copy of that." Inspector David Walker stood at the top of the stairs. "I spent *hours* studying it." He didn't sound lascivious, just melancholy. Anna had known David since they'd both attended Hendon Police Training College in the early '60s. She'd once blagged an Embassy Regal off him in the local pub, then they'd fallen into each others' orbits.

Walker looked like he'd spent years on a North Sea trawler rather than the force. He had a handsome yet weathered face and green eyes which often twinkled with inner amusement.

David was rugby wide to Anna's tennis lithe, so she reversed back off the stairway and let him pass. "Hello, D.I. You've met Fisher, then?"

"I have. Since she's standing right there, it would be difficult not to."

"Only her first week and she's been vomited on twice."

"That's what happens when someone gets partnered up with *you*, Walker."

"It wasn't me who did the vomiting."

"I did guess that. I was making a joke."

"Which made me laugh a lot," replied Walker stone faced, then allowed himself the ghost of a smile.

Pleasantries over, the inspector pulled out his notebook.

"Right. I called you because the deceased is Jeanette West, thirty-three. You know of Jeanette West, I gather?"

Anna looked up at the photographs again. "David, please. I'm not a hermit. Yes."

"Hence why I didn't mention her name on the radio. You never know who's listening."

For years, the press had monitored police frequencies to get early warning on any news worthy incidents, which forced dispatchers and officers to use ever changing radio codes to stay one step ahead.

"So, she has a book out, er," he consulted his notes again, "it's called "Phoenix Rising". Nice title. It's her biography."

"Autobiography," corrected Anna, airily. "If they write it themselves, it's an autobiography."

Walker haughtily crossed out the word on his notebook, then, with tongue between lips in concentration, wrote in a new one. "*Au…*to…*biog…*ra…*phy*. You learn something every day, don't you? So she was making a big comeback. Which is why she called it "Phoenix Rising," see?"

"I did get the reference."

"Right. Her career had gone a bit quiet for a few years but was on the up again, did that BBC comedy with whatsisname, Donald Sinden. She was supposed to be on, er, Pete Murray's Sunday Show talking about her *autobiography* yesterday morning but never showed up and missed an interview with the Daily Mail yesterday afternoon too. Her husband Clive St. Austenne, who's also her agent, is in Los Angeles right now on business. He's been calling, trying to track her down. She doesn't have friends or family local so he called us. Myself and Fisher popped round, knocked, no answer. Then I looked through the letterbox and saw *that*."

He nodded at the broken wine glass on the carpet.

"Jeanette West doesn't seem like someone who'd just leave a glass on her Axminster. That seemed a valid reason to be concerned for the safety of the occupant, you know, preservation of life and that, so we knocked again, then, er, affected an entry."

Anna turned to look at the door, which seemed intact. She raised an eyebrow at Walker who patted his trouser pocket, from which sounded a metallic clanking. "Well, as luck would have it I *happened* to have the Universal Keyring on me. Just in case."

In the course of their work, police would often retain "*helpful evidence*" once a case was over. In this instance, a ring of skeleton keys had proven invaluable in moments like these, when someone's immediate wellbeing was considered in danger. Preservation of life was the first priority when attending any incident.

"OK, noted. Go on."

"We entered at 11:17. Fisher took a look round the downstairs, I went up and, well, you'd better come and see."

Anna sighed and thought, *I've seen too many corpses and every single one has taken up residence in my head, right back to that first one…well, a long time ago.* She prepared herself to add another to that awful list. After attending an incident or autopsy, Leeding would scrub herself raw but couldn't ever wash away those faces. She looked up at the photographs on the stairway again.

Every single one of those is about to be superseded by what I'm about to see, she thought. *To remember any of these photos of Jeanette West, I'll have to go through what's upstairs first. Corpses tend to rise to the top of one's recollections, barge out all other memories of that person.*

"Fisher, the next person through that door is the crime scene photographer. Nobody else, OK?"

"Yes, sir."

Anna turned to Walker, surprised.

"You called for the *photographer*? Already?"

He paused for just a moment but Anna recognised the hesitation. She'd seen it before.

"Uh huh. I'm preserving the scene, but I thought it was best to get a photographer sooner rather than later."

Best for who? Anna wondered, and slowly climbed the stairs. She turned back to the WPC. "Oh, Fisher, once you've admitted the photographer, talk to the surrounding neighbours. Be vague, tell them there's been an incident in the street, see if they offer anything but don't give out any details, OK?"

"Yes, ma'am."

She turned back to Walker.

"Let's get this done, then."

3/ 6th April 1981, Jeanette West's house, London

There were more photographs of Jeanette on the landing and most involved one celebrity or another.

The whole place is a shrine to herself, Anna examined the shots. *So what went wrong? Did Keith Richards stop calling? Did 007 not want you back? What got so bad you wanted out of all this?*

She popped her head round the bathroom door, which was exactly as she'd imagined it. Gold taps on a corner bath, black and white tiling on the floor and walls, a huge mirror flanked by onyx cherubs. Anna opened the bathroom cabinet to reveal various ointments, aspirin, tampons, Elnett hairspray, a big tub of Oil Of Ulay…The bathroom could have come straight from a catalogue, in fact, everything Anna had seen so far totally lacked any kind of personality. Were it not for the photographs, the whole place would be devoid of those little touches that make a house a home.

Looks like Jeanette lived within photographs rather than reality and the main function of this place was simply to provide walls to hang her life on.

Anna stepped back onto the landing while Inspector Walker waited silently outside the front bedroom. He'd seen his colleague work enough times and knew she was forming an overview of the entire area. She flashed a tiny smile at him and opened another door.

Anna stepped into the back bedroom, unsurprised to discover it had even less character than the bathroom. There was a fitted wardrobe, single bed with crisp, folded down sheets and puffed up pillows, bedside table and airing cupboard. *A guest room, perhaps? It certainly has the air of an anonymous hotel suite. But unlike a hotel room, there are no paintings or photographs. The walls are bare. Odd.*

From downstairs came the sound of a knock. Anna heard WPC Fisher speak, then another voice. The door shut then there was a thudding sound as someone made their way up the stairs. It was the photographer and she recognised his voice. *Ah, Daniel. Good, that's good.*

From the back room windows Anna could see down into a small paved yard, with a few plants in pots around the edges. A metal gate stood in one corner and behind that, a thin alleyway.

Anna knelt, looked under the bed and found a brown leather suitcase. She gently pulled it out by the edges, took a fresh handkerchief from her pocket and carefully popped the latches. This wasn't a murder but the scene still had to be preserved.

Inside lay a pair of pleated trousers, a couple of blouses, two pairs of Y-fronts, socks and bizarrely, some white kid gloves. The combination didn't make any sense. There was also an overnight bag which contained a Gillette razor, shaving brush and soap. Beneath was a Maybelline lip gloss, Coty Shape 'n' Shadow eye make-up kit and Boots eyeliner. She frowned, looked over the strange collection and tried to find a context. *Oh, wait, it makes sense. This is Jeanette's overnight bag. The blouses and make up are hers, but the male items were...whose? Must be the husband's.*

Something about the suitcase bothered her, but Anna couldn't work out what.

She went back to the windows and saw the one on the far left had been slid open an inch or so. Anna turned and realised there *was* a photograph in here, but leaned up against the wall and hidden by the bed.

Of course, the photo was Jeanette. From West's appearance, Anna guessed this one dated to the late 1960s/early 1970s, a black and white head and shoulders portrait. Jeanette stared down the lens, head insouciantly titled back, lips parted *just so*. Anna carefully tipped the frame forward and handwritten on the rear was, "DUFFY '71." David Bailey *and* Duffy. This woman really did move in the rarest of fashion circles.

It's a beautiful photograph. Legendary, even. So why's it been shoved behind a bed, leaned against a wall and hidden from sight? Anna wondered. *Jeanette clearly loved to stare at her glory days, so why has this one been demoted? Did she fall out with the photographer? Did it remind her of bad times? If so, why not just put it in the back of a cupboard? Throw it away?*

Jeanette gazed out of the frame and offered no answers. Maybe there were none *to* offer. *Sometimes things have no meanings and we layer our own reasons onto them. Stick to what you know, and guess what? Right now, you know nothing.*

She sighed and headed back to the landing. Photographs presented one face, but now Anna had an appointment with the real Jeanette.

4/ Sometime *before (1)*

In order to understand the present, you must look into the past.

*

Butterflies tumbled around the buddleja and insects hummed about the grass as she sat in her garden and pulled at the daisies. One daisy chain already hung from her wrist and as she worked on another, her tongue poked out in concentration.

It was nice to find daisies, because Father hated them. They were weeds and he despised anything that affronted his sense of order. *"Without order there is chaos!"* His face would redden if a cup was placed on the wrong shelf, a newspaper left open or when daisies grew uninvited. Mother arranged her larder so the labels faced outward; Bird's Custard, Merry Monk Plum Tomatoes, Fry's Cocoa, Bisto, all perfectly displayed as if they were in a shop window.

Mother and Father always cared more about how things *appeared* than how they really *were*.

She'd once gone on a school trip to a recreation of an Elizabethan house and realised her own home was the same. Oh yes, it looked authentic, but was just a Land Of Make Believe. Everything sat in the right place, but like Mother's larder, was only for show.

Visitors were rare except for Uncle John and uncomfortable relatives who sat ramrod straight and silent at Christmas. Eventually they'd compliment Mother and Father on their "exquisite taste," but guests never realised everything had been copied from magazines. This wasn't her parents' genuine style, they'd simply used "Woman And Home" as an instruction manual for life.

She completed her second daisy chain and sat back, cross legged.

Apart from the occasional bird and buzz of flies it was still and quiet. No music ever tumbled from her windows and laughter was rare as a dragonfly. She occasionally saw neighbours in their gardens as they sat together, talked, giggled and happily set out trays of tea and biscuits. They seemed like impossible people who spoke in imaginary languages which tinkled like bells.

There were no clouds today. She looked up at the blue and knew there was a whole world out there and a whole universe *up* there, yet here she was, alone again.

In summer the other girls from school dressed in light, airy skirts. She'd seen them from the back seat of the car as they skipped along streets, held hands with their parents, were lifted up and swung between them.

It was a scorching hot July day but Mother still made her wear layered, starched dresses, as if at any moment it would be time for Sunday Service in her Sunday Best. She was *always* in Sunday Best whatever the occasion, like one of the expensive yet tacky ornaments carefully placed around her house, there to be seen and admired, but no more.

On the street strangers would always compliment Mother on her pretty, beautifully dressed girl. Mother would take the praise and appear affectionate but in reality was simply proud of her achievement. She'd managed to make a shop mannequin look like a real eleven year old daughter.

Everything here was an act. She woke, got dressed, ate breakfast in silence, went to school (and school was another unbearable Land Of Make Believe, where teachers were magically blind and deaf to the taunts, bullying and name calling) came home, ate supper in silence, then went to her pretend bedroom where the few toys were also merely displays rather than objects of pleasure.

Mother and Father *acted* like parents and in company she *pretended* to be a happy daughter because if she didn't, there was always hell to pay later. The Land Of Make Believe had to be real to everyone else, so if she failed to play the part of *daughter* according to her parents' unwritten rules, she would be punished.

She knew what they were doing was wrong. Other children existed, she did not. She saw enough of them to recognise genuine laughter and joy and wondered why she never felt those emotions.

The kitchen door opened behind her.

Mother and Father rarely used her name apart from in company.They'd even named her after a stupid rhyme, which gave the bullies another angle of attack. Her parents would simply start to talk and their tone of voice indicated she was the subject.

"We're going to the Curzon Suite tonight."

She turned to face Mother, who was never anything less than dressed to meet royalty. She couldn't remember ever seeing her in any state of dishevelment. Mother's hair was always perfect, never without its rigid, sprayed structure. She held a cigarette in one hand and grasped the door frame with another as if posing for Cecil Beaton. She resembled Jane Russell, whilst Father nurtured a tweedy, rakish, David Niven image.

The Curzon Suite was a Function Room in town where Mother and Father met, talked, danced and ate with Very Important People. It was an island just off the Land Of Make Believe.

She waited. One never spoke until prompted and she became aware that her hands shook, despite the heat. If Mother and Father were going out, that only meant one thing.

"So Uncle John will be looking after you until our return."

Mother hadn't even glanced her way during this announcement, just stared at the garden, probably to find an errant blade of grass. "Very well, so, that's that. Do whatever Uncle John says." Mother turned and went back inside.

She looked down at the daisy chain on her wrist then grabbed one hand with the other to stop it shaking.

Uncle John.

John wasn't a relative, wasn't even anyone's uncle. Uncles were old and jolly, she'd seen both them and *real* Mums and Dads in books. Uncle John was about twenty-five but still lived at home with his parents up the road.

Uncle John. Again.

She began to breathe heavily and pulled at the stiff starched collar of her dress. *Uncle John is not my friend. He makes me keep secrets.*

She heard a muffled *thump* from the grass followed by a high pitched sound. She turned her head this way and that to locate the noise, then found it.

A tiny chick had fallen from its nest and squirmed on the floor, where its stubs of wings slowly rose and fell in a pathetic attempt at flight. Again, it let out a thin, desperate call.

She searched for the nest but the foliage was thick and the chick's home would be well hidden.

She knelt and looked closer.

"Mother's never coming," she whispered. "Your Mother's never coming. She doesn't care. She hasn't even noticed you're gone. You fell and she *doesn't care.*"

The chick rolled and cried from the grass.

"She doesn't care," she spoke, louder. "She doesn't care. She doesn't *caredoesn'tcaredoesn'tcare.*"

Blankly she picked up a stone from the rockery and brought it down over and over on the bird. The first blow was fatal, but she continued to pulp flesh and bone into the dirt.

"Doesn't care," she breathed hard. "Nobody does. Nobody does."

Only then she realised there'd been a wide smile on her face the whole time.

5/ April 6th 1981, Jeanette West's house.

While Walker waited outside the master bedroom, the crime scene photographer's Olympus *click-fizz-click-fizzed* within.

"Anything?" The inspector asked.

"Depends. Maybe. I don't know. There's always *something*, though, isn't there? Everyone has something that looks dodgy without the right context."

"Ready?"

"Never," she sighed as he opened the door.

The master bedroom had yet more thick cream carpet, anaglypta wallpaper, a Laura Ashley dressing table, built-in wardrobe, frills, pelmets, drapes and lace. *Tick, tick, tick*, thought Anna.

A double bed stood to the right of the door and in her peripheral vision, Anna saw Jeanette there.

"Were the curtains closed, or did you…?"

"Closed," replied Walker.

"OK."

Anna took a deep breath and turned.

Head tilted back, eyes closed, Jeanette had propped herself up against the headboard in a silk robe. West had a full face of make up which still didn't conceal how white her skin had become.

Blood had soaked into the bedsheets and bloomed like giant petals around her hands. The cuts on her wrists went downward, and while movies often portrayed the wounds horizontally, that could cut tendons and make the process impossible to complete. Jeanette had known what she was doing. A razor blade lay by her right hand and at the left, pills spilled out of a plastic bottle.

First impressions.

No signs of a struggle.

Anna looked down at the carpet.

No sign she'd been dragged here. There are no marks on the carpet. The bedsheets are freshly made. Piece of paper on the bedside table. Note? Let's see. No blood anywhere else but by her wrists. Paracetamol and wrist cutting. She meant it, then. Not a "cry for help." Just pills would have made things trickier to determine. People sometimes overdose without suicidal intentions which leaves families left in limbo, but no chance of that here. On first impressions, she took the pills, then cut her wrists, denied any chance of coming back. Paracetamol overdoses often take days to compromise the liver but if the victim really goes to town, they'll go into convulsions before death. Look at the sheets. Jeanette hadn't convulsed, which means blood loss is what killed her. But I don't know that for sure, not until the autopsy. However...this looks like what it is.

WPC Fisher appeared in the doorway, stopped and stared.

"Oh," she whispered then regained her composure. "Do you need me for anything or shall I stay on the door?"

"Your first?" asked Anna, quietly.

"Yes, I've seen photographs, you know, at training college, but yes."

"Anything from the neighbours?"

"Nobody in."

"Doesn't surprise me. Most of these places are second homes, mainly left empty."

Fisher glanced at the bed then down to her feet with a combination of fascination and revulsion. Those were common reactions.

"If you need to go back downstairs I won't stop you."

"No," she replied firmly, "then I won't learn anything. I'll stay if I may."

Fisher took a deep breath and looked at the corpse. For a moment, Anna was worried the WPC would blurt out one of the usual *peaceful* or *sleeping* clichés, but she just matter of factly pointed to a piece of paper on the bedside table and asked, "Is that a note?"

"Uh huh, it is," said Walker, who turned to the photographer. "Got that yet? Can we pick it up?"

Daniel nodded then snapped off a couple more shots for safety's sake.

Jesus, this is so weird, Anna watched the photographer at work. *It's like some kind of sick photo shoot. I can almost imagine him barking orders at her like David Bailey, "Chin up, love! Chest out!" Lenses, tripods, flashes and film, that was her life and now it's her death. Could she ever have imagined her last photo session would be this? Wait. Maybe she did.*

"Am I OK to take a look?" Anna asked Daniel. "Got what you need?"

"Go ahead," he answered.

Anna reached into the breast pocket of her jacket and took out a small Swiss Army knife. She'd lost count of how useful this tool had been over the years. She pulled a little pair of tweezers from the end, then picked up the note by its corner. It was a sheet of Basildon Bond, slightly blue in hue, the kind of paper favoured by old ladies and new lovers. On it were a few typewritten lines. Anna read them out loud.

"I resisted so long, but I couldn't go on like I have before. People have used me, judged me, abused me simply because of my sex. I can't bear to be in this body any more, as I can't bear what people have done to me over the years. Not one of them has paid, apologised or shown guilt for what they did for me. So I am left with no choice but this. I do it with full knowledge that I cannot go back from this step. I must see it through now. No more. From this act, they will all know what they did to me. I have no choice any more."

"Bloody hell," muttered Walker. "She didn't want to be found or rescued. She was going all the way."

"Seems like that, doesn't it?"

"Did she sign it?" asked Fisher.

"Good question." Anna turned over the note but the rear was blank. "No, but suicides don't always sign their notes. Many don't even write one, that's a step too far. By that point, they won't be distracted by notes or reasons, they just take the pills, lie on the tracks or jump. Maybe even typing this was the extent of the effort she could make. I'm not so bothered about the lack of signature than the contents, though. We'll come back to that."

They all stood about the bed silently and Anna realised they must look like a family gathered at a relatives' last moments. Even without the blood, pills and pale face, you would still know this was a corpse. In her experience, Anna felt that dead bodies gave off a final stillness that sleeping ones never did. They almost spread an invisible fog of *anti-life* into their surroundings, a negation of vitality. *Perhaps humans are just hard wired to know the dead.* Anna considered. *Maybe we just pick it up, like a radar finds traces.*

"Any thoughts anyone?" Anna asked. "Anything anybody wants to say?"

She wasn't asking for eulogies but individual perspectives. Anna always encouraged everyone to speak up, no matter how off beam their thoughts and suggestions might be. With three other people present, that meant three more opinions, any of which could be invaluable.

Fisher began, hesitantly. "There were a couple of bottles of wine on the kitchen table downstairs. One empty, one nearly done. The only glass I saw was the broken one on the hall carpet. Perhaps she got drunk, staggered up this way, dropped the glass, came upstairs and…" She shrugged. Nothing more to say.

"Seems plausible. What about the arrangement?"

"The…?" Fisher frowned.

"Look at her. She was a model in life, she's one in death. This is like a cliché suicide scene isn't it? Propped up in bed like a tragic Rossetti, arms by her sides, pills scattered *so* poetically, note on the bedside table. I've seen quite a few suicides and none have looked quite as…artistic, if you forgive the word, as this one. They mainly look sad, lonely, and grotesque."

"What are you saying?" asked Walker.

"I'm not saying anything more than it looks like Jeanette knew exactly what she was doing, knew she'd be found, may have even suspected photographs would be taken. This may sound cynical but I think she planned her last "pose," if you like, to be this. This isn't just her suicide, it's her final modelling shoot. Anyone?"

Inspector Walker took another look at the body. "Possibly. I've seen suicide cases which looked posed, but who knows what someone in that state is thinking? I'm more worried about the note. May I?"

Anna handed him the letter using the tweezers.

"All right. So she writes, '*people have used me, judged me, abused me*' and, '*not one of them has paid, apologised or shown guilt for what they did to me.*' So who are '*people*'? What '*abuse*' did she undergo? What did '*they*' do to her?"

"Exactly. She's using this last *testament*, if you like, to say she was forced into this by others. In which case, a crime may have been committed against her at some point. If so, what and by whom? And why not just name them? If she's killing herself over what she clearly perceived as an injustice, then why hasn't she pointed the finger? She has our attention, then doesn't give us what we need."

"We'll start with the husband."

"Agreed. Daniel? Anything odd stand out from your point of view?"

Daniel Moore looked back around the room once more, as if seeing it for the first time. Anna was glad he'd been given this job. Daniel was quiet, reasoned, efficient, but best of all, didn't take himself seriously like some of the others. This job was serious enough without prima donnas. Anna watched him and noted how he always looked out of place. Even though he dressed soberly and appropriately, Daniel Moore couldn't help his looks and was sarcastically nicknamed "David Cassidy" by some officers. Despite being in his thirties, Daniel had a fresh boy-next-door face that never sat well at crime scenes. He had a ready smile, shaggy brown hair, clear green eyes and was, as Anna's mother would say, "A catch." She often imagined him breaking into, *"I Think I Love You"* at a crime scene, but thankfully, he never did.

Daniel blew out his cheeks. "I can't comment on psychology, or anything like that, but I can talk about what I *see*. That's my job. It's probably nothing."

"It might be something."

"No, I'm just thinking too hard. But, well, she has pictures of herself everywhere by the looks of things, but not in here. That seems a bit weird."

It was true. The rest of the house was a gallery with one repeated subject but here in Jeanette's bedroom, her image was noticeably absent. Anna was surprised she hadn't picked up on it.

There was just one small framed work of modern art, no bigger than a sheet of A4, in a plain white wooden frame. The artwork hung above the headboard about two feet directly above Jeanette's pale, tilted head. It was just one word, written in light blue charcoal on white canvas.

FACE

"Well, West's whole world was about her face, so I don't see your point," huffed Walker.

Daniel brought the camera up and took a couple more shots of the piece. Then he stepped back, went round to one side of the bed and studied the frame up close.

"Well, my *point*, and it's not much of a point, I admit, but look, another picture was hanging up here once." He traced a shape on the wall with his finger. "Look, you can see the slight mark. You asked if I thought anything was odd and," he spread his hands out and shrugged, "that's all I have to offer."

On the wall was a faint dark rectangle which showed the edges of where another, larger frame had once hung. Anna leaned forward, examined the shape, then looked back over her shoulder to the open door.

"Wait a moment." She left the master bedroom and quickly returned holding another picture.

"I spotted this leaning up against the wall in the back bedroom."

It was the head and shoulders Duffy portrait of Jeanette taken in 1971. Anna carefully bent forward and held the frame up against the wall. It exactly fitted over the dark mark there.

"Is that something important, ma'am?" asked Fisher.

"West fancied a change of interior design? Got fed up with seeing her own face everywhere? Although somehow I doubt it. Ah, I don't know." Anna placed the frame down against the bed and turned to the WPC. "You find these little odd things everywhere, in every case. At first they look weird and therefore important, but they're just life. People make decisions that retrospectively look suspicious or out of character, but you know, sometimes we *all* decide to take another route home, buy a new knife, or talk to a stranger in a bar. You have to obliterate all the random noise and concentrate on what counts. This," she pointed up to the picture, "is an oddity, but almost certainly nothing, unlike that note. Jeanette's suicide note alludes to a possible crime or *crimes* that led her to this, so we start there. OK, ask the Los Angeles Police to contact her husband, break the news in person, we'll need to talk to him. Also, this is going to get a lot of press coverage so let's keep everything to ourselves, don't even talk about it to colleagues. Remember," together, Walker and Leeding spoke, "*you never know who's listening.*"

Anna looked around the room one more time, locked it into her memory, turned to leave, thought, then opened the wardrobe door. Inside, under clothes on a rail, a little wooden trunk was pushed into one corner. Anna opened the box and found a pile of press cuttings, photographs and magazine covers, all about Jeanette. Yet more of her life in its own little treasure chest.

Anna's head tick-tocked left-to-right, right-to-left, left-to-right, then she blinked in quick succession five times exactly. Fisher caught the movement, frowned, then looked at Walker. He shook his head and put a finger to his lips.

"Something we should know?" he asked.

"Give me a moment."

She left the room once again, but this time took slightly longer. Meanwhile, as Daniel bagged up his equipment, Walker and Fisher took more notes.

Anna reappeared, face set, and Walker recognised that expression. She'd found something.

"What is it?"

"Uh huh. More like what *isn't* it. I haven't given the place a thorough going over, but…"

She suddenly squatted down, lifted up the bed valance and peered under it. "Nope."

"What?"

She gestured to the typewritten note on the table.

"So let's just posit a scenario. Two days ago, at a time yet to be determined, while her husband is away in Los Angeles, Jeanette West reaches the end of her tether, pushed into utter despair by whatever and whoever has made her so desperate. She drinks a bottle and a half of wine at least. She types a suicide note, staggers upstairs, drops a glass on the way. Then she lies here, swallows an unknown amount of pills then slashes her wrists. Jeanette also leaves the suicide note where it can be easily found. Seem reasonable to everyone?"

Fisher, Walker and Moore concurred.

"But here's the thing, we have the typewritten note, *so where's the typewriter?* West gets drunk, goes to take her own life, leaves a broken glass on the floor but tidies away the typewriter? I've looked pretty much everywhere. There's no typewriter. So when did she write this? And what on?"

Everyone looked back at the lifeless body on the bed as if it could suddenly offer an answer.

Anna stared around the room once again. "Where's the typewriter?"

6 / 6th April 1981, London.

WPC Fisher eased the Rover into the traffic around Harley Street with D.I. Leeding in the passenger seat. They'd left Inspector Walker to secure the scene at Jeanette West's home and wait for forensics and the ambulance.

Anna knew this case was going to attract media attention around the world, but hopefully the LAPD would soon track down West's husband and agent, Clive St. Austenne, to break the news first. Leeding had already begun to formulate a list of questions to ask him, but that particular interview was days away. For now it was a short ride back to Great Portland Street station to write up her report thus far.

Apart from a few anomalies, nothing stood out that made her consider this event anything other than suicide. The autopsy would confirm it one way or another, but the picture in the bedroom and the question of the typewriter were almost certainly oddities that would be explained once she spoke to St. Austenne.

The suicide note, however, asked more questions than it answered.

West had alleged abuses and guilt, so those lines of enquiry would have to be opened. This may have been suicide but its motivation could involve others and Anna was *very* interested to find out who they may be.

"Go around the block would you please?"

"Which direction, ma'am?"

"Turn left here, head up Harley Street toward Marylebone, left into Wimpole on to Cav. Square, round again. I want to remind myself of the area."

"Mind if I ask why ma'am?"

"I just want to see the context, all entrances and exits, if there are any more that is."

Fisher nodded, opened her mouth then snapped it shut again.

"If you have something to ask, please do."

"So do you think there's more to it?"

"Right now, no. But *should* there be more to it I just want to have some first impressions up my sleeve. West has a little garden accessed by an alleyway and I'd like to see where it opens up. Should be round here somewhere."

Anna reached into her inside pocket and pulled out a packet of Benson & Hedges. "Do you mind?"

"Not at all," smiled Fisher, "I'm part of the tribe myself."

Anna offered the pack to Fisher who hesitated, unsure of the protocol, but then shrugged and took a cigarette.

"A fellow smoker, hooray. We are part of a slowly dying breed, quite literally," Anna laughed and lit the WPC's B&H. "I remember when cigarettes were good for you. Then suddenly, 1971, I think, there were health warnings on the packets and smoking became a dangerous pleasure."

"A lot of pleasures are dangerous," Fisher inhaled and smiled.

"Mm, I'm increasingly of the opinion that everything good is bad." London slowly slid by, its buildings streaked black from decades of pollution. The whole place was thickly caked with grime and what was once the centre of an empire now looked like a shambling tramp. Even great landmarks like St Paul's had been painted with a grubby stain of neglect. There were even still a few World War Two bomb sites, which had been added to by the IRA in recent years. *These days, thought Anna, London seems to scowl at me. Maybe it always has.*

"Ah. Here, pull over, please."

Fisher obliged. Anna looked to her left and there, hidden between two buildings, was a tiny, shadowed entranceway. Leeding stepped out of the car and ventured into a thin alley where the only illumination came from the far ends. After a few yards it opened into another passageway at right angles to the first, lined with gates. Anna found West's, was surprised to find the gate open, so carefully pushed it inwards with her elbow and entered Jeanette's tiny yard.

She could see into the kitchen and above it was the rear bedroom window she'd stood at not forty-five minutes before. An iron drain pipe ran up the right hand side of the wall. Anna finished her cigarette, stubbed it out on the pipework and dropped the butt on the floor. Then she stopped and stared. By the drain cover lay the stub of another cigarette. *Wait. Did I see any ashtrays in there? No. And it didn't smell of smoke anyway. Smoke gets into the walls and fabrics like a background noise, you can't Shake'N'Vac it away.* She looked up. *That rear bedroom window was open. Hm, perhaps Jeanette smoked out of it and dropped her butts down here. Perhaps, perhaps.* Anna pulled out her Swiss Army Knife, extricated the tweezers and picked up the remains of the cigarette, just in case. Detectives have a long list of items they should carry at all times, contact numbers, spare pens, a torch, forensic bags and gloves, a fresh notebook…on and on it went, but it this case she'd been lax. She dropped the butt into her jacket pocket. *Maybe something, maybe nothing.*

Leeding was about to leave when she noticed something on the white wall up and alongside the drain pipe. What she'd first thought was yet more London dirt was nothing of the sort. She made a note to get Daniel Moore here to take photographs.

*

Anna climbed back into the Rover. Fisher had finished her cigarette and was listening to Radio One DJ Dave Lee Travis, aka DLT, aka The Hairy Cornflake, blather on about something or other.

"Did you find what you wanted, ma'am?"

"I'm not sure it's what I *wanted*, but…"

She fell silent.

"Would you like me to turn the radio off?"

"No, it's fine, leave it on. I don't mind Radio One, I'm not a pensioner yet."

"I was trying to find the news. See if they'd got hold of Jeanette yet."

"They're good but not telepathic, thank God. Although it's a quiet mews *somebody* would have noticed us going in, I'm sure. And if they didn't, then an ambulance taking away a body will get their attention. In my experience it'll probably break by about five. BBC news will have some vague details, Evening Standard late edition front cover, possibly. Tomorrow is when all hell will break loose. Sun, Mirror, the lot."

"What do we do?"

"We release a very brief statement and let the reporters do what *they* do. Can't stop them."

"It's the happy, happy sound of national Radio One!" trilled some helium voiced jingle singers from the radio. "You're listening to national Radio One," added DLT, pointlessly, "on 275 to 285!"

Following any violent incident, Anna, like many of her colleagues, tried to compartmentalise realities. So after leaving a disturbing scene, she'd quickly attempt to anchor herself back in normality. To an outsider, she knew it could look schizophrenic; one moment, an officer was bent over a blood drenched corpse, the next they smoked and joked. Everyone in high stress, high risk jobs did the same. It was the only way to stay sane.

In Anna's case, the more trivial the distraction, the better; TV, gossip, magazines…anything banal and uninteresting seemed to help dilute the brutalities of her profession. For now the nation's favourite, BBC Radio One, would do just fine.

"DJ's always sound so excited about everything," Anna sighed.

"Well, there's a lot to be excited about these days," added Fisher in sarcastic monotone.

"And once again can I add my congratulations to Britain's brilliant Bucks Fizz after an amazing Eurovision victory on Saturday!" yelled Travis.

"Case in point, ma'am, who wouldn't be excited about Bucks Fizz?" Fisher smiled.

"Oh please God, don't say he's going to play it," Anna moaned.

The deliriously sugary and enthusiastic opening bars of "Making Your Mind Up" began. Leeding groaned, louder. *If the Eurovision Song Contest could be distilled into just a few notes then those would fit perfectly.*

"Yep, shit, he's going to play it."

There hadn't been a war in Europe since 1945, but armed conflict had been replaced with a *ding-ding-a-dong-dong* musical battlefield called the Eurovision Song Contest. The UK's entry, a cheery foursome named Bucks Fizz, had won on Saturday with this breezy number. Undeniably catchy, it was helped to the top by a clever dance move. As the act sang the lyric, *"And if you want to see some…more!"* the two grinning lads had pulled the girls' long skirts off to reveal very short ones. It wasn't subtle but it was a masterstroke.

"You're tapping your fingers, Fisher, that's a bookable offence."

The WPC had been drumming her hands to the beat on her steering wheel, but stopped, embarrassed."Sorry. You know, if some bloke pulled my skirt off in public he'd be arrested, but do it in front of millions and you get a standing ovation."

Anna laughed out loud. "It's a topsy turvy world, officer. If the Bucks Fizz blokes got their trousers ripped off, we'd have come in last."

"Ugh."

The music continued, defiantly upbeat in a country on the edge. The car entered Cavendish Square and circled it.

"So, Fisher. Bucks Fizz. Your kind of music, is it?"

"Ooh, no, ma'am. I was a bit of a punk in my teens."

"No problem. I was a *bit* of a beatnik. How much of a bit?"

"Oh, mohair jumper, safety pin earring. Lots of eyeliner, but not so much of the attitude. More Generation X than The Pistols."

"Didn't mind punk, actually. They caused us a lot less trouble than the Mods, and the Teds when they came back in the early '70s. Mind you, I had a few problems with the Glam Rock crowd, too. I'm interested, Fisher, how does a punk become a WPC? Not many of us women in the police. Only just got a female dog handler a couple of years ago. In fact, I didn't get equal pay to the blokes until '74, I think it was."

"Well, it was almost by accident, really. I started in a desk job like everyone else, but that didn't have much of a career attached. A friend of mine up north joined the force in Manchester, so that got me thinking. I applied but didn't really believe it would go anywhere. Then suddenly I was in uniform and training at Hendon."

"Ah, I went to Hendon. Bugger all there but a good college."

"May I ask what made you join the force, ma'am?"

Anna paused and sighed. "My Dad."

"Oh, was he a policeman?"

"No. No, he wasn't."

From the expression on Leeding's face, Fisher knew she'd reached the end of that line of enquiry.

The Rover pulled out of Cavendish Square into Regent's Street. BBC Broadcasting House was on their left and somewhere in there, Dave Lee Travis had cued up the next record. "Well done, Bucks Fizz, flying the flag! And can I just say, not just the best *song* but the best *legs* in the competition! And I'm not talking about the blokes, ha! Now, as Monty Python once said, for something completely different. It went into the charts at number twenty-four last week, where will it be tomorrow? It's Grey Velvet, and "Ice Age" on Radio One!"

A moody electronic drum beat and pulsing synthesiser began, then a soft vocal crooned, "W*e are in an ice age, dancing on a cold stage, don't you turn our last page, or I will learn and burn and rage."*

"Jesus. Cheer up, love. A lot of this robot music around these days, isn't there? Ah. You're tapping your fingers again."

"I actually like this one, ma'am, more my cup of tea."

"So you went from a punk to a...what are they, a romantic?"

"New Romantic, ma'am, they call themselves New Romantics. Not Really. I don't dress as a Regency Dandy on my days off, I just like the music. Spandau Ballet, Visage, Human League…"

"All Greek to me. Thirty-eight already feels ancient these days. I don't mind this song, actually, I have to admit it's better than Shaking Stevens."

"Shakin' Stevens, ma'am, with an apostrophe."

"I stand corrected. That missing 'g' makes all the difference."

"It does. Shaky would be highly offended if you added a 'g'. "

They took a left into Great Castle Street then another into Great Portland Street, moments from the station. Anna thoughtfully tapped her nails on the dashboard.

"Fisher. Between you and me, I think there *may* be something else to this."

The WPC shot her a curious look as she turned into the station's underground car park. "Something else, ma'am?"

"When I went to Jeanette's garden, there was a cigarette butt by the drain. Did you see anything that suggested she smoked?"

"No. No ashtrays. Not even a lighter, now I think about it."

"That's what I thought. But it's not really about the cigarette."

Fisher pulled the Rover into its designated space, switched off the engine and waited.

"You see, there were scuff marks up the wall round the drain pipe. The window was open in the rear bedroom. It looked like…"

She pondered for a second, then committed to the rest of the sentence.

"…It looked like someone had climbed up it."

7 / Sometime *Before* (2)

She now knew that her primary school had been *heaven*. It hadn't seemed like that at the time, but as her English teacher often said, "You only know what you know," and back then, obviously, she hadn't known much.

What had then seemed like the most awful bullying had been nothing, the equivalent of tapping a dog on the nose. At primary school the girls had made fun of her stiff skirts, the boys pulled her pigtails, there'd been name calling, prodding in the changing room, giggling and whispering in the playground. But that was *nothing* compared to now.

She hadn't been able to tell Mother and Father. She'd tried, of course she'd tried. When she'd returned home with a rip in her stockings she'd cried that Joanne Watson had tripped her up, but Mother didn't listen, just shook her by the shoulders, gone to her bedroom then returned with the piggy bank, wailing and accusing. Mother had taken piggy to the back garden, shattered him against the paving and one piece caught her face, even drew blood, but Mother didn't care. She'd scrambled for the few shillings and pence on the ground, closed her Nivea creamed hands around them and screeched, "Now you can pay for more, can't you? You tear the stockings, you pay for the stockings!"

That had been bad, but then she'd seen Father in the dining room with a pipe in his mouth as if he were birdwatching, intrigued, perhaps, to see where this particular display may go. As he'd taken considerate puffs on the pipe his face became lost in smoke then reappeared as he glared at his daughter like he would stare at his radiogram; as an object and no more.

There'd been no point trying to tell her parents about any of the daily incidents that individually could be shrugged off but cumulatively settled on her shoulders until she slouched under them every morning. That brought the ire of Mother, too, who would slap her on the back of the head and bark, "Straight! Straight! Straight!" like a drill sergeant.

The only blessing was that Uncle John had moved away but she didn't know why. Despite being in his twenties, John still lived with his parents and one night, they'd come round without him. Mother and

Father had talked with them over the evening, but she hadn't dared sneak to the stairs and listen. Soon after that, John and his family were gone.

Good riddance to bad rubbish.

Primary school had been bad but if she'd known what was to come, she would have relished every second of its toxic innocence.

In their final year, children were given the 11 plus exam to decide which kind of school they would attend next; grammar, secondary modern, or technical. Grammar was for the children who were academic and would go on to university, technical for those going into a trade, or secondary modern which offered a bit of both.

She'd been terrified during that exam.

Mother and Father only cared about appearances, so there was no question that their daughter would attend anything but a grammar school. She was one of the smartest girls at primary, which wasn't difficult, since the others only excelled at hair, clothes and dollies. With no toys to distract her, she'd thrown herself into books. Mother and Father had no imagination, so their bookshelves consisted of biographies, historical accounts, atlases and encyclopaedias. She'd learned because there was no other option.

But even so, the thought of failure meant her hand shook throughout the test. The teacher even commented on how her handwriting *was normally so neat, so why have you got lazy today?*

One morning, a letter arrived to confirm she'd won a place in the nearest grammar. Mother and Father's expressions had been those of lions who had brought down a gazelle, a ferocious, predatory satisfaction. They weren't proud of their daughter, but were simply imagining the pleasure of telling "friends" and "neighbours," particularly those whose children had failed the exam. They lived by the law of oneupmanship and it wasn't enough for them to fly, everyone else must fall.

For a while she'd fantasised grammar school would be where the Good Children went. They were the most intelligent, so therefore it had to follow they'd also be the kindest and most empathic. She quickly learned that many of these children had parents just like hers and those apples hadn't fallen far from their trees.

Her grammar was split into two neighbouring buildings, which separated boys and girls so the genders only mixed when they arrived and left. She hated it. Not because she missed male company (Father and others had removed any notion of that) but because girls and boys had different methods of bullying. Sometimes it was a perverse relief to swap one gender's viciousness for another. *A change is a good as a rest,* Mother said, who neither changed nor rested.

But now she was surrounded by competitive and rapacious females. Yes, they looked like children, but were already metamorphosing into the pitiless adults they would soon become. Of course, not all the pupils were like that, but in a room full of mice it only takes one cat to create terror. While there were many mice at school, there were an inordinate amount of cats, too.

It didn't help that she was pretty and she quickly realised there were two types of pretty at school.

Pretty Quiet and Pretty Horrible.

The Pretty Horrible preyed in gangs, the Pretty Quiet tended to be solitary and easy pickings. Once formed up, the Pretty Horribles would often attack each other in some kind of territorial beauty war. Alliances were formed, deals made, leaders elected and deposed, all based on some kind of unpublished "Attractive Index" where girls at the top would wield the most power.

As one of the Pretty Quiet, she tried to make herself invisible but the whole point of pretty is that you get noticed. She deliberately let her hair become greasy and made her uniform as stiff and starchy as possible, but Pretty Horrible always saw through camouflage.

There was one gang and one leader in particular who always made a beeline for her. She didn't know what she'd done to deserve the punishment, but had obviously broken their unwritten rules, so every day they found another imaginative way to erode her.

Used sanitary napkins would find their way into her bag, or, in some cases, hair. Her blazer was defaced with chalk obscenities, books covered in crude cartoons which she supposed were meant to represent her, but couldn't marry the overweight, spotty line drawings with what she saw in the mirror. It was relentless. There was no way she could tell the teachers, and even if she had, they would have probably told her to "stand up for yourself." Then Pretty Horrible would know she'd "told," and would take revenge.

As she cried and shook in bed at night she wished evil upon them all, visualised cutting their pretty faces to pieces, flinging their bodies from cliff edges, burning, slicing, stamping her foot into their perfect features. She wanted to see them beg as she had pleaded, watch them cry as she had wept.

Her school work suffered, progress slipped. She'd been born into a world where one never spoke up, complained nor cried and now she was being educated in that same world. As her reports came back with phrases like *"not trying hard enough," "let down her early promise," "disappointing," "sullen and often rude,"* her parents ramped up their own disappointment. Caught between two kinds of bullies and punishments with different motives, she retreated further into herself.

Everything she *could* have gained from Grammar School had been taken from her. Well, nearly everything. She was still pretty and as she got older she became beautiful. But she hated that beauty because it was responsible for all that had befallen her. If she could have cut it away, she would have, but had to find a way to use her face.

One late night she sneaked from her house and crept to the gang leader's home. That girl would wake and see how her beloved rabbits had been attacked by a fox, dragged from their hutch and ripped to pieces. By this point it was a case of either cutting up the rabbits or herself. *Make it look like what it's not,* she'd thought. *Only I will know and it will be mine.*

As she crept back home again, hands red and eyes wild, her only regret was that she couldn't be there in the morning to watch the anguish.

But part of her was terrified. Not just at what she had done, but the thought that next time she would turn the knife on herself and not be able to stop.

8 / 6th April 1981, London.

Inspector David Walker had opted to remain in Jeanette West's home whilst the other relevant SOC officers made their way over. Usual protocol meant a lower rank officer preserved the scene, but he was worried the press would arrive and didn't want to leave WPC Fisher to deal with *those* vultures. They were very good at extracting information, even from experienced officers, so would work their dark magic on Fisher, no problem. A sergeant had arrived ten minutes ago and soon, Walker would hand over to him and start his logs back at the station. But before that he took one more look around.

He'd known D.I. Anna Leeding for years. They were the same rank but while she'd gone down the detective road, he'd stuck with the uniform. Anna had more of an eye for this kind of work, her initial instincts were always worth listening to, and if she'd had whiskers they'd have twitched from the moment she walked through the door.

Nothing concrete here, he thought, *nothing that jumps out but that's the point of this job. We're not looking for what jumps out, not the Jack In The Boxes, but what's hiding in the* bottom *of their boxes.*

So Walker searched for anything else that wasn't immediately obvious. Once again, David knew he was seeking Anna's approval. A metaphorical tip of the hat and a "good work" from Leeding made his day, so he wanted to go back to the station with a new nugget of interest to offer her.

It was partially because his ego wanted Anna to look at him as an equal and not just in rank. They'd been students together at Hendon Training College, but even back then she had a spark and charisma he still lacked. Perhaps he wanted some of her personal magic to rub off, or maybe he *did* want more from their relationship and never had the courage to admit it to himself.

No, we've been friends for a long time and that's the extent of our connection. That's as far as it goes and as far as I want it to go. Isn't it?

On some long nights at the station he'd mulled over the possibility of getting together with Anna and curiously, the idea hadn't seemed too far fetched, which was strange. She hadn't changed, was still thorough, professional, funny and sometimes remote, so that meant *he* must have changed. At some point in the last few months his attitude toward her had shifted, like he'd reached an internal cutoff point.

He pushed those thoughts to one side because there was a job to do, so Walker went looking.

He traced Anna's footsteps around the top floor but found nothing she hadn't pointed out already. The living room downstairs was spartan, save yet more photographs of West and her show business life. It seemed like Jeanette had been a ghost in her own house and left no trace apart from these images.

David wandered down the hallway to the kitchen, fitted out in the rustic fashion which had become popular in the last few years. Pine shelves heaved with china storage jars and brightly covered pots and pans. Dried flowers, a basket of potpourri, chunky wooden bread board, magnetic knife rack, all straight out of the Grattan catalogue. Everything was in its place, with a place for everything. This kitchen looked like it had never been used for cooking, let alone eating.

A pine farmhouse style table stood by the rear window. As Fisher had pointed out there was one empty and another almost finished bottle of Chateau Latour. He turned to leave but something flashed in the sink, so Walker peered down into it.

There was another wine glass.

One broken wine glass on the hallway carpet, one intact here in the sink. The inspector paused and considered what he had.

What would Anna think? West, suicidal, drinks a bottle of wine, maybe more, ready to have a chaser of paracetamol. She heads down the hall, drops her glass, turns, comes back, has more wine, places the second glass in the sink...No, no, no. She has the first bottle, puts that glass in the sink then decides to open another, has most of that, staggers down the hall, drops the second glass, stumbles upstairs and then...Yes. That makes more sense.

Walker went back to the table and squatted so his eyes were level with the surface. From that angle he could clearly see the faint marks of *two* wine glass rings.

*West's first glass goes in the sink. So this other ring mark must belong to the second glass that got broken. No big mystery, except it could also mean...*David stood up and pondered the other option. *Two glasses. Two people.*

At that moment there was a knock. Walker took a deep breath, headed up the hall and opened the door, where he expected the flash of camera bulbs and bellowed questions. Instead, there was just an old lady.

"Oh!" She exclaimed. "I saw the WPC leave. I wasn't sure if anyone was still here, only got back from my friend's place in Brighton half an hour ago, didn't I? What's happening?"

David went into his standard monotone spiel, designed to bore nosy passers by into doing just that, passing by. This woman would find out from the press soon enough.

"Well, Madam, there was an incident but as you can see, it's been dealt with, really nothing to worry about."

The woman tried to look past Walker into the hallway, but he carefully moved to block her view.

"Is Jeanette all right? I live next door, you see."

"Next door?"

She cocked her head left."Number eight. Is she all right?"

"As I say, there was an incident…" He changed the subject. "You said you've been away. Sorry, do you mind if I take your name?"

He pulled out his notebook.

"Ooh, it's like on the telly, isn't it? "Juliet Bravo," I like that one. I'm Susan Arnold, retired teacher, I'm seventy-nine you know," she said proudly and puffed herself out like a pigeon in a knitted cardigan, "I went to my friend Gillian's in Brighton, we taught at the same school. What happened? Is Jeanette OK?"

"When did you go to Brighton?"

"Do I need a lawyer or something? Like in "Columbo"?"

"No, no. It's…When did you go?"

"Sunday morning, why?"

Walker flicked back his notes. Jeanette West had failed to attend a Radio Two show on Sunday morning, then a newspaper interview in the afternoon.

"Did you see her on Saturday?"

"She's not gone missing, has she? Oh dear."

"Did you see her?"

Susan Arnold thought. "Yes, yes I did, from my upstairs back bedroom. It overlooks Jeanette's garden. So anyway, I was making the bed…"

"What time would that be?"

"Mid afternoon-ish. She came out and opened her back gate, which was strange because we *never* usually open our gates round here, you know, because of robbers. They're getting worse, aren't they? My friend Juliet had two men come round, in suits! And they…"

"She opened her back gate?" prompted Walker.

"Mm, yes."

"Did you see her after that?"

"No, but the next person I saw in her garden was when I was making my bed."

David looked sharply up from his notebook.

"Wait, sorry, did you say, the *next* person?"

"Yes, the next one. About five, five thirty-ish? Maybe a bit later. I was putting fresh pillowcases on and that's when she came into the garden."

"*She?*"

"Mm, she walked in, knocked at Jeanette's kitchen door, then it opened and she went in."

"Jeanette let her in?"

"I couldn't see from my room, but I heard her. Jeanette had this funny way of saying, 'hello,' you see, like she was singing, you know, '*hel..oh..oh-oh-oh!*'" Susan warbled.

"Did you see this woman leave?"

"No, but Jeanette's front door slammed around…" She pondered. "I was in bed, so around nine-thirty. There were some raised voices then the front door slammed."

Jesus, I'm going to have to get this old dear in formally, thought Walker, but needed to ask a few more questions. He couldn't help himself.

"What did this woman look like?"

"Well, that's the funny thing," Susan whispered, then actually looked over both shoulders to check if anyone else was listening.

"I could have sworn it was Lady Diana."

9 / 6th April, 1981, London.

By 19:30 Great Portland Street station had switched over to the night shift. As one group reached the end of a working day, others would take over. One shift would run from 16:00 to midnight, the next from 22:00 until 6. More would come on at 2 a.m. to 10. Therefore, each shift had a two hour crossover period with the one before which ensured there was no time when the district was understaffed.

However, due to rising tensions in the Brixton area, there were fewer officers in the station. The Metropolitan Police had deployed more uniformed patrols to South West London, which took them from other districts.So while Portland Street didn't quite have a skeleton crew, the usual complement was much depleted.

WPC Fisher found herself amongst the mainly junior officers left to hold the fort. Fisher knew damn well she was the "new girl," because that's what everyone called her. Lisa felt like it was the first week in school all over again. Her other nickname was "Juliet Bravo," from the BBC police series of the same name. Once in uniform, Fisher knew that *someone,* police or civilian, would smirkingly call her "Juliet Bravo," and then think themselves the first person to have ever done so.

It had happened again this morning.

One of the constables bellowed, "Here, Juliet Bravo love, tea over here, eh?" and then laughed like a drain. So she'd taken him a cup, smiled and said, "First, Juliet Bravo is her *call sign,* second, she's an inspector, so you're wrong on both counts. You may call me WPC Fisher or even just Fisher, I don't mind. But since you're a police officer, I do expect some degree of accuracy in identification." Fisher wouldn't have dared say that to a higher rank, but she and the "comedian" were on the same level. Plus PC 242 thought he was God's gift, so deserved it.

The other constables sniggered then followed up with a couple of wolf whistles as she'd walked away. Lisa took a deep breath and kept walking. She'd endured whistles trilling from building sites and vans for years, first as a schoolgirl, then a punk (spiky hair or not, a short skirt is still a short skirt) and now even as a WPC. The first time Fisher had gone on the beat she'd been astounded to still hear whistles come her way. "The boys obviously like you. Must be your legs," she'd said to her male colleague, who hadn't appreciated the joke or inference. The streets were one thing, but Fisher hadn't expected casual humiliation within the police station itself.

So tea making, scivvying and Benny Hill style bawdiness had been her introduction to law and order. She was now effectively considered a 1970s issue "sexy secretary" who could also arrest people, which wasn't a good feeling.

During her entire induction and training process, Fisher had wondered what on earth she was doing. It was almost like she'd thrown herself into the most alien situation possible just to see what would happen.

And now every day seemed like BBC children's favourite "Mr Benn." In each episode Benn visited a fancy dress shop and *as if by magic* the shopkeeper would appear. Benn would pick a costume, step into the changing room, then *become* that character; cowboy, spaceman, wizard...anything was possible. Fisher still felt like her WPC's uniform was just fancy dress and constantly waited for people to point and shout, "You're not a police officer! You're a *fake!*"

Now she sat at a spare desk and typed up another dull duty roster.

Huh. Nothing changes. I felt like a fake in 1976, she mused. *Everyone else was a real punk and I just went through the motions. Just like this scratchy uniform, I had all the right badges and everything was authentic. I got my bondage gear from King's Road, but always thought everyone was whispering behind my back. And now here I am in yet another costume and they really are whispering behind my back. But I always carried on doing it, didn't I? I've faked it all my life and I'm still faking it.*

Not for the first time, Fisher thought she may thrive on perversity. She always headed for the road less travelled, the path of *most* resistance. Of all careers, swapping a desk job for the police force really was the height of contrariness. While Lisa's hands mechanically click-clacked away at the typewriter, her mind drifted again.

You're dressing up again, aren't you? Part of her realised with surprise. *Oh my God, you're dressing up again, like you've always done. Right from when you were little, you showed people what they expected to see and they've believed that's what you were. Little girl ribbons and bows, then school badge and tie. Rebellious punk, now WPC. You're dressing up again to hide what you really are. And you know what you are, Lisa, you've always known what you are.*

She pulled the roster from the typewriter, placed the two carbon copies in a file and stood. Fisher was supposed to have knocked off at six but didn't want to leave the moment her shift finished. She wanted to show willing, not that there were many other officers around to see or even care.

She looked about, then walked with purpose over to a row of filing cabinets.

Her heart began to pound.

Don't do this, she instructed herself, but one Fisher never really listened to the other. The *real* Fisher underneath the costumes did whatever she wanted, as long as nobody knew.

She scanned the cabinets as if to find exactly which one was needed, but already knew. With one more look over her shoulder, Lisa pulled out a drawer. Her hands shook just a little as she located a file and opened it.

Fisher scanned its contents and her lips moved silently as she memorised the salient entries. Age, height, next of kin (blank), phone number and address.

She returned the file to its proper alphabetical position; LEEDING, A.H.DETECTIVE INSPECTOR.

Fisher stood, shook her head as if she'd gone to the wrong drawer, then shifted over to the *right* one. A further glance round the room told her nobody cared anyway.

Muttering D.I. Leeding's details over and over again, Lisa returned to the desk, then wrote them on a piece of paper which she pocketed.

Had anyone been watching they may have wondered what this WPC had to smile about.

10 / 6th April 1981, London. 21:15.

Holding a copy of the Evening Standard and a cardboard file, Anna robotically walked into her ground floor flat, walked to the fridge and pulled out a can of Carlsberg.

She enjoyed a social drink but rarely drank at home. Her small cabinet was stocked with the usual suspects; Martini, Cinzano, Cherry Brandy, Blue Nun, Liebfraumilch, Advocaat…but they stood like guests at a party which had never quite started.

The can hissed as it opened. The sound startled her cat on the sofa awake.

"Sorry, Dylan," Anna slumped down next to him. He'd been named for Dylan, the sleepy rabbit in The Magic Roundabout, rather than the nasal folk singer. "Busy day, was it? Oooh, must have been. You're *exhausted.*"

Dylan yawned and placed his head back between his paws, excitement over. "Too tired even to eat, huh?"

She took another gulp of beer and looked down at the Standard newspaper. *No, the press aren't telepathic, but they are bloody good.*

"WESTIE DEAD" ran the headline. Anna supposed some might wonder why the paper was reporting the death of a West Highland Terrier, but they'd be in the minority. The byline read, "TOP MODEL IN SUSPECTED SUICIDE." Ambulance men struggled with a laden stretcher on the front page. It was difficult to tear your gaze away from the covered shape. Jeanette had left her home never to return.

Now it was time to find out what the press did, and didn't, know.

"One of Britain's most famous models, Jeanette *"Westie"* West, 33, was found dead earlier today at her home in Selly Mews, W1. Sources say the model, who became famous in the late '60s, died by suicide, although no further details are available at this time. West's husband and manager, Clive St. Austenne, is currently in Los Angeles, where he is believed to have been negotiating the contract for what would have been his wife's upcoming role in the popular American television series, "Dallas". We have learned that St. Austenne is flying back to the UK in the next twenty-four hours.

It's not known who raised the alarm, but sources claim friends and family became anxious when West hadn't returned calls or attended engagements. She was due to appear on Pete Murray's Radio Two show yesterday to promote her autobiography,"Phoenix Rising"…"

Anna read the rest of the meagre report. The use of words like *"sources," "suspected,"* and *"believed,"* were news speak for *"we're making this up as we go along."* They didn't know the method nor any information about the suicide note, which meant Leeding's little ad hoc team were secure, as she'd known they would be. She trusted Walker and Moore and had instantly warmed to Fisher. Should this be anything more than suicide (and that still seemed remote, despite the oddities) Anna already had a reliable unit in place, should she need them.

Pages two and three were given over to West's obituary. Her star had waned in recent years but this coverage proved how much Westie was engrained in British culture. There were some of the photos Leeding had already seen earlier today; Jeanette with various pop stars and actors, Jeanette naked in Hyde Park, even the head and shoulders Duffy shot. It was fitting there were so many photographs; pictures rather than words would be her eulogy.

There was nothing new in the obituary, but one hitherto unknown and now very important fact stood out.

According to the Standard, Jeanette's husband had been in L.A. finalising a role for his wife in "Dallas." Anna now remembered seeing something about it on the front pages a few weeks ago but hadn't really registered the story. "Dallas" was arguably the biggest hit on worldwide TV. Last year the lead character, a pantomime villain oilman named J.R. Ewing had been shot, which led to a hysterical public whodunit. "Who Shot J.R.?" was *the* question of 1980. T-shirts with the boast, "I Shot J.R." were followed by badges which read, "Who *Cares* Who Shot J.R.?"

The show was a juggernaut and its stars beamed from the covers of every magazine.

And Jeanette had just landed a role in it. Anna stared at West's covered body on the stretcher. *For someone who'd spent the last few years trying to climb back up the fame ladder, this was the showbiz Holy Grail and yet, as her husband was apparently watching ink dry on the contract, she opens her wrists.*

So on one hand there was the despairing, abused, suicidal Jeanette. But on the other was "Westie" who'd written an autobiography called "Phoenix Rising," was about to start a round of high profile publicity interviews *and* begin work on the planet's biggest TV show. It made no sense, but Anna knew most suicides were very good at keeping their intentions hidden until the very last moment. That was the point. Most suicides only revealed themselves once there was no way back.

So when somebody teetered on a high ledge, what did they really want? Anna knew there were two kinds of jumpers; the ones who needed to be seen, know they mattered and that someone cared enough to pull them back from the edge. Then there were those who jumped alone, flew when and where nobody could ever run to help. Their bodies were found first thing in the mornings, crumpled in car parks, broken on pavements.

Those were the ones who dressed, breakfasted, joked, kissed the family goodbye, drove away, connected a hose to the exhaust and left their lives with no warnings. They were like submarines who ran very silent, very deep and when they dived, it was so far and fast they could never surface again.

So was Jeannette a submarine? Or was she stood on a window ledge waiting for someone to save her?

The note suggested she'd made her mind up. West had waited until her husband was away, and not just down the road, but five and half thousand miles across the Atlantic.

*

But now there was one other person positively identified as being inside Jeanette's house during the twenty-four hour window in which she'd died; the woman who'd entered via the back gate and then been let in through the kitchen door.

Anna opened the cardboard file and pulled out Walker's typewritten report.

"At approx. 17:00 - 17:30, on Saturday 4th April 1981, ARNOLD witnessed a white female entering WEST's rear garden at 10, Selly Mews, W1. It was an overcast afternoon, but the witness says she had a clear view of the female for around 30 - 45 seconds.

ARNOLD was in her rear bedroom at 8,Selly Mews and therefore above and approx. 25-30 feet from the female. The female was in clear vision at all times. The female was not known prior to ARNOLD.

The female was described as approx. 25 years old, approx. 5 feet 8 inches tall, although ARNOLD admitted her perspective <u>above</u> WEST's garden may not be an accurate measurement. On entering the garden, the female was wearing "a flat, wide brimmed, bolero style hat" and sunglasses. They then removed the hat and glasses. The female had a hairstyle which ARNOLD described as "like Lady Di's, blonde, flicked at the front and sides, collar length at the back."

She wore bright red lipstick, blusher and thick, dark eyeshadow.

She wore a trouser suit, fitted black jacket and white blouse, frilled or lacy at the neck. ARNOLD could not see her footwear.

The female knocked at WEST's rear door and ARNOLD heard a voice say "Hello" in a "sing-song" voice. ARNOLD identified the voice as belonging to WEST, as she had heard her use a similar greeting in the past."

Anna scanned forward a little.

"At approx. 21:15 - 21:30 ARNOLD was in bed in her upstairs rear bedroom when she heard what she described as,"raised voices" from WEST's home. She could not positively say whether the voices were raised in anger, neither could she identify whether either voice was WEST's as she was hearing them through her walls.

Approx.2-3 minutes after the raised voices, ARNOLD heard a front door slam which she believed to be WEST's.ARNOLD felt no cause for alarm. ARNOLD then heard muffled pop music coming from WEST's home.ARNOLD believes she was asleep by 10:00. She is a light sleeper but nothing woke her."

A little further, this;

"ARNOLD left 8, Selly Mews at approx. 9:15 on the morning of Sunday 5th April, 1981, to visit a friend in Brighton for the night. She neither saw nor heard Jeanette West at any point that morning. ARNOLD returned approx. 13:00, Monday 6th April 1981 and made contact with INSPECTOR WALKER at 10, Selly Mews at 13:25, 6th April 1981..."

Anna flicked back to the description of the woman, who'd been wearing a *"frilled or lacy"* blouse. *Interesting.* The blouses she'd found in the suitcase in Jeanette's rear bedroom had been frilly and lacy, but that meant nothing. Frilly shirts and blouses were the fashion in 1981, worn by either housewives in Laura Ashley or New Romantic kids in nightclubs.

Maybe a friend, another glossy model by the description. But which friend visits through the back gate, and did they stay until the evening, drinking? Did they have an argument with West and storm out, slamming the front door? If so, what about? What did they see?

What do they know? But if they left and Jeanette then played music, that means she was still alive at that point.

Anna picked up the Evening Standard again and considered the front page. *Whoever this woman is, she'll know West is dead by now. So she'll make contact with us, we can talk to her, get more of a picture. Tomorrow, all this will be wrapped up and what looks like loose ends will become obvious. But whoever "Lady Di" is, surely she wouldn't have left knowing West was suicidal, could she? Could she?*

She took another gulp of Carlsberg and shrugged.

Well, if we knew how people thought, we wouldn't need courts, would we? She switched on the TV. *That's the problem with suicide. The victim and the perpetrator are one and if the perpetrator is successful, we can't cross examine them. We have the weapon but often never find the motive.*

BBC 1 was showing "Cool Hand Luke" starring Paul Newman.

A prison drama? No thanks. I have enough of those.

BBC 2 had a documentary about Bombay while ITV was in the middle of "The Sweeney."

Oh Jesus, just what I need. Another "cop" show. How easy life would be if only I could just beat information out of villains like Regan and Carter. Oh well, what else is there to watch? Come on then, Sweeney Todd, you might be worth a laugh.

Something tapped on her window. Untamed bushes grew right up to the front of the flats and in a breeze would sometimes make their presence known on the glass.

Dylan jumped down from the sofa and mewed at Anna.

"Oh, so *now* he wants to eat, does he?"

She stood and walked toward the kitchen but Dylan broke left and headed toward the door. "I see. Going on patrol, then?"

Anna stepped out of her flat and into the shared entranceway.

She pulled open the main door and Dylan raced off to wherever it is cats go at night. Leeding was about to shut out the cold April air when she spotted a long shallow cardboard box on the doormat.

Anna stepped forward then looked up and down the empty street.The box hadn't been there when she'd returned.

If it is for me, obviously. No name, no address.

Although bitterly cold there wasn't much of a breeze, certainly nothing to rustle the bushes and make them tap on her window. Something about the box and its appearance unnerved her, so rather than taking it inside, Anna elected to rip it open on the doorstep.

Inside was a bouquet of shrivelled, faded flowers.

"Oh, what?" she whispered. "Fucking hell, that's weird."

With her top lip curled in subconscious disgust she folded the box shut, held it at arm's length like a dead animal, then threw it into the communal bin.

With one last look up and down the street, Leeding retreated into her flat. She didn't sleep for some time but when Anna finally slipped off, she dreamed as she'd done many times before.

11 / A Dream.

Everyone dreams, even though we don't always remember them in the morning.

Recalled dreams often make no sense when awake, but whilst asleep we find them completely logical. A dream is like several boxes of jigsaws mixed together and those boxes change nightly. One might contain a picture from your present, another, a scene from your past. A further shows people and places from across your life, or completely random images which have nothing to do with you. Those boxes are shaken up, the pieces are spread out, then one's sleeping brain tries to form them into a coherent narrative.

But of course, that narrative is only ever coherent to the dreamer.

So.

Sleep falls, your brain changes its internal waves, jigsaw pieces click together and suddenly...Why, look. You're in a bar with a schoolfriend you haven't thought about for years, but somehow *know* they now mean you harm. You don't question this omniscience, it just happens. But then when you leave the bar, it's days later (time bends but this causes no panic as it is simply part of the dream landscape's twisted physics) and now you *have* to get to a bookshop.Why? Because your exams are about to begin and you haven't revised because you left school years ago. The shop is piled high with revision books, but the one you need is out of stock, the exam starts in five minutes and your life depends on those grades.

Then suddenly you're back in the bar, knowing that old friend still wants to kill you.

Sometimes, dreams are like movies edited by a maniac, where scenes and plots are spliced together with no meaning or continuity. It's hardly surprising that surrealists embraced film so quickly. Throw cuts of celluloid in the air, chop them up, reassemble, see what happens. Horror, comedy, documentary, romance, porn, they all flash past your eyes and while asleep, you have no problem whatsoever with such bizarre internal logic.

But no matter how strange, all dreams are like a pearl. At their heart is a grain of reality which has somehow become surrounded with layers of fantasy.

For years, Anna Leeding had a recurring nightmare which rarely fully faded on waking. Sometimes this nightmare would leave her alone for months before flickering back into the edges of her sleep. Once there, it would stutter up frame by awful frame, like a film sliding from silent black and white to full colour and sound.

Anna's dream always started with running.

As she dream ran, Anna would always give out a little moan made of fear and desperation. Her mouth twitched, eyes rolled, and Leeding's hands fluttered about her face as if to wave away flies or perhaps something bigger, deadlier.

She ran.

It was always night time and the streets were deserted. The map of her dream would change with each performance. Sometimes there were roads she recognised (albeit mixed up from many different locations) while others would be unfamiliar. Despite this, they were always the *same streets*. In dreams, things have an inner identity independent of external appearances. Somebody may have no physical resemblance to your husband, but you know that's who they are.

You just *know*.

So while her sleeping mind redecorated those streets over and over again, they remained the same ones at an identical point in time; a small area of East London, back when Anna was sixteen.

She ran but got nowhere, because those streets were like the backdrop in Scooby Doo when the Gang ran from a monster. The same buildings and landmarks flashed past, but that's how the world works, doesn't it?

Leeding wasn't being chased, no, not quite. But there *was* something behind her, so she tried to put as much distance as she could between it and herself. However, no matter how fast she ran, that *thing* remained at exactly the same point in space. Breathless, moaning, Anna would head for a light in the distance but knew she'd never reach it.

During the race she became aware that people were watching. The silent audience never helped, even though it was obvious this desperate running girl needed assistance.

And that was another odd thing. In the dream, Anna was sixteen, but also thirty-eight, twenty-one, seven, thirty-three…She was all ages at once, not cycling through them, just inhabiting many previous (and current) versions of herself at the same time. She recognised some of the people who stared; friends, relatives, criminals she'd put away and *others*.

Recently, one particular "other" had begun to appear on a more regular basis. This "other" watched as she streaked past through the night streets but Anna also knew they were *right behind her,* not chasing but somehow, simply there.

As she rushed through the repeating dreamscape, Anna's breathing became quicker and her heart rate increased. She would twist beneath the sheets and her feet would twitch, like a dreaming cat's paws. To all intents and purposes this running was real, since her body reacted exactly as it should. A light film of sweat covered her skin and when she awoke, she'd feel its sickly warm moisture.

Anna would then try to claw herself back into reality, where clocks behaved themselves and streets always had an end, but it took time.

Soon enough sleep would claim her again, but the dream never came twice in one night. Once seemed enough to purge herself of it for another few months.

The following morning she would wake, flickers of that sleeping race would return and Anna would know that once again she'd headed into the night to run, run, *run* away from her Father.

12 / April 7th 1981. London.

Leeding walked to work down Tottenham Court Road. She'd lived just off this street since 1975 and like the rest of London, it had the air of a once aristocratic gentleman who'd fallen on hard times. But the road of old could still be found because if one wants to travel in time, then look *up*. Archeologists dig down, but to see a city as it once was, then the view *above* the shop fronts will take you there. The elegant facades of a lost London can still be seen, protected by height from the changes at street level.

Down here on the pavement, Ann knew TCR was a road of two halves. There were high end, fashionable department stores like Heal's and Habitat, where the chi-chi would come for their mass produced individuality, but alongside them were many electrical and hi-fi shops. They had windows and walls but were effectively market stalls by any other name.

Every other doorway led into a cave full of Hitachis, Fergusons, Sharps Binatones, and Pioneers. TV's, video recorders, tape decks and music centres were piled in every available space. What had been out of reach technology a couple of years ago was now mass produced, stacked high and sold cheap.

At first glance what seemed to be typewriters in the windows were actually computer keyboards. Anna knew computers once took up entire rooms and cost an entire year's wages, but yet here they were in cheap W1 electrical shops. She stared down at unimpressive black plastic boxes called *Sinclair ZX81's*. The name alone proved how up to the minute they were, yet these futuristic machines cost just seventy present-day pounds. One ZX81 appeared to be in the middle of a nervous breakdown as it busily spewed out line after line of apparently random numbers and characters. Anna assumed somebody would know what they all meant, but like that song from last year, "Vienna," it meant nothing to her. *I turned my back for a moment and the future arrived.* She peered at the   impenetrable code. *I thought the future wasn't supposed to be here until 1999, at least.*

Then there was the noise. From nine in the morning until closing time at 5:30, these shops pumped out music like factories pump out smoke. If the Tower Of Babel had employed a DJ, it would have sounded like Tottenham Court Road. Anna could only assume the shop owners ran every hi-fi, tape deck and record player at once, all blasting out different tracks. Adverts for "Boomboxes" lined the windows but those boxes were doing a fine job of advertising themselves without any help. They were huge, macho slabs with two tape decks, a radio, massive speakers and plenty of switches and sliders. Level meters bounced into the red and speakers vibrated in their housings.

Anna tried to make out individual songs in the cacophony. Among the waves of sound someone sang about having Bette Davies' Eyes. Bucks Fizz were *still* making their mind up, there was the relentless *thump-blat-thump-blat* of a medley track called "Stars On 45" and if that wasn't enough, Phil Collins was beating up his drum kit on "In The Air Tonight." They were the few tracks she could make out, while the rest blended into an unlistenable thunder of drum machines, synthesisers and wails.

Every day was a carnival on Tottenham Court Road. *I don't know how the shopkeepers aren't all deaf,* she thought. *Or maybe they are, because Jesus, their music taste leaves a lot to be desired.*

She stopped by a newspaper vendor and scanned the headlines. As predicted Jeanette West was on every front cover, since a glamorous death always shifted papers. Anna picked up a copy of The Sun, handed over 12p and flicked through the coverage. West's story was on pages one and two while page three was naturally bursting with today's topless model, a nineteen-year-old called Janine Andrews.

Janine pouted out, Anna stared back. Back at Great Portland Street Station page three girls occasionally appeared on walls as little acts of passive aggressive sexual provocation from some of the more neanderthal officers. Whenever a new page three *lovely* made her debut some of the men would gather round like monosyllabic art critics examining a piece. "Woo, urrrr, hey!" whah, whah *woah,"* "Ooh, aahh, *nice."* Leeding would study the page intently before concluding,"Gentlemen, pay attention, this is what's known as a *girl*. But I'm hardly surprised none of you have seen one *au naturel* before."

The Sun didn't have much more detail than last night's Standard, but they'd run with parts of the official statement. Anna skimmed through the copy before finding the line she'd hoped they'd use.

"Authorities are interested to speak with anyone who was with, or spoke to, Jeanette West `in the days leading up to this tragic incident."`

"Authorities," was a less loaded word than "police," which might infer there was more to the incident than suicide.

She read on.

`"They are also keen to speak with one of Jeanette West's female friends who is believed to have visited her on Saturday."`

Pretty vague but hopefully enough to push our mystery woman into action. Whoever she was, *"Lady Di"* remained the last person to see Jeanette alive.

She'd drunk wine with her then, perhaps, *left in a hurry and slammed the door.*

That person held a lot of answers and Anna needed to hear them.

*

"Ah, Fisher, good morning. So the chief's put you front of house has he?"

WPC Fisher stood at the reception desk with a constable.

"I am the friendly face of the Met, ma'am," smiled Fisher. "He said I should get a feel for everything, hence here I am."

"Here you are, indeed. And much friendlier than Baker here," Anna cocked her head at the constable.

"Charming," grumbled the officer.

Anna put down her copy of The Sun. "Take a look at the coverage. They're asking for West's Saturday afternoon visitor to get in contact. If she does, point her in my direction and my direction only. I assume the other local stations know this one is ours?"

"I believe that to be the case," said Constable Baker.

"Well, belief is wonderful in a church, but here I'd rather have it confirmed."

"Of course."

She turned to Fisher. "So, anything I should know about?"

The WPC checked her log and ran a finger down the entries. "Uh huh. Clive St. Austenne got put through to us. He flew back yesterday night on Concorde. Er…" she squinted at the entry. "God. Terrible handwriting."

"*Charming*," repeated Baker.

"My pleasure."

He took over. "What the WPC is trying to tell you, if she could read my *perfectly* legible handwriting, is we offered to talk to him at his home in Surrey. But he said he'd rather come in, as there are press on the doorstep."

"Time?"

"Sometime around eleven."

"OK," sighed Anna and thought, *it's not OK, it's never OK.* "Sit in with me, would you Fisher? Take notes."

"Yes ma'am."

Except Leeding knew she didn't need Fisher there for note-taking. She just wanted someone else present for support.

She hated this part.

*

Clive St. Asutenne sat opposite D.I. Leeding in the interview room. She'd seen photographs of him over many years but couldn't square those images with the person who stared blankly at her. He looked like the man's badly drawn, empty twin. His hand made suit, cravat, gold cufflinks and bouffant hair were all present and correct but seemed bleached out, like he'd been left in the sun too long.

Clive still had his trademark tan but even that seemed sallow. Grief did that to people, faded them, then replaced the person with an automaton which clicked out moves that looked human at first but quickly revealed themselves to be mechanical. Clive St. Austenne now ran on automatic.

She attempted to look back into his eyes, but their lifelessness was terrifying. The recently bereaved fell into a few categories; they often displayed anger or confusion, attempted to engage with intelligent arguments, or simply tried to negate the awful new reality of their lives. But St. Austenne was almost his own ghost, like *he* was the deceased but just hadn't realised yet.

Papers and photographs were spread across the table. Not pictures of Jeanette, obviously, but elements in the case that were puzzling. Anna wouldn't normally talk with a relative this close to the event, but St. Austenne had dealt with the news as if it were some kind of terrible business meeting. He'd managed Jeanette in life so would now manage her in death.

"I'm sorry," Anna said again. She'd already said it several times, but knew it had no meaning in this situation. "If you want to talk some other time…"

"When, though?" He mumbled, then found some fire. "When Jeanette isn't dead? When is a good time?"

"I'm sorry. Of course, it's up to you."

"Is there something you're not telling me?"

"Not at all, I promise. I understand that this is difficult, impossible, but whenever someone dies, particularly in the way that your wife… you see, a life has been taken. And even when a life is *self* taken we treat it as we would any other case."

"Like a murder," he said, but without venom.

Anna nodded. "We have to look at everything to ensure we understand exactly what has happened, and to leave…" she grasped for a better analogy, but could find only clichés. "No stone unturned, no loose ends."

"I understand."

"So some of these questions may seem odd but they're just us getting to grips, with any, well, yes, loose ends."

Clive spread his hands out to say, *go ahead.*

Anna could see he was but a few heartbeats from breaking down, so shot a look at Fisher who instantly understood then subtly pushed a box of tissues nearer to the widower.

"How often did you stay at Selly Mews?"

"Rarely, our main home is in Surrey, Shere. Do you know it?"

"I've heard of it but never been."

"Beautiful, it's where our friends are. We never had children so friends are our extended family. Ah…"

He took several gulps of air, glanced at the tissues and continued. "We only stayed in the Mews if there was work in London. Shere's only an hour or so away, but if we had business over a few days it made sense to stay in town."

"And Jeanette was there because," Anna consulted her notes, "she had an interview on Radio Two and one with the papers on Sunday."

"And a further few on Monday. I was in Los Angeles. Jeanette likes to stay in London when I am away. It's busier than Shere, more shops, more restaurants."

"Did she have many friends here?"

"As I say, most live near us in Guildford. A few, though."

"Can you think of any friends that look like, well, Lady Diana? Five foot eight, maybe twenty-five. Blonde, flicked hair?"

"Sounds like almost every woman under fifty these days. Could be you, even."

"It doesn't ring any bells?"

"Yes, she has friends that fit that description, why?"

"They're somebody we'd like to speak to. We think she had a friend over on Saturday. They would be very helpful to find."

"Why? Oh, 'loose ends,' yes."

His lip trembled and he pulled out a packet of Silk Cut. "Do you mind?"

"Of course not. In fact, did Jeanette smoke?"

"No. She hated it, was very health conscious."

He lit the cigarette and his eyes teared up. Defiantly, he pulled on the Silk Cut and pushed the emotion away. "Why? What have cigarettes got to do with anything?"

"We're trying to find out who would have seen her before…well, before. It's possible she had, er, another visitor who smoked." Anna had a thought. "Did you ever smoke in the back garden at Selly Mews?"

"Occasionally, but not for a long time. I haven't been there for, God, months, last summer, I think."

So the butts weren't his or Jeanette's, then. The woman's?

"Last summer?"

"Yes, Wimbledon, actually. We saw Borg versus McEnroe, McEnroe got booed. I'm glad he lost, horrid man."

Anna knew he just wanted to find something normal to hang onto.

"So Jeanette was the main occupant. Did you keep an overnight bag there?"

"No."

So whose bag was that under the bed?

"What's that got to do with anything? What's *any* of this got to do with anything?"

Anna saw he was at a tipping point and was either going to break down or slide into anger. But she had to continue.

"We have to look at the entire picture, even things that seem irrelevant. You understand, don't you?"

He sighed and the moment passed for now. Leeding had to deal with the dry, physical facts before she could talk to him about West's emotional state in the days leading up to her suicide. Once she went down that road, she knew he may not be able to offer anything. Anna shuffled through the papers and pulled out a photograph which showed the framed modern art in Jeanette's bedroom that read simply, FACE.

"I know this seems like another strange question, but what does this piece of art represent?"

Clive stared at it, puzzled.

"I don't know."

"You don't recognise it?"

"No. Should I? What relevance does it have?"

"It's hanging in Selly Mews' front bedroom."

"No, no it's not. Jeanette…" He gulped again. "Jeanette has the Duffy portrait in there, that was her favourite. Duffy burned a lot of his work, did you know that? Lucky we had that print because he burned the original, strange man."

"You've never seen this?"

He looked again. "Never. And it's in the bedroom? Perhaps Jeanette…" his voice caught once more. "*Perhaps* she bought it, but she loved the Duffy shot. Why would she take that down and put this," he shook his head, "utter shit up? She hates modern art. Back in 1966, she went to Yoko's exhibition at the Indica, stayed for the champagne, said hello to John then did a runner as quick as she could. Jeanette hated the whole thing, but particularly hated the "art.""

He studied the photograph. "Total shit. Who's responsible?"

Now that's what I'd really like to know, thought Anna.

"And if I may ask again, what has it got to do with anything?"

Leeding had been put in a corner so was forced to tell a white lie.

"Well, I spotted the Duffy print, you see, Mr St. Austenne. It was in the back bedroom up against the wall."

"Up against the *wall?*" He looked affronted.

"So you see I'm trying to get a grip on Jeanette's emotional state. If she took down her favourite photograph before she…Then perhaps that indicates…"

What? Indicates what, exactly, Anna? You're not a psychologist, so tread carefully. You're just trying to get some context for the scene.

The worst was yet to come. She had to push on, but there would never be an appropriate time. Now was as good as any.

"Is there a typewriter at Selly Mews?"

"A typewriter? No. We have one in Shere and a few at the London office, naturally. But at Selly? Not to my knowledge, no. I have to ask *again* what does a typewriter…?"

Anna flicked through the papers, came to a photocopy of the note they'd found by Jeanette's bed and pushed it towards St. Austenne.

"We found this. If you want to look at it in your own time, in private, then I suggest you do so. But it's your right to have it."

His mouth gaped and he began to breathe heavily. "Is this…?" he asked. Leeding gave a tiny nod.

Clive gazed at the note, looked away, wrestled with his thoughts, then stared back at the paper. He scanned the words and his breaths came faster.

"I don't…I don't…"

"Please, we should stop. Let me get you…"

Get you what, Clive? Your life back?

"I don't understand. What's she talking about? I don't know what she means. *Abused*? Who's she talking about? What have *they* done? Who are *they*? I don't know what this is."

Anna stood and put an arm about St. Austenne's shoulders. There was nothing else she could do.

"She was fine," he wailed, the dam burst, his face collapsed and the words poured out. "She was *fine*. More than fine. This," he waved the photocopy in the air, "she would have told me. She told me everything, everything, we had no secrets, if someone was hurting her I would have known. *I would have known*. Look, look…" Anna knew he was trying to bargain with truth. If he could just put everything in order, then all this would go away. "Look. This is ridiculous. She had the book out, the interviews and Dallas. Oh God, *Dallas*." He ran his hands through the now wilted bouffant of hair. "Don't you see? *Dallas*. She was coming back, so excited, like Christmas it was, when she got offered that part. She danced around the kitchen, sang the theme music at the top of her voice, was *fine*. It was all going so well again. So why? Why would she do that when her life was about to leap up a gear? She was happy before… Jeanette never said anything at all about abuse or people attacking her. Look, listen, you know what she said? You know?"

Fisher attempted to both sympathise and take notes.

"We have people I can contact, people you can talk to," Anna said gently.

"Do you know what she said? 'I had the '60s and now I'm going to have the '80s. The '80s will belong to me.' So why would she? I don't recognise the woman who did that to herself. I don't recognise her, I won't have it, I won't have it. I need to speak to someone. I won't have it."

Finally, he crumbled into incoherence. Anna kept her arm around him while Fisher helplessly looked on. Leeding nodded at her and the WPC knew exactly what she was saying;

This is the job. This is what I do. So can you?

13 / 8th April, 1981, London.

Anna scanned the preliminary findings of the forensic report, which were conclusive yet frustrating. She circled entries of particular interest.

"WEST's prints were found on the broken wine glass in the hallway, marked on diagram C(2). No prints were found on the glass in the kitchen sink."

No surprises there, she thought. *It was in the sink, it had been washed. But by who? Jeanette, or the woman who came to visit? And if the visitor washed the glass, why?*

"WEST's prints were found on the bottle of paracetamol (D2) and the razor blade (D3). Other than WEST's there were no other unknown prints in the bedroom. Two clear prints from WEST were found on the note in the bedroom (D4)."

Anna flicked through to print D4, which showed the position of the two prints found on the suicide note. They were both at the top, just above where the typing began.

Leeding's head tick locked, left-to-right,right-to-left, left-to-right, then she blinked exactly five times. She picked up another sheet from her desk, inserted it in the typewriter and noted the position of her fingertips on the paper. They were on the front and rear edges.

She tapped out, "The Quick Brown Fox Jumped Over The Lazy Dog," then pulled out the paper and looked where her fingers naturally fell. Anna's thumb had grasped the top front edge, while her index and middle fingers went to the top rear.

And yet Jeanette's only prints on her suicide note were two clear ones, index and middle, flat on the front.

That makes no sense. Two clear prints flat on the paper, none where you might expect them to be.

She tapped her nails on the desk and considered the puzzle.

There was no typewriter at the residence. So she types this where? St. Austenne said there were typewriters at the London office, so maybe she typed the note there? Then whilst taking it to Selly Mews, her other prints are wiped off and we're left with just these two. Possible. Unlikely. I'm grasping at straws.

"At the request of D.I. LEEDING, the artwork in WEST's bedroom was tested and no prints of any kind were found. Likewise the photo of WEST in the rear bedroom, on which no clear prints were found. Unknown prints were discovered on the windowsill in the rear bedroom (E3) but at present have not been matched. Other unknown prints have been found (E4)."

No signs of foul play, so why can't I shake the feeling that I'm missing something? Jeanette's prints are on the razors and the pills. No other prints are in the room. The note is strange but not enough for me to kick up a fuss. The cigarette butts and scuff marks are odd but don't seem to go anywhere as yet.

So who is the bloody woman who visited? It's been two days now and no sign of her. If we ask the press to push for her again, they'll scent blood, start to circle and I don't want that. For some reason, I want to keep a lid on this for now.

Anna didn't know why, but alarm bells were still ringing. For now they remained distant chimes, but pealed just the same. She had a horrible intuition that soon they would get much louder.

14 / 13th April 1981, London.

D.I. Leeding sat at her desk and leafed through the newspapers, which were extremely depressing this morning. Relations between police and the black community had rarely been good, but they seemed torn beyond repair today.

In January, thirteen black teenagers and adults had tragically died in a blaze at a house party. Some believed the fire was a racist attack and the police weren't investigating as thoroughly as they should. A mainly peaceful protest march followed, which had been marred by sporadic confrontations with the police. The London Standard's coverage showed a bloodied officer next to a quote from one of the organisers which claimed it had been a "good day."

That headline was unhelpful at best, incendiary at worst.

Since then the police had continued to make mistakes. Statistics suggested robbery and violent crime were on the increase in Brixton, so the Special Patrol Group were deployed and "stop and search" powers introduced. Those decisions simply stoked the flames. Locals called the powers "sus law," where "sus" meant "suspicious." Ultimately "sus" meant anyone could be stopped just for *looking* like they might commit a crime, so if an officer with those powers was a racist then surely *every* black face was "*sus*."

Anna knew there was racism in the force, in fact there were *lots* of '-isms,' but this was Britain and sadly bigotry was as much part of the country as fish and chips. So ingrained was suspicion of *others* that the intolerant didn't even class themselves as such; they were just "normal."

Anna knew there were thousands of officers on duty across London but less than one hundred and fifty were from ethnic backgrounds. Those kinds of figures didn't bolster trust in the force.

Naturally, resentment and anger had spread across Brixton like toxic fog and last Friday the fumes finally reached choking point.

Such was the level of community mistrust in the police that an act of compassion was mistaken for one of callousness.

Police had used their patrol car to take a young black stab victim to hospital, but onlookers believed he'd been arrested and rumours spread that the officers let him die. Therefore a metaphorical match was dropped, the accelerant caught and by Saturday afternoon SW9 was alight. Inadequately equipped for what quickly became a battle zone, the force was pelted with bricks, Molotov cocktails and bottles. It had taken most of a day to push back the rioters and achieve an uneasy measure of calm.

Anna looked at the photographs in disbelief and sadness. *Ultimately, however justified their grievance,* she thought, *the protestors turned anger and despair inwards. The police may have been the target but Brixton's own community was collateral. These front pages are a warning. If figurative triggers are not removed, then actual guns can go off. Pubs, schools and businesses were put out of action and nobody won. Not the police, Brixton, nor Britain.*

Leeding knew the UK would have no sudden guilty realisation that things had to change. For many people, the riots had simply reinforced their opinions.

Without purpose and focus, anger only achieves itself, but how desperate must they be? She glanced over at Jeanette's report. *Isn't that what West did? Went so far she couldn't come back, turned all that anger and confusion on her own body? She couldn't deal with the world so rather than fighting against it, demanding answers, justice, she burned her world down. How many more personal riots are going on out there right now? How many fires are being set? This isn't over. This has barely even begun. 1981 has a long way to go.*

Anna flicked through the rest of the paper.

NASA's new spaceship, the "shuttle" was up there in orbit somewhere.

The boxer Joe Louis had died.

IRA member Bobby Sands was on hunger strike and had become an MP.

Bucks Fizz were still number one.

Jeanette West was still dead.

Whoever had visited West that Saturday afternoon was yet to come forward, which Anna found extremely worrying. *Surely when a friend kills themselves and the police ask for help, then people come forward. So why haven't you?*

So "Lady Di" remained unknown. Leeding picked up the transcript of Clive St. Austenne's interview which raised more questions that it answered.

But the press had already moved on from West and there was nothing else that could be done right now. Other cases tapped Anna on the shoulder; a mugging which had escalated into a murder, a gang who dealt in both stolen cars and drugs, another suspicious fire, possibly arson. On and on they went. Crime never took a day off.

Her phone rang.

"Extension 273."

"Anna, *dear*," oozed a cheeky, plummy voice from the receiver. It was Anna's friend Mary Price, a pathologist for the area. They'd known each other since the mid 1970s.

"Mary, how are you?"

"Well, I'm well. What are you doing for lunch?"

"Lunch? Oh, sorry, I'm up to my neck. Can we put something in the diary?"

"Think of it as a working lunch, because there's something I'd like to discuss before you see my report."

"Jeanette West?"

"Mmm. Shall we say Avella's? In one hour?"

"And it's work?"

"Of course. Synchronise watches, Miss Leeding. One hour, see you there."

"Right, yes."

There's something Mary wants to discuss that she'd prefer to do in person. OK. Should I be worried?

*

Avella's cafe is on Mortimer Street, just up from BBC Broadcasting House. It mainly dealt in take-out sandwiches and tea, but had a cosy little backroom where Anna and Mary often met for business and pleasure.

Anna was first to arrive, ordered a Ty-Phoo tea and ham sandwich then waited for the tsunami. Leeding heard Mary before she saw her. The doorbell tinkled then a voice boomed, "Tony! How are you? I'm meeting Anna, is she…? Oh she is? Wonderful! May I please have a pot of Earl Grey and, oh, how posh. I shall have a smoked salmon sandwich. *Lo-ver-ly*. Anna dear, I'm *co-o-ming*."

Mary Price appeared in the doorway, threw a dramatic pose and laughed. She was a handsome blonde woman who still looked much younger than her forty years. Off duty, Mary often dressed like a fox hunter who'd been separated from both the party and her horse, then found herself inexplicably dumped in London. Today she wore a tweed jacket and blouse with a camay brooch between the collars, while a knee-length tweed skirt and brown leather high heels completed the set. Always effortlessly stylish, she often made Anna feel underdressed. Compared to Mary's outfit, Leeding's black jacket, white blouse and sensible trousers made her look like a bank worker on lunch break.

Mary Price was the smartest person Anna knew. She spoke four languages, casually rattled off twenty-thousand word essays for The Lancet and as a "hobby" occasionally supplied The Sunday Times with art criticism. But Mary didn't wield her intellect as a club, but rather like a scalpel; gently, precisely and only when absolutely required.

She gave Anna a peck on the cheek and sat down. Out front, a transistor radio played the ubiquitous Shakin' Stevens.

"Mary, how are you?"

"I have rarely been better. I'm still spending my days with the dead, but my love life has jumped up a notch or three."

Never one for too much bedroom detail, Anna skated over that statement. "Glad to hear. Something more permanent this time, is it?"

Mary winked, became conspiratorial. "Well, as you know, I've been through a few in my time and don't really *do* permanent, but this one could stick around for a bit. Charming, very attractive, game for a laugh and has nothing to do with corpses, which is heavenly after a day at the slabs. To be honest, it's a relief to have physical contact with anyone who doesn't use *eau de formaldehyde*. Why can't they at least make it smell vaguely fragrant, hm?"

"It is outrageous," Anna concurred.

"I'm going to write to Chanel and *demand* they introduce Embalming Fluid No.9. And you, *Miss* Leeding, and you?"

"I'm good. No, actually, I'm OK. Good is a bit much."

Mary turned down the corners of her mouth in sympathy.

"Is it work? Personal life? Oh, not that again. How many times? You did the right thing. It was making you ill! I saw it in your face. You were unhappy, dear, it just wasn't you and you know exactly what I mean. I don't mind a bit of pussy-footing around but as I have already pointed out on numerous occasions, you won't be *happy* until you're truly *happy,* will you?"

"Well, yes. No. Whatever that means."

"You know exactly what it means. Anna won't be happy until *Anna* is happy."

"OK, enough, thanks, Marjorie Proops. To what do I owe this pleasure?"

"Business already? No, we have to do pleasantries first, dear, it's decorum. Oh, tea, lovely, Tony, thank you."

Tony the owner, server and chief bottle-washer of Avella's brought over a tray loaded with tea and sandwiches. "I put some crisps on the side." He gave a flourish with his hands, like a courtier. "On the house, ma'am."

"*Golden Wonder Ready Salted*," whispered Mary in mock awe. "Now I know we're in West One."

"That is the real reason the Langham Hotel shut," offered Tony. "They couldn't compete with our crisps." He retreated backwards, bowed and laughed.

"What a character." Mary smiled, fondly. She looked down at Anna's paper. "Ah, dreadful business in Brixton."

"It is."

"Although despite the best attempts of our esteemed fourth estate, I rather suspect the whole awful affair may be six of one and half a dozen of another."

"I'm not sure yet. But we won't know until we know."

Mary tut-tutted. "*We won't know until we know*? You sound like a member of the cabinet. No, you sound like a back bencher. Even our beloved Mrs T. wouldn't say that and she's capable of some of the most frightful rhetoric."

"I consider myself chastened," Anna laughed. "But I think there'll be more where Brixton came from." She nodded out toward where the transistor blared. "Radio's the only place where you'll find a 'happy, happy sound,' right now. Britain is..." she searched for the right word, "...seething. Yes, it's seething."

"It is, you can feel it. And tolerance is in very short supply, as you and I well know. In fact, intolerance has become somewhat of a national sport hasn't it?"

"I think it always was. So, to better times, Mary."

"Better times."

The two women clinked their cups like champagne glasses and giggled.

"So what particular breed of intolerance killed Jeanette West, do you think?"

"Killed?" Anna put down her tea, all levity gone. Mary waved away the question. "Coroner was particularly sniffy about this one.

Thought it was 'open and shut,' as he always does when he can't be bothered to stay late at work. How did you persuade him?"

"I said it was a high profile case, public interest, newspapers, blah, blah, blah. You know his ego, loves to hold court at parties and talk about his exciting career, so I played on that."

"Nicely done. I'll send on the report but first, I wanted to tell you my findings face to face."

"Why?"

"Because," Mary weighed her words carefully, "I want to watch your expression. My report will stick to the facts as I see them. And it will state unequivocally that Jeanette West killed herself."

"Mm, I can feel a 'but' coming on."

"Well, yes, but all my 'buts' can be explained away. If there was anything I thought suspicious it would be in the report, you know that, don't you?"

"Of course. So why all this?" She waved her hand around the empty back room. "Why the cloak and dagger?"

"Well, I look wonderful in a cloak as you know, but as for the dagger, that's your department."

She took a bite of her sandwich. "Mm, lovely. I don't eat quite enough smoked salmon. So, Jeanette opened her wrists in bed, everything is consistent there. Most choose the bath as a point of exit, but not all. There is no officially sanctioned method of suicide but to put it simply, West died of blood loss, as one would expect."

"But…?"

"That's what killed her, you can announce my conclusion to the world because it is correct."

"*But…?*"

Mary formed a slow and sad smile.

"There was an open bottle of pills. Paracetamol."

"Uh-huh."

"That's strange. Why is it strange, you ask? Because there was no paracetamol in her body. None *at all*. And if that was one of the causes of death, she'd be full of it. Paracetamol poisoning usually takes a long time to build up in your system and even if you do go hell for leather and swallow an entire bottle, you'll be convulsing before you die. No sign of that, no sign of *any* paracetamol. She died as calmly and beautifully as Rossetti's Ophelia. Which may have been her point."

"I thought that."

"I doubt whether a model, even a suicidal one, would want to leave anything other than a beautiful corpse. But then that's just my particular intolerance of the gorgeous since I jealously see them all as shallow and hate myself for it. So, we have a bottle of pills arranged like a prop."

"Yes, it did look that way."

"But on the other hand, perhaps she meant to take them and never got round to it since her wrists did the trick. It's not that big a mystery. As you have pointed out on many occasions, one person's cleverly worked out plan is someone else's chaotic improvisation."

"OK…" Anna wondered where all this was going.

"But I tell you what *was* in her system. Alcohol, and a lot of it."

"Yes, we think she shared a couple of bottles with a person or persons unknown."

"That woman you want to talk to?"

"Perhaps."

"Well, let me tell you something there. Let's pretend West drank *both* bottles herself. Just chugged the whole bally lot down. Her BAC would have been sky high. Not good at all. Stupor, unconsciousness and amnesia are all on the table. Now it's possible she could have sunk two bottles and still managed to kill herself before the full effects made themselves known, but it's unlikely, isn't it? West would have been beyond squiffy, in a whole other place past pissed. And the bottles were *downstairs*. If they were by her bed, maybe, maybe. Then again, perhaps she had a greater tolerance for alcohol. Everyone is different and we know it happens. She didn't strike me as a drinker though."

"Didn't strike you…?"

"I met her a couple of times," she said airily. "Gallery openings, chi-chi, la-de-dah gatherings." Mary's face darkened. "Rather shallow for my taste, but nice enough and she didn't *seem* too drunk. Mind you, alcoholics don't tend to advertise the fact. When she stayed at Selly Mews she could have been a *monster* for it, and West wouldn't have been the first wife to spend cheeky nights away from hubby with Mr Red and Mr White, would she?"

"She wouldn't. So…?"

"So in conclusion, we have pills that were never taken and a greater level of alcohol in her blood than could be expected from someone who'd shared a couple of bottles. A level close to leaving her paralytic, depending on her tolerance. An alcohol level that *could* have prevented her from carrying out such neat and tidy cuts to both wrists. Only *could*, though."

"But still not enough for you to conclude anything suspicious?"

"Not in my report, dear, *not in my report*. Everything is still perfectly explainable." She paused. "Off the record, though, I think something is very rotten in the state of Denmark. Well, in the state of W.1. On paper, it's a suicide, 'open and shut.' But in here, Anna my dear," she pointed to Leeding's forehead, "you don't believe that, do you?"

"Something isn't right, I just don't know what it could be. West's note accused others. Part of me thinks that whoever those "others" are, they could be something to do with it. But why…" She shrugged.

They sat and silently sipped their cups of tea.

"I'll tell you something else that's surprising," Mary piped up.

"Go on," Anna leaned forward.

"Who would have ever thought crisps and smoked salmon would be quite so delicious? Wonders never cease."

15 / 13th April, 1981. London. 9:30 P.M.

In North London, The Church of St Mary's can be found between Camden Market to the West and Primrose Hill to the East. Reverend John Martin was given curacy there in 1973.

John loved the area and its people. The quiet, affluent suburbia of Primrose Hill was countered by Camden's vibrant throb. He remembered the market when it opened in 1974, just a handful of stalls which sold trinkets, second hand clothes and books. At forty-eight years old, John was way past caring about music and fashion but took civic pride in Camden and how far it had come.

These days the area had become the most fashionable *hang-out* in London, eclipsing the likes of Borough and King's Road. Martin would often go to his favourite cafe and watch the world go by. Youth today were more tribal than in the late '60s, when John had awakened to the Lord Jesus Christ. Back then, there were only hippies, mods and greasers, but now only the aviary at Regent's Park Zoo could boast more varied plumages. Some he recognised; Teddy Boys, Skinheads, Punks, the new wave of Mods who'd re-appeared a couple of years ago…But now there were yet more fascinating breeds on display. Zoot-suited kids who looked like South American immigrants from the '40s, white faced androids with shirts and skinny ties, Jazz Funkers dressed in silk and gold, made-up boys who fluttered like Beau Brummell.

John knew many of his parishioners were appalled such fashions and sexual licentiousness were on their doorstep but he viewed youth benignly. *Most of these kids have no time for God,* he thought, *but surely only the Creator could have given them such imagination and lust for life? They're not harming anyone, after all.* The Punks claimed to be nihilists, but while true nihilists rejected all belief and meaning, Punks were *covered* in signs and symbols. In fact the market's many T-shirts proved how these young people ultimately believed in *something*, even if that was, for now, a popular chart band.

We all find our leaders to follow, he'd often thought. *For today, they might believe in "Soft Cell," "Joy Division,""The Human League," or "The Spandau Ballet," but ultimately they will need more and that is where our Lord will enter their hearts.*

He could see God in the life and energy of Camden Market, but then find his maker in the glory of nature at Primrose Hill. For Reverend John Martin, the market and park were two sides of the same miraculous coin, both to be marvelled at. The young people would come round to the Lord in their own time. The reverend didn't believe in forcing his religion on anyone because an enforced faith is no faith at all.

John hadn't always been this way. In his teens and twenties he'd sated his earthly needs with no concern for the happiness of others. He tried not to look back on those wilful and selfish times, but still didn't believe his actions had caused any lasting harm. That's what he'd told himself on many sleepless nights and had almost begun to believe it. He'd rationalised the past, re-wrote his history, painted over parts he couldn't bear to examine in detail and been re-born in God's sight. Therefore if God forgave him, *God the almighty*, then he could forgive himself and surely those he'd *crossed* could forgive him, too. Mercy was all, and when the day of judgement came, Martin knew he could face God with a   cleansed soul and total faith the gates of Heaven would open.

It had been a busy day. Morning service had been relatively well-attended despite the uncommonly cold weather, since St Mary's was warm enough with tea and biscuits, talk and laughter afterwards. This afternoon he'd officiated a wedding and attended the reception, but left before things became too rowdy as it wouldn't do to be seen indulging in high jinks. However, despite many busy marriage services, he'd noticed his congregation had become much older and smaller. But John planned to fill the pews again by organising a music festival at the Church Hall. His friends the market traders could "put the word out," get some bands along, set up a few stalls, create a mini-Camden and hopefully the kids would realise the church wasn't stuffy and *uncool*. St Mary's could be *happening and now*.

If that wasn't enough, John had another youthful trick up his sleeve; he was a runner.

Back in the mid 1970s he'd heard about an American craze called "jogging". If he were honest with himself (which John wasn't, not as much as he'd like) Martin admitted to a little vanity. That came from pride, one of the deadly sins, but the reverend knew he'd become what the old dears admiringly called *distinguished* in middle age. He wanted to keep his weight down and body toned, so running was ideal and also gave him time alone to think.

When he'd first started, jogging was considered weird because only criminals, athletes, and school children ran, and even then only in very specific circumstances. Simply sprinting along the street invited derision from passers-by, but John enjoyed any and all forms of attention. Then, on March 29th this year, over *six thousand people* had taken part in London's first marathon and overnight a niche sport became a national fascination.

John liked to go running at 9:30 p.m. whatever the weather. Once the business of the day was over, he would pull on his bright blue track suit and run the same route; out of the church grounds, turn left, head down Fitzroy Road, right into Regent's Park Road, join Primrose Hill Road, circle round the outskirts adjacent to Euston railway line, then back to St Mary's.

He stood on the church step, took a deep breath of freezing air and set off. This dark and cold Monday evening meant he mostly had the pavements to himself but apart from the pubs, there wasn't much to do in London at night anyway. The city was pretty much shut by eight with only occasional late commuters on the roads.

His breath plumed out, the street lights became further apart and soon enough he joined a dingy and deserted Regent's Park Road.

John glanced over his shoulder. A solitary Austin Maxi passed by and he noticed how the old driver craned his head round with a disapproving expression. *Obviously someone who hasn't caught up with the latest trends. He probably thinks I'm a burglar, but where's my swag bag, granddad?*

Eventually, he took a left into Primrose Hill Road, which was darker yet and tree-lined on both sides. There was still no-one about so it felt like London belonged to him alone.

No other cars went by. A solitary Ford Escort had parked on the other side of the road, which was an unusual place to stop since there were no buildings on this part of the route. The reverend glanced over as he passed. The Ford's headlights were off and the vehicle had pulled up diagonally with its near-side wheels on the pavement.

Then John realised someone was sat inside. He couldn't see any details in the darkness, but they were still and faced ahead. Peripheral movement normally attracts one's attention, but this driver remained motionless.

It was somewhat unnerving, so John picked up his pace. As the reverend put distance between himself and the car, its engine suddenly barked into life then *growwlllllled* like an animal.

Everything happened very fast after that.

Martin barely had time to register how the Escort's engine screamed and tyres screeched like nails on a blackboard. Amidst the panicked, primal clattering of his mind the reverend managed to think *that noise is unholy,* then looked over his shoulder.

The Ford's lights were still dark and John realised with horror that the vehicle hadn't simply pulled away but was fixed on him. It crossed the road then headed into what would have been oncoming traffic if this were rush hour, but it was nearly ten o'clock and completely deserted. Even the horrified moon had slipped behind clouds, unable to watch.

It must have only taken seconds but the motor's revs and squealing tyres seemed to go on forever, becoming incrementally louder behind him. John's legs pumped for his life but were no match for the Ford's engine.

Whyisthishappeningwhyisthishappeningwhyisthishappening? His brain cycled like a siren but then, the strangest thing; John felt his body *pusssssshhhhed* from behind and he took off. Solid ground was now some way below.

Time slowed yet further. Martin became distantly aware his spine and hips had been seriously damaged. Cold air rushed past and his flailing arms tried to find something, *anything* to slow this impossible flight but then the dark icy pavement rushed toward him, ready to break his fall.

He crunched into it and while there was no pain below his waist, every nerve ending above tried to scream at once. His skull bounced off the ground, up, then down again, where it cracked.

John's eyes were still open but his breathing, at first fast and desperate, began to slow and hiss like ancient bellows.

The rev. twitched, spasmed and saw the car was idling maybe twenty feet away. A person stepped out but John's eyes had started to cloud and he still couldn't make out any details.

Not that it mattered, none of it mattered any longer. There was no more pain because his nervous system had nothing else to offer. Pain alerts you to danger, tells you to *get away from this, fast*, but when there is no further need for warnings, what is the point?

The driver sauntered toward him and squatted down.

A childlike part of John's mind managed to think, *perhaps this was a terrible accident and they will help me and take me to the hospital where I will be all put together again like Humpty Dumpty.*

But the person simply stared and made no move to help. The reverend didn't know who they were, their face held no memories for him.

"God forgives, doesn't he?" The person whispered. "But I don't. Remember those long nights? Look at my face. Know my name."

As darkness started to cloud about his eyes and soul, John Martin finally recognised the person who looked down and smiled at him. As he died the reverend thought with horror, *there is no Heaven for me. There was never going to be a Heaven for me.*

Then there was nothing, forever and after.

16 / 13th April, 1981, 11:20 P.M.

Once again Anna returned from work late, taken an unsatisfying bath then fallen exhausted into bed. It was fatigue of mind rather than body, since her brain had been whirring for days. She'd poked and prodded at West's case but still failed to find anything that might take it forward. While Jeanette's mysterious nocturnal female visitor stayed in the shadows there was nothing to get things moving again, so the reason for her suicide remained hidden.

Anna had to stop the mental noise or she'd never sleep, and reading usually worked. Leeding was very good at starting books but poor at finishing, so accusatory folds marked where she'd stopped and never gone back. Along with Stephen King's "Firestarter" and John Le Carré's "Smiley's People" there were sixteen books patiently piled on her bedside table and Anna would often wake with one opened but unread at her side.

She slid out Kit Williams' best-selling literary treasure hunt, "Masquerade." A golden hare worth £5,000 had been buried somewhere in Britain and the book's combination of lush illustrations and cryptic wordplay were supposed to reveal its location. But despite becoming a national obsession, the Hare had eluded capture. Anna had poured through "Masquerade" many times and was now petulantly offended by it.

Of all people, she often sulked, *surely I could solve this puzzle?* But no, like the West case, at first there seemed to be lots of intriguing clues, but they disappeared the moment she studied them in any depth. Anna made herself comfy and leafed through the exquisite paintings until one page made her stop.

In this particular picture a bearded puppeteer operated two marionettes; a boy in short trousers and a girl wearing a green skirt. Wrapped up in the book's mysteries Anna had never noticed how the female looked like her, complete with blue eyes and a blonde bob. The puppet master had pulled the girl's hands up to her eyes as if to suggest she was wilfully blind. Anna frowned. *What if somebody is pulling* my *strings?* Despite several layers of sheets a chill settled over her. *What if they're making* me *hide my eyes from what I* should *be seeing?*

There was no evidence for that thought but the idea wouldn't shift. This female puppet had the ghost of a dumb smile across her lips as the man who pulled her cords stared out of the page. Before, Anna thought his expression benign, but now she looked again the puppet master seemed to smirk.

Don't look at me, Anna imagined him sneering. *Don't look here, silly girl, look* there. *Take your hands away and just* look, *would you?*

The phone rang in her hallway and broke her reverie. She sighed and shut the book. No-one ever called at this time except work, which usually meant bad news. Leeding pulled on her dressing gown, ambled out and picked up the receiver. "Hello?"

Silence.

No, not quite silence. It wasn't a broken connection or dead line because Anna heard an atmosphere from the other end.

"Hello? Hello?"

She listened but couldn't tell if there was breathing or just the ebb and flow of electricity.

"Hello, who's there?"

Silence answered, but Anna got the feeling *somebody* was weighing up whether to speak.

"Pathetic, you're pathetic. What is this? What is the point of this? Don't call again. You're pathetic."

She dropped the receiver back in its cradle, aware her pulse had started to race. Anna stared at the phone and willed it to ring so she could confront the caller but it remained hushed. She curled her top lip in disgust and walked away.

Ring. Ring. Ring.

Leeding turned back.

"Oh, you want some more, do you?"

She pulled the phone from its cradle and wasted no time.

"Fuck. Off." She snarled. "Just. Fuck. Off."

"Ma'am?" It was Inspector Walker and he sounded confused.

"Oh, Christ, sorry, David."

"Just come back from the docks have you?"

"No, sorry. I just had a silent call and thought it was the same person calling back."

"Does that happen a lot?" asked Walker, concerned.

"No. First time. Last time too, I hope. So, it's late and I'm guessing we have a situation?"

"Sorry, but yes, a hit and run, the victim's dead and he's reverend of St Mary's in Primrose Hill."

"A reverend? *Fuck*."

*

Walker picked Anna up ten minutes later and although he ran the Rover's heater on full, cold still got into Leeding's bones. He briefed her on the short trip.

"Hit and run, apparently. A motorist saw the body at approx. 22:00 hours. They pulled over, realised the victim was deceased, drove on to a residence further up the road, called from there. The motorist lives locally and identified him as Reverend John Martin, very well known in the community. Hence why I called you, public interest and all that. I thought it best."

"Uh huh, all right."

"Parker was first on the scene. We've blocked the road but there's virtually no traffic anyway."

"Turn the bloody heating up would you?"

"It won't go any higher and besides you'll feel even colder when we get out. Pull your collars up."

"Yes, dad. OK, anything else?"

"The victim was running."

"Running? From what?"

"No, just running, you know, like people do these days. Track suit, those training shoes everyone wears right now. Unless of course the reverend was also a mugger who dresses very appropriately for his getaways."

Hit and runs came under the Road Traffic Act of 1974 which classed them under the catch-all term, "Reckless driving." When such behaviour resulted in death, the victim was "of interest" and the driver fled the scene, that was within Anna's purview.

On arrival she switched on her torch, looked at the crumpled body, then up and down the road.

First impressions;

There are tyre tracks fifty or so yards behind the deceased which might belong to the vehicle involved. The tracks are on the other *side of the road, though, so the vehicle responsible was in its correct lane, then sped up enough for the tyres to leave a mark, crossed over, and...*

She walked forward, played her torch across the ground and followed the incident's trajectory...*ploughed into the victim. Driver must have had their foot fully down on the accelerator.*

Anna retraced her steps back to the corpse, which reminded her of the limp and lifeless marionettes she'd seen in "Masquerade".

The only illumination came from their torches and vehicle headlights. Otherwise, Primrose Hill Road was coal black.

Skid marks here on the pavement. The victim is struck, the car slides to a halt, then...? Does the driver get out, realise what he or she has done? Or do they just immediately speed off? Why did *they drive away?*

Walker seemed to have read her mind. "For what it's worth and from the marks on the ground, I think this is a drunk driver. He's going along here, it's deserted, decides to put his foot down. But look, the road's iced up. He loses control, the car crosses into the oncoming lane, he mounts the kerb, hits the victim. Driver panics, pegs it. So maybe someone further up the road saw or heard a car at speed earlier this evening."

"Be nice to have a reg. OK, get some officers knocking. I concur. It looks like a drink drive incident." She sighed and rubbed her gloved hands together. "If they hadn't left the scene I'd still be tucked up in bed. It's never normally this cold in April."

"They reckon snow soon enough."

"Jesus, the world's gone mad."

In the distance, Anna saw spinning red lights of an ambulance which would take the body away once all necessary boxes had been ticked.

She walked to the other side of the road where the dark streaks of rubber began. Those tyre tracks bothered her. Leeding now saw the marks were solid as if the vehicle's wheels had spun on the spot. They had the same appearance as the skids "Boy Racers" left when they revved up then sped away. Traffic specialists were better equipped to analyse them. She called over to Walker.

"Have you radioed for a photographer? We need to preserve these."

"Of course. Daniel's on his way."

"Oh, good."

She wandered back to the broken reverend, splashed her torchlight round him then froze.

"Walker," she called, but discovered her voice had dried up. "Walker!" She managed, louder.

The inspector picked up on her tone and jogged over.

"There." She aimed her torch at a spot above and to the right of the reverend. "What is that?"

Written on the pavement in blue chalk, or charcoal, was a single word;

FOG

Walker looked confused. "Oh, road menders often mark pavements and that with little instructions, numbers. You must have seen them."

"Yes, but does it remind you of anything?"

"No. Should it?"

Anna checked no-one else was in earshot since the ambulance crew had started to exit their vehicle. She pulled Walker to one side.

"Blue chalk, charcoal. West's house. The picture in her room, that was one word, "FACE." Same colour here but 'FOG.'"

The inspector finally twigged her meaning.

"Ah, I see. Just coincidence. You see these marks everywhere. It's a repair code or Highway Maintenance. It's nothing. "FOG" probably means fog lights are to be fitted here."

"Just here? In this one spot? And wait, you know as well as I do fog lights aren't fitted on roads, just cars."

She waved her torch up and down the rest of the pavement. "Look, there are no other markings here, none at all. What, the victim just *happened* to land right next to a word written in the same colour and material as at West's home?"

"With respect, you're sounding paranoid."

"Yes, OK. It's what it looks like, just a drunk driver and this is some kind of Highway Maintenance mark. But do me a favour, would you?"

The ambulance crew waited nearby to be given their next move. Walker indicated he'd be over in a moment.

"When Daniel arrives don't make a big thing of it, but make sure he gets shots of that mark, symbol, whatever. I want to check it with the Highways Agency."

"It could just be graffiti."

"Kids graffiti where their work can be seen, that's the whole point, it's a kudos thing. And what does 'FOG' mean?"

"Who knows? Could be a band."

"Just get a photographic record of it. Humour me, OK?"

Walker shrugged, then shouted over to the ambulance crew. "Bear with us, we need to get some photos when the snapper arrives, all right?"

The crew were fine with that and gladly lit cigarettes.

Anna couldn't tear her eyes from that blue word written above the body.

Probably a repair code, possibly graffiti, could be coincidence. So why don't I feel it's any of them?

She shivered and once again the cold had nothing to do with it.

17 / Sometime *Before* (3)

She'd started to keep a journal in her final school year, which wasn't a "diary" in the conventional sense but rather a notebook of every attack, insult and negative event in her life.

She admitted to herself that it was a masochistic hobby. The entries recounted every brutal moment in clinical detail, almost like they'd happened to someone else. She thought once those daily horrors were reduced to "objective reports" it might lessen their impact. Part of her also seemed to take perverse pleasure in writing them down.

But she also believed her "diary" would be of use eventually, to help her look back from a distance and judge events impartially. She hoped the fury would never pass, though. She didn't want time to diminish her suffering.

Of course, not everyone at school was a bully. She had friends, well, more *acquaintances who smiled* and didn't treat her badly. Sometimes that was enough. But the bullies had latched onto her like lampreys and wherever she was, they were too.

One of the ringleaders had become a prefect, which was a joke. That *cow's* report would say she was trustworthy and respected when she was anything but. That *cow* played a very clever game, oh yes, in class she was brightest and best, ready to laugh at the teachers' jokes and collect exercise books. But in the dark corners of the corridors and far ends of the yard she was like a spoiled child who delighted in pulling the wings off flies.

The death of her rabbit hadn't seemed to make any difference. She'd watched that *cow* come into school the following morning and her haughty, self-absorbed demeanour was exactly the same. The brief feeling of satisfaction she'd felt after killing the pet had faded quickly.

Her academic record continued to slide. Mother and Father still exhibited an utter lack of concern about the bullying and any attempts to engage with them were met with petulant lectures on the importance of schoolwork and "sticking up for yourself."

They didn't care. No, that wasn't quite right. They did care, but only about the job she'd get after school. As long as their daughter had the right grades to start a nice, *visible* career in a bank, that was enough. Being able to tell "friends" how she'd secured a career in the High Street Barclays was their only dream.

The only subjects she excelled in were art and drama, both, of course, quite useless. Her art pieces were met with confused stares from Mother and Father. Mother smirked and called them "doodles," Father didn't call them anything, but looked right through the paper as if it were transparent.

She'd started to turn her suffering and anger into art, but anyone who saw the work remained oblivious to its real meaning, which delighted her. Charcoal was her favourite medium, blue the chosen palette. She enjoyed how charcoal blended into waves and washes while blue gave the pictures a dream-like quality. True blue is rarely found in nature, but she *felt* blue. Not the emotional blue jazz singers evoked, but a person made of blue, translucent, without mass. If she didn't really exist then how could she hurt?

Her art teacher, Mrs Butler, was one of the few members of staff who still had patience. Butler praised her work but never really knew what she was looking at. So while *teacher* saw a shimmering picture of a rabbit, *she* knew the animal was dead. Mrs Butler admired ghostly portraits of Uncle John without realising he too was a corpse and had been made to suffer. Her charcoals showed Things That Had Happened and Things That Were Yet To Be, but in code. Nobody else recognised the truth she put to paper.

*

Eight months earlier, Mother had been ostentatiously watering the garden when a stroke came for her. Mother died as she'd lived, acting out a perfect life, always on show while her daughter was kept in darkness and only brought out when necessary. She hoped it was painful and imagined how the blood vessels in Mother's head must have exploded from the pressure of living a lie twenty-four hours a day.

She'd dared to hope Mother's death might make Father see life as precious and engage with his daughter, but no. If anything it made him worse, like he had to embody *both* parents' disappointment. Father treated her as an unwanted lodger and reduced his already meagre communications yet further. "Tidy that away," "heat that up," and "make your bed," were amongst other caring Fatherly announcements that she *treasured*.

Then a few months ago, everything changed.

She'd often fantasised about a boyfriend and occasionally even entertained the idea of a girlfriend, but always pushed that away. She didn't know what she was, not really. Sex was never spoken about in the house (she thought it highly likely Mother and Father had *"done it"* just once and she was the disastrous product of that awful union) and the reproductive act was only giggled and whispered about in school. She knew the mechanics, of course, but never had the chance to try them for herself.

Boys kept their distance. She may have been pretty, but when most girls announced her arrival with a chorus of "creep," "weirdo," "nutcase," and "freak!" she knew it would take a brave lad to dare enter her orbit in case *he* became those things, too. The girls were right, of course. She *was* a freak, because only freaks would kill chicks, rip a rabbit to pieces and fantasise about doing the same to classmates. She believed her body gave off a low level warning that people felt rather than heard, a dark vibration that hummed, *Stay away*. School had forced her into playing this "normal" pupil. In extremis, you wore the face you needed to survive.

The Christmas Musical arrived. She enjoyed Drama because people saw her differently on stage. She often dreamed of transforming into another version of herself, then living as that character for ever after, free of her past.

The musical was "The King & I" and she'd landed the lead role of Anna Leonowens, a Western schoolteacher in an alien culture who eventually falls for its king. She recognised her own life in the story; school was a foreign land and she would never fit in.

The King was played by Danny, one of the most popular boys in her year. Normally lads who took drama were mocked as "poofters" and "Nancy boys" but Danny was a high achiever. The boys liked him, the girls *really* liked him.

At first she'd been embarrassed but Danny was patient and kind. His eyes twinkled during their duets and when they danced, she felt him hold her tighter than the role required. He often shyly glanced her way on stage, which made her heart beat faster. She found it hard to suppress joyous giggles when that happened.

The musical was a hit. Audiences laughed in the right places, dabbed their eyes at others and gave standing ovations every night.

She started to believe this was the turning point, that she'd been accepted. Yes, the audiences had actually related to *Anna*, but maybe it really was a new start and perhaps soon Danny would hold her without need of stage directions.

The final performance garnered three curtain calls. Danny held their hands up high, the audience cheered and she felt tears on her cheeks. It was the happiest moment of her life. Naturally, Father wasn't present, but that only added to the joy. To look out and spot his disapproving face emerging from the dark would have scratched away the shine.

The after show celebration was the first ever party she'd attended with her peers. The rest of the cast were effusive in their praise, and swept away with excitement, she suddenly realised they weren't keeping her at arm's length.

As couples paired off, she'd stared over at Danny and occasionally he'd look back, then coyly glance away.

The performance had given her a new confidence. A few weeks ago she wouldn't have approached any boy, let alone Danny, but she spotted him alone at the buffet table. It took just a couple of moments to re-inhabit the strong persona of Anna, then once the character was in place she marched over without further thought.

She took his arm, flashed her eyes and giggled. "So, would the King like to dance with Anna once more? *Shall* we dance?"

But he pushed her hand away with a cold, disgusted expression.

"It was just *acting*," he hissed then looked about in case anyone had seen them together. "Just acting, you weirdo. You thought it was real? They cast you and I didn't make a fuss, but it was just acting. *They* chose you, not me. I would have never chosen *you*."

Her mouth dropped open in disbelief.

Danny's voice was hoarse, hateful, hurtful. "I did what I had to do for the best performance. It all goes on my report and I'm getting As. It was acting, acting, *acting*, so stay away from me." Then he looked over her shoulder, pulled a face and shrugged. She turned and saw some of her tormentors giggle. "Weirdo," he rasped then broke away toward the popular girls, cocked a thumb her way, shook his head and laughed.

She'd mechanically picked up an egg sandwich as if that was the intention all along. The room had lost its warmth, leeched from technicolour to washed-out, charcoal blue. She smoothed down her dress, painted on a smile, then gave a little wave to no-one in particular. It was just acting.

Just acting.

The only time she'd been accepted was as someone else and once she'd taken off the costume, nobody cared.

She didn't cry. He didn't deserve her tears, none of them did.

Once back home she went straight upstairs and pulled out her charcoals.

She drew Danny and this portrait wasn't in code, but what she wanted to do to him. Then, knowing even Father would recognise her wrath, she ripped the paper into pieces and imagined the strips were parts of his body.

18 / 15th April 1981, London. 7:20 P.M.

Anna sat in the Ten Bells pub in Commercial Street, Whitechapel. She'd been born and raised just a few hundred yards away, but her home had been pulled down to make way for offices. She didn't mourn its passing and had never gone back. Whenever Leeding returned to Whitechapel, she stayed on the very edges of her old haunts. The past could bite.

Anna had lived and worked in Central London for years now, so felt she knew every shopkeeper, delivery boy, street walker, hustler and busker in the area. Around W1 she'd almost always bump into someone familiar, so the East End gave her a welcome anonymity. Anna liked to keep her own company, especially recently.

When she'd walked into The Ten Bells, there'd been curious stares from the locals but that was usual. Women (or "*birds*" round these parts) usually went to pubs with boyfriends or husbands as little female add-ons who lurked quietly at the edges of conversations and nursed half of lager or a white wine for the evening. The only women seen alone in pubs were the barmaids or posters of topless girls hidden behind packets of Big D peanuts. As each packet was removed, a little more flesh was revealed. If a girl was in a pub alone she was either a server or stripper, and if one was there with her "fella" she just shut up and listened. But The Ten Bells wasn't a rowdy inn and Anna could handle East End boys, no problem. She'd grown up amongst them and knew even the loudest *barra-boy* could be silenced with the right comeback. Looking around the old and disinterested clientele, she knew there'd be no trouble of that kind tonight, not least because Leeding was still in her work clothes; black jacket, white shirt, A-line skirt and sensible heels. She was aware this made her look like a bank clerk, but the outfit drew little attention and that was just fine.

She'd stood for a moment in the doorway and remembered female pub etiquette; you were either a wallflower or acted like you owned the place, went straight to the bar and ordered.

So she'd marched straight up to the central bar, ordered half of Carlsberg then retreated to a table. She *could* have had a pint, but if a "*bird*" asked for one she was also asking for trouble, so Anna started with a demure half and would then move on.

Most pubs have a bar which runs the room's length, but that wasn't how it used to be. The Ten Bells still had a nineteenth century *central* bar, an island of alcohol which allowed customers to approach from three hundred and sixty degrees. Anna thought that was a far more efficient and grown-up system.

Excitement over, the regulars went back to their muttered chats, cigarettes, pints and papers while Leeding lit up a B&H and pulled a handful of papers from her bag.

There was another reason she'd chosen The Ten Bells for this informal meeting. With the exception of Walker and maybe Fisher at a push, she didn't want any of her colleagues to know it had taken place.

*

The Ten Bells' lighting was jaundice-yellow and low wattage but still brighter than the dark street outside, which meant people could see *in* much easier than anyone could look *out*.

Anna never spotted the person who'd also alighted from the tube train at Aldgate East, then followed her at a discreet distance out of the station into Whitechapel and up Commercial St.

Sat at a small corner table, Leeding didn't realise she was being watched from the bus stop opposite. Occasionally this observer would cross over, walk past the Ten Bells, glance in, stop outside Christ Church and look up in admiration. Then they'd turn, look through the windows of the pub again and resume their original position. The dark outside and cigarette smoke inside conspired to make the watcher invisible, whilst Anna remained lit and scrutinised.

*

At seven-thirty, Daniel Moore walked in. Once again, faces turned his way and made instant appraisals. Anna noticed the barmaid look him up and down approvingly. He glanced about, saw Leeding, smiled, then made the time honoured mime of *"what do you fancy?"* She picked up her own drink, waggled it and he gave a thumbs-up. Daniel wore a fashionable brown suede jacket plus tight cream slacks and black suede Chelsea boots.

And here he is, ladies, Anna smiled to herself. *Mr April, 1981.*

The barmaid noticed the mimed exchange and looked disappointed. Anna could read her mind.

Only one other bloody bird in here and she's with him. *Typical.*

He brought his pint over, sat down and looked about approvingly.

"Ooh, this is a *nice* boozer. I can't believe I've never been."

"I thought you were from round these parts."

"Nah, little bit further west, more Farringdon way." Daniel looked back over his shoulder. "The bar's in the middle? That's new."

"No, it's old. Lovely, isn't it? It's been here since the late nineteenth century and hardly changed, apparently. Legend says a couple of Jack The Ripper's victims drank here."

"Ooh," he whispered. "Bit creepy. So is that the attraction for a detective, then? A historical crime scene that also sells beer?"

Anna gave Daniel a thin smile."No, that's not why I come here. I see enough nastiness on a daily basis, I just like the look of the place. Sometimes you have to forget the past and just appreciate the present."

"Well, Jack or not, it is very nice indeed. Cosy." He laughed ruefully and shook his head. "You know, when I was little, I thought Jack The Ripper was a made up character like a pantomime villain, twiddling his moustache in disguise while everyone shouted *'beee-hind you!'*. But the pantomime villains always get caught, don't they? Happy endings all round. They never collared Jack, though, did they? I wonder how he got away with it?"

"I'd imagine the usual combination; luck, coincidence and police incompetence."

"Bloody hell, really?"

"Uh huh. Mind you, it works the other way, too. We sometimes catch villains because *we* get lucky, *we* spot coincidences and *they're* incompetent."

"Well, cheers to that. Here's to catching the villains."

They clinked glasses, sipped their drinks and a silence descended. The Ten Bells had no jukebox so the only sounds were pumps hissing and gently muttered conversation. Anna always thought there was something of the church about pubs like this, a weird kind of reverence.

"So what's it all about? This skullduggery?"

"*Skullduggery?*" laughed Anna. "Who are you, Blackbeard?"

"Aaarrr," he nodded in agreement but didn't smile. "Discussing a case out of hours? Out of the station? I'm a little concerned. Only a little, but…" She could see him weigh up his words. "This isn't illegal, is it?"

Leeding smiled. "No, because it's not even a case, just a hunch which I want to check out. I thought this might be nicer than Portland Street."

"And, if you don't mind me saying, a long way away from nosy parkers?"

Anna shrugged, but didn't answer.

"I've brought what you asked for." Daniel pulled out a brown A4 envelope. "Colour, as requested."

"Mm, as I said, I only have the black and whites." She took another sip and realised her half was nearly gone. "Stuff this, I'm having a pint. Bear with me a moment."

Anna went back to the bar and returned with a pint. "I just don't see the point of a half," she shook her head. "It's like having a three wheeled car. Just get the bloody extra wheel."

He laughed again. "So what's this all about?"

Anna had already been through her notion with Inspector Walker and now talked Daniel through what she had. None of it was conclusive and almost all could be rationally explained away, but she still had the nagging feeling that something wasn't right about the art work in West's house and graffiti at Martin's hit and run.

"So it's probably nothing at all, but I've got a bone now and can't stop gnawing at it. May I see?"

Daniel opened the envelope and pulled out some colour stills. Some showed the art at Jeanette's house, the rest were markings from the pavement in Primrose Hill.

"So, what do *you* think?"

"What do I think?" He riffled through the shots. "Well, I didn't really *think* anything about the picture in West's house, it just struck me as weird that her photographs were hung all over the place, but in the bedroom there was just this," he waved a print of the word FACE. "Jeanette could have drawn it though, perhaps fancied herself as an artist. Or just preferred to have one room without herself. Who knows? The fact her husband didn't recognise it is interesting, but hardly suspicious. From what you say, Selly Mews was more West's London bolt-hole than his anyway."

"But what about the graffiti, markings, or whatever you want to call them?"

"OK, so when I turned up to Primrose Hill and Inspector Walker was being furtive, getting me to take pictures of the marks but not make a fuss, that's when I thought, *hello, what's all this about?*" He pointed to prints of the graffiti."Now, I took these shots that night but you piqued my interest, so I went back there the following day."

"You went back?"

"Well, the *West* pictures were taken during the day, but the *Martin* ones were taken at night, so you can't really see if the colours match. Hence I put my detective hat on and went back to take these."

He reached into the envelope and pulled out a few colour prints of the word FOG, but taken in daylight.

"Daniel, you are brilliant."

He tipped an imaginary hat at her. "I hope you don't mind but I put two and two together. If you hadn't called I would have put it down to my over-active imagination and left it there. But here we are."

"Mm, here we are. That's what I thought,too, that I was getting too over imaginative. Now I'm not so sure."

They lay the pictures side by side. The shade of blue used in both the art and pavement markings was identical.

"Chalk, charcoal, " he shrugged. "Is there much difference? Isn't charcoal thicker? But the colour *is* the same, yes. However, blue's a pretty standard chalk colour isn't it?" Daniel frowned. "Nothing? Something? I'm not the detective."

"What does FOG mean, do you think?"

"Not a clue. Maybe just, you know, *fog*. Oh, but I did have one thought, for what it's worth; look at the West picture again."

He pushed the photograph toward her, which showed the framed word FACE written in blue charcoal.

"Now, I'm no handwriting expert, but FOG and FACE both look like they're written by the same person. Mind you, they're in capitals and capitals always look pretty samey." He smiled and sighed. "Or FACE is more likely *just* a piece of modern art and FOG is *just* a marking on the pavement with a perfectly dull explanation. Sorry to be boring, but that's what I'm erring toward. It's an interesting coincidence, but that's all."

"OK, Maybe no connection and no meaning. West killed herself, Martin was a hit and run and I'm being paranoid."

"Well, I hate to say, but it does sound a teensy bit that way. So what else can I do?"

"There is nothing *to* do. If some of my colleagues knew I was talking like this, they'd send for the men in white coats. Right now, there's only you, me and Inspector Walker who know about these two odd little coincidences, signs, clues, whatever you want call them. I'd like to keep it that way. But if I'm honest, there's nothing here I could point to and say, 'this isn't right and we need to investigate further.' Don't you think?"

"Mmm. It's interesting though. Bonkers," he laughed then added emphasis, "but very *interesting*."

"Why does that sound like I'm being damned with faint praise? But in for a penny, as they say. Sitting here in this pub of all places, I'm reminded of something."

Daniel looked about and tried to see what Anna alluded to.

"Jack The Ripper. He allegedly left a chalked phrase on a wall next to one of his victims."

Daniel frowned. "He did?"

"Mm, *The juwes are the men that will not be blamed for nothing*." Heaven knows what *that* meant, and never conclusively proved to be written by the Ripper, but some believe it was a message, directly to the police."

They both looked down at the photographs once more.

Daniel picked up a print of FOG and peered at it. "If that's so, what's the message here?"

*

Anna and Daniel left the Ten Bells at nine o'clock. They'd spun round in circles, gone off on tangents and debated various possibilities but after a while it became little more than a parlour game.

Daniel held up his hands in surrender. "I have reached the end of my expertise in this area, which was almost non-existent in the first place."

"Let's call it a day, then."

"Let's. My head is decidedly fuzzy."

As they walked back to Aldgate Station, Daniel laughed. "Well, that was an interesting but weird date, wouldn't you agree?"

"*Date*? I don't think so."

"No, no, I didn't mean it like that. I meant it was our first social contact outside work. And what do we do? We get weird."

"I've had dates that were weirder. Let's just call it an unofficial work meeting."

"I wish I could have more meetings in a pub."

"Ha, what a wonderful world that would be."

Daniel and Anna laughed and stepped into Aldgate Station, unaware they'd been followed. The expression on their shadow's face was like the April night; cold, bleak and full of dark intention.

19 /16th April, 1981, London.

WPC Fisher was back on front desk duty, which was still far from the exciting police career she'd once imagined. Lisa knew she had to start at the bottom but right now, the only people below her were the cleaners. She was surprised nobody had given her a mop yet.

There'd been drunk drivers and drunk fighters, drunk husbands and wives, drunk girlfriends and boyfriends. She'd seen a lot of shouting, kicking and vomiting. From this vantage point, Fisher was now of the opinion that London was permanently sloshed.

Of course there were other crimes and many officers were still being redeployed to Brixton, but Fisher often thought Great Portland Street Station resembled Last Orders on a Saturday, *all the time*.

Lisa dreaded shifts which coincided with pub closing times. The licensing laws had been created to prevent excessive drinking but in reality they just sped it up. When last orders were called blokes lined up pints as if the world were about to end, which for some, it was.

Consequently the station often smelled like a cross between a men's toilet and hospital ward. Fisher was neither qualified nor interested in working for either.

Today, however, was the nine to five shift; very civilised and mainly vomit-free.

D.I. Leeding arrived at ten a.m. and Lisa watched Anna and Inspector Walker go to a corner then whisper among themselves.

Leeding pulled some photographs from her bag, but Fisher couldn't make out any details.

Walker shrugged, Anna pointed. Walker shook his head, Anna frowned. It clearly wasn't a social chat. The WPC watched their body language and they were obviously professionally close, but nothing indicated a deeper relationship.

Interesting. Very interesting. He looks at you seeking...approval? But you just look at him seeking an opinion. I see who has the power here and even though you're the same rank, it's not you, Walker. Very, very interesting. What's the connection here, really?

At that moment Leeding glanced up, so Fisher looked away, aware she'd been noticed.

Shit. But no harm in just keeping an eye open, that's what we officers do after all, isn't it? Observe developments.

The WPC picked up a random file and walked in their direction as if she had somewhere to go. As Fisher passed, she heard Anna mutter, "blue charcoal in West's place. *Exact same colour* blue charcoal at the hit and run." "Yes, I see," Walker replied, "but…" and then she passed out of earshot.

Lisa watched as Walker and Anna went different ways. She caught the barest glimpse of a blue shape on a photograph in Leeding's hand.

That's from Jeanette's bedroom. So Anna's still thinking about that picture and now she's found more blue charcoal somewhere else.

WPC Fisher went back to the front desk. Although she appeared to be doing her job, her mind was very much elsewhere.

*

A couple of hours later, the WPC looked up to see an old lady who'd appeared from no-where like a magician's assistant.

"Good morning, madam," Fisher smiled, whilst part of her died inside. She'd already endured the police O.A.P. experience, where in the station the abbreviation stood for Obsessed Accusing Pain.

Many pensioners treated the force as a cross between a confession box and witch-hunt. After pouring them a cup of tea, you'd hear their entire life story, then eventually, after your *own* life felt over, they'd come to their grievance, inevitably some kind of point scoring exercise against neighbours or perceived enemies.

The old lady looked around with wonder. "Ooh, it's just like the telly," she cooed. "There are policemen and everything."

Don't say it, thought Fisher.

"And you're just like, whatshername, ah, Juliet Bravo."

You said it.

"Well, it's the uniform," said Fisher, brightly. "That always helps."

"This is only the *second time* I've ever been in a police station," the old dear bellowed, then looked around to make sure everyone heard in case they thought she was a bus-pass-toting recidivist.

"How can I help?"

Here we go. The milkman's stolen her garden gnome. The black kid in the shop stared at her funny. She saw someone on "Police 5" who looked like someone she saw in Woolworths. Her fridge is on the blink and what are you *going to do about it?*

"May I see someone about Jeanette West?"

"Jeanette West?"

"The model who killed herself. I am her neighbour. Ex neighbour.
Well, I'm still her neighbour, sadly she has passed on, but life is better
at Jesus' side. I spoke to a policeman the other day about a woman I
saw. My name is Susan Arnold, I am the *witness*. I have information."

Ah, so you're that old lady. I see.

"Let me fetch you Inspector Walker," Fisher grinned widely.

Over to you, inspector.

*

A few minutes later, Fisher showed Susan Arnold to an interview
room where Walker waited with a notebook and pen.

"Mrs Arnold," he stood, shook her hand and she gave a curious
little curtsey.

"Please sit down. Cup of tea?"

"White three sugars, thank you."

David Walker poured two cups and sat back.

"So how can I be of assistance?"

"Well, you remember me?"

"I do. Number Eight, Selly Mews. Tragic occurrence. You were
very helpful. You saw a woman in Jeanette's back garden," he
consulted his file, "at approx. five, five-thirty, on April the fourth.
We've been trying to identify her since but she hasn't come forward.
Have you remembered something else?"

"Ooh, no, better than that. *I know who she is.*"

Walker paused and his pen hung above the paper.

"You do?"

Mrs Arnold pulled out two magazines. Adam Ant stared from "The
Face" which Walker didn't know, but he instantly recognised "Smash
Hits" since his niece was obsessed with it. Aimed at teens, "Smash
Hits" was a glossy pop paper which featured the latest pouting made-
up music stars, cheeky, ego-puncturing interviews, and lyrics to chart
songs.

Mrs Arnold proudly spread it out on the desk.

Walker examined the cover. A scary looking bald man caked in
eyeliner, lipstick and blusher stared back at him. The headline
informed him that this man, or perhaps his band, was called "*Classix
Nouveaux.*" This issue also featured The Jam, Landscape, Spandau
Ballet, and Teardrop Explodes. Like the rest of his generation, Walker
was more a Beatles and Stones fan.

The Beatles, The Stones, Good names. But Spandau Ballet? Classix Nouveaux? They may as well be called Pretentious, Moi? And what has this *got to do with Jeanette West?*

"My granddaughter left the magazines at my place last week. Frightful, aren't they, today's pop stars. Look at this woman…" She pointed to the bald man on the cover. "If she has a condition, of course I'd be sympathetic, but she could still get a wig! And this magazine costs thirty-five pence! I could get a loaf of bread for that! Daylight robbery!"

"So what does this…?"

Mrs Arnold ploughed on. "So I thought I'd take a look, see what Gail, that's my grand-daughter, is into. That's what they say these days, don't they? 'I'm *into* this,' 'I'm *into* that.' I was 'into' Douglas Fairbanks and Ivor Novello when I was sixteen. Proper talents."

The inspector let her meander. She'd get there, they always did.

Susan opened the magazine and flicked through. Walker caught sight of lyrics for "Fascist Groove Thang," "Up The Hill Backwards," and a poster of some serious looking men with what looked like teacloths round their necks. Then she stopped at a photo of a rather attractive girl in a black suit.

The title identified her as *"Sam Bizarre - Grey Velvet."*

"That's the woman. I'd recognise her anywhere. Not my cup of tea, but striking, isn't she?"

Walker had to admit "striking" was one word. Samantha Bizarre *did* look a little like Lady Di. She had a similar blonde flicked hairstyle, high cheekbones and her heavily kohl-lined eyes flashed you a coy come-hither look. But that was as far as the resemblance went, since Sam wore a sleekly cut black suit and thin red leather tie. She leaned on an umbrella, hands in black leather gloves. Her head was tilted back, red lips slightly parted as she sized you up, feline. Sam's right hand held a bolero hat.

Not my cup of tea either, thought Walker. *But she has* something. *Looks like she wouldn't suffer fools gladly.*

"You're *sure* this is her?"

"Inspector, she's not exactly run-of-the-mill, is she? And that was the same hat she was wearing when she visited Jeanette."

So if Mrs Arnold is right, that may explain why Sam Bizarre hasn't come forward. She's a pop star, so wouldn't want controversy, death *even, anywhere near her career. Bad publicity.*

He studied that insouciant, attractive face again.

Or maybe…no. Who was it that said, 'there's no such thing as bad publicity'? Being the last person to see Jeanette West alive would be a hell of a story. Pop stars aren't known for being shrinking violets, after all.

Samantha Bizarre gazed out at him, certainly no wallflower.

So, Ms. Bizarre, why haven't you come forward?

He turned to an interview on the page opposite. It featured lyrics from Grey Velvet's "Smash Hit," "Ice Age". His brow furrowed as he glanced through them.

```
"We are in an ice age, dancing on a cold
stage, don't you turn our last page, or I will
learn and burn and rage."
```

Walker grimaced. *Bloody hell, lighten up, love. What's wrong with "yeah yeah yeah"? Sam Bizarre must be a* really *fun date.*

David had flicked through his niece's "Smash Hits" a few times, so was used to its breathless one hundred mile an hour unashamedly teenage prose. It was a new style for new sounds.

The headline was a mixture of ice blue and fire red, which declared;

```
"SAM BIZARRE AND GREY VELVET - THAWING OUR
ICE AGE!"
```

"Do you mind if I have a read?"

"I have my tea. Go ahead."

He scanned the article.

```
"It's like punk never 'appened! From Essex to
Eee,Sexy! Grey Velvet's (literally) glacial
synth-pop is taking them to the top of the
charts, alongside fellow lipstick-and-liner
faves like Depeche, Ver League, Visage and
Spandau. Your Uncle disgusting may not like
them, but here at Hits Towers, we're all for
wrapping ourselves in a bit of Velvet, grey or
otherwise.
```

And that's in no small measure down to the rather lovely Sam Bizarre. Let's be honest,those cheekbones could cut you. Sylvian, Bowie, Toyah, you'd better watch out, because Bizarre's after your (blusher encrusted) crowns."

None of this makes any sense to me. Have these people not heard of the English language?

"At just twenty-one,Sam's a face and force to be reckoned with in the New Romantic scene and *Ice Age* hasn't been off Hits Towers' record player since its release on Chrysalis Records three weeks ago. We met Sam in swinging Soho to find out what makes Grey Velvet tick.

"This *is* a new ice age isn't it?" Bizarre asks, sipping swanky Italian coffee in a swanky recording studio."People are becoming colder, icing over. I know this sounds dreadfully old fashioned, but in the '60s, it was technicolour, vibrant, full of life. Nowadays, everyone's grey, overcast. Even Visage sung about fading to grey as if that's a good thing. It's not!"

"*Bu-u-uttt,*" we venture,"doesn't your band name have "grey" in it?" Sam laughs."Fair point! But remember "Grey" is followed by "Velvet" and that's lush, warm, soft. You see? Contrasts! I love contrasts, I mean look at me!" Oh, we *do*. Bizarre continues,"We want to splash some colour and warmth over everything again. Bring back glamour!" What kind of glamour? We ask, admiring those unfeasibly, *unfairly* long eyelashes."Classic glamour! Look at Twiggy, Shrimpton, look At Westie," Bizarre purrs, fluttering those impossible 'lashes…"

Westie? Walker stopped reading. *Of all people, she's directly mentioned Jeanette West. OK, that's interesting.*

"I love Jeanette West. She's still one of the most glamorous women that ever lived. If I could look ten percent as good as Westie, I'd be happy."

Go on, Sam, Walker thought. *Now's the time to mention you're a friend of hers. That would make sense. Go on.* He turned back to the magazine cover. *It's dated 2nd to 15th April, so printed before West's suicide. Sam had no reason not to mention her friendship.*

"There's a lot of bleepy synthesisers in the charts right now, we point out. What makes Grey Velvet different? "Synths are just another instrument. They suit the songs we're making right now. Next week, I might decide to use a banjo, or bang two sticks together like a neanderthal. Whatever works." But you're not going to swap your look for furs and a club? "Ha! The only club I'm interested in is Club For Heroes." With those looks and this success you'd expect him to be as glacial as an "Ice Age" but Sam Bizarre is one of the nicest guys we've met from ver Scene…"

Wait. What? He? Him? Walker re-read the last two sentences and flicked back to the poster. *He? Him? That can't be right. It must be a typo. Sam Bizarre is a* man?

"…One of the nicest guys we've met…"

Not Samantha. Samuel. *Dear God. Jeannette West's husband is out of town. A man visits, but not through the front door. A* man *who's talking about how much he loves her. Anna found a suitcase full of shaving gear and spare men's clothes under the bed, it didn't belong to*

Clive St. Austenne, but I bet those clothes fitted Sam Bizarre. What the hell is going on?

"There's another picture of her in "The Face" if you'd like to see." Mrs Arnold piped up. "Is everything OK, dear? I don't suppose you have any custard creams?"

20 / 16th April 1981, London.

"Saddle up, Constable, you're relieved. We need to go and talk to someone." WPC Fisher looked up to see Anna stood at the front desk, one eyebrow raised. "And by the way, it seems you're on reception a lot more than the other constables." She mimed looking through binoculars at the rest of the station. "I wonder why that could possibly be?"

"No idea, ma'am."

Leeding clicked her fingers at another constable. "Ah, Barker. Hold the fort would you? Skirt not required. Men can do reception too, you know."

"Yes, ma'am," the PC sighed.

"You'll need to grab a cape," Anna pulled on a jacket. "It is *bitter* out there."

"We're not driving?"

"No, it's a five, ten minute walk at most, depending if we march or not."

"In that case, I'll just take gloves if you don't mind. The capes make me feel like Batman, or rather, Batgirl."

Anna laughed. "Well, we are crime fighters."

"We are. Where are we going, ma'am?"

"Soho. I thought it might be worth you sitting in on a bit of questioning, you know, as part of your on the ground training."

"Questioning? May I ask who?"

Anna held up the copy of "Smash Hits" magazine and smiled.

"We've found our mystery woman and here's a surprise. I had to look twice. She's not even a woman." Leeding opened the magazine to the poster of Sam Bizarre.

"Pretty, isn't he?"

"Not my type," replied Fisher.

"You never know. You like this kind of music, don't you? Well, how do you fancy meeting a real life pop star?"

*

Nigel Blundell sat in Trident Recording Studios in St Anne's Court, Soho and stared at his reflection in the control room window. Except this wasn't *his* reflection, because the bright red lipgloss, eyeliner, blusher and flicked blonde hair belonged to Sam Bizarre.

Two years before, Nigel had been lead singer of an Essex mod group called "Vespa" who'd got no-where. But a change of wardrobe and name led him and his band here to one of the most famous studios in London. They'd found a second hand Korg synthesiser in the classified ads, bought an Elizabeth Arden make up box from Argos, chose a suitably pretentious name from a suitably pretentious Italian murder movie (*"Four Flies On Grey Velvet"*) *et voila*, their debut single was in the charts, easy as that.

As "Ice Age" climbed the Top Thirty, Chrysalis Records wanted the album finished quickly to capitalise on its success. The working title was "4FOGV," *exactly* the kind of name which would sell bucketloads in 1981.

Nigel/Sam looked around the control room again. He still couldn't get used to the idea this was where The Beatles, Queen, even Ziggy *Fucking* Stardust had recorded. Top of the range synthesisers blinked in corners and a Linn drum machine bumped away as the producer tweaked dials and pushed faders.

Sam stared back at his reflection, which wasn't his reflection. The eyes which stared into his looked terrified.

We're so close and now this, he thought, lit up another cigarette and realised his hands wouldn't stop shaking. The band had recorded BBC chart show "Top Of The Pops" yesterday afternoon at TV Centre. Spandau had been there, The Beat, The Cure…Once an act appeared on "Top Of The Pops" they'd officially made it. Grey Velvet had a party planned to watch the programme tonight and Sam was dreading it.

No-one knows, he thought. *Nobody knows about anything. I just keep my mouth shut and all this goes away. If someone knew, if the* police *knew, I'm easy enough to find. The place was empty. Why did I leave by the front? Doesn't matter, the street was deserted. No lights on. Nobody saw. It was two weeks ago. I'm in the clear. Nobody knows.*

"A little more top on my Sigma, Martin, mate. Bit wooly, isn't it?" said the keyboard player. *Three months ago he'd never even touched a mixing desk*, thought Sam. *Now he's Tony Visconti. Jesus Christ, it's so pathetic, all a big act. We don't know what we're doing. Look at us, we're not real. The only thing that was real in my life is dead and I'm responsible.*

Sam buried his head in his hands.

"Alright, Sam?" asked another member as he poked away at a Roland Jupiter 8. "Boring you, are we?"

"No, just a bit of a headache."

"Hope that's not what reviews say."

Shut up. Just shut up. Everyone just shut the fuck up. Why did I lose my temper? Why do I always lose my temper? Whenever things are going right, I sabotage them and I sabotaged this one right into the grave. I should have done an Ian Curtis, just topped myself before I did any damage.

The drum machine thump-thump-*thumped*. It had been thumping for days now. *How long does it take to get a bass drum right? It's just a bass drum.*

Sam's head thumped in time to the rhythm, just as it had started to thump that night in Jeanette's place. He'd been drinking, they'd both been drinking. Then...Sam didn't want to think about it.

She hadn't told anyone, just as we agreed. It was just between us. She wouldn't have done, couldn't have done. If she had then the papers would know. The police would know and if the police knew, all this would be over. We're on Top Of The Pops *tonight. It* can't *be over.*

The drum machine thumped and the synths pounded. Martin the producer rewound the tape so Sam's voice sang the same line over and over. "Out and down and out and down and out and down, I'm out but I'm not down..."

"Oh Jesus," he moaned. "I can't do this."

Everyone in the room swivelled round to look at him and at that moment the studio telephone buzzed. "Good excuse everyone, let's take five," said the producer and picked up the phone. "Rushent here." He listened, then stared directly at Sam. "The police? OK, well, shall I send him down?"

Before anyone could digest those nine words, Sam Bizarre had jumped to his feet and bolted for the door.

21 / 16th April 1981, London.

Anna brought Fisher up to speed as they walked up Great Portland Street.

"How do you know where he is?" asked the WPC.

"By paying attention to the little things. That's lesson one, if you're interested, which you should be."

"I am."

"He's a pop star, so naturally, Smash Hits Magazine told me where he is, well, gave me an idea. They said Sam Bizarre was in Soho at, I quote, 'a swanky recording studio.' There's only one 'swanky recording studio' in Soho and that's Trident."

Surprised, Fisher looked round at the D.I. "With respect, how do you know about recording studios, ma'am?"

"I've gone to Soho many times over the years, professionally I should stress, and Trident itself once or twice. Pop stars being pop stars, if you know what I mean. Puffed up and drugged up, never a good combination. I was always surprised it existed there. Abbey Road, yes. Nice little leafy bit of St. John's Wood, very refined. But Soho's grim and yet massive stars turn up in limos every day. Maybe it's the grimness they like, the authenticity."

"But you don't *know* he'll be there, do you?"

"I don't. But it's on our doorstep and worth a punt. I *could* have called Chrysalis, but that would have given him warning. Lesson two; in a case like this, I prefer not to give a witness time to think too much about their statement. I want first impressions. Are they nervous? Cocky? Do they seem like they're holding something back? So I want to get Sam Bizarre's unadorned, unrehearsed thoughts."

"That's clever."

"Oh, I'm full of clever," Anna laughed. They came to the end of Great Portland and stepped into Oxford Street.

It was almost lunchtime and the pavement was packed, but pedestrians parted as an intense looking man in a suit, tie, and Breton cap slowly walked toward them. He held a sign written in strident capitals above his head; "LESS LUST, BY LESS PROTEIN: MEAT FISH BIRD: EGG CHEESE; PEAS BEANS: NUTS. AND SITTING." Some passers watched him quizzically, others with amusement or open hostility. He was a well known fixture of the street, like House Of Fraser, John Lewis or Centre Point.

"Stan," said Anna.

The man nodded in recognition but said nothing and passed by.

"You know him?" asked Fisher. "I've always wondered what that's about."

"Well, everyone knows him, but nobody *knows* him. He just walks up and down all day. As for what that sign's about, I have no idea. Something to do with how your diet can change your morals? Who knows?"

The WPC watched him head toward Oxford Circus.

"But I know one thing, Fisher. He's probably the most honest person on the whole street. He's being true to himself, even if that means getting laughed at. He's real, even if most people don't like his reality, and that's to be admired." She sighed. "We should all be more honest about ourselves. The world would be a better place."

"I never thought about it like that," pondered Fisher.

Despite its glamorous reputation, Oxford Street was a chimera. The high end flagship department stores were the exception rather than the rule, since most of the shops could be found anywhere; Mothercare, Ratner's, C&A, Millets and Wimpy were all present and correct. But nestled between them were tacky little gift shops selling tacky little souvenirs, cheap clothing outlets stacked high with knocked-off Made In Taiwan studded belts, chunky bangles, leather jackets and this week's fashions. Currently the trend was T-shirts with Japanese writing, but next week it would be something different again.

"When I was younger we used to think going up west was the coolest thing ever." Anna looked around at the retail chaos. "Do people even say cool any more? But it's just another street, isn't it?"

"I always wanted to go there." Fisher pointed at a little sign above a tiny doorway which read "100 Club." "Back in 1976, when I was sixteen. It was where all the punk gigs went on." She sighed, wistfully. "Never made it. In fact, I never even saw The Clash until 1978, Rock Against Racism in Victoria Park."

"I was there."

The WPC turned to her boss, shocked. "You were?"

"In uniform, Fisher, working, not pogoing. It was a very...ah, *interesting* day. I'll tell you about it sometime."

"Yes,please. I *was* pogoing, I'm proud to say."

"Back when you were smashing the system."

"Well, back when I was smashing teacups,'cos my Dad wouldn't let me wear a safety pin in my ear. I always wondered why it's called the 100 club."

"Well, that might be because it's 100 Oxford Street," Anna replied, drolly. "Pay attention to the little things, Fisher. Sometimes even the big things, too. That's lesson three; sometimes the obvious is right in front of you."

They crossed over toward Wardour Street then entered Soho.

"This place gives us no end of hassle." Anna sighed. "If it's not the pimps beating up prostitutes, it's the customers or the prostitutes slapping each other."

As if on cue a couple of girls in a doorway giggled. One shouted over at Fisher. "Nice outfit, love, what do you charge?" The WPC shot them an angry look, which made them laugh louder. "Lesson four," Anna paid them no notice. "Choose your battles. Every crime is important to somebody, that's what makes them crimes. But we don't have the time nor manpower, or womanpower in our case, to tackle them all. So it's like crime scene rules. Preservation of life is priority, then work your way down from there."

Soho was more schizophrenic than Oxford Street. The neon signs in Titty Bar windows were designed with brevity in mind. Most said, "SEX! SEX! SEX!" or if that was too many syllables for the punters, just "GIRLS!" Dirty magazine shops stood next to esoteric book stores while Greasy Spoon cafes faced some of London's best (and yet little known) restaurants. Tiny seedy cinemas competed with peep shows which offered "NON STOP EROTIC CABARET!" Fruit and veg stalls were set up outside shops which sold toys that *weren't* for children, and at night, the clubs pumped music into the streets; Le Beat Route, The Whisky A' Go Go, Le Kilt…The list went on and queues of peacocks snaked about the Soho nights, whatever the weather. On top of all that, people actually *lived* here.

"It's like a city within a city, isn't, officer? You walk into Soho and just know they do things differently. They should have their own police."

"Like Vatican City."

Anna laughed. "Yeah, just like Vatican City, but with less corruption and fewer hookers."

The entrance to St Anne's Court was an extremely thin alleyway that linked Wardour with Dean Street. After yet more strip joints stood an anonymous building which outwardly gave no clue to its famous purpose. The alley was dark and dirty, far from the kind of place Ziggy Stardust should have chosen to land in 1972.

"Right. If he's here, I'll talk, you take notes. If he's not we go to plan B and call Chrysalis. Not ideal, but beggars can't be choosers and remember, he's just a witness. There's no evidence he's done anything apart from visit her, but I want to know why he hasn't come forward. Other than that, we're not charging him with anything because there's nothing to charge him *with,* OK?"

"Yes ma'am." Fisher pulled out her notebook and pen.

"Oh and lesson five, are we up to five? In a situation like this don't ask questions, make statements. You'll see what I mean. Right, let's go and swap make up tips with Sam Bizarre."

The WPC looked up, confused.

"A joke, Fisher, a joke."

They rang the buzzer. The door opened a fraction and a young woman peered out. Her eyes widened when she saw Fisher's uniform and Anna with her warrant card.

"Nothing to worry about ma'am. D.I. Leeding and WPC Fisher from Great Portland Street Station. You have Sam Bizarre here. We'd just like a quick word, if we may. He's not in any trouble, we just need a little help with one of our enquiries."

"Oh," said the woman. "Yes, of course. Come in."

She motioned them into a tiny reception area where a single thin staircase led upwards. "One moment."

The woman picked up a phone and pressed a button.

"See? I didn't *ask* if he was here," Anna whispered. "I *told* her he was."

The receptionist began to speak. "Mr Rushent? Yes, sorry, the police are here. Yes. They'd like to speak to Mr Bizarre. Erm, I'll ask…" She turned to Fisher and Leeding. "Do you want to go up?"

"Yes, that's fine."

Then the woman held up a finger and frowned. "Oh. Apparently he's just, er, run out."

There was a *thump-thump-thump* from upstairs and Anna watched in surprise as a pop star almost fell down the thin stairway. Sam's kohl rimmed eyes blinked in shock when he saw the visitors. They'd blocked the main entrance so he simply carried on down the next flight.

"Hey!" Anna shouted. "Mr Bizarre, we just need to…"

But he disappeared through another door and slammed it shut behind him. Leeding started after the singer. "Where's he going?" she said over her shoulder.

"It's the basement," the receptionist answered, confused. "There's an exit to a light well, but after that, nothing."

"Mr Bizarre!" Anna called out, aware that it was the most stupid thing she'd ever shouted after someone on the run. Leeding ran down, pulled open the door and stepped into the basement. Inside, an exit was wide open and the women rushed through.

There in the light well they were confronted by an androgynous man trying to climb onto the neighbouring walls. Above, back doors of restaurants stood open and it was clear this was his ad hoc plan of escape. *Why* he was trying to escape, however, was not so obvious.

Sam Bizarre's black suede pixie boots scrabbled against the brickwork, but were designed for posing, not climbing, so found no purchase. His black pleated trousers flapped about like sails.

"Sam. *Sam*," said Anna. There was no more need to shout and she really didn't want to say, "Mr Bizarre," again. It felt unseemly.

Sam's legs stopped kicking and his entire body slid slowly back down the wall. What could have been construed as mildly comic moments before became rapidly tragic. Sam Bizarre wept and retched as he tried to catch his breath. Eyeliner and mascara ran down his cheeks, which gave him the impression of a painting left out in the rain. He clutched at his hair, shook his head and Sam's shoulders shuddered as his eyes tried to force out more tears than they were physically capable of.

Anna tenderly bent down to him. "Sam, it's OK, we know about you and Jeanette. We just want to hear your side. It's OK."

He couldn't look her in the face but simply stared at the ground between his splayed legs.

"It's my fault," he managed to say in between gasps, "it's my fault. It's all my fault."

Leeding glanced up at Fisher. "Call for a car to meet us in Dean Street. Be discreet." As Fisher went inside she looked back over her shoulder one last time, concerned.

"We need to talk, don't we?"

Sam still kept his head down, unable to look anywhere but the floor. "I lost my temper," he muttered, then louder. "I lost my temper."

Jesus, what the hell do we have here? But take it slow. Don't rush to judgement. Don't rush. Never assume. Remember 1964.

So reluctantly, she did.

22 / 7th June 1964, Marble Arch, London.

Following school, Anna Leeding spent a brief but soul destroying few years behind a bank desk. A dramatic change of career was needed, so for personal reasons she applied to the police force and was judged a suitable addition.

Anna spent June the seventh 1964 on the four a.m. to midday shift, so depressingly her alarm rang when even *milkmen* were still asleep. She shared a house in Waterloo with two loud girls so getting to bed at a reasonable time was almost impossible. While tissue paper in the ears drowned out some of the noise, summer evening sunlight and heat weren't so easily blocked.

The night bus journey from Waterloo to Marble Arch police station only took twenty minutes, which she mostly spent in a semi-comatose state. Officers never travel in uniform, so Leeding wore regulation skirt, shirt and tie under a plain coat then picked up her WPC's jacket and hat at work. She was always amazed how a simple change of appearance could completely alter people's perceptions.

So far her new career hadn't involved much excitement. She'd dealt with pickpockets, robberies, domestics, suspected arson, walked about W1 and even been asked the time, as the cliché demanded. There'd been talk of a deployment to Brighton, which had become a battleground for feuding Mods and Rockers, but the call never came.

Leeding had made more cups of tea than she could count, typed up reports, filed papers, shined her shoes, taken statements and talked to endless aggrieved visitors. There was one small benefit; Odeon Marble Arch gave free tickets to police on the understanding they'd step in if there was any trouble during a performance. She'd seen "The Pink Panther" and "Zulu" but the cinema had been demolished in March, so that was that. Both times she'd gone alone, which was still preferable to sitting in her tiny room at Waterloo. Anna was attractive but couldn't flirt with men like her friends did, and ninety-nine percent of the males she met as a WPC weren't exactly dating material.

In life and work, Anna wanted to stand out. As only one of two WPC's at the station, she knew many eyes appraised her, but not for the right reasons. She fantasised about medals on her uniform and mentions in "Police Review" magazine, but also knew how shallow that daydream was.

On the summer evening of June the sixth, 1964, she'd lain drenched in sweat and stared at her alarm clock in frustration as the hour grew late. The window was wide open but any benefit of a breeze was cancelled out by the roar of Waterloo outside, so Anna barely made it through the next day's shift without nodding off.

She finished just after noon, which left an entire afternoon and early evening to fill. As Leeding left the station, a heat haze shimmered above workers, shoppers and summer tourists who crowded the Marble Arch pavements. Going back to a stuffy rented room wasn't an option and thanks to her woollen knee-length skirt, neither was a trip to boiling Hyde Park.

Anna's early morning coat now felt tight and oppressive but the C&A clothes shop opposite gave her an idea; she'd buy a cheap cotton dress, change into it straight away, then head to Hyde Park suitably attired.

That decision was to have far-reaching consequences. If she hadn't been so tired, things may have gone very differently.

Anna started to cross the road when *something* made her stop, a peculiar mix of déjà vu and apprehension. She froze on the pavement and her head tick-tocked, left to right,right to left, left to right, then she blinked exactly five times. Anna turned and tried to locate the source of her unease, a peculiar talent she'd developed over the last few years. Leeding believed her *subconscious* mind spotted irregularities, then rang alarm bells until her *conscious* mind registered them.

She continued to turn in a slow circle and her head tilted like a dog trying to focus on a sound. She quickly eliminated the traffic and shops, since there were no shouts or screams which might indicate an incident. Some people grumbled as they pushed past, annoyed she'd blocked the pavement. Anna didn't even notice.

It was a person. Yes, I saw a person and...what? Something rang in my brain. Who did I see? What made me stop?

She scanned the crowd, stepped back to where that *apprehensive déjà vu* had occurred, then studied the pedestrians and extrapolated their movement. Like a falcon instinctively calculates where its prey *will be*, Anna stared at a spot as yet unoccupied, but soon *would* be.

Then she saw him.

He had short dark wavy hair, deep set eyes and a red wine stain birthmark on his neck. He wore a bright blue cotton shirt and was over six feet tall, thin and wiry.

Why do I know you?

Anna took a step toward the man, leafed through files in her mind, then discarded the ones that didn't fit. In a matter of moments, she had him.

Montagu Square. Oh Jesus, it's you.

Back on February 14th, while couples celebrated Valentine's Day, a horrific incident had taken place in Montagu Square, just a few hundred yards from where Anna stood.

That night a seventeen year old girl had been attacked by a tall, wiry assailant with short dark wavy hair and a distinctive birthmark on his neck. The victim eventually managed to give a description, but back then it was winter, when the birthmark had surely been hidden by scarfs and collars, so no sightings were reported. However on this hot summer's day, that identifying stain was on show.

Jesus, the arrogance, thought Anna. *You raped and tried to kill a girl not five minutes walk away and yet here you are, enjoying the sunshine like you're untouchable. Oh God, the blue shirt.* Anna now remembered another part of the description. *A bright blue cotton shirt, with distinctive pearl buttons.*

The man's pearl buttons flashed.

He looked up the road toward Marble Arch and Leeding saw his shoulders tense as a bus came around the corner. He clearly intended to catch it, but was no-where near the bus stop.

At that moment, options flashed through her mind;

I could try to follow him, find out where he lives, then return with back up. But look at the streets, look at the roads, it's the height of summer. If I lose him, then what are the chances of picking up the trail again?

Or I could try to apprehend him right now. But I don't have any handcuffs and he has height and strength on his side. Plus,he tried to murder *that girl. What might he do to me in order to get away? No, look, the street's full of people who could help, even if it means just blocking his way. I could identify myself and hope the pedestrians will assist.*

Another unwelcome thought filled Anna's head. She pushed it away, but the idea circled back.

If you do this by yourself, you'll be someone. *Commendations, recognition, respect. Pull this off and doors will open.*

She realised the opportunism was shameful but couldn't let images of medals and citations go, so pulled out her warrant card. "Police! Police! You! That man! Stop! Stay where you are!"

She rushed toward the suspect as passers-by watched. Anna knew what they were thinking; *she doesn't* look *like a police officer. Where's her uniform?*

The man looked confused, which made Leeding waver for a moment. She'd expected recognition, then anger, determination, fight or flight, but the suspect just stared as she closed in.

"Police! Assistance, please!" As people swivelled to look, the man's eyes widened then fear flashed across his face and he bolted for it.

"Police! Stop! Help!" Anna shouted but it made no difference. The crowd were too surprised to become participants, so remained a fascinated, detached audience.

"Stop! I need assistance!"

The man's long legs gave him a clear lead but the pavements were choked with pedestrians, so he broke left into the traffic toward Park Lane.

Oh God, no, Anna managed to think before she chased him into the road. He weaved between fast moving vehicles and headed for the Park Lane entrance of Marble Arch tube station.

"Police! Stop!" Anna's shouts may as well have been in a foreign language. A car braked and the driver furiously sounded his horn as she skittered into its path. Leeding had to trust the vehicles would stop, but wasn't confident of that outcome.

Park Lane is fed by three lanes where traffic often slows down, but at that moment the lights at Bayswater Road changed and cars rushed forward. A Vauxhall Cresta missed her by inches. The driver shouted insults but his abuse was lost in road noise. As a Sunbeam Alpine sped past with no intention of slowing, Anna instinctively put up one hand to stave it off.

The suspect lithely bounded across the road like a gazelle, although Anna didn't feel too leonine. Distantly she thought, *I really should cut down on the fags.*

He'd almost reached the station entrance when a Norton Atlas motorcycle darted between two vehicles and struck him at speed.

It's often noted that shocking moments are perceived in slow motion and Anna found that the case as bike and suspect collided. Hands to her mouth, she skidded to a halt and traffic around her did the same. Silence *seemed* to fall, although of course engines still growled, people shouted and London hummed. Leeding felt like she was in the centre of a snow globe, fixed in position as the frozen scene whirled about her.

Then the bubble burst and life crashed back in full colour, at full volume.

Anna rushed between the stilled vehicles and stared down at her suspect, smashed into the tarmac. Someone screamed but the sound was fuzzy and muted. The motorcyclist stood over his fallen vehicle. "He just ran out," he gasped. "I couldn't…He ran out. I couldn't…He ran out…"

The man's head was at an impossible angle to his body and blood had started to spread from it. Anna thought wildly, *cracked egg, it's a cracked egg, cracked egg, Humpty Dumpty.* His eyes were wide open, but blank. "Somebody call for an ambulance, please! I'm a police officer! Go into a shop and call for an ambulance!" But an ambulance was superfluous, since there was no life to preserve here any more.

"He ran out," the rider muttered on repeat, a mantra he obviously hoped would make all this go away. "He ran out. Did you see? He ran out."

"I'm a police officer," Anna repeated to the crowd and held up her warrant card as if it were a shield. "I *am* a police officer. You need to move back, give him space." Everyone knew he had no need for space, but did as they were told. "Has anyone called for an ambulance? And please, someone call Marble Arch Station, explain where we are." Nobody moved and she screamed on the edge of hysteria. "Get into a shop and call Marble Arch Station!"

"I will," somebody said from within the wall of faces.

Anna waited with the dead man, waited for the ring of ambulance bells and patrol cars, waited as the crowd stood about her, as they waited for the next act of this performance to begin.

Oh God, a man is dead and I am responsible, whirled around her mind. The fact he'd left a girl for dead offered Leeding no succour. *I am responsible and justice has not been done.*

*

His name was Terry Emmonds, twenty-eight years old, lived with his mother, was unemployed and had suffered from mental illness most of his life. He had occasional paranoid episodes and panic attacks.

Terry had a distinctive red-wine birthmark up the right hand side of his neck. The Marble Arch attacker's stain was on the *left* side.

On February 14th 1964, Terry Emmonds had attended a family party at The Crown pub in Islington from approximately six p.m. to ten-thirty. There were over thirty witnesses to attest to his presence, including an off-duty policeman.

It had been a cluster of dreadful coincidences. Terry's appearance had *happened* to fit the description of the attacker. Months later, he'd *happened* to be in the vicinity of the attack, wearing a similar shirt. He suffered from mental illness and paranoia, so when a police officer had made herself known and raced toward him, he'd run.

Naturally, the press jumped on the story. A man had died in front of literally hundreds of witnesses, pursued to his death by a young, pretty WPC who'd made a tragic error of misidentification. The front page of the Evening Standard put her photograph alongside Emmonds' under the headline, "A FATAL MISTAKE".

Anna was asked to stand down during the enquiry. She'd done so gladly, and hid in her oppressive Waterloo room whilst Emmonds' large and vocal family demanded justice. She attended hearings and went over the same story over and over again. Witnesses testified the victim had behaved in a suspicious way when confronted by a WPC and many assumed he was guilty of *something*. "There's no smoke without fire," came up a few times.

The attacker's photofit and photographs of Emmonds confirmed they were incredibly similar, although his birthmark was on the opposite side. But the hearing conceded the fact he'd run from the WPC may have clouded her judgement. Shown the two men side by side, most officers said they would have made the same decision.

Within the force, there was great deal of sympathy for Anna. With the evidence available, the enquiry concluded she'd acted correctly. How was Leeding supposed to know the suspect ran because of a mental condition, not guilt? It was just a tragic matter of seconds that put Emmonds and a motorbike on the same trajectory.

The press had quickly backed away from the case once it was obvious the event was due to a series of awful coincidences. Normality slowly returned for Anna but it was a different kind of normal. Leeding had made a (forgivable, understandable) mistake, but only *she* knew the motive behind it. Anna had wanted approbation; she'd received condemnation.

She returned to the force exonerated but aware she'd always be the WPC who'd chased an innocent man to his death. Whatever she did, wherever she went, she'd never erase it from her record. Leeding had toyed with quitting the police but that would have been running away. Anna decided to stay, then train to become a detective on the unspoken understanding she wouldn't make assumptions, rush to judgement, let pride inform her decisions or allow another innocent person suffer through *her* mistakes.

They never caught the Marble Arch attacker.

23 / 16th April 1981, London.

D.I. Leeding and WPC Fisher sat in the offices of Jenkins & Dacre Solicitors in Holborn. Sat opposite them was Nigel Blundell, AKA Sam Bizarre, solicitor Mark Jenkins and an Artist & Repertoire representative from Chrysalis records. Anna thought they made an odd collection. On her side, two soberly dressed and uniformed members of the Metropolitan Police. On the other, an androgynous pop star, a balding solicitor in a corduroy suit, and a record company representative who wore a horrible brown leather jacket with a white silk scarf.

Although witnesses don't legally require a solicitor in an interview, they are entitled, so Chrysalis insisted on one given the sensitivity of the situation. Anna had briefed the solicitor beforehand and they in turn privately talked Sam Bizarre through the purpose of the meeting. After those formalities, it began.

"Can I just re-iterate we are interviewing Mr Blundell as a witness and no more. He is not suspected of any crime, there is no evidence that he has committed one, but we believe he may have information that might help us understand elements of Jeanette West's death which are puzzling."

"Are you happy with that, Nigel, er, Sam?" asked the solicitor.

"It's Nigel," he whispered. "It's always been Nigel." His drained and white expression found some venom. "Sam is nothing, just an act."

Given Sam's job description, the interview was conducted at the solicitor's offices rather than Great Portland Street. In a witness interview, police can suggest a location most beneficial to a relaxed and productive meeting. To bring a pop star into the station would set tongues wagging and Anna knew the press would be on their doorstep within thirty minutes. She had no desire for Sam Bizarre's connection to this case to be made public. It would be of no benefit to anyone and Leeding knew that Great Portland Street wasn't as secure as she would like it to be. The newspapers had an uncanny ability to sniff out crimes and Anna believed they were given inside knowledge.

"Do you mind if I have a fag?" asked Chrysalis Records' leather man.

"I'd prefer not, I hate smoke," said Sam. The record company representative had to defer to the only pop star in the room.

OK, thought Anna. *So he doesn't smoke. Or* says *he doesn't. But for now let's assume the butts in West's back garden weren't his either.*

"Sorry mate," said Chrysalis.

"I'm not your mate," hissed Blundell.

"Let's get moving then," Anna nodded to Fisher who was ready to take notes. "I know you'd much prefer to be back in the studio."

Sam looked up at the clock. "We're on Top Of The Pops tonight," he said with no pride or enthusiasm. "And I don't even care."

"Well, let's get you home in time, shall we? Nigel, you're here because we believe you were the last person to see Jeanette West alive at 10, Selly Mews, West One, on Saturday the fourth of April. Do you understand?"

"Uh huh." Sam stared down at the table.

"Before we talk about that day and get some background, may I ask why you didn't come forward when you discovered Jeanette had killed herself?"

He sighed then, a long gasp that seemed to roll from somewhere impossibly deep within. "Because I wasn't supposed to be there, obviously."

"Obviously? Is that why you tried to run from us at Trident Studios?"

He shrugged. Back in Soho he'd fitted in, but here the remains of his make up, fashionable clothes and feminine hair were incongruous to say the least. "I panicked. I panicked because I hadn't come forward and I knew that was wrong, but I just couldn't."

"Nigel, I need to reiterate you're not suspected of anything. Just tell us why you didn't come forward."

"Jesus," he shook his head angrily. "Not much of a detective, are you? Because *we were having an affair*. Isn't it obvious? We were having an affair and that's not something you broadcast, is it?"

So that's one suspicion confirmed, Anna thought. She waited a moment and carried on. "Take your time. It's OK."

"It's not OK, though. *Clive St. Austenne…*" Sam sneered as he said the name. "Clive loved her, she was certain of that. But have you *seen* him? He's like her dad, or something. No, he was like a cross between her dad and a puppy. Maybe they were suited once upon a time, but not any more. She wanted me. Well, I thought she wanted me." His eyes began to well up again. With nothing to do, the Chrysalis man pushed a box of tissues his way. "I didn't know...I didn't know she was so...You wouldn't have known, nobody would. I didn't think she'd...do..." Nigel grabbed a handful of tissues from the box and plunged his face into them.

Anna took a chance. "So you had an overnight bag there and whenever Clive was away, you came to stay."

Sam/Nigel looked up sharply and managed to pull himself together. "How did you know about...?"

"I found your bag under the bed in the spare room. I thought it was *women's* clothes, plus a man's razor and stuff, but it wasn't. It was all yours, right? Frilly shirts, pleated trousers.The current fashion." She motioned toward Nigel's clothes. He nodded.

Second suspicion confirmed, Anna mentally ticked a box in her mind.

"Bit brazen, leaving your bag there. What if Clive found it?"

"He never went to Selly Mews, well hardly ever. It was Jeanette's bolt hole from him and I only went there when he was *very* out of town, I mean, like, in another *country* out of town. I was her little secret, she was my big secret." His mouth began to tremble again and he put his head in his hands.

Not just a fling, was it, Nigel? Anna thought, sadly. *You adored her.*

"Since you're not charging Mr Blundell with anything," wondered the solicitor, "perhaps you might explain exactly why he's been called here as a witness? He didn't see Ms.West actually commit suicide." He turned to Sam, who looked as if he was about to get violent.

"Of course I didn't! Jesus Christ! What are you saying? That I *watched*?"

"No, we're not saying that. There are some anomalies at the scene we want to, er, tick off, and hope you might be able to help. Your private life and relationship with Jeanette is only of interest to us in that regard. Now when we came to see you in Soho and you had your panic attack, you said, I quote, 'it's all my fault,' and, 'I lost my temper'. Now, I want to get some clarification on that in good time, but first, I'd just like some context, background, if it's OK. How long had you two been having the...how long had you been together?"

Nigel/Sam looked upward into his memory. "Since July 26th last year."

"That's a very precise date."

"It was a very memorable night."

"So where did you meet?"

"H.M.S. Belfast."

Anna sat back and shot a glance at Fisher who jotted it down, equally surprised. "*H.M.S. Belfast*? The warship moored near Tower Bridge?"

He nodded, sadly.

"Why were you on a warship?"

"Oh, it wasn't a warship that night. It was a nightclub."

Anna frowned.

Mr Chrysalis puffed himself up, glad to add something to the proceedings. "OK, you know Spandau Ballet?"

Fisher nodded. Anna shook her head.

"Band of the moment, on our label. They didn't want to do conventional gigs, they wanted to do *events*. Gigs are Seventies, man. Band stands on stage, lights flash, encores, all a cliché. *Bo-ring*. But the kids now, they want more. So Spandau decided to do a gig on H.M.S Belfast. You know, military chic. Exclusive."

Nigel sighed. "I don't think they want a fucking press release."

"And that's when you met Jeanette? At a music concert?"

He nodded again. "I just want to know why she did what she did. That's all. I'll tell you whatever you need to know, if it'll help explain. I need to know, I have to know. I want answers, like you. I want you to know what she was like. Jeanette just wasn't *that kind of person*. If I could go back to that night, you know, in Selly Mews, I would and I'd change things. But I can't."

Leeding waited. It was best to let witnesses say whatever they needed to and then decide what was relevant later. For now, she'd let him fill the silence, take his time and talk about what *he* thought mattered.

"So, July 26th 1980," he said quietly and examined his painted fingernails as if there was some truth to be found there. "That's when I met her. She was…magnificent."

Nigel Blundell remembered, but he had another name that night.

*

Sam Bizarre climbed down into the bowels of the H.M.S. Belfast. He was supposed to feign an ice-cool insouciance in keeping with the attitude of the day, but couldn't stop smiling. Grey Velvet had signed to Chrysalis Records two months ago and that gave him V.I.P. access to album launches, single playbacks, parties and gigs. So he'd been out clubbing most evenings, stamped his face over London nightlife, added his voice to the sound of the crowd.

Things had changed, fast. It seemed this new decade had quickly brushed away the Seventies and said goodbye to squalor, hello to glamour.

Once upon a time, there were only four night-time destinations; pubs, concert halls, discos, and Gentlemen's Clubs. All four remained unchanging bastions of pleasure for the conservative and conforming. Having fun in the Seventies meant strict uniforms and behaviour, and even Punks had become assembly line copies of their original anarchic ideals.

But then 1980 tore up the rule book. Music, clothes and world views were different, but crucially for Sam, the clubs were *very* different.

Over the last year, little pockets of resistance had started to form. Kids had taken over empty little bars and deserted poky clubs during the week then made them their own. Generally those venues were vacant from Monday to Thursday, since their usual clientele were sat at home watching "Tomorrow's World," without realising tomorrow had arrived. *Tomorrow* was busy dancing, laughing, drinking and loving in basements and back rooms, all dressed up with somewhere to go.

Sam and his band had *the look* and were instantly accepted into the clique. At first the press didn't know what to call this new dandified movement; Peacock Punk, The Cult With No Name, The Now Crowd and Blitz Kids were all thrown into the (Stephen Jones designed) hat, but soon enough, a name stuck; New Romantics.

Sweaty gigs at The Rainbow and Lyceum were obsolete. Intimate but equally sweaty gigs by word of mouth became the new normal and Spandau Ballet led the way. They'd played their first gig at a rehearsal studio, then The Blitz Club in Covent Garden. A cinema followed and now the H.M.S. Belfast, all part of a carefully orchestrated hype to make record companies eat out of their hands. Chrysalis were desperate to sign Spandau and that meant Sam had highly sought after tickets. It was easier to attend the 1980 Olympics in *Moscow* than get your name on the guest list for this event.

So on that July evening, Sam descended into a warship. Just another normal night at the New Romantic office. Outside in the predictable world, Don McLean, Olivia Newton-John and Odyssey had all scored number one singles over the last month but they were the old guard.

The DJ blasted out the *new* sounds of 1980. The Human League, Gina X, Shock, Ultravox…Sam felt like this was the epicentre of Here And Now and the entire world had converged on this lump of grey metal in the Thames. The usual suspects were all here; George, the cloakroom attendant from The Blitz, nightclub overlord Steve Strange, Stephen Linard, Degville…anyone who was anyone had crammed into these tiny booming corridors. There was a camaraderie here but also a cautious circling and suspicion, as everybody wanted to be first to *really* stake their claim on the 1980s.

Look at us all, Sam thought. *We're going to rule this decade. How couldn't we? All that is past is prologue. Oh, that's a good name for a song.*

The band had set up their equipment at one end but the ship's metal roof was inches from their heads, so Spandau would have to fold themselves around pipes and columns in order to play. The Belfast was aesthetically and culturally perfect but as a venue, it stank both figuratively and literally. The music reverberated and clanged about the bulkheads, sure to result in a mass migraine before the night was out.

"Oh my goodness," a voice purred in his ear. "You look ab-so-*lutely* stunning."

Sam turned and found himself face to face with his past, with *everyone's* past. He couldn't quite compute what he was seeing. All around him, pirates, gangsters and dandies were trying to get each other's attention, but right here was a star that eclipsed them all; Jeanette West.

She was dressed in a suit and had ringed her eyes with thick kohl. Crimped blonde hair exploded from the edges of a bowler hat and formed a halo about her face. She looked like 1980 condensed into one person. Jeanette waved a can of lager his way.

"Hm, better than *me*, actually," she frowned, "for which I am extremely jealous. Look at those eyelashes, real, too! For a moment, I thought you were the most beautiful girl here, but up close…nearly, but not quite. Oh, I'm sorry." She extended a hand his way. "Jeanette West."

"I know," he managed. "You're famous." Sam grimaced internally. Of *course* she was famous. Despite their outward cool, the other guests enviously glanced their way. Steve Strange clearly hated how she'd chosen to talk to this *nobody*.

"Well, I *was* famous," she shrugged. "And will be again, I suppose. Things go round in circles, don't they? Look at all you beautiful people, finding fashions from worlds gone by and making them your own. Round and round." Jeanette spun on the spot, nearly fell and giggled. She'd obviously had a few drinks before his arrival. "Do you have a name, you gorgeous boy, or shall I just stare at you in silence?"

She's flirting, he thought. *I'm being flirted with by the Face Of 1968.*

"Sam Bizarre."

"*Sam Bizzzzaaaarrrrre*," she rolled his alter ego about her tongue. "Wonderful. And why is Sam Bizarre here? I was invited by Chris Wright. Know him?"

"He's my boss at Chrysalis."

"Oh! He's a lovely man! Wait, your boss? So you're a *pop star*. Of course you are! How couldn't you be?"

"Well, we haven't had any hits yet."

"You *willlllllllll*." She brought her face closer to his and her eyes slowly took it in, from chin to fringe. "Oh, they'll come to you. People do, you know, gravitate toward beauty."

Sam decided to flirt back. "Which is why you're so successful."

She threw her arms around him and laughed. "I *love* the way you use the present tense."

She must be ten years older than me, but she could be twenty-one. She's amazing.

"This reminds me of the sixties." She stared around the cramped concert in wonder. "Funny, isn't it? We all got colour TV in the seventies, but the *world* went black and white. Now colour's creeping back. It feels like everything is changing for the better. I *hated* the seventies but here we are, the eighties already and I want to be part of it. Perhaps we could be part of it together?"

Fast mover, he thought. *That's fine, though. But isn't she married? Yes, Clive someone-or-other. Better check.*

"So is your husband here?" He looked over her shoulder as if searching for him. She gently pulled his face back and *tut-tut-tutted*.

"Nice, very nice, Mr Bizarre. Don't think I haven't heard that fishing trip before. No, he isn't. Not his thing, very few things are 'his thing,' if I am honest, and I am. But this is *my* thing."

She grabbed his hand and began what had become known as the New Romantic dance. She pushed herself toward him, then away, while they waved their joined hands back and forth.

"I was worried I might be the fuddy old aunt in the kitchen at parties, but I feel right at home."

"You look right at home."

She stopped dancing and stared at him seriously. "We should get to know each other. I need to learn all about 1980, since I intend to live, love and work here."

"My pleasure. I'm happy to be your tour guide."

"Good. Then get to know each other we shall."

There was a squall of feedback which made everyone wince. A synthesiser whooshed and crashed, white horses of noise, then the bass drum reverberated about the hull like cannon fire.

"Oh. The band are starting. How exciting."

Yes, it is, Westie. In more ways than one.

"So as my Holiday '80 guide, how long do you think they'll play for, Mr Bizarre?"

"Well, last time I saw them it was about forty minutes or so."

"Then what *shall* we do for the rest of the night?" She whispered in his ear. "If only we had somewhere else to go. Oh, wait. I happen to have a little London *pied a terre* for when the music stops, as it always does, alas."

Sam Bizarre was just about to reply when she kissed him.

*

Nigel gazed into the middle distance and Anna knew part of him was still on the Belfast and maybe always would be. The room was silent as everyone waited for him to come back to 1981.

"She was so alive," he stared back nine months. "She was more alive than anyone I'd ever known. She was," Sam/Nigel searched for the right description, "*vital*. Jeanette occupied life, she shone, inspector. She shone. So the idea that she would just…turn off, go dark, end it…I just don't…"

"How often did you see her?"

"We spent the night together after H.M.S. Belfast and the night after that. We didn't leave Selly Mews. It was perfect, really. Most of the houses there are empty, no-one to see our immoral goings-on." He smiled. "But anyway, most of her time was spent at home in Shere with *him,* you know, *St. Austenne.* Jeanette only came into town on business or if *he* was away. So we didn't meet as often as we wanted but what choice did we have? We'd occasionally *bump into each other* at parties but most of our relationship was spent locked away together in the Mews. We were like castaways, the Mews was our island and nobody knew we were there."

"Did she ever talk about getting a divorce?"

"Yes, a lot. But only in the same way people talk about going into space. You know, yearning, but never really taking it seriously. More like a silly fantasy."

Anna paused again, went over the options in her head, then asked the question. "Were you in love?"

He stared at the table again and his shoulders shuddered as if a great weight had been placed on them. "Yes, we were, but it wasn't real. No, it *was* real, but only within the Mews. Outside that, we were on different planets.I couldn't stand it."

"What would have Clive St. Austenne done if he'd known?"

Sam blew out his cheeks. "She never spoke about it. That option wasn't even real to her. I don't know if it was wilful naivety or a genuine disconnection from reality, but when the door to the Mews was shut there was only us."

"What do *you* think he would have done?"

He laughed, a cackle from the borders of hysteria. "His wife is fucking someone half as old as him? What do you think? A very public divorce, she'd lose everything, be dragged into court, have to confront dirty reality? She didn't want that. Our relationship wouldn't have survived, I'm sure of it. She would have found another reality to live in. He's a powerful man, you know. He would have made things impossible."

"Violence?"

Sam's laughter dried up and he thought for a long while. "He was Jeanette's husband. She couldn't stand violence, wouldn't have stayed with him if he were that kind of man, I know that much. No, his only aggression toward her would have been legally sanctioned. So we stayed in the dark."

"You accepted that?"

His black-rimmed eyes flashed in anger. "Of course I didn't. I wanted to be with her, open and honest. The only thing I *accepted* was her love, the rest of it was…anathema to me."

Anna glanced over at Fisher. *You getting this?*

The WPC tapped her notebook. *Yes, ma'am.*

"Do you think I can help?" Sam looked like a little lost girl. "I mean, help to understand why she did what she did?"

"I hope so. We all want to understand, to make sense of it."

"That's all what I want, to make sense of it. Ask me anything and I'll tell you, if it can only help make some fucking sense of it." His lips quivered again.

"OK, Nigel," Anna said, softly. "You know what I must ask now. You ran from us. You said you lost your temper, that it was your fault."

He nodded, then looked round at Mr Chrysalis and the solicitor as if they could answer for him.

"Mr Blundell, remember you're a *witness*," said the solicitor. "You say as much or as little as you want at this stage. If you have something to charge him with you'd better do it now."

Anna shook her head.

"No," Sam straightened up like a child about to answer a question in class. "No, I'll tell them. Because they want to know what happened, and so do I."

Leeding leaned forward. "Very well. What happened on April the 4th?"

Sam Bizarre looked up to the empty heavens, back at the detective inspector, then began to speak.

24 / April 4th 1981, London.

Sam Bizarre/Nigel Blundell climbed out of a black cab and darted into the back alleyway that led to Jeanette's home in Selly Mews. He was dressed almost identically to the outfit he'd worn for the "Smash Hits" poster. Nigel wished he could go incognito, but Jeanette preferred him as Sam. On the one time he'd arrived anonymously, she'd almost gone into a sulk. "Where's my Sam?" she'd laughed, but there was an edge to her voice. "You wouldn't be happy if I was bare-faced in a muumuu eating baked beans out of the can, would you?" He'd acquiesced but part of him *did* want to arrive and find her unadorned. "There's not enough glamour out there," Jeanette had admonished him and pointed vaguely at London. "So I expect it in here! I met Sam Bizarre, I want *Sam Bizarre*!"

Sam's fame was on the rise, but only within a very small constituency. "Smash Hits" fans knew who he was, New Musical Express readers either didn't know or didn't care. He was sometimes glared at in the street but mainly because of his image, not through recognition.

For now he was able to come and go with relative impunity, but often wondered how long that would last if Grey Velvet became successful. Soon, Jeanette would be forced to make a decision; lover or husband. Every day brought that choice closer.

The back gate was open as expected and he walked into her tiny box-garden. Sam wore a bolero hat and sunglasses for anonymity, but his feminine features and make up meant most people passed him off as just another kooky 1981 girl. He took off the hat and glasses then realised Jeanette was in her kitchen. "Hel-oo-oo!" she trilled in the sing-song voice she used when excited. Sam smiled, gave a little bow and entered her house.

A bottle of wine was already open on the kitchen table. From Jeanette's giggly, little-girl demeanour, Sam could tell she'd already enjoyed a couple of glasses at least.

"Let the party begin!" West yelled and span on the spot.

"Looks like it already started without me."

"Ooh, *somebody's* cross today." She teased. "What? Had a spat over lipgloss with Phil Oakley from The Human Leagues?"

"It's Phil *Oakey* and *League*, singular." He grumbled. "It would be nice if you weren't a few glasses ahead."

"Well, poo to you." She gave a moue, put a hand on her hip and he laughed. "That's better, grumpy chops."

Jeanette poured him a glass of white then wandered over to a shiny new stereo system. "I got this delivered yesterday," she said proudly. "Beats my old music centre. Look, tape deck, radio, it's got a Dolby, a whatsisname, strobe thing to get the speed right," Jeanette waved her hand over some albums lined up beneath the stereo, "*aaaaand* I went to Virgin on Oxford Street. Got up to date on what's groovy."

"Nobody says groovy any more."

"I know. That's why I said it. I need to know what's happening so I can keep up with you. Music and fashion have always gone together and I should know, I am an *expert*. The fashion bit I'm *au fait* with, but I needed to raise my bar on the music front. I may as well be an OAP." Jeanette mimed being an old woman with a walking stick which she then dramatically threw away. "So for our listening pleasure, I have Bowie's new one, "Scary Monsters," "U2" by Boy."

"Other way around."

"I prefer my way. "Boy" is a good name for a band, "U2" sounds like some hippy nonsense. Anyway, er, "Zendoatta Mondyatta," or *something*, by The Police. "Kings Of The Wild Frontier," by Adam And The Ants."

"Ugh."

She stuck her tongue out at him. "Hendrix wore a Hussar's jacket first you know. Er, "Visage," by Visage, that's your mate isn't it? See? La-de-dah-de-dah. I shall be a Blitz Kid yet and *most* importantly, I got this…" She held up a seven inch copy of "Ice Age." "*Aaaaaand* this…" Jeanette picked up the twelve inch version and squinted at the cover. "It's a *remix*. How exciting. It's longer, so you can dance to it more."

"I know, I was in the studio when we did it. They had twelve inches in the seventies, you know. Remember disco, all those decades ago?"

"Saucy! But argh, disco, no thanks. I waited for you before I played it." She put the twelve inch on the slip mat and switched on the record player.

"Wrong speed. You've got it on thirty-three," Sam laughed.

"But it's the size of an album," Jeanette protested.

"But it's the speed of a single. Forty-five, my dear, forty-five."

She adjusted the speed control and "Ice Age" *whiiiiiirrrrred* up to the proper revolutions per minute. "Come on, let's dance!"

"It's a bit early for dancing."

"It's time for dancing when the first people start. So let's start."

She grabbed him by the waist and they twirled around her kitchen. But Jeanette couldn't see Sam's expression. He wasn't smiling.

*

The evening progressed and wine flowed. One bottle went into the bin, another was opened. Soon that also began to dwindle. Eventually, they meandered into the living room and sat down to watch The Eurovision Song Contest. Jeanette got fidgety after half an hour. Drunkenly, she leaned over and whispered. "Let's go to bed."

"It's only nine."

"I didn't mean to sleep."

Sam went silent and watched some brightly dressed Europeans cavort about in Dublin.

"*Bed*, bed."

"No."

It took Jeanette a moment to register his response.

"No?"

"No."

"You never say no."

"I do tonight. We need to talk."

"That sounds ominous."

He put down his drink and turned to her. "I can't keep doing this."

"This? What's *this*?"

"This," he gestured about the room, "this, sneaking about, only meeting in private. London's out there, it's just *there* in the next street, and we never go out together."

"You know we can't. People would see, people would talk. Clive would find out. We've been through this."

"I know." Sam felt himself getting worked up. They *had* been through it before, but clearly she hadn't been listening. "But you don't love him anymore. You love me. So why can't we just…"

"It's complicated."

"Jesus, no it's not. People get divorced all the time. It's not 1935, there's no shame in it."

"Oh and you'd know, would you? Mr Marriage expert, there," she slurred. He could see her eyes roll a little and try to focus. "You'd know? Out there with your friends, clubbing about, posing around, pretending life's just one big masquerade ball."

"It's more than that."

"Oh, no it's not. We thought we were different in the sixties, too."

"Oh, not the bloody sixties again."

"Yes, the 'bloody sixties.' We thought we were changing the world, but were just changing ourselves. The world carried on fine, same as always, we just turned up the colour a bit. That's all, and it's all you're doing, too." She staggered over to the TV and turned the colour dial so the picture took on a nauseating vivaciousness. "Turning up the colour, dah-ha-ha-*harling*. But some things are black and white. Marriage, for example. *Comprendi*? *Verstehen*? Understand, *sweetheart*? So do you want to fuck or not?"

Sam had never seen her like this, bitter, spiteful, vicious. For a moment he saw past the beauty at a cruelty she'd kept well hidden. He was shocked by its ferocity and a little scared, so tried a different tack. He wasn't as drunk as Jeanette, but certainly on the same train. "I love you. I do."

"Oh and I love you, too, but that's not enough sometimes, is it?"

"Yes, it is."

"Oh, grow up. This is where our love stays." She spread her arms around the house as if in the middle of a country estate. "Maybe one day, maybe once I move to America for Dallas."

"You're going to move?"

"Well, only when we're filming. Not forever."

"You never told me." He felt his anger rise. That wasn't good. Once he started to boil, he couldn't switch off the pressure. It would just continue to grow until he exploded. "When were you going to tell me?"

"Tonight."

"Liar." She looked like he'd slapped her.

"I have never lied to you. Never, you *shit*." She stumbled back toward him, picked up her drink and weaved toward the living room door. "I'm going to bed. You can join me if you want. It's up to you. Maybe I'll pass out. You can fuck me then, if you like, I wouldn't care."

He followed her out into the hallway. Dozens of Jeanettes of different ages stared down at him from the walls. She'd lived an entire life he wasn't part of. "We haven't got a single photo together. How much would it hurt to have a picture?"

"Oh, well why don't we just get a photographer to snap us fucking, *the special way you like*, then hang that up, shall we? *A picture of us.* Ha. What are you thinking?"

The anger took control of him at that moment. He surrendered to it.

"It's me or him." Sam said quietly, but with menace. Jeanette took a moment to process the words.

"What?"

"You heard, me or him. If I walk out without an answer you will never see me again."

She blinked then, a rapid succession of flickers like a tremor had passed through her. "You don't mean that."

"Try me."

"Oh, you spoiled child."

Sam didn't know what happened. One moment she held a wine glass, the next it had flown from her hand, smashed against the stairway and fallen onto the carpet, where its lethal shards pointed straight up. Jeanette slowly looked down at the broken glass then back up at Sam. "Look what you did," she said quietly. "Look what you've done."

"Me? You threw it! Him or me. What's it to be?"

"I can't make that decision. You can't ask."

"Him or me? Him or me? Him or me?" The genie was fully out of the bottle, the rage took and held him. He grabbed her by the shoulders. "And if you choose him, then fuck it, I'll tell everyone anyway." The words had flown before he could take them back. She pulled away, an expression on her face somewhere between fear, defiance and an acidic fury. He recoiled from it.

"You wouldn't *dare*."

"I would."

She stumbled against the wall, held herself up with one hand and raised her head. Jeanette's hair had fallen across her face and she stared through the fringe pitifully. "But I love you."

"Then prove it. Him or me? Him or me?" He shouted. Jeanette waved her hand as if that could diminish the volume.

"Him or me?"

She looked round at her life framed on the walls. "I can't leave all this," she said desperately. "It's me. It's who I am. Don't make me, please. Please don't tell anyone, we can make it work, we'll find a way."

"ENOUGH. HIM OR ME?" He thundered.

In moments, West switched from pleading lost girl to cruel banshee. "Oh, fuck off," she shrieked, "little painted boy, little fucking painted boy. I've eaten more than you for breakfast, had Stones and Beatles, you think you're special? Don't you know who I am? Look at this, look at all this…I'm Jeanette West and you are a *little painted boy*. Fuck off."

Then she simply stared at him and her vicious glare said it all.

Sam didn't even give her dramatic parting shot. He simply threw open the front door, rushed out, then looked over his shoulder.

Jeanette West was slumped against the stairway, head in her hands. He curled his lip in disgust and slammed the door.

25 / 16th April 1981, London.

Anna felt the already small solicitor's office had become tiny. The only sound was Nigel's breathing but after a while, Blundell hesitantly picked up where he'd left off.

"So I grabbed a cab from Oxford Circus back to my place in Shoreditch, went to the offie opposite, got a bottle of vodka then waited for her to call, but she didn't. I know why, now. But I was furious, thought she'd acted like a spoiled brat. So I sat and drank then passed out."

OK, we'll check that with the cabbie and the offie, thought Anna. *They'll easily remember someone like you, Sam Bizarre.* But out loud she said, "You can't blame yourself." *Ah,* she cursed herself. *What meaningless, cliché bollocks. Of* course *he blames himself, who else is there?*

"That was our first argument," he said. "I swear. It just happened. But she wouldn't have…She wouldn't have done *that* after one fight. I would have come back, I was just angry, I would have come back, I swear I would. I was just being bolshy, I didn't mean it."

Leeding let him talk. She knew these thoughts had haunted his every moment over the last two weeks. However whenever reality hit, Nigel Blundell could paint his face, lipgloss a smile and escape into the role of Sam Bizarre. But Anna knew every act must leave the stage eventually and when *Sam* took his final bow, then *Nigel* would be back for good. Perhaps this was that moment.

"So do you know why she did it?" He asked with desperation in his eyes again. *You need exoneration, proof Jeanette's suicide was the result of something deeper, darker and out of your control.* Leeding thought. *But I don't think I have that yet.*

"Is there anything else?" He carried on. "You said there were loose ends.Has what I told you made any difference? Has it helped?"

Anna slowly nodded but chose not to answer that question for the moment.

"Nigel. There are five people in this room. Nobody will say a word about what's been said. Your relationship with Jeanette will stay private." She flashed a look at Mr Chrysalis Records, the only person with anything to gain from releasing this information. "Understand? Nobody wins if the press get hold of this. Nobody."

Mr Chrysalis nodded. "No-one at Trident will say anything, it's not in their interest. And when you work for a record company, you might as well have your office in a confession box. We release records, we keep secrets, that's my motto."

"Good, and that applies to you, too, Nigel."

"I'm hardly going to go to Smash Hits and tell them about it, am I?"

"No, but I just need to ask a few more questions."

"More? *More?* What else is there?" Sam barked. For a moment, Leeding saw the fury he'd just described.

"I know, I know." She held up her hands in supplication. "But I have to ask, OK?"

His rage passed for now. "So do you know why Jeanette…*why?*"

Anna decided to skirt around the edges of what she knew (or thought she knew) and see what revealed itself.

"Some of these questions may sound odd but just humour me. As I've said, they're loose ends. I need to cross them off my list."

"OK, ask, I'll answer, if I can."

Anna picked up a file, rooted through and pulled out a photograph of the modern art from Jeanette's bedroom wall. Written in blue charcoal was;

FACE

"Do you recognise this?"

Nigel peered at the photograph with a blank expression. "What is it?"

"You sure you don't know?"

"Why should I? Is it an album cover? Or that magazine, "The Face"?What's that got to do with all this?"

"It was hanging on the wall above Jeanette's bed when we entered the property."

"No, no." He shook his head vehemently. "No, she had the Duffy portrait up there. She loved that photograph."

Another question confirmed, Anna thought. *First St. Austenne and now Sam have both denied the FACE picture was there before.*

"You're sure?"

Nigel took his leave for a moment and *Sam* was suddenly back in the room, dark and sexual. He appraised Anna through those kohl-ringed eyes. "I slept in that bed enough, we *fucked* in that bed enough. I looked at the picture enough." Sam suddenly gulped and Nigel returned. "Wait. Was that where she was? She did it in the *bed*?"

"We'd like to keep some details private, if we may. You must understand."

"She did, didn't she? Oh God, she did it in the bed we slept in. Oh God, why there? Was it really so bad? Was *I* really so bad that she wanted to do it *there*?"

"Nigel. *Nigel*." Anna forced his attention back onto her face. "You have to trust me. This wasn't about you. I can't go into details, but there were other things going on in her life."

He grasped at the hope offered. "Really? Oh God, what?"

"In time. So you've never seen this picture before?"

"No, I said."

"Was it there on Saturday the 4th?"

"I never went into the bedroom that day, I told you. So I don't know. Why are you so interested in a picture?"

"We're trying to get an insight into Jeanette's mental state. We think she took down the Duffy portrait and put this art work up in its place. We're just wondering if it's significant. What it means, whether she drew it or not. We know she loved the Duffy photograph so taking it down seems out of character."

"It is. You've seen her house, the only pictures are of herself. There are no other photos, paintings, art, anything. So in her home, this," he pointed at the charcoal work, "this is unique."

"Any ideas what it could be?"

"You'd have to ask an art collector or an expert. Means nothing to me."

"All right, thank you. You said you don't smoke and Jeanette didn't either. Are you sure she didn't have a little crafty puff now and again?"

"No, she hated smoking. It was one of the reasons she preferred not to go out to clubs and whatnot, all the smoke. Why?"

"Just background."

Leeding went to pull out Jeanette's suicide note but stopped at the last moment. Generalities would suffice.

"You were saying how much energy and life she had. Was there anything," *careful now,* "that was bothering her?"

Nigel looked puzzled. "Bothering her? She was in a loveless but convenient marriage but had come to terms with that. I wish she hadn't. No, nothing really *bothered* her. Life was too much fun to be *bothered* by things."

Yes, that's the picture I'm getting, thought Anna. *I know Jeanette West far more than I did half an hour ago and she doesn't seem like a person who was* bothered *by much at all. Even her faded fame was being fixed, with that role in Dallas. The Jeanette I'm hearing about doesn't seem the same woman who'd write;* 'I resisted so long, but I couldn't go on like I have before. People have used me, judged me, abused me simply because of my sex. I can't bear to be in this body any more, as I can't bear what people have done to me over the years.' *But that's suicides, they rarely seem like the kind of people who do what they do.*

"She never talked about anyone mistreating her?"

"No. Well, I mean, there were a few little bitchy stories from the sixties, other models trying to trip her up on the catwalk, gossiping behind her back, but just the usual girls being girls stuff. Mistreating her? How? And why do you ask?"

"As I say, just following a few threads."

Sometimes we all keep things inside for years and even those close to us never know what's beneath. That's just called being human. So what did Jeanette keep down for so long? What troubles rumbled down there and erupted after one stupid argument on one single night?

"She said nothing that would make you think there was anything desperately wrong? Anything she needed help with?"

He sighed but this time it was frustration rather than sadness. "Never, and she'd have told me." His rage rose again. "Do you think for one *fucking* moment if she had a problem that made her suicidal I wouldn't have helped her? That I'd have done what I did that night? 'Oh, my girlfriend is on the edge, tell you what, I'll make an ultimatum, then walk out on her, because that's exactly what depressed, suicidal people need, isn't it?' A stupid, spoiled little shit." He began to cry again, "A spoiled *shit* walking out on them. That's what they need, isn't it?"

"I'm not saying…"

"I know *you're* not saying, but *I am.*"

So what happened to Jeanette that made her write that note? What was she keeping so far down inside nobody would ever find it?

Nigel pulled himself together again. "Sorry, I'm just…I'm just so…confused."

"I understand."

"Do you understand? Do you? Do you really, honestly think *you* know *anything* about…"

Anna looked him directly in the eyes and what he saw there shut his mouth quickly.

"Yes, Nigel, I do." She realised her hands were shaking.

You stay down where you belong, memories. Don't you dare *surface now.*

Nigel thought for a little while.

"Well, there were the letters, I suppose. But she wasn't *bothered* by them. If anything she thought they were weird, even a bit funny, sometimes."

Anna's head snapped back up. "Letters? What letters?"

"Fan letters. She still got the occasional fan letter, usually wanting an autograph or signed picture. But there were a few of them that were a little odd."

"In what way?"

"A bit more obsessive."

"We get them all the time," piped up Mr Chrysalis. "Some fans can overstep the mark. You should see some of the things Billy Idol gets sent. Knickers, bras, stories about what they'd like to do with him. Sam's already had a few. Ha, do you remember that girl who sent you some of her pubic hair? Jesus…"

Sam shot him a look of withering disdain and he shut up. "Yeah, Jeanette had a few letters from some girl. Sarah was her name, she'd write these long, rambling letters, first declaring her love for Jeanette then they'd *turn* halfway through, start getting hysterical and bitter. Then they'd go all lovey dovey again. Very weird. Jeanette felt sorry for her. But she'd also laugh. It was difficult not to at points."

"Threats?"

"Not threats as such, more…" Anna could see him try out a few descriptions in his head before settling on one, "…violent declarations of love. Talking about how she'd protect Jeanette from *them*, you know, paranoia. But they could also be very funny. It was like the writer would sometimes catch herself being mad and laugh about it. But then she still sent the letters."

"How did the…did you say her name was *Sarah*?"

"Sarah. That's what she signed, yes."

"How did this Sarah send the letters?"

"To Jeanette's Fan Club P.O. address. They just got sent straight on."

"Jeanette never replied?"

"God, no. She had enough crazy communications in the sixties. Yeah, I think she felt a bit sorry for her, too, but not enough to get in touch.That's just madness. As I say, she kept them because they amused her. Now I think about it, that's not very kind, is it?"

I'm not surprised, thought Anna. *I'm increasingly unsurprised by West's behaviour.*

"And to be clear, she didn't feel threatened by them?"

"No, as I said, she really wasn't bothered about anything." Anna saw his Adam's apple move up and down as he tried to swallow the grief. "But I suppose it turns out she was bothered, she really was."

"One more thing, Nigel, did she keep the letters?"

"Some of them I think. She was quite a hoarder when it came to herself, as you saw."

"Where might they be now?"

"She had a box in her wardrobe, full of clippings, photos, tickets and God, everything. If she hadn't got rid of the letters they'll still be there."

Anna turned to Fisher. "Let's get hold of that box, OK? Will you call Clive St. Austenne and arrange it?"

"Yes, ma'am."

"Blue ink." Sam sighed out of no-where.

"Sorry?"

"That Sarah, whoever she was. Always used this light blue ink, beautiful handwriting. That was what made the letters so odd. She'd be ranting, going off on tangents, but it was all written in this lovely blue Copperplate. The *look* of the words and the *meaning* were quite different. You know, like a tiger. It looks beautiful but its *nature* is something else. Maybe Jeanette was like that, too."

Anna felt like the solicitor's office had just shrunk in size again.

26 / Sometime *before* (4)

With grinding predictability she left school with low grades in all her exams except art and drama. And as equally expected, at the age of sixteen she found herself behind a desk at a high street bank mourning a future that had never arrived.

The other girls from her year were no-where to be seen. They'd left school and taken their beautiful, clever, two-faced smiles to gullible employers. But she hadn't forgotten them and never would.

Her "diary" had become several volumes. Some entries were neatly written in blue ink while others were scrawled, vicious blots and slices that cut through the paper. Both the list of crimes against her and guilty parties involved had grown. She documented everything from outright hostility to a sly glance on the bus and had lost count of the times parts of her were chipped away.

As she wrote about these events she was able to watch herself from a distance, both emotionally back in the moment yet detached and clinical. It had become increasingly apparent that insanity was part of her DNA, as inevitable as eye or skin colour, therefore, she simply accepted it. When a flower grows wild one doesn't question the seed's origin but simply admire its tenacity.

As she'd grown into womanhood her madness had flowered but nobody saw. She kept it well hidden.

Artistically, both her charcoal work and acting skills blossomed. At school she'd played a wallflower who quietly blended into the background, but it was a one-note act. Playing the role of Anna had shown her how easy it was to shed one "reality" and pull on another persona. In the seconds between side stage and spotlight, she'd folded *Anna* around herself until she *was* a strong willed widowed teacher in Siam. She watched this transformation from afar and marvelled at the realism of her performance. The emotions she fashioned on stage were indistinguishable from the real thing. She *almost* felt them herself.

So *Anna* was kept ready even after the curtain fell. In social situations she pulled out facets of the character as required, smiled, laughed, even looked interested in people she had nothing in common with.

The act worked up to a point, but ultimately she was just a waxwork that moved. Eventually everyone would instinctively move away, as if they subconsciously sensed her unreality. Men would be drawn to her looks, then after a while she'd see their eyes glaze over and they'd find an excuse to break off the conversation. One can instantly tell if a dog intends to bite and she thought perhaps that aura of menace emanated from her, too. It was as if she were a slow-acting poison gas. People would enter her orbit then slowly back away to safety, unaware they were doing so.

Oh, but *she* always saw.

After Mother died Father quit his job and started a new business, like he was clearing the decks. Mother had existed and served a purpose but now she was no longer present, Father moved on. The "family" of two moved to a new address but it was just the same; simply walls to keep the cold out.

Father didn't offer her a job, which was just fine; she didn't want to work *and* live alongside him. The only time he barely smiled in her direction was when she handed over her share of the housekeeping. She was saving to move out, but on bank wages that would take some time.

While she was a waxwork, Father was an optical illusion; simultaneously physically close whilst emotionally broadcasting from afar. She didn't care. His only purpose had been to supply half of the equation that led to her birth, but beyond that, he was nothing. There would be a reckoning one day, though, of that she was certain.

The men at the bank were almost all old, bald and kept sad families trapped in tatty frames on self important desks. There were some younger men, boys really, but despite her looks they never got close. Like everyone else, she repelled these *boys* as if they were opposing sides of a magnet. They'd suddenly veer around her desk, pushed away by an invisible wind.

The younger girls were polite but nothing more. She knew some had resented her physical appearance before gleefully realising she was no threat whatsoever. The older women looked down on her as they would at a dirty, wounded animal; somewhere between contempt and pity.

But every day her act became more refined. Male customers started to linger a little longer, females would compliment her clothes and hair choices. But eventually they would all begin to drift and become uncomfortable in her presence.

She had more finessing to do but knew eventually one act would fool everyone. And when that day came, she could really get to work.

That December, one of the slightly older boys held a Christmas party for some of the bank staff and friends. His mum and dad were taking a weekend away and had foolishly trusted their oldest to look after the house. In retrospect that turned out to be a very bad idea.

To her surprise she'd been invited. It was the first party she'd ever been asked to attend. The disastrous "King & I" after show didn't count, as they'd *had* to invite "Anna". But this was different. Somebody actually wanted *her* company.

His name was Nicholas. He'd never really spent much time with her so hadn't experienced the creeping sensation of unease she created in almost everyone else.

Nicholas had sidled over one morning and sat on the edge of her desk. That in itself was thrilling but what happened next shocked her into laughter.

"Hello," he looked directly into her eyes. "Haven't spoken to you as much as I should have, really."

She formed a smile and switched on part of *Anna's* "King & I" personality. "And what can I do for you, today, sir?"

He'd understood the role he was supposed to play. Nicholas pulled up a seat and sat opposite, client and bank clerk.

"I'm having a Crimble do," he'd smiled. She'd nearly gagged, as "Crimble" was what Mother called the festival, but "Anna" prevailed.

"How lovely."

"And I'm inviting some of us lot. That includes you, naturally. December the ninth, are you around?"

She'd found herself experiencing a rare emotion; happiness. She gave a disbelieving laugh then remembered to stay in character.

"The ninth," she made a play of checking some papers on her desk. When she looked up he smiled and his eyes slid about her features. "Yes, I believe the ninth is fine. I shall pop it in my diary."

"Pop away," said Nicholas. "Great, I'll see you there."

"You will."

As he walked away she looked him up and down.

I think I've just been flirted with, she thought. *But not like in The King & I where 'The King' flirted because of expediency, but actual flirting. Genuine interest.*

This thought was tempered, of course, by the knowledge that her side of the exchange had been a performance.

*

She found herself a new outfit for the party. Since leaving school she'd tried out various fashions for size to find out where in the teenage food chain she sat. No-one had seen her outside the bank so were used to a stuffy A-line skirt and blouse. Therefore she decided to *really* put on a show.

The party skirt was shorter than anything she'd ever dared wear, but knew her legs could carry it off. She'd chosen something very "now" for the blouse, a puffy cotton affair with geometric patterns, and invested in a copy of Vogue for make up and hair tips. It was all surface but then again, her entire personality was surface, too. She'd told Father not to expect her until late but he'd simply glanced her way, appraised her legs, shrugged and gone back to his book.

She hadn't known what to expect. A party, a *real* party, where people would drink, smoke, laugh and dance? The idea intoxicated her. The guests may even do *other things*, too. She'd read magazine articles about throwing parties but they were purely academic, because now she was going to a real one.

Nicholas's house was big enough to fit thirty or so guests. From her research she knew turning up at the invited time was simply not done, so arrived forty-five minutes later. Music blared from the windows, open despite the December chill, and smoke billowed out alongside the sounds. She saw shapes move in the darkened living room, heard laughter and noisy conversation.

It's happening, she thought. *It's really happening.*

The door was opened by an unfamiliar young man with a drink in his hand. He looked her up and down, puffed out his cheeks, whistled and said, "I don't care if you're gatecrashing, *you,* darlin' can come in." She'd smiled, entered, then was surprised to feel his hand grab her backside. She knew such things happened at parties but no-one had touched her there for a very long time and the previous experiences had been anything but pleasurable. So she hid her shock, dropped into character, then flashed a look over her shoulder, one she'd seen in Silvikrin hairspray adverts; coy yet alluring, forceful yet welcoming.

"Cheeky," she purred.

The boy on the door laughed. "I can be cheekier."

"Tut tut *tut.*" She'd found a new facet of her "Anna" character, "The Vamp" and she liked it.

The alcohol made everyone more welcome than usual. As the drinks flowed, inhibitions relaxed. She supposed it helped that her outfit was a dramatic change from daytime wear, so both girls and boys were curious. *It's "My Fair Lady" in reverse*, she'd thought. *No Professor Higgins required. I've gone from high class to street level and it suits me.*

She'd never drank alcohol like this before. There'd been sips of sherry and Cinzano when Mother and Father weren't in the room but nothing like the amount she consumed that night. Cans of lager and bottles of Babycham stood on the kitchen sideboard and there were funny little snacks in bowls, even wine. It felt like a posh society gathering and yes, people smoked, drank and laughed, just as she'd imagined.

She'd spotted couples pair up in darkened corners and wondered what that felt like. She watched fascinated as boys tried their luck with blouses and skirts, some succeeding, most failing. The alcohol gave everything a fuzzy glow. She felt like an astronaut who'd visited another civilisation, and walked like one, too. Her feet seemed to float above the carpet.

Then suddenly Nicholas was there, an arm around her shoulder. "Having a good time?"

"Oh yes," she'd beamed, and really was. No act was required. "I love the music."

"Oh, I love music too," he slurred and made no attempt to hide how he looked down her top which had fallen open "Listen. Oh. No, listen. Oh. Tell you what. Come with me, come on, come."

He pulled her toward the stairs and she didn't resist. It was past eleven thirty and the party had thinned out somewhat. Although the kitchen was still full, the lights of the living room were off and forms moved on sofas in slow motion.

She allowed him to guide her upstairs, wondered where the adventure would take her next. "You like music? You should see my record collection. You should see it." He stumbled a little and pushed open a door. "Come on," he whispered and put a finger to his lips. "Come on. You'll like it."

She walked into his bedroom and it was true, there were shelves full of LP's and singles.

"Wow," she said, genuinely impressed.

"Yeah, yeah," he said, then turned a key in the door. "Get some privacy," he mumbled. "Yeah? Get some privacy. You'll like it."

"Like it? What?" She asked but knew what he meant. Her heart begun to speed up in anticipation. She didn't know *exactly* what was going to happen. The events of her childhood were something different and far away, but this was now, she was in control. This moment was what she wanted, wasn't it?

He licked his lips and looked her up and down. His expression had changed, darkened. She'd seen that aspect before.

So her childhood *wasn't* so far away and she *wasn't* in control.

"I don't think...Nicholas, I don't think..."

He pushed her onto his bed. That was a surprise, because the couples in the living room had been so languid with their explorations.

"Nicholas, I..."

"Yes, yes, you do," he contradicted a statement she hadn't even made.

"Please, I..."

"You do."

*

Nicholas had finished, silently rolled away, pulled up his trousers and crept from the room. He'd whispered, "Thank you" on the way out, a gentleman to the last.

So this is how it is, she thought. *How it always is. Doesn't matter who, when, where, how old I am, this is how it is. This is all I am. It wouldn't have mattered whether my skirt was short or ankle length, my top loose or tight. None of it matters. I am just this thing. Whatever character I play, I am always just this thing.*

She lay on Nicholas's bed and stared at the ceiling. Once again she disassociated her mind from the reality.

How do I really feel? Like nobody and nothing. All this is just a performance where the players don't see the stage. Tonight I played the victim, he played the guilty. Tomorrow it may be something else again. The scripts change. But soon I will write the lines. I will cast the characters. I will decide.

She lay there for a while. Downstairs the sounds of conversation and music died down. The front door opened and closed as guests left. There would be people asleep on sofas, or fumbling in corners. She'd read the magazines and knew how these events played out.

Eventually, she rose, turned, sat on the edge of the bed and idly curled a lock of hair around her finger. Her expression was blank but her eyes burned, fixed into the middle distance.

She stood and left the room.

Nicholas was asleep on the landing, leaning against the wall, breathing heavily with his mouth open.

So you leave me used up on the bed and that's as far as you got, is it Nicholas? Just had your fun and fell asleep a few feet away from your conquest? Couldn't sleep next to me, could you? That would have been too close to the truth, wouldn't it? So here you are and here I am.

She looked at him for a long time.

It was almost silent downstairs.

She cocked her head to one side and listened. Nobody moved down there. She may have been the only one awake, perhaps everyone else was anaesthetised by alcohol.

She squatted down next to Nicholas, stared into his face, gently stroked his cheek with a finger, traced the outline of his lips and smoothed down his hair. He didn't react, wrapped in sleep and beer.

"Rockabye baby," she sang quietly, "on the treetop, when the wind blows, the cradle will rock..." she kissed him on the cheek, "...and when the bow breaks, the cradle will fall, and down will come baby, cradle and all."

With one hand and barely any effort she pushed Nicholas down the stairs.

27 / 17th April, 1981, London.

Clive St. Austenne had readily agreed to hand over the box Jeanette kept in her wardrobe. The suicide note implied she'd taken her life because of being *used, abused* and *judged* by others, so he wanted to get to the bottom of those claims and was prepared to help the police in any way he could.

Now the box sat on Anna's desk at Great Portland Street Station.

It was slightly larger than a toolkit and made of stained wood with a brass handle on top. There was no lock, which implied Jeanette wasn't bothered about anyone else rooting through her life. Anna knew West was an exhibitionist so wouldn't have been particularly sniffy about privacy. *Except,* she thought, *when it came to having an affair, naturally.*

Anna had already looked inside that day in Selly Mews so knew no Pandora style surprises were about to fly out. Papers, magazines, envelopes, contact sheets and yet more photographs were stacked up to the brim.

Leeding put on gloves and began to examine the paper trail of Jeanette's life. Sat on top was a thick red leather book with "DIARY" embossed in gold on the cover. Anna's heart fluttered in expectation that it contained the inner workings of West's mind, but soon discovered it was little more than appointments, going back several years. Restaurant reservations, work meetings, photo shoots and more were recorded there with brevity. Just single words, initials, addresses and times covered the pages. There were no emotional insights to be found so Anna put the book to one side and started to dig through the rest of West's trove.

There was Jeanette on the cover of "TV Times" with Ed Stewart, Ingrid Pitt and Mickie Most publicising their joint appearance as judges on "New Faces". "Look In" magazine featured her with a "WESTIE POSTER FULL COLOUR." There was a front cover of The Sun newspaper, which dated back to last February. The main headline shouted "MY SHY DI" and featured Charles and Lady Di. Charles appeared to be giving his future wife a shoulder massage and the paper promised, "FOUR PAGE ROYAL ROMANCE PULLOUT STARTS ON PAGE 13".

God, there was still seven months to go until the wedding. How many times can the papers keep telling the same story? And starting your Royal Romance Pullout on page thirteen *doesn't augur good luck, now, does it?*

Jeanette hadn't kept the paper for royal posterity, however. The side bar featured a recent shot and the headline, "WESTIE GOES WEST - MODEL STUNNER FLIES TO U.S. TO JOIN 'DALLAS!'" Anna scanned a few lines of the story, which basically repeated the headline but with more words. *So what made you give that up, Jeanette? You announce to the world you're back on top, then pull the plug on your life. Why?*

There were party invitations and concert tickets (including one for Spandau Ballet which featured the guns of HMS Belfast) menu cards, odd little scraps of paper that must have meant something to West but were meaningless outside of her context.

Then there were photos which dated back to the sixties and documented Jeanette's social, personal and professional lives; Jeanette meeting Princess Anne, Jeanette high-kicking with the Bay City Rollers, pouting in a photographic studio somewhere, dancing with Diana Dors, modelling her own line of dresses for the Grattan Catalogue, dressed as a valkyrie on a record sleeve by the band Roxy Music.

Bloody hell, thought Anna. *Aboriginals believe you lose a part of your soul every time your photograph is taken. By this evidence she had no soul left whatsoever.*

Jeanette was a hoarder of information, but only about herself. Looking through this box, Anna realised anything outside West's frame of reference simply didn't exist. There were no photographs of anyone else unless she was with them and not one headline or magazine clipping featured other people. Jeanette was the centre of the universe and unless you orbited her, you floated in the void unnoticed.

I do believe that I'm going off you, Anna thought. *Not that I was particularly "on" you to start with, but the ego here is...vulgar. Yes, that's the word. There is a wanton, vainglorious vulgarity here and I don't find it attractive at all.*

She leafed through a few more photographs and felt guilty. *OK, perhaps this is how she dealt with things. Playacted happy, smiled for the flashbulbs. Perhaps keeping everything* two *dimensional kept the* three *dimensional at bay. Perhaps, perhaps.*

Then, between two magazine pages, she found an envelope and the handwriting on it made her shudder.

It read, *"Jeanette West, P.O Box 242"*, exquisitely written in light blue ink.

Anna gently eased the paper into the light and saw the letter was written on Basildon Bond paper. Jeanette's suicide note was typed on the same, but that had little significance. The brand was incredibly popular, they even used it here in the station. Anna read what the writer had to say.

"15th December 1980.

Dearest Jeanette,

What a tragedy! John Lennon killed by an evil man. I saw you talking about dear John on the Nine 'O' Clock News. You were saying what a FUNNY and warm person he was. You looked extremely pretty and made Angela Rippon look very dowdy in comparison!! How could dear John Lennon have been gunned down in such a cruel way? The world is a cruel place, isn't it? I do hope he is at peace now. Poor Yoko Ono, she must be lost without her soul mate.

I know we are soul mates you know, you and I. Although you haven't replied to <u>any</u> of my <u>many many previous letters</u>, I forgive you, because you are so very busy and of course I know that you can't and I accept that. But I know you will be thinking of me, for we are SOUL mates. I knew that we had a connection when I first saw you on "Shang A Lang" on the television in 1975. I wonder what "Shang A Lang" means? It sounds like a skin condition doesn't it? Like all the other girls I watched it for the music, but then suddenly YOU were on talking with Eric, Woody and the boys about modelling and you turned to the camera and said, "there are models just like me out there watching this right now. Models just like YOU." And you *pointed directly at the camera at ME. I was so happy. You'd noticed! I do wish you would reply though. I always need to know that you know you and I are connected. It would be very nice if you replied. I do get angry with you sometimes! If I knew where you lived I could come and we could have tea and I could tell you all about myself face to face. But I know we can't. Oooh, what a game we play! We have to be discreet, you and I.*

I think you would be proud, too! I just got a job in fashion! Well, if you can count uniforms and work blouses as fashion!! But we all have to start somewhere. Who knows where I'll be next?

I love you and believe me, I will protect you from any cruel man like Mark Chapman. I would leap right in front of that bullet! I would! Which is more than Clive St. Austenne would do! His hair is too greasy, I do hope you've spotted that. You should tell him. It looks like a cat that's fallen into Swarfega! I know there's no way you can reply, but I still don't like it when I get angry with you. It makes me SAD. When I get sad I drink and I smoke more and both those things are very bad for me. PLEASE don't make me sad or angry, life is sad and angry enough, as John Lennon has found out. I sent you some more flowers to the fan club address, your favourite, roses. Did you get them?

Yours with love,
Sarah.

Anna read the note again, then found two more letters in the same hand, dated 1977 and 1979.

The writer had underlined the words "many many previous letters" in the 1980 communication, which suggested Jeanette had either not received them, or thrown those away. The other two letters followed much the same pattern. Warm yet odd greetings followed by a mention of a TV appearance or magazine article which featured West, then a turn in tone to slightly threatening. *But only slightly,* Anna compared the pages. *There are no death threats here, not even any intimations of violence, just these off-kilter streams of consciousness flipping between puppy love and childish tantrum. If Jeanette had brought these to us, I wouldn't have found much to say except, "Let us know if they become more serious or if you feel threatened in any way." But there's no return address on any of them. Even if Jeanette wanted to reply, she couldn't.*

Anna flicked through them again and found her answer.   In the 1979 letter, the writer had said;

"As you know, I provided you with my new address in last year's letter. I do not wish to put it in writing any more than necessary. As we are both aware, there are <u>those</u> who wish to hurt people like us, who do not understand our love and want to tear it to pieces. If they find me, and know of our true selves, I am scared what will happen. Keep my address safe, my darling!"

There are no other "Sarah" letters in the trunk so her address is lost, for now. OK, so she's paranoid then, of course."Sarah" believes she's in a secret relationship with West they can't acknowledge because society won't accept it. Perhaps she even thinks Jeanette doesn't respond for fear of revealing her "true self". Who knows? But one thing's certain, these letters surely couldn't have led to West's suicide. There's nothing in them that could have sent her over the edge like that. But still, but still. Blue ink? Coincidence? Of course it is. Loads of people use blue ink. If it had been blue charcoal, then...Then what, *Anna? You're tying yourself in knots because of this but in reality isn't it just a lot of weird coincidences and inconsistencies that* look *like they're going somewhere but add up to nothing.*

She sighed.

You know why you're fixating over this, she admonished herself. *You know damn well but you're doing it anyway, so just drop it. There's nothing here.*

Anna was about to return the papers back to their envelopes when she noticed something on the 1977 letter. The writer, normally fastidious, had blotted some of her ink and there was a tiny partial fingerprint on a corner of the page.

Wait. Wait a moment.

Anna stopped and her head tick locked, left-to-right,right-to-left, left-to-right, then she blinked exactly five times.

What have you missed? What should you be putting together? These letters and something else?

She pulled out her desk drawer, found the report from Jeanette's suicide at Selly Mews and scanned through, not actually knowing what she was looking for.

Then she lighted on it.

"Unknown prints were discovered on the windowsill in the rear bedroom (E3) but at present have not been matched. Other unknown prints have been found (E4)."

Partial unknown prints on the open windowsill.

It's a very long shot but worth a go. I should get these letters printed. Perhaps, perhaps they match, highly unlikely, but…There were scuff marks up the wall. Did somebody climb the drainpipe, grab on to the windowsill? Pull themselves up to look inside? Maybe even go inside? What if prints on the letter *match the prints on the* windowsill? *What would* that *mean?*

Anna dragged herself back to reality. *Ah, this is all just conjecture, and like everything else, it's an interesting game which probably goes nowhere.*

Leeding tapped her fingers on the note.

No, there's something else.

She looked back through the letters then returned to the report, but couldn't find another connection.

Because the connection isn't in the report, *is it? The connection is in your head.*

She stared at the 1980 letter.

Something in here, something throwaway. No, wait, something thrown *away.*

There it was.

"When I get sad I drink and I smoke more and both those things are very bad for me."

Cigarette butts in the garden drain. Butts that didn't belong to Jeanette, Clive or Sam Bizarre. So did they belong to this "Sarah"?

Anna put the letter down and thought for a long time.

Lost in her reverie, she didn't notice Inspector Walker staring intently at her from across the office.

28 / 17th April, 1981, London.

Inspector David Walker watched Anna. She'd intently worked her way through Jeanette West's ego-treasure chest, lost to the world.

He was worried about her.

Yes, he admitted the West suicide had some oddities but Anna wasn't normally this off-road. *Suicide itself is full of contradictions,* he thought. *It's counterintuitive, goes against that most basic human instinct, self preservation. And now Anna's behaving in a counterintuitive way but I know why. What was it that song last year said? "Suicide Is Painless"? Surely written by someone who'd never experienced it. There but for the grace of God go I.*

He hadn't plunged that far in his own life but had teetered.

*

Five years ago David's wife Barbara had died suddenly from meningitis. The speed between first indications of illness then diagnosis and death had been impossibly, horribly fast.

She'd complained of a splitting headache at lunchtime then quickly became feverish. They'd both put it down to a sudden onset of flu and Barbara had taken to her bed. That's when David saw the rash, a constellation of terrible red stars. Trained in first aid, Walker had rolled a milk bottle over the marks. Normal rashes fade to white under pressure, meningitis spots stay vivid.

These had remained bright and malignant.

He'd rushed his wife into hospital where the nurses took one look at Barbara then sped her into intensive care. She'd complained of the headache at lunch. By dinner she was dead.

His life had been turned inside out in less time that it took to complete a shift. David had gone into the hospital a married man and left a widower. There'd been no time to prepare for the loss, no slow running down of the clock, because Barbara's clock had simply stopped ticking.

In the weeks after, their shell-shocked families came to visit then sipped tea and ate unnecessary sandwiches, their silence punctuated with self-conscious clinks of cutlery on china. But eventually they always left him alone with his thoughts and Barbara's ebbing presence.

With no children, David had nobody else to refocus his energies on. He was given compassionate leave but the last place he wanted to be was at home with her ghost. But even leaving the house was heartbreaking. David couldn't *bear* to hear couples talk at the supermarket, blissfully unaware conversing with the one you love was a fragile luxury. He asked to come back to work many times but the bosses gave him no choice, because a distracted police officer who can't engage with their responsibilities is a danger to both themselves and the public.

Anna had taken her entire holiday allowance to look after him. She cooked, cleaned and revealed a talent for housewifery previously kept well hidden. But most of the time she simply sat and only spoke when required.

"Sometimes there is no sense, David," Leeding said one evening. "Look at our job, what we see on a daily basis. We are the human face of law and order, but laws only work if people obey them and order is more delicate than we'd like to admit. Things happen and often there is no sense to them. We just have to accept that chaos and meaninglessness is part of this world. We don't have to like it, but we must accept it. There are some things you cannot fight."

Anna was very good at putting things into context. Sometimes he thought she treated his healing process like a different kind of case. *Preserve life. Preserve the scene. Find what is important, discard the distractions. Then discover the reason, if there is one to be found.*

There'd been times when he couldn't get out of his darkness. In those jet-black moments he'd considered staying in the shadows for good, but Anna had always pulled him back into the light.

He loved her for it. Not in the way a husband loves a wife, there was no physical attraction (not at that point, physicality was a foreign language) but rather a deep need.

Slowly, the times in that darkened room became further apart and he went back to work. At first colleagues tiptoed around him, as we all do in the presence of the bereaved, not knowing what to say and scared their grief may soon be ours. But to Walker's surprise, eventually he found his lips could make a smile and voice form a laugh.

He'd felt guilt, of course. Everyone who's lost a loved one goes through a period of self-loathing when they drop back into disrespectful, unbecoming emotions like *happiness*.

But what's my alternative? He'd often thought. *To dress in black for the rest of my life like Queen Victoria? To deny life, just as life had been denied to Barbara? Except* she *hadn't been given a choice. I have.*

The last five years seemed like no time at all and yet, an eternity. Sometimes he couldn't picture Barbara's face, his memories were a jigsaw with parts missing. He'd see her eyes but Barbara's mouth wouldn't appear. He'd remember her hair but then discover his wife's body was blurred.

David thought memory's leeching was being disloyal and hated himself for it. But it was just life, and life moves on. Sometimes clichés exist because they are true.

*

He watched Anna and was worried. There were piles of cases still to bring to a conclusion and yet she remained fixated on West.

He knew why of course, and had known it since they'd first attended Selly Mews. He'd seen Anna's stoic expression in Jeanette's suicide room and known his friend was thinking about another place, another time.

Elsewhere, *elsewhen*.

But David couldn't say anything because that part of her past was *verboten*.

He watched as she pulled letters from the box then read and re-read them, a faraway expression on her face. She cross-referenced with files and he saw lights going on in her eyes as she made real or imagined connections.

Come on, he thought, sadly. *West killed herself. The Reverend died in a hit and run. Other than some random blue charcoal there's nothing to link the two events but clearly* you *believe they're connected.*

David knew Anna was looking for sense in the present because deep inside she was still trying to find a meaning in her past.

Walker wanted to wander over, gently shut that box, smile and ask her out for a drink. But he knew that look on her face. Anna had *something* and now wouldn't let it go. In this particular case he doubted her suspicions would reveal anything concrete. Whatever Leeding thought she'd built so far was made of sand.

No, not sand, *blue charcoal*.

*

Anna looked at the clock, yawned, stood and stretched. The Yorkshire Grey pub was only two minutes walk and David was desperate to ask her for a drink. He looked at Leeding's sleek profile as she pushed the blonde fringe from her eyes.

Why has someone with so much had so little attention? David wondered, and not for the first time.

Over the many years they'd known each other, Anna had kept her private and professional lives almost completely separate.

He remembered her with a trainee officer at Hendon, a broad, rugby playing man, the total opposite of Anna's personality. One day they'd been together, the next he was no-where to be seen.

Walker recalled a long-haired musician type at some point in the seventies who'd also suddenly become a Nowhere Man. Then she'd turned up at a Christmas party with a middle aged sleaze ball in a flash suit. He'd disappeared, too, thank heavens.

And most recently there was Robin, who'd also vanished into the Bermuda Triangle of Anna's personal life. Robin was a quiet, thoughtful type of man; polite, interested, clearly besotted with Leeding and hung on her every word. Walker wasn't sure if the feeling was mutual. She was obviously fond of him but they didn't have that spark he'd seen in other couples. Robin wasn't the smartest man David had ever met, but also certainly not the most unattractive, in looks and personality. As a police officer one developed a sixth sense for bullshit and Robin was clean. He'd metaphorically patted him down and found nothing suspicious but then, maybe six months ago, the guy had obviously climbed into Anna's magician's cabinet and, *pooof*, gone. Like the non-people in Orwell's "1984" he just stopped existing. *Robin? There was never a Robin. I've never even known a Robin, what are you talking about?*

Walker didn't find Anna's secret Merry-Go-Round of lovers a problem.

She's just looking, but never found the right one, that's all. We try on people like we try on clothes. Some fit, some don't, some suit us for a while but then we no longer feel comfortable with them. And occasionally some become our favourite outfit.

She turned, spotted him and smiled.

Go on, David, he thought, *make the "fancy a pint?" mime. Point down the road, toward the Yorkshire Grey. Smile. Shrug. Stand up. Offer her your arm. Walk. Find a table, drink. Laugh. Talk. Laugh more. Tell her stories about yourself she's never heard. Drink until closing time. I'm only five years older. It's nothing. Walk her home. Go on. Do the "pint" mime, that's an order.*

But his arms stayed put and refused to get involved with the fantasy.

"I'm knackered," she called over to him.

Do the mime. Smile and do the mime.

"It's getting on," he agreed.

Do it.

"Homeward bound, then. Tottenham Court Road has never seemed so appealing. Oh, I found something interesting, we'll chat about it tomorrow, shall we?"

No, let's chat about it now. Do the mime.

His arms weren't interested. They lived in the real world, unlike his heart.

Anna picked up her bag, waved over her shoulder and left.

Walker watched her go. Life always moves on and sometimes clichés exist because they are true.

Fifteen minutes later he left too.

*

Anna wandered back through cold, empty London. At night she always found it hard to believe this was the capital city, because after sundown it resembled some long forgotten town at the tip of some long forgotten county.

Today was Friday, officially start of the weekend, so pubs had a few more drinkers than usual but other than their lights, the pavements were made of shadow.

London was starting to shake again. She could almost feel it beneath her feet. The tremors that had spread out from Brixton a few days ago were still rolling and there was a heaviness in the air, like just before a storm breaks.

Anna knew the riots weren't over, just on hiatus. The police had backed off recently but no amount of *softly-softly* could stop a riot determined to have time in the sun, when any excuse could serve as its midwife. The idea of riot was in the air, like a virus. It had infected people across the city, perhaps even the entire country.

Riot was out there somewhere.

So London waited in the dark. Drinkers drank, New Romantics danced, the homeless hid in doorways, police walked their beats and riot capered, a pied piper to disaffected, disenfranchised, victims and violent. All the city could do was wait for it to emerge.

It didn't take long for Anna to make her way back to Tottenham Court Road, just as deserted and shuttered as the rest of the city. At the junction with Oxford Street, the Dominion Theatre's lights blazed. Even from here she could hear muffled music. A band called "Dexys Midnight Runners" were playing tonight.

Funny to think there are thousands of people crammed together just a few yards away, Anna thought. *And yet here I am, all alone. Aw, poor me. Ha, same planet, different worlds.*

A few minutes later, Leeding was back home. As she let herself in the phone began to ring. At the kitchen door, Dylan the cat shouted that he was *famished*, but Anna ignored him and rushed over to the telephone. A call this time of night was usually bad news.

"Leeding, hello?"

Silence.

"Hello?"

Once again, it wasn't a completely dead line because an expectant, dark ambience floated through the receiver.

Is that breathing? Oh Jesus, not again.

Police advice on nuisance calls was simple. Don't engage with the caller because that's what they want. Hang up and *if the problem persists we will work with British Telecom to find a solution and hopefully track down the culprit.* In reality catching a nuisance caller was unlikely, since offenders mainly dialled from public phone boxes then melted away once satisfied.

Anna could definitely hear someone breathing. To get their kicks, nuisance callers needed their victims to know this wasn't a technical fault but a deliberate act.

Ah-ah, not tonight, you sick fucker. She put the phone down.

It rang again.

Nope. I'm not playing.

Anna unplugged the phone and knew the caller would soon lose interest. It was a cold night and even the hardiest pervert wouldn't want to stand in a phone box any longer than they had to. The low temperatures tended to reduce the size of a man's *excitement*, as it were.

As she walked away from the phone a thought struck her.

It rang the moment I walked in. Could be coincidence, but what are the chances of someone calling at the exact *moment I get home? How would they know?*

There was a phone box on the corner of her street.

Anna gingerly picked up the lead like it was about to bite, then plugged the wire back in. Within moments the phone rang again. She grabbed the receiver and listened. Far away, but enough to make its presence known, there was once again the sound of breathing.

Leeding backed away from the telephone and headed out into the street. She looked up to the corner where a red telephone box stood.

Someone was standing in it.

From this distance and in the dark she couldn't make out whether it was a male or a female. The box had been vandalised months ago and the internal lights still hadn't been repaired.

Thanks Buzby. So what do you do now? Arrest some bloke calling their Auntie? Confront a girl who's just ordering a cab?

Anna started to walk slowly towards the box when the person inside turned in her direction. They quickly put the phone down, stepped out and walked briskly away. "Hey!" she called, but the figure swiftly disappeared round a corner. She heard the clatter, *taptaptaptaptap,* of running footsteps and knew there was no point pursuing whoever-it-was.

Anna stared at the empty phone box.

What happened? Was that something, or nothing? Was the person in the box the same as the one on the phone?

Finally she felt the cold so rushed back to her little ground floor flat , which suddenly seemed very vulnerable.

29 / 21st April 1981, London.

It was the end of a Bank Holiday weekend but rather than rested, the people of London felt anxious and afraid because more trouble had flared up at Finsbury Park, Ealing, Wanstead, and Peckham.

Some called the disturbances "riots" but in reality they were sporadic outbreaks of mugging and violence carried out by feral gangs. The fact some were black led the press to compare the disorder to Brixton's events one week before, but the truth was simply a few young men just wanted a riot of their own. This new unrest was a desire for pandemonium rather than social change. Just as Alex and his Droogs committed ultra violence for fun, these '80s Droogs wanted to experience the thrill of destruction for themselves. There was no societal motive, just the rush of targeting Bank Holiday funfairs and running amok amongst stalls and rides, as the gangs stole, smashed and laughed.

It was like Brixton had fired a starting pistol on parts of Britain's youth and sent them racing into chaos. While families cowered for cover in London, seaside towns across England echoed with the sounds of breaking glass and sirens. Just down the road in Southend On Sea, Essex, gangs rushed at each other on the beach. They weren't angry with the police or society and had no racial argument to prove, but fought simply because some were Mods and others weren't. Back in the sixties Mods and Rockers had faced off at coastal towns and now their sons followed the tradition. Who you punched depended on whether they wore a fishtail parka or leather jacket, rather than the colour of their skin or a police uniform.

At every disturbance, girls stood on the sidelines and watched their boys on the front line. Those girls would sometimes laugh and point but often their expressions were terrifyingly blank as they chewed the cud of their gum and observed the tumult with dead eyes. Punks, Mods, Rockers, Teds, they all came to stake their claim on sandy battlegrounds. New Romantics were no-where to be seen, which was a shame. The image of a police constable being attacked by a dandy highwayman or foppish pirate would have made an unforgettable headline. Britain was fraying at the seams. Sociologists and commentators tried to explain youth's descent into anarchy using historical precedents and sociological contexts but sometimes truth is self evident. The young were running wild *because* they were young. Sometimes youth is its own reason.

And Bucks Fizz were *still* number one in the charts, *still* making their minds up.

*

Finsbury Park was just up the road from Nick Atkey's flat. As a wheelchair user he generally avoided busy streets but this Bank Holiday he'd braved the crowds and, as usual, found that people looked straight through him or were suddenly surprised (and even a little annoyed) when he was in their path. "Oh," they'd say and *tut-tut*, as if he'd *chosen* a wheelchair just to inconvenience them.

But once in a while he forced himself to face the mob because it meant he was around real people face to face, rather than voices at the end of a line.

It had been another ordinary public holiday until he'd noticed heads turn in the park's direction and then people run from it. Parents swept up their children, teenagers screamed and alarm rolled his way. Panic spreads between people in a wave, blooms out from its point of origin. Those at the edge often remain unaware of the cause but find themselves carried along in the torrent. So it was that afternoon.

In his wheelchair Nick was effectively the height of a child, unable to see beyond the pushing bodies. He couldn't move left or right, so was forced to sit powerlessly as they flowed about him. "What's happening?" he shouted at the fleeing mob but knew they couldn't or rather, *wouldn't* hear him.

"What's happening? Hello? Can someone help?"

A black teenager stopped by his side. "Are you OK?" he asked.

"I'm fine, what's happening?"

"Let me get you out of the way, over here, is that all right?"

"It's fine, I can do it."

Nick managed to reposition himself in a shop doorway. Sirens sang like Muezzins in the distance.

The black kid sighed and wiped his forehead. "Bunch of wankers," he spat. "Bunch of *wankers*. People out, having a nice day, right? Families, kids, then…bunch of *wankers*."

Somewhere terrifyingly near a shriek of breaking glass cut the air.

"What? Who?"

"They start throwing stones at the Old Bill, no reason, probably thought they were in Brixton, you know? Hundreds of them, *hundreds*. Beating people up, smashing up the fair. Why did they do that? Just people having a nice day."

Police cars sped past. The crowd had thinned and now Nick could see groups of young men breaking shop windows and throwing bins into car windscreens. Atkey tried to remember their faces and clothes because he'd gone from pedestrian to witness in a few short minutes.

"I think we need to get out of here," said the kid. "They're coming this way. If you don't mind, I know you can do it yourself, but I think I can push you faster than you can roll yourself."

"OK, but please be careful."

"Where do you live?"

"Drake Road."

"I know it."

Nick found himself suddenly accelerate and became alarmed. He knew nothing about this kid. What if he were taking him to an alley somewhere? What if this were an elaborate mugging? But then he hated himself for the assumption, because it was those attitudes that caused riots in the first place.

A police officer ran toward them and stopped.

"Everything OK with you two?"

"Yeah. This guy was stuck on the pavement, I'm getting him home."

"It's no place to be on wheels," added Atkey.

"It isn't," agreed the officer. "Good work, son, stay safe."

"I saw some of them," said Nick. "I can give you descriptions."

"That would be very helpful." The officer looked up the road at the chaos which unfolded there. "In time. What's your address?"

"17, Drake Road."

"17 Drake Road. Got it. I'm P.C. Watson. Call the station, we'll arrange a time for me to get a witness statement. Just get to safety for now, quick as you can."

"Don't need to tell me twice," said the kid and they were off.

On the way home Nick started to rant about the state of the nation, since he considered himself an expert in that field. The black kid made suitable noises of agreement and commiseration but generally just let the angry man in the wheelchair speak. "The world's going crazy," moaned Nick for the umpteenth time as he rolled through streets soundtracked by alarms and sirens. "They shot John Lennon. They tried to shoot Reagan. We had the S.A.S. in action at the embassy in *Kensington* last year! The S.A.S! In Kensington! Kids running wild at funfairs. I don't know whether to be angry or just totally in despair."

"I know, I know. It's a weird world," agreed the kid, "not far now, right?"

Nick didn't answer. He was normally the listener, so it was a novelty to have a captive audience. "National Front marching," he sighed, "but 'The lady's not for turning.' Ah, God, I hate it. I really do. I feel so helpless. Just look at it." He waved his hands vaguely at North London. "It's not going to get any better. I know people. It'll just get worse."

"Look on the bright side," offered the kid.

"I try to, but there isn't one."

*

The kid's name was Patrick and he declined an offer of a beer once they'd got back to Nick's bungalow. "No problem, just your average good samaritan," he'd said and saluted. Nick wheeled himself back inside, watched television for the rest of the day and waited for the news to tell him what he already knew.

Nick wasn't surprised by what he'd seen because he knew *people* very well. He received just £21 a week in benefit and worked as a volunteer for a charity called "Listen To Disability" which resembled The Samaritans but with an emphasis on disabilities. Nick had two phone lines in his home, one private, the other linked to the charity. He advised callers on their rights, offered suggestions and solutions, but mainly sat tight and made sympathetic noises when required. Oh yes, he knew *people* very well. He was well aware some of the so-called "able bodied" had a strange perception the disabled were somehow more noble and kind in character than themselves, that their disability granted them a wiser, more tolerant demeanour. Utter bullshit, of course.

Nick spent hours listening to vitriol. He'd heard it all from racism, to violence against women, whining self-justification, bitterness, blame, self-pity...No, wheelchairs and white sticks didn't negate human failings. He'd worked out around forty percent of calls fell into the "vicious" bracket, extrapolated that into the wider world and decided there were forty percent of people he simply wouldn't want to be around, whatever their physical condition.

Back in January, Nick almost choked on his tea when he'd heard the United Nations had declared 1981 to be the "International Year Of Disabled Persons." So far, he hadn't seen any evidence of that. Travelling on the tube was almost impossible unless you only wanted to visit parts of London with lifts, and even if you made it underground, getting on the trains was a case of sheer luck. Nobody wanted to clear space for a wheelchair as they obviously all had very *important, urgent* places to go. The "able bodied" just didn't notice how many doors were at the top of steps, how many toilets were unusable for those on wheels, how few cinemas had ramps or seating areas…The list went on and on. At times, Nick felt that bile rise in himself. So here he was, invisible because most of the time he couldn't even enter places where the "average" worked, shopped and played.

"The International Year Of Disabled People" was a joke and he was the punchline.

*

The day after the "Finsbury Park Riot" as the press had predictably dubbed it (if white kids, then it was a *rampage*, if black, a *riot*) Nick once again spent his time listening to people's lives.

He often wondered how different his life would have been had things not turned out this way. Stuck in a chair, he lived in a bungalow with bars on the walls and every facility two feet lower than in an "able" home. But even this tiny amount of self-sufficiency made him proud.

After a day's worth of listening and talking, he was always ready to knock off at five o'clock. "Listen To Disability" was a twenty-four hour service but Nick couldn't bear evening and night shifts. As a volunteer, he dictated his hours and if nine-to-five worked for most of the population, then that was his choice too.

He mixed up some Smash instant mashed potato, grilled a crispy pancake, heated some beans, then, tray on lap, Nick rolled into his boxy living room and switched on the TV.

John Edmunds was reading the evening news. The disturbances at Finsbury Park and British seafronts led the roundup. The USA had given Saudi Arabia one billion dollars for arms and in sport, young Steve Davis' world champion snooker win was still the big talking point. The magazine show "Nationwide" followed with a mix of consumer advice, quirky reports and "wacky" presenters. Nick let it all wash over him. The dumber the programmes, the better; they diluted the anger, heartache and helplessness he experienced on the phone. To that end the next show was perfect, as Rolf Harris presented his "Cartoon Time." Why the BBC put kids cartoons on during adult hours was a mystery to Nick but he sat back and laughed at Tom'n'Jerry all the same. A documentary about the pop star Sheena Easton followed. She wasn't Nick's cup of tea musically but he simply couldn't be bothered to wheel over and switch channels, so she stayed on.

Eventually he needed the bathroom, which was always a tiresome, depressing, degrading process. It was marginally easier in his own home and damn near impossible anywhere else but eventually he manhandled himself onto the bowl. In times like these he often thought about the thin line between his life as it was now and what it could have been.

And all because of a stupid party.

He'd been working at a bank back then, his parents had gone away for a December trip and he'd decided to have a sneaky "do" in their absence. Ostensibly it was a Christmas celebration but his real motive was to fill the house with girls, ply them with drink and see who he could persuade upstairs.

I was drunk, he thought again. *Yes, I was drunk, but she wanted it. She came up there willingly. Yes, she was drunk too, but had plenty of chances to say no and didn't, did she? She never said no. If she'd said no, I would have left her alone.*

He tried to stop these thoughts when they began to circle but it was impossible. The red line between his potential future *then* and its reality *now* had been drawn on that December evening.

She did *want it. She didn't resist. And besides, even after everything, she never told the police, did she? Or they'd have come for me and they never did. If it had been so bad, why didn't she tell the police? She liked it. I know she did. She was moaning. She loved it.*

He'd persuaded himself this version of events was the truth but somewhere deep inside him a little voice would whisper, *liar, liar, liar.* They'd made love (and that little voice cackled with derision every time he described it so) he'd left her to rest (*To rest, he says! To rest!*), then the combination of excess drink and post-coital exhaustion (*And guilt, Nicholas, guilt!*) made him slide down the landing wall and fall asleep.

He'd come to in hospital with his neck in a brace and no feeling below his waist. Once the events of the night had been pieced together, it was concluded that in his drunken slumber he'd tipped forward and fallen head first down the stairs.

If you hadn't slept with her (Raped! Raped!),you wouldn't have even been there, his mind accused, as the two rival voices competed for attention. *You wouldn't need bars on your walls to help you go for a shit. You'd have girlfriends, a wife by now. A great job, a life. A* fucking *life. It was her fault. She wanted it. She went to the bedroom with me. Her fault.*

But what was, *was,* and could not be changed.

He fought his way back into the wheelchair.

There was a knock at the door, a sharp, businesslike, *tap, tap-tap-tap-tap.*

That was very unusual as Nick never had visitors. "Hang on," he shouted and rolled out into his hallway. His front door was mottled glass and he could see the shape of a woman there.

"Be with you!" he called out and opened the door.

A WPC stood on the little ramp and smiled.

"Ah," Nick took her in. She was attractive *and* wearing a uniform, which was two big plus points in his book. "You must be here about yesterday?"

She looked confused for a moment then smiled again. "Yes, yesterday, that's right."

"I spoke to one of your colleagues, Watson, you know him? Tall chap. Well, you're all tall, aren't you. Nice fella. Come in, come in, it's freezing."

She'd dressed for the cold in leather gloves and a scarf pulled up around her neck. Her hat was tipped down a little further then usual and she carried a large leather bag. The WPC glanced over both shoulders then stepped inside and looked up and down the hallway. Nick trundled toward the kitchen. "Would you like a cup of tea?" he asked.

"I'm fine thank you. Here by yourself?"

"Alas yes, but now I have company!" He tried to flirt. It felt odd coming on to a police officer but ultimately he thought, *a bird is a bird is a bird.* "So, yes, I made some notes about the kids I saw yesterday. I'll just fetch them. I got a good look at a few, sure I could pick them out of a line-up thingy thing that you have."

She followed him into the tiny kitchen and stared around it. The officer appeared to be appraising his life. It was a peculiar feeling. *That's the police for you,* he thought. *They make you feel guilty without even trying.*

She smiled once more.

"Would you like to sit down?"

She didn't answer the question but walked around the oven area and studied it. The WPC appeared to be looking for something. Nick began to feel a little uneasy but had no idea why. "So do you need to take notes?"

"Notes?" she turned to him. The officer leaned down and slowly considered his face, top to bottom. "Hm," she nodded to herself. "Well, well, well. Well, I never."

Nick frowned. "Is there something wrong?"

"No, *noooo*," she laughed, waved a gloved hand in front of her face and stifled a giggle. "I'm sorry. Please. Let's hear these descriptions you have for these, er, kids. In your own time. Take as long as you need."

She rooted through her bag then pulled out a notebook and pencil.

"Dreadful, isn't it?" he said. She raised an eyebrow at him. "You know, these riots, all this stuff. Dreadful. But I suppose they'll get a slap on the wrist in the end, won't they? They all do, these days. The Yorkshire Ripper will probably get five years or something." Nick realised he was gabbling, but then always did around attractive women.

"Oh, no, the guilty always get what's coming to them," she smiled and revealed bright white teeth. At that moment the WPC looked somewhat predatory. "Always, even if it takes a *loooooong* time."

"Well, that's something."

"It is. Do go ahead with your, er, descriptions. Don't mind me, I'm just taking notes. Nice place, by the way, very you."

Very me? Thought Nick. *What does she mean very me?*

"Right. Well, the first guy, he was tall. Six two, three, something like that. I know I'm in a wheelchair, so people all look tall, but I'm a good judge of height, I think…"

"Uh huh," she walked behind his chair. "Carry on."

"And he had this big afro with a red hat on top, so it was kind of spilling out all round the sides. He was quite recognisable."

"Right," she said from behind him. "Here we go, just relax."

"And he was wearing this striped jumper, like Dennis The Menace, and…"

"Oh, " said the WPC, still out of his vision. "Sorry to interrupt. Before we talk about riots, might I just take a diversion? I don't suppose you've ever seen that children's show, "Sesame Street?""

"Sesame Street?" he asked, confused.

"Mmm," she laughed, then put on an eerily accurate Californian accent. "'*Todaaaaaay's* Sesame Street is brought to you by the letter R.'"

"Sorry, I don't know…"

She leaned round from behind the wheelchair, looked over Nick's shoulder and pushed her face into his.

"You know. *R*. R is for riots, and oooh, let me think, R is for Christmas *Rave*-ups and Rape. *Rape*, Nicky boy. Here's another, R is for *remember*. Remember me, your old Christmas conquest? *I* pushed you down those stairs, *I* put you in that chair. R is for *revenge*, too, and well, look, here we are."

His eyes widened in realisation, but then suddenly Nick Atkey couldn't breathe.

30 / 22nd April 1981, London.

Patrick was worried about the man in the wheelchair he'd taken home yesterday. He'd arranged to meet friends at Finsbury Park funfair, but then everything kicked off. Kids started to grab things from the stalls, then the situation had escalated as stones were thrown and madness descended. Many of them were older than him, but Patrick was shocked to see looters and wreckers aged maybe only ten or eleven.There was no reason for any of it.

For a while he'd been too shocked to move, since the whole scene was like something from a TV show like "The Professionals" or "The Sweeney". He'd seen footage of riots on the news, but this wasn't two opposing sides lined up in Brixton, more like the January sales where greedy, hysterical people simply grasped and pushed in all directions.

After a minute or two Patrick had come back to reality and realised he needed to get out, fast. There were only a few police to control hundreds of untamed kids but soon there'd be many more and he was the wrong age and definitely the wrong colour to be anywhere nearby. Even though it was now the eighties, being black still meant you were *always* in the wrong place at the wrong time.

So he'd joined the running crowd and split as fast as he could.

Patrick hadn't meant to stop and help the man in the wheelchair. In his panic, he hadn't even noticed him. But then, amongst the tumbling crowd, he'd seen this vulnerable guy. Patrick's Nan used a wheelchair and he'd suddenly pictured *her* lost in that awful chaos, so he'd turned back and offered to take the man home. Patrick hoped someone would have done the same for his Nan in that situation.

The guy was called Nick and he hadn't stopped talking all the way back. He'd flipped from violently angry to quiet and despairing, sometimes even the middle of a sentence. Patrick's Nan had been like that, too; bright as a button in the morning, dark and miserable by the afternoon. Nan topped herself last year. The 'authorities' said it was a terrible accident, but Patrick knew better. She'd rolled out in front of a Routemaster and they are difficult to miss, *very* big, *very* red and with *very* loud horns. But somehow Nan failed to spot it ten feet away.

Patrick thought she'd had enough of her darkness and done something about it.

So now he was worried about Nick.

*

After much thought, he decided to drop in on 17 Drake Road just to check. He wouldn't make it a big deal, just knock on, ask if Nick was OK "after all that excitement," and that would be that. Part of him still felt guilty about Nan, even though there was nothing he could have done. But perhaps one little visit to Drake Road might make all the difference to Nick.

He wandered back to the bungalow, had a moment of uncertainty, but then marched up to Nick's door and knocked. To his surprise, it swung open. The door had been pulled to, and the latch was engaged.

This put Patrick in a difficult situation. Gangs of black kids had just run wild and if someone saw a teenager like himself walk into someone's house uninvited the consequences could be dire. But then he remembered the police officer they'd met yesterday, who would confirm Patrick had helped a member of the community get home. Satisfied he had a reasonable excuse he pushed open the door and walked inside.

"Hello? Hello Nick? It's me, Patrick. I walked you back."

Music played faintly from a living room to his right. The television was on, but the BBC closed down between eleven a.m. and twelve forty-five, so only the test card was on screen. It showed a little girl playing noughts and crosses against a green balloon and a clown's head. The girl looked out at the viewer, just as she'd done for years, frozen in the middle of a never-ending game. Jaunty music played, a creepy counterpoint to the silence in the rest of the place. Patrick noticed a tray on the table with remains of food and began to feel very uneasy.

Who leaves their telly on the test card? He wondered. *Food on the table and door unlocked?*

"Nick? Nick, it's me, Patrick."

He looked left into a tidy bedroom where the bed was made. The bathroom was equally empty.

"Hello? Hello?"

That left a door at the hallway's end, which Patrick stared at for a long time unsure if he was ready to find out what was behind it. Incongruously cheerful test card music continued to chirp from the living room.

For some reason, he knocked on the door first. "Hello? It's me, from yesterday."

Silence.

The door opened inwards a foot or so but then stopped.

Whatever's prevented it opening any further is soft, like a cushion, or something, he thought. *I'm not sure I want to know what that* something *is.*

Patrick pushed a little harder and whatever-it-was gave way just a little more. "Hello?" he tried again, but his throat was dry.

Although he could now squeeze his head around the door, there was nothing in the world Patrick wanted to see *less* than what was behind it. But we all look eventually, because like Bluebeard's wife, we can't help ourselves.

He shut his eyes to delay the moment a little longer, put his head around the frame, took a deep breath like a diver about to plunge, then opened them.

It took a moment for Patrick's mind to process the scene in front of him. But when reality finally focussed he gagged, put a hand to his mouth, stifled a scream and ran.

*

WPC Lisa Fisher and Inspector David Walker sat in a Rover SD1 heading north.

When London's Metropolitan Police were formed in 1829, the "Peelers" or "Bobbies" travelled on foot over clearly defined routes. Criminals knew if officer X passed by at ten o'clock he wouldn't be seen again until ten thirty. It was thought Jack The Ripper exploited this predictability in Whitechapel. Whatever its faults, the "beat" remained an important and visible sign of policing on London's streets until the car arrived. Psychologically, officers on foot remained the best way to reassure the public, but cars quickly became another symbol of efficient and conspicuous policing. In many ways four wheels had replaced two feet as the "beat" and today, Fisher and Walker were on the road.

As the Rover slid through London they talked of their profession, the default conversation of most colleagues. They spoke of burglaries and beatings, of fraud and fights, and David Walker soon realised this was a teacher/pupil situation. Fisher wasn't just making idle chat, but probing him, and he was happy to oblige.

In fact, Lisa was talking around the houses, slowly homing in on the real object of her interest. Eventually, once she was satisfied he was ignorant of her intentions, Fisher casually threw in a question she'd wanted to ask for a while.

"Oh. D.I. Leeding. What's she like?"

With interest she noted the little smile which flashed across David's lips, then just as quickly disappeared as his "professional face" returned.

"Well, I hope by now you've seen she's one of the good ones. By which I mean she's thorough, detailed, professional. I trust her instincts. You could learn a lot from her, probably more than from me, if I'm honest."

He went on to tell her about training together in Hendon, their parallel career paths and some of the cases they'd worked on. There were anecdotes and little lessons, but, Fisher noticed, nothing too private. Walker spoke about Anna as more of an idea than a person.

She risked going a little further. "Sir, she has that thing, you know, the…" Lisa tick-tocked her head left right and blinked, "I noticed it a couple of times, I wondered…"

Walker shot her a dark look and she shut up.

Too far, Lisa, too far.

"I wouldn't mention that again if I were you." He seemed on the verge of anger, which was a first. "If, *if*, she ever wants to tell you, which I doubt, then that's her prerogative, not mine. It's personal."

"I'm sorry, sir, I just wondered if it was anything I should know about. So, you know, I don't put my foot in it."

He softened a little. "Yes, of course, but it really is down to her and as I say, with respect, you're a WPC, not a friend, so I doubt she'll ever take you into that kind of confidence. Honestly, Fisher, your best bet is to watch Anna at work. That's the best way to know her."

"I will, thank you. Do you mind me asking something else? Related to Anna, but not about her?"

"Why are you so interested?"

Careful now. Be very, very careful.

"Well, it's not really her I'm interested in, but a case. The Jeanette West suicide."

She noticed his shoulders stiffened for a moment. "Go on."

"Well, there was that odd picture, right? The blue chalk thing."

She sensed him on the defensive. "Blue charcoal, right."

"As you know, I'm doing a lot of filing right now, which is fine, you start at the bottom and all that. And I'm trying to read as many reports as I can to get a feel of work on the ground. We did a lot in training but there's nothing like the real McCoy, is there?"

"There isn't."

"I saw a report about a hit and run in Primrose Hill. There were photos, some graffiti or something in the background and it was blue charcoal too. So I was wondering if they were connected."

Walker sighed. Mechanically, he explained that there are oddities and coincidences at every crime scene and while some go on to be important, many are exactly that, just curiosities. "Interesting little diversions, Fisher, but in police work one must always guard against them and keep one's eyes on the evidence."

"So just nothing, then?"

"In my opinion, yes."

"And what about Anna? Does *she* think there's more to it?"

"You'd have to ask her," he grumbled. "But between you and me I wouldn't. D.I. Leeding will ask *you* if she wants help or an opinion."

"Of course."

Fisher could see Walker considering his next words. He puffed out his cheeks and ploughed on. "She likes you, thinks you've got what it takes. I can tell, you know. She doesn't have to say anything out loud but I see how she treats you as an equal, not a WPC. I hope you've noticed not every PC gets that kind of treatment, she doesn't suffer fools and you're clearly no fool. But don't push it. If she wants your help, she'll ask, and that's not something I could say about most of the PC's at GPS. Many of them need their hands held. You don't."

"OK, thank you, sir, that's very kind." Fisher turned to stare out of the window. Waker couldn't see, but she raised a quizzical eyebrow at her reflection and nodded, slowly, almost imperceptibly.

*

Ten minutes later Fisher and Walker were required to attend an incident in North London. A body had been discovered in Drake Road. Walker had consulted his map, worked out a route and muttered, "*This* is when we need a cabbie."

On arrival they discovered an ambulance in attendance, while neighbours silently watched from their gates and doorways.

The ambulance crew had already entered the property and ascertained the person involved was beyond any kind of help, so waited outside for police to secure the scene. "Suicide," said one of the crew, "in the kitchen, male, about thirty-five." He performed a none-too-subtle mime of a hanging, complete with crossed eyes and lolling tongue. "This fella found him." A young black kid nervously chewed his nails next to the ambulance.

"Fisher, talk to him," said Walker, "get his story while it's fresh, find out who the subject is. I'm going to take a look."

"Not much to see," said the other ambulance man and repeated the tasteless mime.

"I'll be the judge of that," replied Walker and stepped inside.

In the living room the test card and its jolly library music were still on show. David knew normality carried on oblivious to trauma; car radios continued to pump out pop songs from recently devastated vehicles, birds sang and dogs barked as bodies were dragged from rivers, children played outside whilst a victim of domestic abuse wailed inside. Sometimes you only had to travel a few feet to leave horror behind.

I wonder what the kid was doing here? Walker thought. *Friend? Relative? Passer by? God, I hope not a passer by. That makes things tricky.*

He remembered one case where a stab victim was discovered one evening in Regent's Park. It transpired the "passer by" was responsible and had tried to cover up the attack by posing as a random Good Samaritan.

Don't assume anything, he thought, *think like Anna*. He knew all about her Marble Arch incident in 1964. *Have hunches, yes, intuition, fine, but only use those as springboards, not foundations.*

He glanced into the tidy bedroom and bathroom, noted the handrails about the place. *So he has a disability.* Had *a disability. OK.*

Walker stepped into the kitchen, taking care not to touch anything. When death was involved, *don't assume* became the only position to take. There *had* been murders made to look like suicides but they were rare and, as with so many homicides, often the perpetrator was known to the victim. *So did that black kid know this guy? Fisher will get his story and then we'll go to work on it.*

The deceased hung from a noose attached to a handrail fitted around the work surfaces. A wheelchair was upended, its back on the floor in front of the corpse, which bent in front like a Muslim at prayer. The cadaver's arms hung by its sides and the man's open eyes stared at the tiled floor.

Walker looked at the scene for a while and tried to work out the trajectory of events. Anna always started with quick fire first impressions like snapshots, then decided which ones stood out.

OK, first impressions. He's a wheelchair user. Do those bars mean he had limited walking ability?

The inspector looked around the kitchen but there were no walking sticks anywhere to be seen.

Possibly not, then. He could have taken over this home after it had been converted for another kind of disability. Well, we'll soon find out. So he ties the noose around the bars. They'll be really solid, to take someone's weight. That noose is well tied. He meant business.

Walker looked at the ceiling. There was nowhere a noose could have been tied up there. *But if this man needed a wheelchair, he couldn't have stood up anyway.*

He studied the tipped wheelchair. It was one of the lighter models with a low back and tubular construction, designed to be small as possible and give the user their greatest chance of negotiating a world built for bipedal travel.

So he ties the noose, puts it round his neck. He sits facing away from the handrail and then just...flips the chair from under himself. It rolls forward and onto its back, he's left here hanging. He can't move his legs in any way, so they just fold up under him, his weight bends him forward and...the inevitable. That's first impressions, anyway. We'll need to hear the black kid's story and what the neighbours have to say.

Walker turned to leave when he noticed something strange. The arms of the corpse were hanging by its side, hands palms up on the floor. As he looked closer, David saw the fingertips were stained light blue. He bent down to get even nearer. It wasn't paint, but a chalky residue.

Oh. No. No, that's too much. No, surely not.

Walker turned and looked around the room. The dead dominate their surroundings and draw your entire attention, so he hadn't even *seen* the rest of the kitchen other than to register its most basic properties. In front and to the left of the corpse was a kitchen table, slightly lower than a "normal" one. On the table, propped against a glass, was a small piece of paper which faced the far wall. Lying alongside was a light blue stick of charcoal.

Chilled, Walker went round the other side of the table to see what was written on the paper;

WOE IS ME

He stared at the note for a long while then realised his mouth had been wide open the whole time. David turned from the kitchen and walked out, slightly unsteady.

*

The black kid sat on a wall and smoked a cigarette. While neighbours still watched and waited, Fisher sat in the Rover going through her notebook. As Walker got in she looked up and frowned.

"Are you all right, sir? You look a bit pale."

"Who's the deceased?"

"Haven't had a chance to get much detail from the neighbour, but…Nick Atkey, thirty-something, lived here for five years or so, works for a Samaritans type charity answering phones. Quiet, fairly unsociable, didn't really have much to do with anyone, worked from home, rarely left the house."

"Tell me about the kid."

Fisher told him Patrick's tale, from helping Nick out of danger, to meeting Officer Watson then getting Atkey home. Patrick had explained how desperate, angry and sad Nick sounded, which was why he'd wanted to check in on him today.

"OK, obviously we'll corroborate that part with Officer Watson. Anything else?"

"The neighbour opposite saw the kid and Mr Atkey yesterday at the time Patrick mentioned. He went inside, the kid left, and that was as much as she saw. It checks out with Patrick's version."

Walker nodded. Fisher waited for him ask another question, but he remained silent.

"Is everything OK, sir?"

He glanced back at the house, where the two ambulance men waited to remove the body. Walker sighed and made a decision.

"It's probably nothing, but I'd like you to come in and take a look."

"OK. What am I looking at?"

"You tell me."

*

Fisher stared down at the corpse of Nick Atkey.

"This is your second body, right?" asked Walker. "And both have been suicides."

"Uh huh," Fisher replied and walked around the deceased. "Sir, is this a test? Would you like me to talk you through the scene, like training?"

"No, we can compare notes later. Just get a feel of it. I'm going to get forensics in and a photographer."

Fisher looked up at him sharply. "You think there's something else?"

"If we have any reason for suspicion then we act on it, you know the rules. A young man takes this guy home then *happens* to discover him dead the following day. What do you think?"

"The neighbour said Patrick didn't enter the house."

"Not at *that* moment. But did he come back later? Then, to cover his tracks, do a "good deed" and "discover" the corpse?"

Fisher bit her lip.

"You're not convinced."

"With respect it seems quite far fetched, sir."

"You'd be amazed how far fetched some things seem until you start unravelling them. He left a note. Not all suicides do, but some need the world to know *why*. It isn't much of a note, but…"

He pointed over to the piece of paper propped on the table. Fisher frowned, then circled round so she could see the front. Her eyes widened. "It's written in…"

"That's right," said Walker quietly. "Blue charcoal. He had residue of blue charcoal on his fingers. If you look, you can see some prints on the paper. I have no doubt they'll be his."

"*Woe is me*? Not much of a statement is it?"

"Well, he worked for a charity listening to people's woes. Perhaps they got to him in the end, ground him down. Didn't the kid say he sounded desperate?"

"Yes, desperate and sad."

"We'll need to get a full statement from him, naturally."

"Woe is me," Fisher whispered, "I suppose that's every suicide note boiled down to just three words, isn't it? Woe is me. When you can't deal with woe any more, you..." She stared down at the body.

"I suppose so. But aren't you going to point out the elephant in the room?"

"I didn't want to, sir. I thought you might think I was being silly."

"But the elephant is?"

"Blue charcoal. Again."

"Right. Blue charcoal. Professionally, I think this is just one of those weird coincidences. We've dealt with God knows how many incidents since Jeanette West died and 99.9% have had absolutely zero blue charcoal involved. It just so happens that this, Primrose Hill and Jeanette West did. I just thought you should see, so you could understand that these things do happen, and how you can tie yourself in knots trying to find an explanation when there simply isn't one. So that's something to always bear in mind."

"I will, sir."

She continued to look at the three word note.

"Was there something else, Fisher?"

"Do you mind if I ask a question, sir? It might sound presumptuous."

"Go ahead."

"Well," she chewed her lip again, uncertain, "you just said *professionally* you thought this note was a coincidence. Does that mean that *personally*, you..." She let that thought hang in the air.

He looked around the kitchen one more time. "Secure the scene, Fisher. Wait for forensics and the photographer. I'll send someone to relieve you as soon as I return."

"Yes, sir."

He started to leave, then turned back. "For now, just keep this," he waved airily at the note, "between ourselves, OK?"

"Yes, sir."

He nodded and left.

Fisher turned back to the suicide note. "Woe is me," she read, then looked at the body knelt in supplication on the floor. "Woe is you," she whispered, sadly. "Woe is you, Nick Atkey."

31 / 22nd April, 1981, London.

Inspector Walker finished his shift at six p.m. There'd been more reports and incidents to deal with but for today he was done, or as 'done' as any officer can be. He often thought police work meant you were never really 'off,' just occasionally, 'on hold.'

He took off his jacket and unclipped the tie. Police ties were easy. They clipped on, so if anybody tried to throttle you, the tie just came off in their hands.

He put on his 'civilian' coat then turned to find D.I. Leeding had magically appeared behind him. She held a few typewritten papers.

"Oh so you read that one, then?" he said, casually.

"You know I've read them, which is why of all the stuff you've typed up today, you *happened* to leave this particular report on my desk."

"I thought you might be interested."

"Well, I did wonder why you wanted me to look at another suicide."

"Sorry, I didn't mean to…"

"It's fine. Well, your report seemed fairly cut and dried but then, just thrown away in the middle of a paragraph, there's this." Anna flicked through the pages, found the section she was looking for then cleared her throat in a pantomime way. "Ahem, ahem, I quote, 'the deceased appears to have left a suicide note stating, 'WOE IS ME' brackets, 'caps,' end brackets. 'The note was written in blue charcoal. There are clear fingerprints on it which have been given to forensics to identify.' End quote."

She raised an eyebrow at Walker, tapped her fingers against the papers and he shrugged. "I have to report exactly what's there."

"I know you do David, and what was *there*, was blue charcoal."

"I'm not saying it has any significance. It's just how he chose to write his suicide note."

"If it *was* a suicide note."

"He left it propped up on the table to be found."

"Well, that's supposition." She sighed. "You know, with this kind of situation, there's only one thing we can do now."

He frowned and waited for her answer. She didn't say a word, but raised a hand and mimed drinking a pint.

Oh, he thought with surprise. *So that old saying is true. My heart really did just skip a beat.*

*

A few minutes later Walker and Leeding had found a corner table in the snug of Langham Street's Yorkshire Grey. The snug itself was exactly that; a cosy space with room for maybe ten people with a welcoming little hearth which banished the freezing evening outside. The snug was separated from the rest of the pub by a wooden partition with tiny etched glass windows that could be rotated to let the air, or rather smoke, flow freely.

"One Carlsberg, ma'am." Walker handed a pint to Anna.

She waved a cigarette and asked, "Do you mind?"

"How could I? Everyone else is. Yours would hardly make any difference."

"You're always so *accommodating*," she smiled and lit up. "Can you believe how bloody cold it is out there?"

"They're predicting snow soon."

"Doesn't surprise me. Brass monkeys." They sat for a while, drank their pints and enjoyed the fire, comfortably silent as only old friends can be.

"We really don't do this enough, David."

No, we do not, thought Walker. "But when do we get the chance? We're either on different shifts, or knackered."

"True. Do you still go to that pub near your place? The Devonshire?"

"Uh huh. I've become one of those blokes who sits at one end of the bar all night, yacking."

"I can imagine. But you're still getting out, seeing people, right?"

He knew the subtext of that question; *you're not sitting at home alone again are you?*

"Oh yes, when I can, when the *crims* let me."

"Hear, hear," she raised her glass and they clinked their pints together.

Go on, she's given you the opening, take it, he thought.

"And you? Get to leave law and order behind much?"

"Ah well, you know me. I don't mind my own company, in fact, I still go to the cinema alone. Remember I used to do that during training?"

"Yeah, we all thought you were sneaking off with some fancy man."

"Well, I was. Me and Michael Caine, or Richard Burton."

"You do pick them. Actually, if you don't mind, what happened with that guy Robin? You haven't mentioned him for a while, everything OK?"

As soon as the question was asked David knew it was inappropriate. Anna looked down at the glass, tapped her fingernails on the table and went quiet for a little while.

"Sorry, I didn't mean to pry, I was just wondering."

Finally she muttered, "We weren't really compatible. That's always been my problem, compatibility."

"Sorry, I'll shut up."

He hoped she'd wave a hand in the air, smile and say, *no, no, it's fine, actually I'll tell you all about it, wow, what an idiot* he *was!* But she just sipped her pint.

The fire crackled and the two friends withdrew to silence again, but this time it was uncomfortable.

"OK, here's a thing," she said eventually. He felt like a curtain had been drawn over the previous conversation and opened on a new one.

You blew it, David. You just blew it, he thought miserably.

"Jeanette, the reverend, now this suicide. What do you *really* think about the blue charcoal? As always you've been neat and professional in your report…"

"That's me. There's still more to add, that's just preliminary. I need to properly talk to that kid Patrick and then there's forensics."

"I do know how it works, David. I was asking what you *didn't* put in your report. Be honest, am I finding something that's not there or is the charcoal just too weird and precise to be coincidence?"

"Right. You want an opinion? Well, as you may notice," he pointed to his head, "I am *not* wearing my inspector's hat."

She squinted at his hair. "Indeed you're not."

"Ha. So whatever I say is with the proviso I have no evidence, nothing concrete, *nada* that would stand up in court."

"It's OK, this isn't a disciplinary hearing. Ooh, but imagine if it was!" She held up her pint. "We'd be queuing up to be disciplined."

He laughed, then got serious. "Professionally, I think the charcoal is pure coincidence. But *personally*, why do I feel it isn't?"

"That's exactly how I'm feeling. In black and white, typed up, carbon copied, there's nothing going on. But in here…" She pointed to her heart. "You know, that bit police are never supposed to use, in *here* it feels significant."

He nodded. "It makes no sense at all. Or rather, we just haven't found a way to *make* sense yet."

"I agree. It's like we're missing something huge."

"Yes, so huge it might not even be there."

She sighed. "That would be the most obvious answer. We're chasing rainbows and they keep moving every time we get near. Do you want another drink?"

"Same again, please."

He watched her go to the bar and noticed a few of the other customers did the same. She smiled and made chit-chat with the barman, who puffed himself up a little as he poured the pints. *I don't think you have any idea, do you, Anna? You say you're not compatible, but you're compatible with everyone. Look at the way the barman's staring at you. I wish you'd stare like that at me.*

She returned with more alcohol.

"Oh, since we're talking about work, I should have said, you know those weird letters Jeanette West kept? From "*Sarah*"?"

Walker had glanced over photostats of the fan letters a couple of days ago and found them odd, but nothing to worry about.

"I got the fingerprint results back. Remember I wanted to see if there was any comparison between the prints on the fan letters and those we found on Jeanette's rear windowsill?"

"And?"

Anna did a little drum roll on the table with her hands. "Ladies and Gentlemen, well, gentleman singular, our guys found *six* points of similarity. *Six* similarities between the prints on the letters and those on the windowsill."

Walker frowned. "No-where *near* enough to get a conviction, not without other overwhelming evidence."

"Yes, but six points, that's still pretty high, considering, don't you think?"

He considered it for a while. "Come on, you know it's not. You wouldn't get it past even a cack-handed defence, not unless you have a few witnesses testifying to having seen the suspect *at* the property, *in* the garden *at* the time. And you don't, plus, I might add, you don't even know who this mysterious "Sarah" is in order to either eliminate her or take it further."

"Thankyou for telling me my job."

He shrugged.

"But come on David, it's worth just keeping an open mind about should anything else turn up, don't you think?"

"I wouldn't waste too much time on it."

She smiled, a big knowing, Cheshire Cat smile.

"Ah, my dear inspector, but what if I then told you the prints on the windowsill were outwards, not inwards? In other words, somebody had grabbed on to that sill from *outside* with one hand?"

"What? Somebody climbed the drain pipe then tried to get in? Is that what you're saying?"

"I'll go one better. What if *Sarah* climbed that drainpipe and *did* get in?"

32 / Sometime *Before* (5)

She hated both her work *and* her name. Mother and Father had taken it from a nursery rhyme, which was the extent of their creativity.

Unfortunately the bank job required a name badge, so she'd heard every wisecrack about it several times over. Internally, she wanted to leap over her desk and pull the jokers' mocking tongues from their heads, but on the outside, she'd giggle. It wouldn't do to reveal even a fraction of the rolling fury inside her, since there were special places she'd be sent and in them, cutlery was plastic and walls padded.

After two long years behind this desk she'd perfected a new character, "The Worker," who gave every impression she enjoyed both the job and her colleagues' company. Despite that, other girls who'd joined at the same time had risen up the ranks while she'd only managed a small pay rise. She'd carefully noted their names in her diary.

The only positive was that she never had to see Nicholas again. She often pictured him tumbling headfirst down the stairs and the memory never failed to make her smile. He'd been paralysed below the waist, which she'd found highly poetic. Nicholas had made her numb down there, now he was permanently dead in the one place men put above all others. It was a beautiful punchline.

Nobody suspected her. She'd gone back to his bedroom, feigned sleep, eventually heard shouts from downstairs and soon after that, a siren's song. She'd pretended to wake up and be *shocked* at the terrible accident. Nicholas had been too drunk to remember anything. She'd considered visiting the rapist in hospital wearing the shortest of skirts and tightest of tops just to taunt him, but didn't want to see his face again.

Well, not until she was ready, whenever that day might come.

Sadly, Nicholas wasn't the only male she contended with at work. When the old and greasy manager leaned over, he'd always manage to brush against her body.

"Oh *sorry*," he'd wink.

"No harm done," she'd smile then imagine how it would feel to break his fingers one by one.

For appearance sake she'd always attend office parties ("The Worker" was a slightly ditzy party kind of girl) and inevitably one or more of her drunk co-workers would have an opportunistic feel. She externally channeled Barbara Windsor at those moments, gave a saucy giggle and lightly slap the offender. Then she'd make a note of which glass was theirs and spit in it. *Little defeats, little victories.*

She had a handful of what might be called friends, but preferred her own company anyway. These micro-friends were just accessories for this new character and like human jewellery, she could take them off at the end of the day when they had no further use. Most of the time she would sit in cafes and cinemas alone. Her favourite actor was Michael Caine, who was born Maurice Micklewhite, but had reinvented himself as a cool man-about-town. She enjoyed the idea of reinvention very much.

So, like Caine, she decided to reimagine herself. She'd saved enough money to quit the bank job and start again with a different name and new address.

She'd always vowed to change her name one day, so tried out many options then spent evenings practicing autographs in different handwriting styles. Because after "The Worker," a new role would be required. Just as she'd cast aside the character of "Anna," "The Worker," would be retired soon enough. Occasionally she'd still try out "Anna" for size, put her on like an old outfit to see if it still fitted. "Anna" worked best with older people who reacted better to a sensible kind of girl rather than "The Worker," who was slightly airy.

So she created a new identity and moved out of the "family" home. It was so easy. She'd opened a bank account under her latest name and paid cash upfront to rent a pokey bedsit at the edge of town, but even that was preferable to living with Father and his new woman.

Father was so predictable. He'd met someone else only a few months after Mother's brain had burst in the back garden. This Mother replacement was no different to the model death had traded in for him. Ten years younger than Father, she was just as prissy, stuck up and socially obsessed as his previous bedmate. At first, the New Woman had wrongly believed that Father, like most other dads, put his daughter on a pedestal. She'd quickly realised the house had no pedestals for anything but money. Before long New Woman had adopted the same attitude as Old Mother; *ignore and if one couldn't ignore, belittle.*

She'd hoped New Woman would also fall asleep at the top of the stairs, but Father's latest barely drank except at *"celery-berations,"* as she called them. And even then, after a couple of Cinzanos she'd flirt outrageously with the other guests. She thought Father was probably turned on by the show, since New Woman had zero sexuality except after a drink, when she became a hideous cross between Naughty Matron and Slutty Housewife. But the act was obvious, had no subtlety and was only worn drunk. She watched New Woman with pity at these events, sneered at the obviousness of her lines and moves. Father's latest was a dilettante compared to Father's daughter. Am-Dram against Oscar winner.

So she'd gleefully moved out and downsized but the bedsit was a stop gap, because she had a plan.

Along with acting, her real talent was art. Most of her pictures would never see the light of day, so were enjoyed privately, sweet memories of *little victories* against her enemies. But she was proud of her more "acceptable" pieces, still in charcoals, with blue the colour of choice. She believed those works stood out and had something different to offer.

Therefore her next character would be "The Artist". She'd worked out her image down to the tiniest detail, created a new speech pattern, phoney history and fake relatives. She was certain "T.A." would be her ticket to respect, even acceptance.

She discovered the prestigious Royal College Of Art held open days for potential students to look around and meet the staff, so booked herself a slot and started to rehearse the character of "The Artist". She bought a new,"arty" wardrobe; thoughtful, but not too dowdy, contemporary, yet not too painfully "hip". She invested in a beautiful leather portfolio case from Liberty in Regent Street then counted down the days until her new life would begin.

In her mind, once The Royal College saw her work, surely they would offer her a position, possibly even a scholarship. And if that didn't transpire (*and it must, it must, I cannot go back behind a desk for one moment longer*) then at the very least they'd suggest career paths for her obvious talents.

Soon enough, the day came. And soon enough, she wished it hadn't.

*

She arrived for her appointment an hour early to look around and was pleased to realise her outfit fitted *just so* into the general ambience of the place. Clearly she already belonged and soon her presence here would be formalised.

At 1:30 p.m. she walked into a classroom for her meeting with Professor Paul Birch and a lecturer, Helen Thompson. They were behind a table at the far end and she felt self-conscious on the long, slow walk to get there.

Helen Thompson was in her mid fifties and looked every inch an art teacher, with brightly coloured kaftan, greying hair piled up high, and glasses on a gold chain.

My god, she thought, *you look like you've been cast in this part. Just like me.*

"Good afternoon dear, and you are?" Helen consulted a clipboard. Without thinking, she gave her real name. It came out automatically and internally, she squirmed.

"What a lovely name," said Thompson.

"I don't really like it. I'd prefer to be known as…" and then gave the fake name she'd chosen for,"The Artist".

Professor Paul Birch sighed loudly and dramatically. "Well, we're not here to debate names, dear, are we? I mean, we *could* call him Donato di Niccolò di Betto Bardi, *or* Donatello, but his art remains the same, does it not?"

"So tell us a little about yourself. I'm Helen Thompson, senior lecturer, this is Paul Birch."

"*Professor* Paul Birch," he corrected.

"Of course, *professor*."

She looked at Birch, also in his mid fifties but a far less appealing character, dressed in a knowingly ostentatious red velvet jacket. His hair was greasy and combed over to hide a bald spot but the lonely strands had failed to achieve the desired effect. Birch's face was puffed, florid, and his expression veered between predatory curiosity and a sneer. He looked her up and down and she knew he'd gazed that way at many girls before and would to many after. She knew his type and her internal sonar pinged something crucial about Birch; it took one to know one.

You're a liar, professor. This is all an act, isn't it? The velvet jacket, the manicured hands, that ridiculous way of speaking…all pretence. I see through you, Paul Birch. You cannot fool a master. You are in the presence of greatness and don't realise. You could talk to me from now until forever and never see the joins, never see this as a performance. But I know *you.*

He gestured limply for her to sit and she formed an expression of hope and gratitude, neither of which she felt, since there was no need for hope. Even *Professor* Paul Birch would have to concede the RCA needed her.

She told them about her fictitious background and family, then her genuine hopes and dreams. Birch looked bored but Thompson was attentive. The professor tapped his long manicured nails on the desk after a few minutes then gestured to her like a Roman emperor would call a slave.

"Well, the proof of the pudding is in the pictures," he chuckled, pleased with his wit, "let us see what your art inspires in us."

She stepped forward, opened her leather portfolio and placed it on the desk. As she did, the stench of alcohol rose off Birch.

He's drunk, she thought with shock. *To me, this is important, to him, it's just an intermission between glasses.*

She showed no sign of offence.

Birch slid her pictures from the portfolio as if they were infected. She'd included an overview of all her styles; some were abstract waves and lines, others still life, landscapes, portraits. Many were single words, written in capitals, like SIN, QUESTION, ALONE, SKY and ART. They weren't a complete example of her oeuvre, but many of her other works were too revealing by half.

"Very blue," sniggered Birch. "In fact," he riffled through the pictures, "*all* very blue."

"Is there a reason for…?" asked Thompson.

"It resonates with me. I think we are all colours, just as we are all different parts of the spectrum of personalities. Mine is blue."

Birch stifled a giggle which he badly turned into a cough. "Mine is red, like wine. What is yours, Helen?"

Thompson shot him a dark look, easily translated as *shut up.* Birch was either too drunk to notice or care. "Some of these are very…" Helen searched for a description. "…Very soothing, I could lose myself in them."

Better, she thought. *At least the lecturer can see my potential.*

"Ignore my colleague," said Birch. "She is the kind of naive Samaritan who puts splints on a broken wing. I, however, prefer a more realistic approach." The professor took a few shuddering breaths through his nose like he was sniffing wine. "These are derivative at best, badly executed at worst. Your monomaniac use of blue charcoal doesn't interest me. Yves Klein already ploughed this field and Picasso gave us his blue period decades ago. You however, are no Picasso, far from it."

She felt herself redden. This wasn't how she'd imagined it by a very long way.

"All art is subjective," offered Thompson. "There are many, for example, who consider Picasso a charlatan."

"Yes, yes, all is art is subjective, *Helen*, that is what makes it art. A glass is a glass is a glass. There is no debate on that front. You might argue its form, but you cannot argue its purpose. Great art should make you argue both. And what should I be asked to argue and feel from these?"

He picked up the edge of one of the pictures as if something nasty might scurry from beneath it. "What do I feel? Nothing. I see blue, I see endless blue. I see abstract, but while a natural pattern in the sand can be abstract, that does not mean it is art."

"Well, I think," she began. He held up a hand and pouted his wet, buttery lips.

"What *you* think, dear, is of no consequence. Alas for you, what I think and to a lesser extent, Helen, *is* of importance in this room and in this college. You wish to study art? Then take this advice which I offer from years of experience and for free. If you wish to study art, then *study art*. Go away, learn technique, *then* you can pervert it. Even the most abstract of artists had technique. Look at Hans Hartung, a genius of modernist art, but who still had classical technique in his armoury to subvert. You, my dear, are running before you can walk."

She tried to appear grateful for this professional insight. Birch looked straight through her.

"What is it you want?" he mused, "I cannot see anything beyond the surface of these daubings. You do not know who you are and in consequence, this "art" does not know what it is. You need to stare into the mirror before you stare at the paper, decide exactly what and who you really are inside before you express it outside. I only see confusion." He tittered. "Of course, confusion in art can be celebrated. The obscure can tell us much about ourselves when we react to it. But these," he waved a hand over the pictures, "these are obscure to the point of irrelevance."

"There is potential though, professor," said Helen.

"Oh there is *potential* in everything, is there not? So that phrase is meaningless if considered. Yes, my colleague splints the bird's wing. I prefer to put the creature out of its misery."

"Is there anything you can offer?" she grasped at straws.

"I have offered all I can," he said imperiously. "Now we have other people to see."

He carelessly shoved the pictures back into their portfolio then pushed it back to her.

She wouldn't cry, wouldn't give him the satisfaction, but looked into his eyes for a long time. He broke the stare first.

Little victories.

"Thank you for your time," she managed.

"Please, do take the professor's advice and come back when you have solid grounding," said Helen.

"A *very* solid grounding," he added.

"I'm sorry we couldn't be more…" Thompson shot another disapproving look at Birch, then mouthed the word, "sorry," one more time.

She turned and tried not to run from the room.

Once outside she allowed herself a few tears, which were an unusual expression of emotion. She reached up to feel the wetness on her cheeks, recognised the drops of salt water as self pity, so switched them off. They served no purpose and were a waste of energy.

Her potential future had been dashed in less then ten minutes. She'd already mentally shed the character of "The Worker" but for now it seemed, "The Artist" was not an option. She needed to regroup, rethink, recreate.

But one day, professor, you will *know my work and tremble before it.*

33 / Saturday 9th May 1981, London.

Life had moved on for Anna. There were new cases to investigate and old ones to close in the never ending round of criminals and victims that made up her professional life.

The strange coincidence of three recent cases which all involved blue charcoal was an interesting diversion but led no-where. In the end they were just a strange series of *apparent* connections that melted to nothing when light was shone upon them.

Other than the vague accusations of "abuse" in her note, West's suicide wasn't suspicious. The details of any alleged crimes had gone with her to the grave. The fan letters from "Sarah" were another cul-de-sac. They contained no threats and the small similarities between fingerprints on the letter and prints on Jeanette's windowsill weren't enough to pursue further. Since there were no prints which matched in West's bedroom, that was where the matter ended.

The hit and run case involving Reverend John Martin was still open, but it had taken place a few weeks ago and Anna suspected there'd be no break now. Martin's death would probably join the Met's long list of sadly unsolved crimes.

As suspected, there was nothing untoward in the demise of Nick Atkey either. The kid's statement all checked out. Patrick's prints were found in the hallway exactly where his account claimed, with none in the kitchen. Officer Watson confirmed he'd spoken to them both on Bank Holiday Monday and a neighbour had witnessed Patrick drop Atkey off, which left his suicide's motive as the only remaining mystery.

Atkey's boss said he was a, "Serious, sensible man who perhaps felt things a little too much." Anna thought that may be one explanation. The day before, Nick had witnessed kids smash up a funfair for no reason, so perhaps he didn't want to imagine what the future held. But in the end it was all conjecture. He'd died by his own hand and tragic though it was, there ended Anna's interest in his case.

So she'd moved on.

Today, Anna had Saturday off. She enjoyed a lie-in until ten, then picked up cigarettes and a paper.

The trial of Peter Sutcliffe dominated the news. It had started last week and while Sutcliffe's guilt was a foregone conclusion, the judge wanted a jury to decide whether his crimes were due to insanity. Anna thought that question was redundant. If somebody murders thirteen women and attempts to kill another seven, surely that indicated a mind wired horribly differently to others. *Also,* she savoured her first cigarette of the day, *it's Catch-22. To kill thirteen people, you have to be insane. But to kill them and get away with it for so long indicates more than just luck, it shows guided intelligence, no matter how twisted that intellect might be. Sequential killers in masks don't lurch around slashing teenagers, no matter what "Friday the 13th" might say.*

"Friday the 13th" was a horror movie that had delighted teenagers and offended authorities last year, exactly as its makers intended. Anna understood the plot was basically a series of gruesome murders, each more graphic than the last. Viewers fainted, vomited, and had to be helped from cinemas by ushers. Today's newspaper featured the sequel, imaginatively titled "Friday the 13th Part Two," which had just premiered in America and produced the same audience reactions as its predecessor. Therefore in the space of just a few pages the paper had reported on a genuine mass murderer *and* a Hollywood version. Lines were blurred everywhere in 1981.

It's so weird, she skimmed over the piece, *all over the world people are queuing up to watch a fictitious multiple killer and yet we have the real thing on trial at the Old Bailey. People can deal with it on screen, but not in life. It's too real.*

The article went on to report a wave of "video nasties" that had come from *somewhere* to the UK and were currently rotting the minds of young people. *Something had to be done,* the paper opined. "A generation are now growing up believing such atrocities to be normal behaviour."

Well, I remember when rock and roll spelled the end of civilisation and television was going to make us all drooling idiots. Every new advance and culture shift starts a panic. A few years ago it was punk, now it's VHS tapes.

The arrival of home video recorders meant police now dealt with crimes no-one could have foreseen a few years before, since new technology inevitably led to novel ways of breaking the law. "Video hire shops" had started to open and with the right nod you could rent "special" tapes kept under the counter. The police had already raided a few and confiscated extreme films of all kinds.

People like to watch, don't they? And some people like to be watched, no matter how depraved they are. We are a very visual species.

That thought bounced about her mind a little longer. There was something important about it, but Anna couldn't make the connection.

She idly flicked through the rest of the paper. In sport, today was the F.A. Cup Final, which meant Anna would stay in this afternoon and early evening to avoid elated or depressed Tottenham or Manchester City fans. Anna pitied the officers working *that* one. With sport, you were guaranteed half the spectators would end every game in a vengeful mood.

So she'd pottered about her tiny flat and Dylan the cat was glad of the company.

Evening arrived and Anna prepared herself for an unusual event. She was going out.

*

Part of going out involved the ritual of getting ready.

A bugle sounded, a horse galloped, then Adam Ant shouted, "Stand and deliver!" from Anna's radio. She couldn't keep up with pop these days, the charts were full of Ants, Spandaus and Fizzes. Sam Bizarre's group Grey Velvet had stalled at number two behind the all conquering Adam and his Ants.

Sam's secret affair with Jeanette West had remained hidden from the public and Anna was glad. Out of his make up, away from the record sleeves and posters, he was a little lost boy. To have the love of his life destroy herself had torn him to pieces, so this chart success must have been bittersweet. She hoped Sam, or rather Nigel, could find a way through his grief.

Anna rarely went out but when those occasional nights arrived, she liked to get ready with a loud radio and deep glass of wine or two. She kept wine for special occasions and tonight definitely counted as one.

Although much of today's pop music passed her by, she didn't consider herself ready for BBC Radio Two or Radio Four quite yet. Radio Four was just too serious and her day job was sober enough. Radio Two felt like a coffee morning at an OAP's home, so the dial always slid by that station, which meant this evening's soundtrack was provided by London's Capital Radio.

She stood in her bra and knickers and turned in the mirror.

Not bad, all that nervous energy's keeping you slim at least. Still not bad at all. "Stand and deliver!" she sang along to the radio, gave a little spin here, waved her arms there. "Come on Dylan," she called over to the cat, who remained asleep. "Join in! Ah, you're no fun." She hopped on the spot then span again, aware she must look deranged.

Hidden at the far end of her wardrobe, Anna kept clothes which were only ever worn on these rare outings. She flicked through the hangers, pulled out a few combinations, held them up against herself, then mentally awarded the ensembles points out of ten.

Eventually Anna settled on an outfit she'd never normally wear, but that was the whole point.

Leeding sat down at the dressing table and laid out her make up. At work she wore the barest amount of foundation, mascara and lipstick, enough to highlight her features and no more. But tonight was different.

Anna consulted a copy of Vogue on the bed. She'd chosen a particular look from the magazine and went about replicating it on her own skin. She didn't have Vogue's expertise but enjoyed the process of transformation and reinvention. Tonight, *Anna* would be staying in while this other person took care of things. After a while she'd managed an attractive simulacrum of the Vogue model. Anna turned her head this way and that, pouted, stared and took another swig of wine. It wouldn't do to be drunk, but tipsy would help this evening. She had to become somebody else.

She played with her blonde bob then shook her head. Anna rooted through the dressing table drawer and pulled out some hair clips. Leeding placed a few between her teeth then clipped up her hair. She opened another drawer, went through the contents, picked them up one by one, held each to her face.

Yes. That one. Dark. Jet black, in fact.

Anna pulled on a wig and carefully styled it.

The radio played "The Sound Of The Crowd" by The Human League. The band entreated you to *get around town* and that was exactly what Anna had in mind.

She sat for a long while and stared into the mirror, unrecognisable even to herself.

34 / Saturday 9th May 1981, Central London.

Professor Paul Birch was drunk. Not falling-over intoxicated but a warm, fuzzy condition Birch called, "On the edge of swirly." He was also jet-lagged from yet another speaking tour in New York.

He sat in his Southampton Row home and poured another glass. This afternoon he'd watched the F.A.cup and willed his beloved Tottenham Hotspur to win but the game ended in a draw. Although still better than losing, the result left him unsatisfied and grouchy so he'd continued to drink steadily throughout the day, safe in the knowledge he'd developed quite a tolerance for alcohol.

He would still be *relatively* sober and *completely* wonderful company by the evening, F.A.cup win or not.

Colleagues were always surprised to discover his passion for football. Traditionally professors of art treated sport with disdain, but Birch had cultivated a maverick personality full of contradictions. He'd astonish dinner party guests with an extensive knowledge of individual matches, fixtures and players. He liked to keep people on their toes. "There is as much artistry in the feet of Ricky Villa as there is in the hands of Frida Kahlo," he would exclaim and guests would laugh, without a clue who Ricky Villa was.

But oh, he was *so* angry with Spurs today, who'd played like a Third Division team. An almost certain Manchester City victory was thankfully sabotaged by Tommy Hutchinson's own goal.

But at least he still had something to look forward to this evening.

In fact, it was his very favourite thing.

Art had been very good to Professor Paul Birch. He'd risen to Dean of the RCA School Of Arts, but then life had taken an even more thrilling turn after he'd written "Behind The Canvas," a biography of Picasso which had become a surprise global hit. Since then, he'd been *everywhere* to talk about Picasso. Birch had become "hot property," shuttled between TV and Radio stations, glittering receptions, museums and galleries. "The only thing more read than my book is my passport!" was one of his favourite witticisms.

Along with huge financial benefits he'd also discovered an upswing in his love life. The professor's wife often stayed at home in Kent during his tours, which meant he could take advantage of both free and paid bedtime company. Mrs Birch didn't suspect these nocturnal exertions and seemed more than happy to enjoy the extra money his success generated. These days, everything was *highly* acceptable; life, love and lucre.

So this little house off Southampton Row had become his secret London love nest, a convenient place to eat, drink and screw someone attractive who wasn't his wife.

He hoped tonight would be successful in that regard.

Birch had received a phone request for an interview from a flirty sounding freelance journalist who knew her stuff. He found any woman who sparred with him over art incredibly arousing and over the line, this one sounded *delicious*.

She'd given him her name and he'd cleverly pretended to recognise it. "Haven't we met before?" he'd asked.

"I think you probably saw me around at some of the openings," she'd rattled off a few art parties from the last year or so.

"Do refresh me," he'd fished for a description.

"Oh, I'm thirties, slim, black hair, fairly tall…" she'd paused and then breathlessly added, "some say I have the look of a young Elizabeth Taylor, and I *wish* I did, but I suppose there is a distant resemblance."

A young Elizabeth Taylor! How his mind had played with the possibilities. Then Paul went ahead and reeled her in. He'd become quite the expert in *"fishing for filly."*

"Let me think where and when would be a good place for an interview. Alas, I am away on quite a few dates but, ah yes, I am back in London on the seventh. Oh, Damn! But then I am to fly off on another dull talking tour by the eleventh. Such a shame."

He'd let *her* put the pieces together. "Oh dear, professor. But is there any way I could interview you that weekend? The weekend of the ninth?"

Slowly, slowly.

"I suppose it would be possible. But I am chock a block during the day. Also, it is the F.A.cup and I cannot miss Spurs play."

"Oh, same here! They're my team!"

"Really?"

"Oh yes. Born and raised Spurs, in fact, I grew up in Foyle Road, two minutes from White Hart Lane. I'll be watching with my Dad. It's a tradition, so I completely understand."

Here we go, gently now.

"Perhaps after, then? Town will be ghastly though, being the Cup Final." He'd pretended to have a sudden idea. "Wait. I am based very central. My London home isn't much but you could come here, if that was acceptable. I have some very good wine, perhaps some canapés? I do hope that's not too forward, but work should be as enjoyable as play, don't you think?"

There'd been a silence at the other end and for a moment. Birch thought he'd blown it. "That sounds like a wonderful, generous idea, professor. Hopefully we'll be able to celebrate a Spurs win together!"

"There will be no *hopefully* about it, dear, none at all."

"That's the spirit."

So arrangements had been made.

Obviously, no-one else had to know. And if things went the way he hoped, once she'd written up the interview, Paul would ask her to locate it in a less compromising location.

She arrived at exactly seven thirty as arranged. Birch smoothed down his remaining hair and opened the door wearing what he considered his most seductive expression. The professor thought he looked cheeky, alluring and very intellectual. In reality he resembled a dirty old man on a nudist beach.

What he saw on the doorstep made his heart sing.

Bent over picking up some papers was, as promised, a slim dark haired woman. Her coat was open and she wore a low cut blouse, so Birch could see straight down it. What he saw gave him great satisfaction.

Oh hallelujah, hallelujah. Thank you, God, he thought.

She looked up and smiled.

"Professor! I'm so sorry. As I knocked, I dropped my notes."

She brushed the black fringe out of her eyes.

Yes, you do have the look of a young Elizabeth Taylor, he thought. *My goodness, is it Christmas already?*

"Let me help," he offered, with no intention of doing so.

"No, it's fine, honest." She bent over and he enjoyed the view again.

"Come in, come in. What a shame about Spurs, is it not?"

"It is, but at least we get a replay."

"And we shall prevail! Here, please go into the drawing room."

He let the journalist walk in first in order to enjoy her figure properly. She glanced over her shoulder, saw him look and smiled.

"What a gorgeous room." She scanned the bookshelves. "Oh, a bound copy of Rosenberg's "The American Action Painters"! What I would *do* for some of these."

And what would *you do?* Wondered Birch. "Wine? I have a Chateau La Gaffeliere '71?"

"Exquisite, thank you."

He poured two glasses. "And should you become peckish I have some prawn canapés and a rather delightful Roquefort and sable grapes, which are *so* complimentary to the Gaffeliere."

"I am being spoiled!"

"My dear," he looked into her eyes. "I rather feel that I am the one being spoiled."

She laughed, opened her notebook and clicked a pen into life. "Well, to business. As we discussed on the phone, I'm really after an overview of your life outside Picasso. Everyone associates the names of Paul Birch and Pablo Picasso together but I'd really like to know more about you, the man "behind the canvas" as it were."

Birch smiled. "Touché, dear."

"You spend so much time writing about others, your own life is a cipher which we must decode through your reactions *to* and criticisms *of* art. That's how I see it, anyway. A fair comment?"

The professor found himself become just the tiniest part aroused by that. "Well," he puffed with false modesty and crossed his legs. "The truth is, I am but the medium, the art is the message."

She scribbled that down. "I'd like to know more about the *medium*, if I may." The journalist crossed her legs, too. Birch tried not to look and failed.

He talked for some time and she was always ready to top up his wine. Birch was so lost in his own importance he didn't notice the journalist had drunk just one glass to his three.

"I heard a fascinating rumour," she said once he'd reached a natural break in his life story.

"About me?"

"Of course about you, silly. Who else is there?"

"And what is this fascinating rumour? Is it something," he fluttered his hands over himself, "personal?"

"I suppose it is." She put down the notebook, crossed her legs again and fixed him with those dark eyes. "I heard you have an original Picasso line drawing. A camel, I believe?"

"You heard correct. I did mention it once or twice a while ago in interviews but stopped in fear I would be burgled for it. Mind you, the piece is only worth around £1000. A lot, you would agree, but not as much as one would hope for a Picasso, even a small one."

"I would love to see it."

He pretended to be embarrassed. "I would be happy for you to do so but I should tell you, it is in my bedroom."

She uncrossed her legs and stood up.

"Yes," she purred. "I heard that, too."

He stood, weaved a little then gestured to the door and stairway. "Please, ladies first."

She demurely tipped her head at him, picked up her handbag and walked on. She mounted the stairs slowly and as he followed, Birch gazed up, hypnotised by her body moving beneath the tight skirt. Once the journalist reached the landing, she turned and he stopped behind her.

"Professor, may I just ask one thing?"

"Go ahead."

"Picasso's Blue Period. How do you feel about it?"

"Well, there's so much to say," he spluttered, frustrated they were so near yet so far. "Perhaps we could sit in the bedroom and I could tell you."

He reached up to touch her shoulder but she swatted his hand away.

"Do you *like* his Blue Period?"

"Well, it is by nature sombre, since Picasso was in a depression at the time."

Birch tried to softly push her back toward the bedroom but she stayed rooted at the top of the stairs and stifled a big stage yawn. "It's just you were somewhat dismissive of *my* Blue Period. A period, I might add, I am still very much within."

"Your blue…?"

The journalist reached into her bag, pulled out a piece of paper and slowly unfolded it. "Let me remember. You described this and my others as, 'derivative at best, badly executed at worst.' You said my use of blue was 'monomaniacal,' and didn't interest you. Now, was that fair?"

He squinted through the red wine at the picture. He recognised it. *Where do I know that charcoal from?*

"Obscure to the point of irrelevance," she went on. "Remember? RCA? An open day a lifetime ago?"

The memory returned. *There was a girl. I criticised her work. But surely this wasn't...couldn't be her.*

The journalist's beautiful face had become twisted and dark.

"You only had to be nice, Professor. You only had to be *fucking* nice but you couldn't, could you?"

"Oh, oh, you need to go. You must get out of my house. Now."

She sighed. "You only had to be fucking nice for ten *fucking* minutes."

Then she pushed him backwards.

*

She'd enjoyed breaking Nicholas Atkey's back so wanted a repeat performance on someone else. *Professor* Paul Birch fitted the bill but unlike Atkey, couldn't be allowed to live and 'enjoy' his new reality.

From this moment, jet-setting, globe trotting Paul Birch wouldn't be going anywhere else. His days of travel and temptation were nearly over.

She languidly walked back down toward his crumpled body. One leg was bent forward at an impossible angle and his right arm had twisted backward. Birch's eyes rolled as he looked up. "You pushed..." he squealed, shocked. "You *pushed* me. Get an ambulance."

She checked the tips of her fingers. They were still coated with the glue which erased her prints, but she'd need to clean her wine glass and remove any other evidence the professor had "enjoyed" company tonight.

She squatted down in front of him. Even in extremis, he still looked up her skirt. "Sometimes, *prof*," she said quietly, "you can't even see a work of art when it's right in front of you. I am a work of art. I am both frame and picture, oil and canvas. I have painted myself anew so many times but never used my real signature. What was it Wilde said? 'All art is quite useless'? Do you realise that, now, Birch? You have lived your life in the pursuit and explanation of the useless when art itself is its own explanation."

"Ambulance..."

She tut-tutted.

"We both know that won't happen and I can't finish until *you* are finished. Nobody knows I am here, do they? You're *so* discreet about your little conquests and tonight that discretion is my gain and your loss. So let's get this done and you'll need to be big brave boy for me. Can you do that?"

She reached for his head, held it tight by Birch's cheeks.

"Can you be a brave boy? It'll only take a moment. There, there, my big, brave soldier."

"No," he pleaded. "No, please, I…"

"Sssh. You've already said too much, haven't you?"

She twisted his head and heard a satisfying snap from within his neck.

Then she got to work.

35 / 12th May 1981, London.

"Why am I here?" Anna Leeding stood outside Professor Paul Birch's Southampton Row home. Inspector Walker waited on the doorstep while an ambulance idled in the road.

"Quite a big philosophical question for so early in the morning."

"Don't be smart, David. I got an urgent call from you to attend a domestic accident but no more detail. Why urgent? I don't "do" domestic accidents."

"I know, but the deceased is high profile. And that means you *do* "do" this one."

Anna groaned. "I'm up to my neck with so much stuff. I've got reports to file from *days* ago. OK, let me take a look and get back to my massively busy desk." She sighed and started to walk into the house. "Shall we?"

Walker shifted position to block her and she looked up, surprised.

"Quick recap, ma'am. The deceased is Professor Paul Birch. Ring any bells?"

Anna looked up and to the left, searched her memory. "Is he the art guy? Oh, yes, I remember, he was on Russell Harty's show last year, when that pop star threw a temper tantrum."

"Grace Jones. Yes, he's the "art guy". Critic, museums, galleries, theatres. He moved in very exclusive circles and Prince Charles was a fan, apparently. He wrote that best seller about Picasso."

"I'm more of a Walter Sickert kind of woman." Anna circled her index finger to say, *and get to the point.*

"He counts as high priority so that equates to a very visible, thorough investigation, which means *you* need to be here. You know how it works. The dead famous always gets the whole dotted i's and crossed t's treatment."

"Yes, I know, I don't understand, or agree with it, but I do *know* it. So can we…?"

"He was found by the postman. That's him over there." Walker pointed to a shocked looking Royal Mail worker who waited by the Rover. "He had a big parcel to deliver, naturally it wouldn't fit, so knocked on. No answer, so postie takes a look through the lead lighting, identifies the owner lying on the floor, calls us from a neighbour's house and here we are. It looks like the professor had been drinking and fallen down the stairs. For what it's worth I think he's been there a day or maybe two, but obviously we'll need confirmation on that."

"So can I just come in, take a look and get back to my real work?"

Walker's expression darkened. "This *is* your real work, I think."

Anna picked up on his change of tone.

"There's more to it?"

"I'd rather you take a look and tell *me* if there's more to it. I brought my skeleton key and it worked, thank goodness. I prefer not to smash my way in if I can help it."

He gently pushed open the door with a gloved hand. Walker stepped to one side and gestured Anna inside, like a butler.

She silently scanned the hallway.

First impressions.

Richly decorated. Money. A little too sumptuous for my tastes, too aware of its own worth. This professor wanted visitors to be overawed when they entered. Mind you, he was an art critic, so everything would have been about appearances anyway. He would have decoded meaning in art, so I wonder what meaning he wanted visitors to decode from this place? It looks like a high class brothel, if I'm honest. Perhaps that's the meaning he was after.

To the left of the door she saw a figure on the floor and a telephone table on its side. The phone itself had been thrown into the middle of the hallway, wrapped in its own cord. Anna didn't look at the corpse just yet. She walked forward and glanced into a living room on the right. Two bottles of wine stood on a table, one empty, the other almost finished. One solitary glass had a few mouthfuls left in the bottom.

That looks familiar, Anna thought. *Why does that image bring back a memory?*

Then she had it. The tableau resembled a similar set up in Jeanette West's house.

I think you'll find lots of people drink wine alone, Anna, including yourself. Right, let's take a look at the professor. The ex professor.

She examined the deceased. He was face up, finely dressed in a jacket, tie and shirt. He wore tasseled slippers, except one had come off and lay alongside his leg which bent forward at an almost complete right angle. Part of Anna always found bodies in this condition horribly compelling. Crumpled into ways nature never normally allowed, they didn't even look human. Since your brain couldn't compute such unnatural shapes, one denied their humanity at first. *Nothing is in the right place, the angles are all wrong. Bizarrely, it's like a Picasso*, she thought, *If Picasso's models actually looked like his paintings in real life.*

The professor's arm was twisted almost completely behind his body into a position even a contortionist couldn't manage. But his head was the most difficult to take in. It bent over so far, Birch's cheek touched his shoulder. His eyes were wide open and stared up the stairs.

Dressed up to the nines, weren't you? Or was that your default style of dress? Were you going out? Or expecting a visitor? She caught a whiff of aftershave from the corpse. *Expecting to impress someone, but they never arrived? Or left early? Or were you just another sad, lonely drinker?*

Anna looked up the stairs and then, careful not to touch the handrail, mounted them. She reached the top and surveyed the scene.

OK, he must have fallen from pretty high. You don't often get injuries like that if you trip down the last two steps. It's possible, but unlikely. He fell completely out of control. His right arm is twisted behind him. Did he try to grab on to something on the way down?

Paintings lined the right hand wall of the stairway. One wasn't hanging straight.

Perhaps he tried to grab onto this painting, automatically. No, if he'd grabbed it, this picture would have been wrenched off the wall with the force of his fall and weight. This frame has just been brushed *against, enough to tilt it a little.*

She looked back down at Birch's twisted right arm.

OK, try this. He grabbed onto the rail with his right *hand as he fell. I need to find out if he was right handed. If he was, he fell* backwards*, not forwards. He got to the top of the stairs, lost his balance and fell backward, possibly. Does that make any difference, though?*

Inspector Walker watched Anna from downstairs and silently waited for Leeding's mind to draw the pieces together.

He's drunk. He goes upstairs for whatever reason, trips, slips, who knows, falls backwards. His left *hand brushes the painting, his* right *hand tries to grab the rail, it twists him round, breaks the arm, he tumbles, hits the floor, the left leg breaks and...*

She descended back to the hallway and considered the fallen telephone table.

...His head strikes the table, which snaps his neck. It would have taken a second or two, at most. Alive at the top of the stairs, dead by the bottom. Jesus, life is so fragile.

"Any thoughts?"

"Well, from here it looks like what it is. He's drunk, he falls, he dies. So what's with the drama?"

"I thought the same. Or perhaps that's exactly what we're *supposed* to think."

"Supposed?" Anna looked around once more in case she'd missed something.

"Uh huh. That's what we were supposed to think until we turned the light on. Its quite dim, isn't it, this hall? The dark furnishings don't help, either. I wanted you to see this exactly as I did when I first entered. But now look again. What do you see?"

He reached up with his gloved hand and switched on the hallway light.

Anna bent down to the corpse, studied it up close, then stepped back and glanced around. "I don't see…"

"Not his body."

Confused, Leeding peered about the rest of the hallway. Then her gaze stopped on the wall above Birch. Without thinking, she put a hand to her mouth.

The professor lay broken on his fine, thick carpet. Above him was a framed picture, which had waited unseen in the relative darkness. After all, a corpse does have one's complete and undivided attention.

The picture was small, not much bigger than a Gideon's Bible.

It featured just one word, in horribly familiar light blue charcoal.

GO

36 / Friday 15th May 1981, London.

After Reggae pioneer Bob Marley died last Tuesday, his back catalogue was rightfully filling the airwaves. Lisa Fisher had lost count of how many times she'd heard "No Woman, No Cry," and Radio One was playing it again this evening.

Fisher lay back and gently sang along in the bath. She'd liked Marley ever since her time as a teenage punk. Punks and Rastas became unlikely allies in 1977 so it wasn't unusual to see a Reggae sound system at Punk gigs and vice-versa. Both attracted outsiders and Fisher definitely considered herself a misfit.

Punk's exciting times were only recent, but Lisa already felt her memories of them seemed false. She couldn't work out if they were actual experiences or fake impressions her mind played back as the real thing. Fisher's recollections of Punk were like the music; fast, distorted and open to interpretation.

Was I even really a Punk or just playing a part? She wondered as the audience noise from "No Woman…" died away. *Then again, aren't we all? Isn't everybody just dressing up? Right now I'm dressing up as a WPC. How real is that?*

"Had to start with that really, didn't I?" crackled D.J. Annie Nightingale. "The late, very great and much missed Bob Marley, here on BBC Radio One. I'm setting you up for Friday evening until ten, when Tommy Vance will be turning up some ROCK, but for now, how about "Treason," a bright shiny new single from The Teardrop Explodes!"

The track blared from Fisher's transistor radio, and she sunk under the water until it became just distant echoes of brass and bass.

*

Last Wednesday had been weird for two reasons. First, news broke that Pope John Paul II had been shot in Vatican Square. For a while it was touch and go whether His Holiness would survive but clearly God was on the pontiff's side and JPII had been taken off the critical list.

Fisher had been shocked by the event, but not because she was religious. She'd attended Sunday School as a child, more for her parents' community reputation than to save her soul. When the news flash happened her first thought had been, *how quickly the world reaches for its guns these days.* In the last few months, Lennon, Reagan and now the Pope had been shot. She abhorred this rise in random violence since it offended her sense of justice and order. The increasing use of guns also meant one day she might find herself staring down a barrel. *I can handle myself,* she thought, *but nobody can handle a bullet heading for their head.*

Fisher believed only cowards used guns. If the police ever put armed officers on the beat she'd hang up her hat and leave. Lisa considered herself better than that.

The second reason Wednesday was weird involved Inspector Walker.

Fisher was typing when Walker had sidled over like a kid at the school disco who'd plucked up courage to ask for a slow dance. For a moment she thought he was going to invite her for a drink and the hairs on her arms bristled with embarrassment.

"Ah, Fisher!" The inspector said breezily, like he'd just bumped into her.

"Sir?"

"D.I. Leeding asked *me* to ask *you* what you're doing on Friday evening."

She'd blinked in surprise and tried to translate that phrase into English, because it made no sense. Therefore, her reply was equally nonsensical. "Sorry sir, D.I. Leeding asked what I'm doing? Me? *Friday? Friday evening?*"

He'd rolled his eyes. "I didn't mean it to come out like that, sorry."

"It did sound a bit odd if you don't mind me saying so, sir." Fisher had enjoyed his discomfort and found it quite cute to see a superior officer squirm.

"Yes, well, I apologise. She'd just like an informal chat with you, me, and Daniel Moore. She wants us to go for a curry to discuss something."

The expression on Lisa's face made Walker roll his eyes again. "It's not a *work party*, Fisher. It's an informal chat which D.I. Leeding would like to take place in a casual setting away from the station."

The WPC thought for a moment. "Should I be worried, sir?"

"No, if anything, you should be flattered she wants your opinion. She's booked the Gaylord round the corner for eight thirty. You're not on, I checked your shifts. So is it OK? Yes, or no, where 'no' is not on the table, of course."

"Yes, of course."

"Good." He started to walk away when she spoke up.

"Sir, is it anything to do with the blue chalk?"

"Charcoal," he replied absently. "Blue charcoal. And we'll talk about whatever it is on Friday. Back to work, officer."

Interesting, thought Fisher. *And something to look forward to, I think.*

*

So Friday arrived and Lisa had spent most of the evening in a quandary. What *does* one wear for "an informal meal and chat" with their superior officers and a man she'd only met once at the scene of a suicide? It wasn't exactly an ordinary meal out.

In the end Fisher opted for a black all in one suit pulled together at the waist by a red leather belt. She'd slicked her already short dark hair back and added a little bit more eyeshadow, eyeliner and lipstick than normal. Lisa wanted to look like she'd made an effort but not as if she also intended to head out for a night at The Blitz.

Fisher hoped she wasn't overdressed and prayed she hadn't underdressed.

I want to blend in, she thought. *Because I want to observe D.I. Anna Leeding up close, off duty. See if I can work out what makes her tick. See if my suspicions are correct and the more I get to know her, the more I think they are.*

Her tiny garret flat was above a pub in Holborn, but even though it was a short walk to Oxford Circus she decided to hail a cab.

Fisher wasn't used to wearing heels much these days.

*

At eight fifteen, Anna was first to arrive at the Gaylord Indian Restaurant, where she'd booked a far corner table. Walker was next, followed by Fisher. At first, the WPC was understandably uncomfortable.

"I feel like I'm sixteen and on a dinner date with my teachers," she laughed. "I don't know the form, ma'am, sir. Are we still at work?"

"No and yes," replied Anna, cryptically. "But tonight I'm Anna and this is David, just for tonight."

Fisher looked around the restaurant, impressed. "It's nice here. I don't really know Indian food. " She started to babble nervously. "I had that Vesta instant curry recently. You know, just add water. And I've tried Homepride curry from a can but I've never actually been to an Indian restaurant before. Is it like Chinese? I like sweet and sour. Wow," she whispered, "there are a *lot* of Indians here aren't there? That must mean it's good, right?"

"This place has been here since 1966," said Walker, "trust me, it's good."

Fisher looked through the menu and shook her head. "None of this means a thing to me."

"Don't worry, I'll help you out. It's just different spices, that's all. You have to adjust your taste buds a bit but might really enjoy trying something new."

"I hope I like it."

"There's no such thing as the wrong taste, Fisher, just your own taste," added Anna.

Leeding and Walker both ordered a pint of Indian beer. Fisher did the same. "It's not that different to Carlsberg!" she said through a foam moustache.

"Beer is beer, Fisher, for which we should be truly thankful."

"Yes, sir, we should."

Daniel Moore arrived at eight forty, flustered and apologetic. "Sorry, I was running late, didn't even have time to shave." He rubbed his chin and grimaced. "So rather than the bus, I drove, *then* got lost, *then* couldn't find a parking space, *then* got lost again. On foot."

Anna tittered and waved away the apology. "It's Central London on a Friday, Daniel. What did you expect? And don't worry about a bit of stubble, makes you look rugged, very Lewis Collins."

Daniel laughed. "First time I've ever been called 'rugged'. I like it, I might even put it on my business card, er, if I had one."

"Enjoy the compliment, thanks for coming. Inspector Walker you know and do you remember WPC Fisher?"

"Of course I do." Daniel took off his jacket, which was taken by a waiter who'd materialised from nowhere. He slid in next to Fisher, offered his hand and they shook. "Nice to see you again," he said, looked her in the eyes and smiled shyly. "But much nicer circumstances, thank God," Lisa smiled back, but then quickly glanced down.

"I suppose I could have a half, that would be OK, wouldn't it?" Daniel asked. "I guess you carry a breathalyser at all times, inspector?"

Walker patted his trouser pockets. "Damn, left it at the station."

Daniel ordered a half of lager and the four colleagues chatted for a while about the week's events; Bob Marley, the Pope, IRA hunger strikes, Andrew Lloyd Webber's new musical ("it's something about cats, but I can't remember the title," joked Daniel) and the mysteries of an Indian restaurant menu were all discussed. Fisher eventually took Walker's advice to order chicken korma and then the group waited for their food to arrive.

Daniel was first to mention the as yet unmentioned.

"So, ma'am, sorry, Anna. I'm intrigued. Lovely though all this is, what's the real reason we're here? David was cagey on the phone. Mind you, he's cagey at the best of times."

"I can't comment on that statement," Walker huffed and everyone laughed.

Anna looked down at the table, took a deep breath and began.

"Well, David knows the whole story. Daniel, you know some and Lisa, I don't think you know much at all. But the reason you're here, Lisa, is because you were with us at Jeanette West's, which is where I think..." she grasped for the right description, but couldn't grab it, "... *whatever this is* started. If indeed, anything has started at all."

She looked around at three blank faces.

"I couldn't have said it worse myself," said Walker. Fisher tittered.

"I know, I know," Anna held up her hands. "OK, I'll give you the big statement and work my way back from there. Just bear with me, it sounds dramatic." She took a deep breath. "All right, I'll just say it. I think we have a sequential killer here in London. You're here tonight to play devil's advocates or supporting witnesses to that statement. I just want to lay down what I know and hear your opinions. Is that OK?"

"Is it to do with the blue chalk thing?" Daniel leaned forward, interested.

"Blue charcoal," Walker corrected.

Fisher looked between them and frowned. "But with respect, ma'am, er, Anna, if that's the case and we're discussing *murder* we shouldn't be doing it here should we?"

"I understand your concerns but to cut a long story short, this is all just supposition and instinct. We're not discussing a case because there *is* no case. Think of tonight as a training exercise, or a game. In the past I've jumped in too early and made mistakes. I don't want to go into detail but I have deep regrets for not having all the evidence to hand before I acted on assumptions."

She looked round at Walker, who nodded, *carry on, I know, it's OK.*

"So I'm suggesting something potentially...yes, all right, I'll say it, potentially crazy. But it's also potentially real. I'm going to give you the bare bones, let's see if we can put some flesh on them. But yes, for tonight, treat this as an...intellectual game, if you like."

"OK," Daniel mimed rolling up his sleeves. "Let's play."

Anna reached into her bag and pulled out some photocopied sheets. "Rather than repeating myself I typed up this overview of what I know and what I *think* I know. As you can see it's really not very much. But take a look through and then we can talk."

The food arrived as she handed out the papers, so the colleagues silently ate and read the documents.

The pages summed up what Anna had; the presence of similar blue charcoal words at the deaths of West, Martin, Atkey and Birch. No witnesses to anything suspicious. No forensics which might indicate foul play. Partials on West's windowsill which had a few comparisons to prints on fan letters from the mysterious "*Sarah*". Those letters had also been photocopied for everyone to study.

One by one, the four colleagues put their papers down and waited for Anna to speak.

"As you can see, it's really not very much," she shrugged. "Nowhere near anything I could build a case around. So why do I feel there's *something*? So let's play. Devil's advocate, defence or prosecution, I just want to hear whatever you think. Who wants to start?"

Daniel put his hand up like a schoolboy. Anna laughed. "Yes, Moore?"

"Yes, teacher! Sorry, you wanted a truthful opinion, here's mine. With respect, your idea there's a multiple killer doesn't work, logically. Let's assume this person is trying to commit perfect murders, make them look like suicides, accidents, or a hit and run. If it wasn't for these charcoal "messages" you'd be none the wiser. They'd have got away with it. So why *announce* them as murders, why leave a clue? Isn't that the surest indication this is all just a massive coincidence?"

"Because they *do* want us to know, don't they?" mused Fisher. "That's the point. Why commit a perfect murder if nobody knows it's one? They *want* somebody to realise."

"But why?" asked Daniel. "For what purpose?"

"Because they're so *clever*, aren't they? I'm only playing Devil's advocate here but why go to all the effort to commit perfect murders if nobody can marvel at how smart you are. The killer would be overjoyed to know we're meeting like this to discuss him. If there *is* a killer."

"Do you think there's one, Lisa?" asked Anna.

"I think there's something very odd here. But whether it involves murder, well, I'm on the fence with that."

"For the record, I'm not convinced there is a connection," said Walker. "I admit it's odd but for the sake of this, er, game, I'll go along with it. If these are the works of one person then surely the question is, why *these* four victims? What do they have in common?"

"Exactly," said Anna, "I've looked into their backgrounds and there's nothing I can find to link them. West and Reverend Martin were from the same area, my neck of the woods, East London. But Birch came from Nottingham and Atkey grew up in Brighton. They had *wildly* different backgrounds, occupations, were different ages. However at time of death they all lived in a relatively small area, which might suggest the killer, if there is one, lives in the same vicinity but not necessarily. The Yorkshire Ripper lived in Bradford but killed as far as Manchester and the outskirts of Leeds." She held her palms open. "So it doesn't neatly fit the pattern of previous sequential murders I've looked into."

"Which would suggest, with respect, there *is* no pattern because there are no murders," said Walker.

"What about the words then?" asked Fisher. "WOE IS ME? FACE, GO? FOG? I've tried to make a sentence out of them, you know, by jumbling up the letters, but I can't find one."

"I tried," sighed Anna. "The best anagram I could find is COFFEE MAGGIE WOOS which only suggests Margaret Thatcher is on a killing spree because she can't get a decent cup of Nescafé. And I don't think the Prime Minister is *that* psychotic."

"I wouldn't put it past her though," muttered Fisher.

"So it looks like the only way to prove there's a killer at large is to find a connection between the victims then work out what the blue charcoal words mean. If they mean anything."

"I'm afraid so, Daniel. Does anyone have any other thoughts?"

"This korma is lovely by the way, I can't believe I've lived this long without trying one," said Fisher. "Right, since this is a game, I'm going to be Quincy, or Columbo." She squinted and went into an impressive impression of Peter Falk. "Ah, just one mwah ting…"

"That's pretty bloody good," laughed Daniel.

"I'm a great actress," replied Fisher, primly. "OK, I'm going to assume these are deliberate acts. Is our possible "killer" leaving messages, or statements? Are they for us to find or are the words relevant to the victims? I mean, FACE makes sense for a model, doesn't it? WOE IS ME might relate to how Nick Atkey worked for that phone charity but FOG means nothing for a reverend, and GO doesn't really work for an art critic."

"I did think about that," said Anna, "and got stuck in the same cul-de- sac."

Fisher waved her fork to make a point. "To me, it seems the only evidence of any motive comes from "*Sarah*"'s fan letters, so shouldn't you be working to track her down? If there's a chance "*Sarah*" visited West's home then she's the best person to start with. *If* Jeanette was even murdered, that is."

"I agree," said Anna. "Of course we should identify "*Sarah,*" if only to eliminate her as a suspect. But how? There's no address, no witnesses, we have no idea what she looks like and the fingerprints don't match anything in our records. Not that I can find, anyway."

Everyone picked at the food and looked at their papers again.

"Hang on, what about this?" Fisher held up her photocopy. "Listen, she writes, '*I just got a job in fashion! Well, if you can count uniforms and work blouses as fashion! But we all have to start somewhere. Who knows where I'll be next?*'" Lisa studied the date. "OK, so "*Sarah*" wrote that on the 15th of December last year. Which means around that time, she got a new job which involved fashion, or at the very least, 'uniforms and work blouses'. That's something isn't it?"

Anna looked at the WPC, impressed. "Yes, that *is* something. Excellent."

"So," Daniel piped up, "a uniform could mean she might be working in, what, fire, ambulance, police, military, or…as a waitress?"

Fisher looked round at a couple of the waitresses, raised her eyebrows and mimicked a Bela Lugosi horror voice. "You *ne-eever* know, she might *eveeeen* be *riiiiight here.*"

Daniel chuckled. "That's good, too. You've missed your vocation, clearly."

Lisa shrugged and giggled.

"Or she could work in a shop?" added Walker.

"OK, that's an avenue to think about," said Anna. "Anything else? It doesn't matter how farfetched, don't hold back."

"I think we should start at the start, as it were," Fisher read from Jeanette west's suicide note. "'*I resisted so long, but I couldn't go on like I have before. People have used me, judged me, abused me simply because of my sex.*' With respect, join the club, Jeanette. But if you're saying she was murdered rather than killed herself, is this even a suicide note?"

"Ah, exactly," said Anna, quietly, "I wanted to see if any of you put it together."

"Put what together?" asked Walker.

"May I?" Fisher turned to Leeding, who nodded, *go on.*

"Isn't it obvious? If West was *murdered*, that means she never wrote this suicide note, the *killer* did."

"If true, that rather puts a whole new angle on it, right?" Anna read the whole note out. "*I resisted so long, but I couldn't go on like I have before. People have used me, judged me, abused me simply because of my sex. I can't bear to be in this body any more, as I can't bear what people have done to me over the years. Not one of them has paid, apologised or shown guilt for what they did for me. So I am left with no choice but this. I do it with full knowledge that I cannot go back from this step. I must see it through now. No more. From this act, they will all know what they did to me. I have no choice any more.*" She let the words hang.

Walker stared at Anna, agog. "So if the killer wrote that, then these murders are, what, payback?"

"Call it what it is, David," replied Anna. "Revenge, pure and simple. If true, the killer's working their way through people who have *used*, *abused* and *judged* them over the years. That's one potential connection. I'm glad you made it, Fisher. I thought I might be out on a limb."

"You still could be," said Walker.

"Wait, hold on," Daniel piped up. "The note talks about 'my sex'. No *bloke* talks about '*their sex,*' do they? No bloke even considers their gender an issue. So if a possible murderer wrote it, does that suggest they're a *woman*? Jesus. And if that's the case, we, sorry, *you* should try to identify "*Sarah*" as a priority, right? But look, I just point and flash, so don't take anything I say as gospel, it's just an opinion."

"But I agree," said Anna. "Although we're in free fall, aren't we? It's all 'might' and 'perhaps' and 'possibly'. The *fact* is we don't really have anything at all, not really. Just this game and our assumptions. And as you know, I don't like to assume anything. But for one moment let's indulge ourselves and pretend that yes, there is a killer. Yes, they are leaving messages, either for us or some other purpose. Yes, their victims are connected because they have all done him, or her, wrong in the past. That there may be more to come. The big question, the *real* question therefore, is very simple yet incredibly difficult to answer; *what are we going to do about it?*"

*

As the group debated that point, none of them realised someone had been watching them for a very long time from across the road. Hidden in the shadows, they muttered to themselves and clenched their fists in fury.

37 / Friday 15th May 1981, London.

By ten thirty the meal had reached its natural conclusion. After much debate, the question of a potential sequential killer was put to one side and the conversation felt its way back to more enjoyable subjects.

Anna weaved a little on the short walk home to Tottenham Court Road. Friday nights were normally spent with the cat, a drink, maybe some TV and a book, which, as always, would remain unfinished. The meal reminded her how much she missed company. Despite the group's short wade into dark conversational waters, the evening had made her laugh a lot. That was a welcome change as she'd become unfamiliar with laughter recently.

But Lisa had been the real surprise. From the first time they'd met at Jeanette West's, Anna was sure she could rely on this new girl. In uniform, the WPC appeared calm and thoughtful, but tonight the real Fisher had come out to play; funny, smart, knowingly silly, involved, and always smiling. Leeding was drawn to people who enjoyed life as it happened, unaware they wore that pleasure on their faces.

It's a shame I'm her superior officer, she thought. *Because if I got to know Fisher outside of work, I think we could be friends. The kind of friends who go out on a Friday night, sit in a pub for hours, just talk nonsense and laugh.* That image made her a little sad. There was no way a detective inspector could hang around with a WPC, it would be like a lecturer socialising with a student, although at least now they had a connection.

But wow, *Anna, wouldn't you just be the most* fun *company? "Hi Lisa, fancy talking about murder over a drink?" "Hey, want to pop to the Yorkshire Grey and go over these crime figures?" Ha. God, I need to get out more. I'm not some spinster in a Kensington maisonette, I'm only thirty-eight for God's sake. It's time I just bit the bullet and spent time with people.*

She walked on but her mind had other things to say.

Oh, but you do *spend time with people, don't you? It's just they don't know who you really are, do they? But then you're suddenly in their homes and flats and they don't have the faintest clue.*

Anna caught sight of her reflection in the window of Rumbelows electrical store. Their display was made of banks of blank televisions and their dead screens were like rows of mirrors which all broadcasted the Anna show.

She stared at the multiple Leedings, twisted this way and that, drunkenly appraised her reflection. *You're all right. Come on, you are. Not gorgeous, not a STUNNA as The Sun might say, but all right enough just as you are.*

She wore a simple white blouse and black jacket, combined with a shorter skirt than normal plus black suede boots. *Is that skirt too much?* She wondered, turning again. *Mutton dressed as lamb? Trying too hard to compete with the Romantics?* Anna put two fingers up at the window. *No, sod you, Romantics. The outfit works. I work. It's 1981, I'm here and I've worn far more outré combinations.*

The whole ensemble was fairly conservative but she'd noticed how Walker had still covertly looked her up and down.

Oh David, we've known each other for years and yet it only takes a short skirt for you to become A MAN. She supposed it was quite sweet. *He's a bloke and he's going to look, it's not a big deal.* The many Annas stared back and didn't look convinced by her argument.

As she pushed open her door the phone began to ring.

Anna went to pick up then thought better of it. She quickly ran back outside and looked toward the phone box, which was empty. Inside, the phone stopped ringing.

Dylan waited on the doorstep, confused. First Mum had returned from her foraging expedition, then she'd left again. He mewed loudly to remind her he was hungry then scampered into the kitchen to make doubly sure she'd got the hint.

"Yes, Dyl, yes," Anna laughed. "I get it. Mum's eaten, you haven't for, oh, at least five hours. You must be famished." She began to dish up Dylan's late night snack when the phone rang again.

She picked up and assumed it must be Walker. "I'm too tired and tipsy to talk any more, so this better be good."

Silence.

Not this again, for God's sake.

She was about to slam down the phone when somebody spoke.

"Had a nice time with your new boyfriend, have you, Anna?"

It took her a moment to recognise the voice.

"*Robin*? Robin, is that you?"

"I saw. Yes, I saw you. Having a lovely time with your new boyfriend. I saw you tonight and I saw you in Whitechapel, too, the Ten Bells. Having a lovely time."

"Robin? You *followed* me? What are you doing? What's this about?"

"You know. You *know,* you bitch. You know. You said, you said and you lied."

"Robin, I don't know what this is, but…"

She suddenly sobered up.

"Robin, was it you on the phone? Have you been calling? Did *you* leave those dead flowers? It was you in the phone box, wasn't it?"

"Just checking to see if you were alone or whether your new boyfriend was around. You *said* and you *lied.*"

"Jesus, Robin, what's this about?" He was extremely drunk and his words tumbled from the receiver, garbled like a badly tuned radio. He sounded angry and yet full of self pity.

"Robin, you're drunk. Whatever this is, why don't you call when you're sober and we can talk, but I don't know what we'd talk about, to be honest, we're over. You know we're over."

She tried to sound authoritative but failed. Her *police voice* didn't work on a man she used to sleep with. Part of Anna was scared. She'd worked on cases where ex boyfriends spiralled out of control and they were never pretty. And now, out of nowhere, it had happened to her.

"Robin, you cannot do this."

"You have no idea," he screeched and his voice sounded like distorted static. "You have no idea what you've done. But you will. You will. Going to take action, Anna!" He giggled like an ancient child. "Going to take action! You'll see!"

*

Anna had met Robin Taylor two years ago on one of her rare visits to a pub. It was a colleague's birthday and she'd found herself somewhat drunk at a busy bar trying to remember a huge order of drinks.

As they'd slowly stacked up, a man next to her had whistled. "Wow. Shall I go to the phone and call for an octopus?"

"Sorry?" She shouted over the noise.

"All those drinks," he leaned in closer so she could hear. "You might need an octopus to help with them."

She laughed. "Oh, yes, right. Yes, if you know of any octopi nearby, I'd be very grateful of the help."

He'd made a play of thinking. "Actually, no, I don't. I think there's a squid for hire in Pimlico but you have to book in advance."

"Oh, that's a shame."

"I don't have tentacles, well, not last time I looked, but I could give you a hand."

He was an instantly likeable guy. "That would be great." Then, maybe because of the drink, Leeding decided to dive in and introduce herself. "I'm Anna by the way."

"As in Karenina? I'm Robin, as in Christopher."

"Christopher...?"

"Winnie The Pooh. But as you can see, I don't wear shorts because I don't have the legs to carry them off." He put a hand to his forehead and swooned a little. "I will never play for Chelsea."

"Oh, ha, yes. Nice to meet you."

"And you."

They'd shaken hands formally and laughed.

So he'd helped with the drinks and they'd talked for the rest of the evening. Anna wasn't normally the kind of woman who got chatted up by strange men (and chatted them up in return) yet she'd flirted and giggled like all the other girls in the pub.

Part of her whispered on repeat, *this isn't you. You know it's not you. You don't do this. It's never been you.*

But another voice whined, *but you're lonely and what difference does it make? A person is a person and company is company. So what does it matter? Perhaps this* is *you, after all.*

Anna's romantic history was made of one hundred percent failure. She could count her boyfriends on one hand, her longest relationship had been six months and there were always long, fallow periods between lovers, if she could even call them that.

In retrospect, boyfriends were more like pleasant company she happened to sleep with, so each relationship would slowly dwindle until one partner (usually Anna) called off the whole sorry affair. She'd been "dumped" exactly once, by a long haired musician called Gary who'd become fed up with the lack of what he called "Mattress Sports." She'd let him think he was in control, as it made splitting up convenient.

Of course there'd been one night stands, illicit, faintly guilty meetings for no other reason than to satisfy a basic urge. But then there were seemingly *real* moments that promised fireworks. When those happened, Anna always got scared, backed away and left the potential unfulfilled.

It wasn't that she *resisted* commitment, no, she was *terrified* of it, afraid to admit somebody could be *the one* she couldn't live without. That depth of self admission would take a scary amount of honesty which Anna still didn't think she was capable of.

Then along came Robin Taylor and she'd fallen into their relationship without effort. Not because she loved him, no she hadn't loved any of them; been fond of, yes, attracted to, yes, even enjoyed their company, but loved? No.

Not one of them had been compatible. That was the word, the problem, the be-all and end-all; *compatibility*.

But Robin was easy going and fitted in with her small clique of friends. Anna even liked how he became *very* slightly jealous when she talked to other men. It made her feel desired and yes, to her shame, like she was somehow *his*. Their relationship had been intimate, yet strangely distant. They laughed together but were equally happy to sit silently lost in TV. It seemed all Robin wanted was to be alone with her and his intense need for attention made Anna perversely happy.

But in love? No. She'd asked herself that question over and over again.

But you must love him. You've been together for a year now. That must mean something, you just haven't admitted it to yourself.

No, I don't love him.

But have you ever been in love to know, Anna? Have you?

I would know. I would crackle and my heart would leap and I'd shine when I see him and yet none of those things happen.

So why are you with him?

Because I...enjoy him.

You enjoy him? Like you enjoy a pet? A meal? So why put Robin through it? Why make him think there's a future?

There is, isn't there?

No.

Because I don't love him and I know I never will, because I can't.

Those arguments went on and on but Anna was a coward. It was easier to let both of them drift rather than jumping overboard.

At least I'm not alone, she often thought and hated herself for it.

Eventually, Leeding knew it was once again time to go back to the safety of her own company. There hadn't been one event that made up her mind, because the negatives were cumulative and the end inevitable. Their "relationship" had run its course just like all the rest.

Anna severed the already weak tie last October and it had been easier than she'd expected.

Leeding had arranged to meet Robin at The Lamb And Flag pub near Covent Garden. She chose that venue because it had two exits which led to different streets so they could both leave alone, in opposite directions. She'd already prepared the ground by cutting phone conversations short and finding excuses not to meet up. Over the years she'd become quite an expert in putting up signposts for her boyfriends to follow, even if they didn't know where those signs ultimately led. So she'd followed the same pattern with Robin, hoping he'd see which way the wind blew and then choose to tack in another direction. Sadly, he hadn't. They never did.

So over a pint which remained untouched, she went into her spiel, rehearsed over many nights in front of the mirror.

She felt they'd drifted apart.

Work took up more and more time and she couldn't give him the commitment he deserved.

She just didn't feel the same way about him (not that there had ever been a "way" in the first place).

Leeding admitted she was finished with relationships for a very long time. "I just don't think I'm that kind of woman, I'm better off alone, that's the way it's going to be."

Anna hadn't exactly used the words, "It's not you, it's me," but came pretty close.

He'd listened, nodded, frowned, hadn't interrupted or become angry. Robin had quietly sipped at his pint and after she'd repeated herself a few times and pulled appropriately apologetic faces, he'd stood.

"OK, OK, I get it. This is where you are now. You want time. I understand."

Part of her wanted to push him back into his seat and shout. "No, I don't want *time*. I want this over, for good." But she was spineless, so let him believe an empty promise because it made the whole process easier for her.

"Maybe, Robin, maybe. But I really don't think I want another relationship for as long as I can see."

He'd smiled and nodded. "Well, we'll find out won't we? We'll see."

Then he'd walked away, turned, waved and disappeared into Floral Street. *Oh,* thought Anna. *He thinks this is temporary. OK, well, I spelled it out. He'll soon get the idea. He'll come round. He's not a bad guy.*

She was totally wrong on that score.

*

"Robin, I thought you understood. It's been six months. Why now? You were OK with it."

"You said you were finished with relationships," he spat. "You lied. You lied, you lied, you lied. I saw you with *him*. That man. You were laughing. Good, is he? Better than me? Makes you scream, does he? Makes you *mooooaaaaaaan*?"

Anna couldn't reconcile this twisted voice on the phone with the man she'd been with for so long. It was like he was possessed.

Maybe this is the real Robin, she thought with horror, *and the one I dated was an elaborate act.* Then, that little voice inside her added, *and he wasn't the only actor, then, was he?*

"Robin, I can't talk to you like this. You need to sober up and then…perhaps we can talk about how you feel. But you can't call me and hang up. You can't come to my home and…watch…and you can't follow me, for God's sake. You understand that, right?"

"Makes you scream for more, does he?"

"The man you're talking about is a work colleague."

"That's what you're calling it now, is it? Enjoy his work, does he? Physical labour, is it?"

"Robin, listen, I don't know where this has come from. This isn't you."

"Oh, it's me!" he screamed. "It's me, it's me, it's always been me! Do you know what you did? Do you know what's happened to me? You were supposed to take me back. You were *supposed* to take me back and you never called. You were supposed to take me back! What was I supposed to do? I had to know what you were doing, and you lied. You said you were finished with relationships and you're a lying dirty bitch because you are fucking that man, you are fucking him and others and *loving it* and my life is ruined because of you. Because of you, because of you, because of you!"

"Robin," she said slowly. Anna recognised this kind of behaviour. It wasn't just the alcohol, there were so many other tremors inside that head, convulsions he'd managed to skilfully hide the whole time. *You gave my acting skills a run for my money,* that long away part of her mind whispered. She needed to tread carefully.

"Robin, I think you need help. I can find it for you."

"No, what I need is for you to suffer like I suffer. There's nothing for me. Nothing for me. Nothing for me any more. Will you do that for me, Anna? Will you suffer like I suffer? Will you do that? Will you promise?"

"I can't promise that."

"Oh, you don't need to. I can't trust you to suffer, so I'm going to *make* you. I'm going to *make* you, going to make you! Make you suffer. Ready? Ready Anna? Think of me when you fuck. *Do* you even fuck him? I know what you are. *I know what you are.* I followed you. I saw! I saw, Anna! I saw! What are you? *What are you?* Think of me, me, me, think of me, me, God, no. No. No. I can't. No. Yes. Yes."

Then there was a scream and a dull thump from the other end of the phone.

"Robin? Robin?"

Only silence answered.

No. Please God no, no that, anything but that. Please, no, no, no.

Anna had a horrible feeling she knew what Robin meant when he'd promised she'd suffer. Leeding's hands shook uncontrollably as she put down the phone and then dialled another number.

"Ambulance, please," she waited, gave an address, then a description of her suspicions. Then D.I. Anna Leeding hung up and burst into gulping, shaking tears.

*

The ambulance men forced an entry to Robin Taylor's room and gently took his body down thirty minutes later.

38 / Sometime *Before* (6)

It had taken her a while to get over the incident with Professor Birch, although *get over* wasn't the appropriate term. She would never *get over* it in the commonly understood sense.

Outwardly, "The Worker" still giggled at her desk but inwardly, she was a volcanic landscape. Every person who'd done her wrong became a rock in that molten river and there were so, *so* many of them now.

As her "diaries" filled, she conceded some of the entries were based on perceptions rather than reality, but didn't really care. She was queen of the empire inside her skull and would therefore rule it in any way the subjects deserved. She knew it would be impossible to punish every single name in her pages, so come the reckoning only a select few could be chosen for special treatment. How and when she'd pick them remained unclear but the time would come. She needed a plan which would provide the maximum amount of vengeance and satisfaction, yet still allow her the time and freedom to complete it.

A half finished revenge would be none at all.

So she placed retribution to one side. A method and time would present themselves.

"The Worker" continued to fool customers but the other employees still kept her at arm's length. They were polite and some even pretended to be friends, but she knew they laughed behind her back, so their names and crimes all went into the diary. In rare moments of munificence, she thought some really *were* her friends, but quickly disabused herself of that notion, since no-one could be trusted. *I am the one true human in this world, even if my truth has to remain unseen.*

But she couldn't stay at the bank much longer. She was an artist and if the world wouldn't come to her work, then she'd take it to them. The diary was her creative inspiration, full of hundreds of unknowing muses who daily pushed her to greater heights, *or,* as she often thought, *depths.*

But the bank job was a means to an end and she'd finally saved enough money to begin the next phase. She wasn't sure what her new profession might be, but had many options to consider.

Then the strangest thing happened.

Suddenly she found herself playing a new role, one she learned and mastered very quickly; girlfriend.

Damon Whitehill was an aspiring businessman. He'd spotted how a little pizza restaurant in Soho made big profits, so wanted to replicate its success. Damon had come to the bank for a loan and she'd been involved in the paperwork. He was mid-twenties, tall, good looking, *and obvious, obvious, sooooo obvious,* muttered her cynical mind. But part of her had to admit it was attracted to him. Although the feeling seemed mutual, after Nicholas Atkey she was understandably wary. But at least women would now be safe around Nick after he'd *accidentally, tragically* tumbled down the stairs and broken his back.

She thought any relationship with Damon was doomed before it could start. To share her already complex life with someone else *and* play another character with that degree of intimacy might be too much to ask. *But still, but still, it would be a challenge, fun, even.*

Then as she waited at the bus stop one rainy morning, an MG Sports car pulled up opposite. Damon waved from the window, so with a newspaper over her hair she rushed through the downfall and wondered what on earth he could want.

Perhaps I forgot to fill in Clause IV, subsection VI.

"Hi, love, would you like a lift? It's dreadful out there."

She considered the offer for a moment. If he tried anything funny she could easily ram her Parker pen into his skull and to hell with the consequences.

"That would be lovely, thank you."

The journey only took twenty minutes but as they'd chatted and laughed, she realised a new character had formed right there in the passenger seat.

"*The Worker*" was rather staid and sensible. Despite a promising start the short skirted, low topped, "*The Vamp*" had been a disaster. She'd enjoyed the party boys' attention, but forgot men are unsubtle creatures when sober, let alone full of alcohol. She'd thought *The Vamp* was a clever exercise in deployed sexuality but they'd only seen an invitation.

Then again, even after such a short time on earth she knew some men considered a woman's mere *existence* as an invitation.

"*The Artist,*" well, she'd singularly failed to live up to the character's name.

She smiled out of the window then mentally cracked her knuckles in preparation for another performance.

She guessed Damon wouldn't be interested in *"The Vamp"*. Like all men, he was extremely vain and *"The Vamp"* would make him look cheap. She decided this new character should be like his car; sleek, stylish, attractive and, above all, a classic.

So that short car journey birthed somebody different, *"The Professional."* Her creative process was similar to the way musicians try combinations of notes to eliminate discord from harmony. She played with subtly different kinds of speech, expressions and body language, discarded those which failed to get a reaction, ramped up others which did. Quickly, "The Professional" was born; an intelligent girl with strong opinions, but who also demurred and listened. She tuned into the way Damon reacted to both feminine and masculine traits, sometimes in the space of a single sentence.

Just twenty minutes later, "The Professional" existed. What started as an exercise to flex creative muscles had produced an exciting new addition to her human wardrobe. She'd opened the door, stood, smoothed her skirt, saw him glance there then received vindication as he asked,"If it's raining, would you like another lift tomorrow, perhaps even tonight?

"I'm out with friends after work," she'd lied. "But tomorrow morning would be very helpful, particularly with this awful weather."

After a few more days of flirtatious journeys, once again he'd asked if she'd like a lift home.

"Well, I'm going out for a drink," his face had fallen. "With you, Damon, with you, so don't bring your car. I rather disapprove of drink drivers."

So their relationship started with a lie and progressed from there. He'd simply fallen for a script and costume that she always discarded when alone. Her process involved total immersion in the character, which was exhausting at first but soon became second nature, easy as taking off one outfit and slipping into another.

Whenever they went out, she'd step back and watch *"The Professional"* in action from a distance. Sex was a particular joy. She observed their lovemaking from afar as "T.P." became yet another version of a character which was already a lie. Even when she was *literally* naked, Damon never suspected he was fucking a highly complex automaton. While she appreciated the physicality, her real enjoyment came from the lie's sheer audacity.

But throughout it all another voice whispered in her ear, a tiny mutter that spoke from the end of a very long line. *Some of this is real,* it said. *You're playacting, but basing this on a reality somewhere very deep inside you. And if you are in "love," then you know what that means, don't you? He will hurt you, won't be able to help himself. That's what they all do. He will become bored with his toy and throw it away. You think you are strong, that you've built a shell around yourself that nobody can penetrate, but never forget, part of you is true and it is within that shell. You have to stop, and stop now. Turn and run, run, run away and never see him again. Because you will not weather the storm when this ends.*

She always managed to drown out that voice, but over long sleepless nights it would return and purr in her ear, on repeat; *you are on a collision course with yourself.*

She ignored that traitorous commentary, because this act had become her new reality and even *she* couldn't see the joins any more.

The relationship ended, of course.

*

The way it died was like something from a bad drama. She'd wanted to meet Damon on Friday but he had to work because his head waiter was off ill. So she'd arranged to meet him on Saturday lunchtime instead.

But by Friday night she was bored of TV, so decided to surprise him. Damon lived above the restaurant a couple of bus rides away, but she had a dirty twinkle in her eyes and a long coat. She planned to arrive just as he turfed out the last few diners and staff, then casually let the coat fall open and reveal she wasn't dressed for anything but staying in.

On arrival she was surprised to find the restaurant locked and dark with a *CLOSED* sign up, even though he shut at eleven and it was barely ten thirty. She rang the bell but there was no answer. Obviously standing on a street corner in a coat and little else was a bad idea, so she set off for "Pymm's Steakhouse" nearby with the intention of using their phone.

But she felt uncomfortable and worried. Weekends were obviously Damon's busiest nights, so *CLOSED* made the ground under her feet shift a little. She started to regret introducing an element of surprise into the evening.

So she walked round to "Pymm's Steakhouse," aware there was only a thin layer of coat between London and her silk underwear. The restaurant was busy and its windows ran with condensation. She was about to push open the door when her hand froze mid-air.

In fact, the entire world froze. It was the oddest feeling. The people inside became mannequins which posed as customers. Damon and a girl were sat together in a far corner. He leaned forward then kissed her full on the lips.

Freeze frame.

She recognised the girl as one of Damon's seventeen year old waitresses, but these two weren't work colleagues out after a long shift. She knew the look on his face and a kiss like that could not be misconstrued. Time restarted and she smashed open the door. The customers looked up in shock, but she noticed how Damon was slow to register her presence and read his mind;

Who's that? What? How could you be here when you should be at home, you stupid bitch, because that was what we'd arranged?

The shocked seventeen year old's mouth opened wide and she held up her hands as a shield. Damon rose, palms open, as if to say, *no, wait, wait, don't cause a scene, I know what this looks like, but it's not.*

None of it mattered. She grabbed a steak knife from the nearest table, traversed the length of the restaurant in less than two seconds then plunged the blade into Damon's chest. He looked down at the impossibility of it all and shook his head as if to deny reality. She let the long coat fall open, pulled out the knife, smiled, fluttered her eyelashes and pushed her face into his. "Enjoy the view Damon. It's for old times' sake, and the last thing you will ever see, so enjoy the view, *fucker.*"

She didn't know how many times she pulled out the blade and brought it down again but was distantly amazed at how easily mere bone deflected its progress. *Who'd have thought how strong ribs are?* She wondered. *Not strong enough though, honey, alas, alas.*

Somewhere on earth people screamed and ran, but that was OK, because nobody else was *here.*

Right here there's only me and Damon, enjoying one last intimate moment.

Except none of that happened.

As she started to push open the door, her hand froze and those violent images strobed in her mind. But instead of acting them out she fell backward against a wall, gasped and retched. Nobody inside saw her collapse.

She *wanted* to plunge a knife into him, needed it more than anything else in the world. Well, *nearly* anything else, because if she acted on the fantasy then all those *others* in her diary would get away with what they'd done and that thought was intolerable.

She had to get herself under control, couldn't risk a moment's bleak satisfaction divert from the full fury of her vengeance. Damon didn't deserve to die quickly, no, one day he would suffer and know *she* was the agent of his torment.

Somehow she made it home, but if anyone had seen her that night they would have been terrified. Still wearing coat and heels, she lay on her single bed, stared at the ceiling, barely blinked, hardly breathed and looked for all intents and purposes like a painted corpse. But while her body was in stasis, her mind silently screamed. Once it finished screaming many hours after dawn, she began to plan.

Those hours lying still and silent marked the beginning of a new life and purpose. She now knew what she had to do and although there were many details to finalise, the big picture had focussed. But first, Damon had to atone; not with the full price, but a down payment.

*

She called him at work the following day with a note perfect performance. She was hesitant and added a slight breathlessness to her voice as if on the edge of guilty tears. She explained how things *weren't the same any more* and that she'd started to feel *increasingly distant*. She said sorry a lot, wanted Damon to know it *wasn't his fault*, that he didn't deserve to be dropped like this *by a selfish, spoiled brat*.

He made appropriately sad noises and said accordingly disbelieving replies, but wasn't much of an actor.

In reality she knew Damon was overjoyed, since he'd just been given a parachute to bail out of their relationship with. He could now play the mistreated, jilted boyfriend for all it was worth and had free rein to sleep with whoever he wanted. But then again, he'd obviously been doing that anyway.

It was crucial Damon felt this was a clean break and would never see her again, so he'd be off guard.

Six months passed.

This latest change had been coming since she'd first tried on another personality and enjoyed the fit. Over the years, she'd become "*Anna*," "*The Vamp*," "*The Artist*," and "*The Professional*," but none had set her free, made her happy or accepted.

Drastic action was therefore needed. A wildly different character had to be born, one who would surely become her greatest creation yet. Perhaps even her last, because once that role was fulfilled, where else could she go?

She started to throw away her old life and told the bank she was moving to a (*fictitious*) address far away to start a (*fictitious*) job in freelance accounting. No-one asked any questions and nobody suggested a leaving party.

She started to develop the persona she would inhabit until all this was over. In contrast to her previous efforts, it was painting the Sistine Chapel compared to childish daubs. This new character would be the most radical yet, but the role had to be totally convincing, or all else would fail. It took lots of fine tuning and dress rehearsals at bars and pubs as she tried this *new her* on strangers to see if anyone became suspicious, but nobody did.

Eventually she found a new flat, just as small and pokey as the last, but in a more central location. She took it on in her new name with a cash downpayment and no further questions were asked.

A different person required a distinct wardrobe and she finally settled on a selection of outfits that suited the role. She was still vain enough to enjoy the attention her latest creation attracted. There were appreciative glances in the street and occasional "*phwhooooaaarrrrs*" aimed her way. She'd often give a cheeky wink at her admirers as she strolled past, like an actor acknowledging a standing ovation. She'd always secretly smile whenever sexualised attention like that came her way, but never felt like an object, simply enjoyed the *little victories*.

She cast about for a career that would suit this part. There were a few options that seemed to suit her new personality, but eventually, she attended a training course and discovered with delight her masterpiece was totally suited to this change of profession.

She never gave Father the new address, because there was no point. Most parents would have been distraught if their daughter disappeared but he was probably relieved. That was fine because she'd eventually *get back in touch* and what a family reunion that would be.

New flat, new name, new look, new life, new job.

There was just one thing a previous *self* had to take care of.
Damon.

*

Reoccupying *"The Professional"* hadn't been too difficult. Once her outfit, hair and make up were in place, the character's basic facets were easy to regenerate. She only needed to play her for a little while, so any missing nuances would never be spotted.

So one Saturday morning she became *"The Professional"* again and took the nearest tube to Damon's restaurant. She knew he arrived at around nine thirty and would be alone on the premises.

A builder wolf whistled at her from the top of a ladder. She was used to that, but wasn't in the mood to be objectified today. She glanced about and was delighted to see the road was deserted, so turned on her heels and pushed his ladder away. He squealed on the pavement with limbs at obscene angles, so she laughed and blew him a kiss. As he screamed after her, she accentuated the roll of her hips and looked back over one shoulder, a finger to her lips, *sssssssssh, now, silly boy.*

This is liberating, she giggled. *I will never play this person again so whilst I am her, I can do whatever I want. In another hour or so she will cease to exist. Nobody will ever find her. I could burn this city down and she would never be caught.*

The idea put a spring in her step but she wouldn't act on it. There was too much still to do and prison didn't appeal. Soon enough, she was at the door of Damon's little restaurant.

She played it brilliantly.

He was behind the bar, stocking up. She walked past, did a double take, stepped back to the door and smiled.

"Oh, hello!" she said.

He clearly didn't know how to reply, but her outfit dictated his response just as she'd planned. This was *"The Professional's"* last hurrah and was going out in style.

"Oh, hello, come in," he stared at her body, couldn't help himself.

She pushed open the door.

"How are you?"

"I'm fine. Things are fine." He looked her up and down.

"Good, that's good." She sighed and ran a hand through her hair. "I'm here seeing a friend, but I was kind of hoping you'd be in because I wanted to apologise in person. I know it's been months but what I did was unforgivable. I should have met up with you, told you face to face."

"It's OK, wasn't the first time I've been dumped. I coped."

"Well, I didn't. I keep thinking about it, you didn't deserve what I did. It was selfish and spoiled of me."

"Honestly, don't worry, I've moved on."

"Good, good. Do you mind if I...?" she pulled out a packet of Benson and Hedges.

"No problem. I didn't know you smoked."

"I only just started. *Terrible* habit."

She lit up and slowly walked toward him.

"I hope you don't think this is weird, but I'm not really here to meet a friend. I just wanted to see *you* again."

"Oh, er, good? No, no, it's fine, I appreciate you coming. You don't need to apologise though, people get together, they split up. It happens."

"Mmm, it does."

She leaned on the bar and he bent forward. "I think I owe you something," she purred. "One last intimate moment. What do you think?"

"One last...?"

She put one hand behind Damon's head and ran it through his hair. "Something to remember me by."

She pulled his face towards hers, opened her lips in anticipation and he willingly allowed himself to be drawn.

Then she pushed her lit cigarette into his right eye.

He screamed, fell backwards and grasped at his face.

"I saw you at the Steak House," she snarled. "Yeah, with the waitress. You were having a rare old time so I didn't want to interrupt, thought I'd leave it for a bit and well, goodness me, what do you know, 'a bit' has passed."

He writhed on the floor, hands to his eye.

"You're not who I thought you were, but guess what, *me old china*, I was never who you thought *I* was. All this..." She waved her hands up and down. "None of it exists. I'm fucking smoke, like what's coming out of your eye. And as you've just found out, my darling, smoking is so very, very bad for you."

Damon attempted to speak, but just gurgled.

"Think of me every time you look in the mirror," she hissed. "And every girlfriend you'll ever have will think of me, too. With one eye, you'll never have the same perspective again. This isn't the last time you'll see me, by the way. I'm really looking forward to the next."

She started to sing, spread out her arms and high kicked in time to the words. "We'll...*tah!* Meet again...*tah!* Don't know where...*tah!* Don't know when...*Tah!*"

She giggled, left the restaurant and savoured Damon's cries as they receded behind her. She would miss "*The Professional,*" but everyone retires eventually.

And her new life would be such *fun*.

39 / Thursday 21st May, 1981, London.

Anna stared blankly at the TV. She'd been doing a lot of that over the last few days, watched as 1981 collapsed in on itself.

In the news Peter Sutcliffe, the Yorkshire Ripper, had been found guilty of murder on all counts. The Ripper's defence contended he'd suffered from mental illness and delusions but the jury decided Sutcliffe had faked those conditions to get a lesser sentence.

It seemed like the world was full of actors these days.

The Brixton riots enquiry had begun, although Anna thought that was premature as the riots had more to offer. Israel threatened to attack Lebanon over Syrian missiles but Britain didn't care, because Princess Anne had given birth to a baby girl this week.

However, all headlines were irrelevant between twenty past seven and eight o'clock on Thursday nights, because that was when the BBC's premier music show *Top Of The Pops* enjoyed its weekly party. Anna wasn't invited. Balloons bounced about the screeching audience's novelty-hatted heads as DJ Dave Lee Travis introduced Duran Duran. Travis wore a wacky multicoloured beret while the band were dressed in leather trousers, frilly shirts and earnestness. The singer busied himself with *"careless memories"* and Anna could relate. Her memory wasn't reliable, either.

She remembered Robin Taylor as a nice, normal kind of person. But the more she dug through those surface recollections, the more she found them faulty. What she'd taken as adoration had been intensity and what she'd believed to be devotion was possessiveness. He'd tolerated rather than accepted her friends and in truth hadn't wanted to share her with anybody.

How could I have been so blind? Anna wondered again and again but the question was rhetorical. *I was blind to the contradictions in his personality because I didn't care about him, so didn't even look for any problems.* Over the years, Anna had used her few boyfriends as cover for her own deficiencies and lack of honesty. She'd coasted through their liaisons then cast the men aside once they served no further purpose.

You thought it was just being realistic. But you were selfish, plain and simple, too selfish to go without company, then too selfish to keep it. You're a liar, to him and to yourself. And now look at what's happened, your indifference has come back to bite you.

She'd had offers of tea and sympathy from both Mary Price and Daniel Moore but could only relate to one person right now, and that was her oldest friend, David Walker.

Walker sat on an armchair with some papers next to him. While Anna stared at Top Of The Pops, he waited for Leeding to break her silence. When Duran Duran finished, Dave Lee Travis ran down the chart to reveal Adam And The Ants were *still* number one, *still* standing and delivering.

"I don't mind this actually," said Anna, monotone. "At least it's not Making Your Fucking Mind Up."

"Small mercies," agreed Walker.

She watched Adam and his gang hold up stagecoaches and gatecrash banquets for a while.

"Anna, you really can't blame yourself."

Leeding replied without looking away from the screen. "Really? He called to tell me it was my fault so I think that's pretty clear where the blame lies. I think his exact words were 'my life is ruined because of you'. Yep, pretty unequivocal."

"His life was ruined because of *him*, Anna." He picked up the papers. "Can I please tell you what I found? It will make a difference."

She sighed. "I doubt it. But go on, then, tell me it's all none of my fault and I can go skipping back to work tomorrow."

"Right, as I said, I've done some digging over the last few days, actually, I didn't have to dig too deep." He looked up from the documents. "Didn't you ever think to check him out, you know, before you got too involved?"

She rolled her eyes. "It's the Met, not the bloody Gestapo. That way lies madness and you know it, David. If we start checking out everyone we come into contact with we'd become gibbering paranoiacs and have no friends. We may be police but sometimes, you know, you have to trust people, especially ones you sleep with. So no, I didn't check him out. If I had, what would I have found? A deeply disturbed individual?"

"That was the least of it."

"Am I going to need a drink for this?"

"I think so, yes."

Anna plodded through to the kitchen. "I've got Carlsberg. You want one?"

"Please."

There was a *hiss-fizz* then Leeding reappeared with two cans of lager. "I assume you don't want to bother with a glass?"

"No, I'll take it like a football hoolie, cheers."

She smiled wanly and sat back down. Walker took a deep breath and began.

"First, his name wasn't Robin Taylor. He was born Peter Simons."

"*What?*"

"Mm, lived in Nottingham until...1976, was in a relationship with a girl called Polly Reynolds. They split up, she didn't see him for a few months, got a new boyfriend, then the next thing she knows, he's standing outside her flat every night. Calling up, insulting her. She reported him to the police, they warned him off and he left Nottingham."

Throughout, Anna sat open mouthed. "You're kidding."

"Sadly, no. And that's just the one we know about. I bet there were girls before who got similar treatment but just never reported him. You don't just go from nought to psycho overnight, this is repetitive behaviour. He seemed totally normal, pretty nice until somebody split up with him, then Mr Hyde came out to play."

Anna took a long drink of her lager and whispered, wonderingly, "So I wasn't the first."

"Nope. He was building up to you, building up to, well, what happened. So he left Nottingham and moved to Oxford, where he told people his name was Andrew MacKenzie. Got a job in Radio Rentals where he chatted up an...Andrea Charles. They became an item and guess what?"

"She split up with him."

"Bingo. He'd become too possessive. Once again, he drops off the map until she gets herself a new fella, eight months later. *Eight months*. Then, he pops up like some horrific Jack In The Box, starts appearing at her place of work. She'll be in the pub, turn around and he's on the next table. There's knocking at her door in the middle of the night and she sees him running away. Letters full of pornographic photos are posted to her, with notes explaining how she's just the same as the girls in the pictures. She reports him to the police and he backs off. For a while, anyway."

"Jesus."

"It all comes to a head mid 1978 when she's walking home one evening. He jumps out on Andrea, starts shaking her by the shoulders, screaming in her face. Luckily a member of the public intervenes and he runs off. He's charged with assault, pays a fine, disappears from Oxford. Then I lose trace of him for a bit until he materialises in London, at the flat you knew in Limehouse. He gets a job at HMV in Oxford Street, as you know. And suddenly he's Robin Taylor. Then in 1979 you bump into him at a pub and the rest, well, the rest you know."

"My God. But he seemed so ordinary."

"That's what people like him always seem to be. As we both know damn well, most psychotics aren't frothing at the mouth and carrying axes, most keep their psychoses under the waterline. Look at Sutcliffe. They're human icebergs."

"But suicide?"

"OK. He was extremely unwell, as is obvious. You split with him last October, right? Par for the course, you don't see or hear from him in months, then, somehow, for whatever reason, he gets ideas that you've moved on from him. Who knows? He must have been keeping tabs on you. Perhaps he saw you leave the station with someone or got some kind of idea you were in a relationship."

Anna thought out loud. "Well, he was obviously following me in Whitechapel and must have been outside the Gaylord. But I started getting the nuisance calls before then. No, wait, he sent me the dead flowers first, just after Jeanette West's suicide."

"Well, whatever sparked him off was just part of his breakdown. He was cautioned at work for turning up drunk then back in December last year just after Lennon was shot, he got into an argument with a customer at HMV. Told the guy he laughed when the news broke. The customer gets offended, there's a fight in the album racks and "Robin" is sacked. In January the council get called to his flat in Limehouse after neighbours complain about rubbish piling up outside. Inside it's a tip, he's living in squalor, drinking heavily. So he's removed while they clean the place up and put in a hostel but he makes trouble there too."

Top Of The Pops finished and the sitcom "Are You Being Served" began. Chart music was one thing but canned laughter was another. Anna got up and flicked off the TV.

"So he was heading for some kind of collapse for years. "Robin" was two people. Seemingly well adjusted, charming even, until his ego got challenged when a woman broke up with him. Then when that woman met someone new, or he *perceived* she did, he flipped into this vengeful, possessive, jealous, violent character. I don't want to say it,

Anna, but you were lucky he turned that rage inwards at the end, rather than toward you. It's possible the very last part of his self control stepped in and killed himself rather than you. I know that sounds dramatic but we both know it happens. We've seen the cases."

Anna sat for a while and pondered what might have been. "If I'd known, I *could* have helped him, pointed him in the right direction."

"I don't think he would have listened. You lit the blue touch paper when you split up with him so he was always going to melt down from that moment. So when I say it wasn't your fault, I mean it. You have to accept that. It could have been anyone, it happened to be you. If he'd turned left rather than right at that bar, he would have talked to someone else. You were just unlucky."

"He was nice, he really was."

"No, he was *acting* and you were his co-star but just didn't know he was working to a script."

Then we were both lying, weren't we? Anna had one more question which she didn't want to ask, but had to.

"When he...did it...was there a note?"

Walker coughed and shuffled his papers. "Well, no, not really. So you see…"

"Don't change the subject, what does 'not really' mean? He either did or didn't. Tell me, tell me everything."

Walker sighed. "He hung himself from a pipe on the ceiling at the hostel. Facing him on a table was a photograph of you and a piece of paper." The inspector paused, then went on, quietly. "On it was just one word,"bitch." So…"

For a moment Leeding went to ask another question but Walker got there first. "No, Anna, in black biro, not blue charcoal."

She pictured the scene. When "Robin" self destructed, he'd made a dark little shrine. *The last thing he would have seen was a photo of my face. Robin wanted to stare at me as he died,* she shuddered. *Suicide notes*, she thought suddenly. *Wait. Suicide notes. West's note. Atkey's "WOE IS ME". What is it about them? In fact, what is it about the placing of all the blue charcoal words?*

She recreated the scenes in her mind. West's bedroom, the hit and run, Atkey's kitchen, the professor's hall…She placed the words in their correct places.

Above the bed.

On the pavement.

On the kitchen table.

Hanging above the professor's body.

*"Robin" had placed his note and the photograph of me where he could see them. But the blue charcoal words were...*what *were they?*

She tried approaching the scenes from different angles but couldn't work out what gnawed at her. "Don't think about too much," said Walker from far away. Anna snapped back into the room, the thought lost. "You were *not* to blame."

*

It took Anna a long time to get to sleep. When it finally took her, once again she dreamed of running screaming through the streets, away from her Father.

*

She was back at work the following day. Cases and reports needed her attention, there were many plates to spin and all of them were wobbling.

She looked up from her typewriter to see Lisa Fisher. The WPC was actually wringing her hands. Leeding thought that only happened in Greek tragedies yet here was Fisher doing it for real.

"Are you OK?"

"Yes, ma'am, but are *you*? I hope you don't mind. I know what happened and I'm so sorry."

Anna smiled up at the nervous officer. "Thank you, I appreciate it."

Lisa nodded but didn't move. Anna raised her eyebrows, *and...?*

"If you want to talk about it, I'm here. You know, it's good to talk, especially about things like that. You shouldn't keep them in. So what I'm saying is, I'm around, if you want to have a drink, or a cup of coffee, or, you know, anything."

"That's very kind, Fisher. Lisa. I think I've done all the talking I want to for now but I'd like that, I'd like that very much. So, yes, perhaps. Let me think about it."

"Of course."

"It happened to me, too," she said quietly.

"Happened? What happened?"

"An ex killed themselves. It wasn't because of me, I don't think. He had issues, all kinds of issues I didn't know about. He kept it all in then suddenly, I suppose couldn't keep it in any more...Jumped off a building. So, I know, you see. I know where you are right now."

"Oh God, Lisa, I'm sorry."

"Thank you. So I've been where you are and if you like, I could go back there to that time, talk about it."

"Thank you. If you're all right with that. Yes, let's talk. I think it would be helpful."

Fisher's eyes grew wet and she turned away before her face collapsed.

The WPC had *almost* told Anna the truth.

Almost, but not quite.

40 / 15th June 1981, London.

June had already been a good month for Damon Whitehill. He'd bet on a horse called Shergar at the Epsom Derby and it had romped home *ten lengths* in front of the nearest competition.

Then Damon opened his very first "D's Pizzeria" in Scotland, which brought the chain up to twenty-six outlets. The restaurant's opening party was full of attractive women and he'd "persuaded" one to join him for the night. The vodka he'd secretly topped her drink up with had helped in that regard.

He'd appeared on the front cover of June's "Investor's Review Magazine" holding a *huge* slice of Margherita. The headline read, "Damon Whitehall; Pizza's Very Big Cheese!" which made him laugh a lot. Shares in "D's Pizzeria Ltd" had risen by nine percent in the last few weeks which meant another excuse for celebrations and liaisons.

Last Thursday the Queen had opened the new Natwest Tower in the City Of London. Damon was a VIP guest and the party had carried on *way* past bankers' bedtimes. A rather regal Lady Someone-Or-Other had caught Whitehill's eye and he'd "persuaded" her back to his eight bedroom home in Putney.

Whitehill could be *very* persuasive.

A couple of days later a fame seeking teenager had shot at the Queen in Horse Guard's Parade. Thankfully his gun was only a starting pistol and the boy was quickly disarmed by members of the Scots Guards.

Damon had seen opportunity in crisis; he'd offered free pizza for life to the heroic guardsmen involved and put up their pictures in the new Glasgow branch of "D's Pizzeria". That had made the papers in Scotland and given him no end of free publicity.

God Bless Her Majesty and disturbed teenagers with guns, he'd thought.

That same day National Front skinheads had clashed with black kids in Coventry. Ironically, an anti racist concert by the band The Specials had also taken place. The Coventry branch of "D's Pizzeria" was wrecked and photographs of the smashed restaurant appeared in every paper, a symbol of British success brought to heel by thugs. Once again it was almost a free advertising campaign; when the name "D's Pizza" is on every front page the price of a few broken windows faded into nothing.

Damon knew his real genius wasn't mozzarella and tomato but the ability to spot opportunities, whether practical, financial or sexual. So if Britain wanted to tear itself apart he'd cheer from the sidelines with a cheese grater in one hand and share certificates in the other.

For once he was alone this Monday night. He didn't enjoy his own company and preferred to jump from one West End hotspot to another; Stringfellows in Covent Garden, The Talk Of The Town in Charing Cross, maybe even one of Soho's new "cooler" clubs where the kids hung out. But tonight he was tired after a weekend's celebrations. The Queen and skinheads had made him a lot of profits last week and the party just hadn't stopped.

It was a hot evening so he'd spent an hour in his outdoor swimming pool then relaxed poolside with a jug of sangria.

Damon rubbed his ruined eye. Normally he wore a patch, which had become his trademark and given him a rakish, piratical air that certainly worked on some women. Whitehill supposed he should thank *her* for that, but *in every crisis find an opportunity* had become his motto.

Damon would never forget the morning she'd walked back into his first restaurant. He hadn't seen her since she dumped him and for a few exciting moments he'd thought they were going to bed. But then there was *fire* inside his skull and he'd collapsed in exquisite agony. She'd spoken to him but the pain had dulled her words. It was *something* about meeting again but that had never happened.

Then she'd disappeared off the face of the earth. The police contacted her employer for a forwarding address but discovered the road she'd given didn't exist and her name was false, too.

As his personal fortune grew and money became no object, Damon had hired private detectives, but they'd turned up precisely zero. She'd ceased to exist.

Damon really, *really* wanted to meet her again. He had it all planned; eventually, one of his detectives would find her, then he'd have the bitch drugged and brought here to a basement very few people saw.

He'd have her tied to the metal table there and then blind her right eye with the same method she'd used on him.

But that wasn't all. He intended to slowly ruin her beauty and force the bitch to watch in a mirror with her one remaining eye. He'd imagined the process many times, relished the idea of reducing her femininity to a twitching pile of screaming flesh. The Bible spoke of an eye for an eye, but he didn't like that trade. Damon only dealt in profit and he would take more than she ever did. Their happy reunion would come, he was sure of it. So with a drunken smile on his face Damon Whitehill fell asleep by his pool.

*

"Wake up. Ooh-ooh, wake up, fu-u-u-cker."

Somebody lightly slapped Damon's face. He came to on his sun lounger, but no, he surely wasn't awake, because the world had become very strange indeed.

Damon's mouth was covered and his arms and legs were immobile. But that wasn't the most terrifying aspect of this awful dream. It had conjured *her* up from his past.

She leaned over him, dressed almost identically to the morning he'd been blinded. Despite the passing of years she still looked young and beautiful. "You know what they used to say in the Music Hall, Damon? *Heeeeere we are again!* And here *we* are again, so come on darling, I don't have all night. *I'mmmmmmabusybusybusybusy* girl, so wake up, you fucker."

"Mmmm, mm-mmm," he tried to speak, but she held a knife to his face.

"No, no, *nooooooo*, you don't speak, I do the talking. You try to speak and I'll put out your other eye, do you understand?"

Damon began to moan as he realised this really was happening, *right now*.

"Sssh, shhh, don't be a baby. You really should pay more attention, I've been hidden here in your garden for hours." She yawned theatrically. "*Soooo* bo-ring. I slipped something strong into your sangria when you went inside, maybe too much, if I'm honest. I didn't expect you to be out this long, but hey, I'm in no hurry and neither are you."

He tried to fix her with a look of pure hatred from his one good eye, but she just laughed. "Ooh, scary." She held her thumb and forefinger a tiny distance apart. "*This* scary, actually. I'm not afraid of you and especially not afraid of somebody strapped to their sun lounger."

Damon looked down and saw his hands and feet were tied to the lounger's tubular construction with soft wool. Its bright colour looked incongruous.

"No bruising, see? Can't have any bruising, no evidence that I was ever here." She tut-tutted. "You know, I nearly didn't choose you. I had a rare moment of leniency, thought that perhaps sticking a fag in your eye was more than enough punishment for cheating on me with a seventeen year old. Seventeen! Bit old for you, wasn't she? You were so close to living your life and never seeing me again. Do you like the look, by the way?"

She rotated on the spot to show off her outfit and gave a scarily accurate impression of Bruce Forsyth. "Give us a twirl, give us a twirl, Anthea!" she laughed. "Good game! Good game! I kept the whole shebang for old times' sake, thought I'd bring back *The Professional* for one night only. That's what I called the character you knew, *"The Professional."* That's right, she was just a character I played, made of a bunch of signs and signals that really pushed your buttons. But even though I stitched her together like a Savile Row suit, a perfect fit just for Damon, she still wasn't enough, hmm? You had a roving eye and then *literally* had a roving eye, singular. Let no-one say I don't think about those kinds of details. I like to find a poetry in pain, sonnets in screams, verse in viciousness and yes, I did work *very* hard on that line. But hey-hey-hey, what do you say, *The Professional* is here, just for you! Brought out of retirement for one last performance, *Laydeeeeez and Gennellemen*, I thank you, I thank you!" She curtseyed and waved to an imaginary theatre. "Looks good, doesn't she? Nice to see her again, is it?"

She lit up a cigarette and pulled over a plastic chair.

Damon struggled with his ties. "Mmm! Mm, mm, mmm!"

She put a hand to her ear, pantomime style. "I can't *heeeeeaaar* you," she singsonged. "So don't even try. Yes, you were so nearly off the hook but I thought I'd better do some digging, just in case. In my line of work I have all kinds of contacts, you know. People tell me all sorts, mostly rumours about girls of a certain age. Nothing anyone could really pin on you, 'cos money keeps lips shut, doesn't it, or in your case, gets them open. I had a little look around your pad, Damon. *Jesus*, I don't even want to know what you do and who you do it to down there in your basement. But here's the good news, by tomorrow, the whole world will know what a despicable excuse for a human being you are."

He started to screech and she held the knife up to his face again.

"What's that? I can only imagine you're offering me money to be quiet. No can do, Damon old chap, no can do. Or wait…No, I know what you're trying to say. I bet that basement of yours was all set for a special guest one day and might that special guest be me? Tell the truth and it might set you free. Were you planning on giving *me* the treatment down there? The truth, if you please."

He nodded, slowly.

"Good, that's good, and possibly the first time you've told the truth in a very long while. So here we are and while I'd love to sit and jaw-jaw, it would be a bore-bore. I have somewhere to be and you do, too. Your friends will be so puzzled when the news breaks. 'Oooh, he was such a strong swimmer' they'll say, but the police will find excess alcohol and sleeping tablets in your system then conclude that must have been it." She put a hand to her forehead and swooned like a silent movie actress. "Oh, what a tragic accident."

Damon's body convulsed as he tried to free himself from the lounger.

"So handy these things are on wheels, isn't it?" She began to push him toward the pool. "What was that? They'll know someone did it when they find your body tied to this chair? Honestly, Damon, did you think I'm that stupid? Once your lungs are full of water and no longer fit for purpose, I'll cut you loose and leave you floating. Face up, or face down? You know, I haven't thought that far ahead, I was just going to enjoy the drowning. But face down, I think, *so* undignified."

He squealed and shook but couldn't extricate himself from the bonds.

"Well, then," she sighed, "think about the upside. Your entire pizza chain will go under and your name will be mud, for ever and after. I have performed a great and honourable service tonight and one day the world will know my name. When I said *upside* I meant for me, of course."

She began to tip the sun lounger toward the dark water. "Isn't this exciting?" she giggled. "What was it Peter Pan said? 'To die will be an awfully big adventure'? Well, that adventure starts right now for you. Do enjoy it, I'm almost jealous. Only *almost*, mind. "

She pushed him in.

It took a few minutes for the bubbles to stop rising but she left it a few more just in case and then got busy with blue charcoal. She was in no hurry.

41 / 17th June 1981, London.

When the body of Damon Whitehill was discovered all hell broke loose. The nationally famous businessman's death revealed him to be a sexual predator with very specific tastes.

After Whitehill had failed to answer the phone or attend business meetings, police were called to his Putney home where they found him floating face down in the swimming pool.

But that shock was quickly usurped by the contents of his basement. Today's newspapers squawked with excitement because the story had everything; fame, money, sex, scandal and death, a perfect storm for any headline writer. *Everybody* knew Whitehill, who stood alongside other self made British business icons like Richard Branson, Clive Sinclair and Alan Sugar. He'd played up to his public image as a playboy but clearly that had been a front to hide the darker side of his sexuality.

This case was under the jurisdiction of Wandsworth police, so Anna read the latest developments in today's Telegraph. "*Under-age images*" had been found, which translated to child pornography. The papers used a code which allowed them to report the most salacious details under cover of prissy Middle England prose. The basement was full of "*curious sexual implements*" and "*abnormal sexual devices*". Damon was portrayed as enjoying "*unusual erotic practices*" and took his pleasure from "*young victims and paid participants*". Anna was amazed he'd got away with it for so long, but knew some men walked between the rain drops and never got wet, no matter how hard the downpour.

Of course she'd heard rumours and hearsay was helpful to a point, because it lit distant flares which got your attention. But once you got closer, those flames were often revealed to be damp squibs. Bizarrely, fame helped; the bigger the name the more likely people were reluctant to believe there could be a rotten core. Some celebrities were part of Britain's cultural landscape and therefore everyone was complicit. *If we can't spot a predator right in the middle of the herd, what chance do we have?* Most people were content to look the other way. Anna knew of *at least* one nationally famous DJ and children's presenter whose young sexual predilections were whispered about, but nobody ever came forward and so the whispers stayed just that.

But *Damon Whitehill!* How many families had eaten in his restaurants, how many kids had posed with Pizza Pete, "The Friendly Slice Of Happiness"?

1981, she mused, *a surprise round every corner and we're only half way through.*

"You're reading the wrong paper," Inspector Walker placed a copy of The Daily Mail on Anna's desk.

"And you're reading the *right* one? Never had you down for a Mail man."

"I'm not, I nicked this off Charlie in the canteen."

The Mail's headline read "MILLIONAIRE SUICIDE SEX SCANDAL".

"Wow," said Leeding. "They managed to use all their favourite words on one page."

"Uh huh. Papers love the word 'scandal' don't they? As if they're somehow whiter than white."

"They *are* whiter than white. The only coloured people on Fleet Street are the cleaners."

The byline read, "PIZZA BOSS SEX SHAME DEATH".

"Well done Daily Mail. 'Sex' twice on one front cover just in case we didn't get it first time, oh, and a *colour* photo. Goodness, they're pushing the boat out today." Papers rarely used colour photographs but this was a real scoop. Somehow one of the Mail's snappers had peered over the tall bushes which surrounded Whitehill's garden.

The picture showed police officers at the edge of his pool in bright sunlight with the title, "WHERE HE WAS FOUND". The water reflected blue sky and it almost looked idyllic, except for a black dot on the surface which the paper had placed to cover Damon's floating corpse. "*We have obscured Mr Whitehill's body to avoid any distress,*" explained the Mail. The journalist theorised Damon had been so consumed by shame and self loathing that he'd taken his own life.

Anna looked up at Walker. "It's a mess, isn't it? But you know, I have The Sun, so I don't really need to read the story in stereo."

"Yes, but The Sun doesn't have this photo."

"I've seen enough bodies, David, I'm not some newspaper reader who gets a thrill from death."

"It's not the body I wanted to show you."

He produced a magnifying glass from his jacket pocket and Anna giggled. "Elementary, my dear Walker."

The inspector didn't laugh. "Look on the wall behind the body."

She frowned, took the glass and stared at the photo. "Oh my God."

"Uh huh. Oh my God."

Written in blue on the wall, barely visible, was the word **LOVING**.

"I thought it was an interesting coincidence. Should we tell the boys in Putney?"

"Oh my God," Anna repeated. "No, no, don't tell anyone anything, it could blow up in our faces."

"That's what I thought. So I called a mate at Wandsworth station, ostensibly to arrange a drinks night out for my birthday, which is next week, don't forget."

"I didn't. Go on."

"So I pretended to be interested in the latest, did a little digging, nothing too obvious just, you know, officer to officer gossip."

"Please tell me you did't mention the writing."

"Of course I didn't, not least because I'm still unconvinced there's actually anything concrete going on. And this…" he tapped the paper, "…hasn't changed my mind. So, no witnesses, nobody sees or hears anything unusual. First reports say Whitehill had a lot of alcohol in his body plus some under the counter sleeping tablets which they found on the table next to his jug of drink. The Daily Mail may be right, he could have topped himself or just misjudged his capacity for drink and drugs, went for a dip and…glug, glug, glug."

"*Glug glug glug?* Remind me not to ask you to deliver my eulogy."

"There were more tablets in his basement so the thinking is he used them to make his victims compliant."

"Has anyone come forward? Any women?"

"Not as yet but you know how these things play out. People like Whitehill get away with it because of the shame. Victims think *they* are responsible somehow, they're ashamed, bury the ordeal. I'd imagine most of them don't even remember it if they were drugged up."

"So if you don't think this has anything to do with West, Atkey and the rest, why show me?"

"Because there's a very slim chance it might. And even if there's the smallest possibility then you should know about it."

Anna examined the photograph again then opened a drawer and pulled out a file. "I keep this handy just in case, and this feels like a 'just in case.'" Leeding found a photocopied sheet. "I know West's suicide note by heart, but listen, '*I resisted so long, but I couldn't go on like I have before. People have used me, judged me, abused me simply because of my sex. I can't bear to be in this body any more, as I can't bear what people have done to me over the years.'"*

"I know where you're going."

"So we have the possibility this note *wasn't* written by West. Just go with it, humour me, OK? And *maybe* the writer is the same person who's left blue charcoal words at death scenes. The author of the note talks about being abused because of their sex. Well, that's what Damon Whitehill's stock in trade was; abuse." Anna's head tick-tocked left to right and she blinked five times. "So what if all those people, West, Martin, Atkey, Birch, Whitehill, what if they were all part of some ring of abusers? And this person…"

"This *possible* person," corrected Walker.

"This *possible* person is killing them one by one as revenge?" She sighed and threw up her hands. "Ah, listen to me. I sound insane."

"I'm afraid you do." Walker ticked off points on his fingers. "No witnesses to anything strange at any of the cases. Reverend Martin was the only death that we could link to an external suspect and even that's probably a drunk hit and run. We've found nothing inconsistent with suicide or accident, and I bet we could dig forever and find zero contact between these so-called "victims". The only thing you have are letters to West from "Sarah," whoever she is, and fingerprints on those same letters that *might* match some on Jeanette's windowsill."

"I know, I know. But what about that, huh?" She stabbed her finger at the blue writing on Whitehill's wall, **LOVING.**

"Anna," said Walker gently. "I showed you this because I didn't want you finding it for yourself and jumping to those conclusions alone. I admit it's extremely weird but go *one inch* below the surface and it all collapses into nothing."

She nodded. "OK, but you agree we should still try to find "Sarah" if only to eliminate her from the enquiry?"

"Of course," he replied reluctantly.

"I'll keep this if I may," Anna held up The Daily Mail. "You never know."

"No, you don't."

He stood by her desk a while longer and eventually spoke up. "Do you want to go out later? Have a drink, talk about things?"

"By 'things' you mean Robin, I'm guessing."

"Well, anything you like."

"That's very kind, but maybe another day. I'm already booked up tonight."

She saw the disappointment on his face and wondered why it was so obvious."How about Friday?" she asked.

He brightened immediately. "Friday is good for me."

"Then it's good for me."

David smiled and walked away.

Anna turned back to the paper and tapped her nails on the photograph.

Why can't I drop this? Is it because there's still something I'm missing, something staring me in the face? What is it about these words, these artworks? Something connects them, I can feel it. Something so obvious yet I can't grab it. If I can, I know this will all open up to me.

She riffled through her file and found photographs of the various words found at the scenes. *Maybe coincidence, but* two *people having almost identical art works above their bodies? And another* three *with similar words near theirs?*

Still nothing presented itself.

Wait, whoah, wait. Art works. Art works. *If I could identify the artist behind these, might that open doors? Who do I know that's into art?*

Mary Price.

Mary Price, pathologist, occasionally wrote art criticism for the Sunday Times.

Any excuse to meet up with Mary and this is a very good excuse.

It looked like Anna Leeding was going to have a very sociable few days.

*

At seven that evening Anna walked into the Horse And Groom pub opposite the BBC. WPC Lisa Fisher waited at a corner table.

"I took the liberty of ordering you a pint. You drank pints at the Gaylord, so…"

"Thanks, that's great. Can we go into the back bar? It's nicer, snug."

"Of course." Fisher and Leeding picked up their pints and walked through to the pub's back room. There were a few stares from the mostly male clientele but the bar's proximity to the BBC meant customers were generally a little more liberal. It would be unusual to get a wolf whistle in here.

Fisher still wore her white police blouse and black skirt but had changed into a denim jacket, so looked like just another secretary out after work.

"Thanks for meeting up like this," said Anna.

"That's OK, I hope I can help."

"Let's not get into that quite yet, if it's OK."

"Of course."

So the two women sat and chatted about everything and nothing. The Damon Whitehill case was covered ("world's better off without him, sick pervert" was Fisher's sum up) and Lisa's tenure so far at Great Portland Street. They compared notes on their past histories which both involved dull desk jobs that led to a desire for more excitement and responsibility. They talked of riots and royals, frilly shirts, dandy highwaymen, how *crazy* 1981 had already been, and laughed a lot. But after a couple of drinks Anna told Fisher about the Marble Arch incident in 1964 and how it had made her extremely reluctant to make assumptions. That in turn led to a reappraisal of the bare facts behind the possibility a murderer was behind the blue charcoal words. Leeding had brought some relevant files and photos in case the subject came up.

"Inspector Walker remains unconvinced," Anna sighed.

"Well, it's good to have dissent, someone to keep asking questions. For what it's worth I think there *is* something to it, but what, I have no idea. I mean, at first glance it's *possible* "Sarah" had been abused by Whitehill, but by all the rest of the 'victims'? Unlikely."

"I know."

Throughout the conversation, Anna found her gaze drawn to a RESERVED sign on the next table. It faced the front of the pub so guests who'd booked would know where to sit, but Leeding didn't know why she'd become fixated on it.

"So how are you feeling about things now?" asked Fisher, once all other conversational avenues had been explored. "It's been a couple of weeks. How are you?"

"I go round and round it in my head, wondering what I could have done differently, you know, like Marble Arch in 1964. Should I have realised it was Robin calling? But why would I? It had been months since we split and what could I have done anyway? Had him arrested? Sectioned? What for? I didn't know anything was wrong until the very last moment of his life and by then it was too late."

"Mm-mm," Fisher let Anna talk. They both lit cigarettes and Leeding felt the weight lift just a little from her shoulders.

"It was the same with mine." Lisa took a deep drag of her B&H and Anna noticed her hand shook. "He was a little intense at times, but nothing that made me suspicious. This was in 1977. I was so young, he was a few years older, so I think I was flattered, actually. More flattered than in love if I'm honest. He seemed worldly wise, like my guide to a whole new world. He helped me find myself, find who I really was. I owe him that at the every least."

"I have a friend like that, Mary. You should meet her, you'll like Mary, she's a piss taker."

"Yeah, I like piss takers," Fisher smiled. "But here's the thing. While he helped me discover *myself*, he still wasn't happy with who and what *he* was, couldn't live in his own skin. Isn't that funny? Well, funny peculiar rather than funny ha-ha. Maybe he was living vicariously through me, you know, his young protégé. I was happy with who I was, but he hated it, was in conflict with himself. Did I love him? No, I adored him, admired him, wanted to be like him, but ultimately, that wasn't enough. I didn't love him, not really. I know that now."

"I never loved Robin. I don't think I loved any of them, actually."

"It happens. So, from what I could piece together later, we spent the night together at his high rise near Islington. He worked for the council sorting people's homes out, so he turfed me out first thing, said he had work to do before he went into the office. That was weird because he'd never done that before. And you know as I left, he called my name. I turned round and he sort of looked me up and down, like he was fixing me in his head. That's what it felt like, or maybe I'm retrospectively fitting that to the memory. He said, 'thank you,' I asked what for, he just smiled and said, 'well, you know.' I nodded, but I *didn't* know and I still don't. Then I left. About thirty minutes later he swan dived out of his window. No warning, no hints, no nothing."

"Jesus."

"I wondered exactly the same things you're thinking about now. Could I have done anything differently? Should I have noticed? Could I have helped?"

"Probably not. Both your fella and Robin were too far down that road."

You've never mentioned his name, Fisher, Anna suddenly thought. *That's your right, it's painful, but not to even say his name? Does this go even deeper than you're making out?*

As truthful as they were being together, Anna couldn't bring herself to ask why that was the case. They talked for a while about their shared experience, which was cathartic for Leeding, but she still felt her eyes drift to the RESERVED sign. Fisher followed her gaze.

"I noticed you look over there a couple of times. What is it?"

"I'm not sure," Anna replied. There was another event from her past she wanted to tell Fisher about, but couldn't, not tonight. Very few people knew about it and they were old, trusted friends. Leeding got up from her table and walked back a few steps. Lisa watched, intrigued.

Anna faced the table with its RESERVED sign and began to talk to herself.

"So, think about it. That sign faces outward, so people who booked the table and bar staff can see it, right?"

Fisher nodded, but knew the question wasn't directed at her.

"It wouldn't make any sense to face it the other way, to the back of the pub. It wouldn't fulfil its function facing that direction. The people *behind* aren't meant to see it. The people in front *are*."

Anna's head tick-tocked and she blinked five times. Leeding sat back down and finally engaged Fisher directly.

"When Robin killed himself he put a photo of me on his table, with a note that said, 'bitch.'"

"Oh God, I didn't know. That's awful."

"But the point is, the note and photo was where Robin could see it, right?"

She rooted through her file and pulled out a photograph from Atkey's suicide. It showed the WOE IS ME suicide note propped on the table, where it faced the kitchen wall. "You were there, right? So did you spot anything unusual about this?"

"Well, it was a suicide and that's unusual enough, I suppose."

"The pub's RESERVED sign is placed where people can see it. *Face out.* But look at Atkey's note, look where it's placed. Think about it."

She demonstrated with a napkin. "Look, I'm Nick Atkey. I place my suicide note on the table, but either facing *me* or facing the door where it will be seen by the first person to enter, like that RESERVED sign. But look at this."

She indicated the photograph of Atkey's blue charcoal note. "It's facing the *kitchen wall*. It's on the table, propped up, *facing the kitchen wall*. Why? Why, if you're going to kill yourself, would you go to the trouble of propping up your note facing a bloody wall?"

"Well, he was obviously disturbed, so he'd be acting irrationally."

Anna waved away the suggestion and pulled out the other photographs from the scenes. "Look at the placing of all these words compared to where the bodies lay. They're arranged to be seen from a certain angle. *They're not meant for us*. If Atkey had intended his note for whoever found him, it would have faced the *door*, not the *wall*. And it wouldn't need to be propped up, either. His table was low because he was in a wheelchair, so anyone could have just looked down and seen it straight away. Let's be honest, blue charcoal stands out."

Fisher began to nod. "The words weren't for us to find. They're for…the killer to enjoy?"

"Uh huh. Like a tableau. Posed."

She found the photo of West's suicide scene. "I knew this looked weird. Too perfect, too dramatic, too *suicidal*. At first, I thought that's because Jeanette wanted to go out looking like a painting, you know, vanity kills and all that. But if the suicide note wasn't written by West, then *it's part of the image*. These are staged scenes and the words are part of the backdrop."

"But why? Why stage them?"

"Because they're art, Lisa. Because they're *art*."

*

By ten p.m. Anna and Lisa decided that enough was enough and went their separate ways. Leeding weaved her way back to Tottenham Court Road feeling light headed, but also lighter hearted. The evening had been surprisingly helpful but also comfortably enjoyable. Fisher had proven to be insightful in both Robin's death and the possibility blue charcoal may be more than a coincidence. But most of all Anna felt like she'd made a friend.

She returned to her flat ten minutes later, went straight to the phone and dialled with a purpose.

"Price." Mary Price always answered as if demanding the cost of something.

"Mary, it's me."

"Anna, dear. Goodness, bit late, isn't it?"

"I know, I just wanted to ask a favour."

"Oh, get straight to it, why don't you? How about starting with 'sorry to interrupt your evening, but how are you? Haven't spoken in ages, are you OK?' How about starting with that?"

"Yes, sorry. To be honest, I'm a little bit drunk. How are you, sorry to interrupt your evening, er, what was the other stuff you wanted me to say?"

Mary laughed. "Drunk? I'm jealous. I've spent the night watching a dreadful Nevil Shute drama with a cup of tea. Me, not Nevil. Please tell me you weren't drinking alone."

"No, out with a work colleague," Anna slurred. "She's very nice, I think you'd like her. In fact, I mentioned you."

"I'm flattered. But you mentioned a favour, which would imply sadly that this isn't just a drunk social call."

"Well, I've got a lot to tell you about. Not all of it good," she trailed off.

"Oh dear. Well, I'm here, I'm comfy, talk away."

"No, in person would be best, but I'd like your advice, regarding art."

"Art? Well, that makes a nice change from corpses. This is becoming ever more intriguing, is your art query work related or just aesthetic?"

"Work. I need to show you a couple of pieces, see if you know who the artist is."

"*Very* intriguing. What kind of art is it? What style?"

"Modern, I think. Pop art? I don't know, not my field."

"Not really mine, either, but I'll try my best. What do they look like?"

Anna went to light a cigarette but dropped it. "Balls."

"It's pictures of *balls*?"

"No. Ha, no. I just dropped my fag. Look, I'll pop some copies of the pictures over to you. Then can we meet? I'll tell you all my news, maybe Saturday lunch?"

"That I would like very much. Shall we say Avella's again? Saturday at twelve thirty?"

"That's a date."

"Wonderful. Send me the pictures and I'll see if I know the artist responsible."

"Thank you. Ta-ta, Mary."

"Ta-ta, Anna dear."
Leeding slept dreamlessly that night.

42 / 20th June 1981, London.

Brrrrrnnng. Brrrrrrnnng. Brrrrrrnnng.

"Anna Leeding, hello?"

"Anna, dear, bingo, full house."

It was early Saturday morning. Leeding wore a dressing gown and a confused expression.

"Mary?"

"Yes, dear, are we still on for today? Twelve thirty? Avella's?"

"Yes. Sorry, what does 'bingo' mean?"

"Bingo means bingo, dear. I received the art works you wanted me to identify. Alas, as suspected, they're not really my field or my taste. Simply writing, "FACE" and "GO" doesn't really float my boat, isn't that what the young people say?"

"*Young people?*" Anna laughed. "You sound like a pensioner."

"The ripe old age of forty feels like one, dear. So I hope you don't mind but I showed them to a few friends here and there. Friends who are a lot more knowledgable than I on that particular style. I'm incredibly interested to know why you want to identify the artist, by the way. Am I going to be party to that information or is it all a case of keeping Mum?"

"No, I'll tell you what it's about when we meet. So what does 'bingo' mean?"

"*Bingo* means *bingo* means *I have an answer.* After a few non starters, one old chum thinks she recognises the work. Would it be dreadfully forward of me if I invited her to come for lunch? It's easier if she explains everything to you face to face."

"Of course. But can she come for one thirty? I'd like to speak with you privately first."

"*In-tri-guing.*"

"See you at twelve thirty, then."

"You will."

*

Anna sat in the back room of Avella's cafe off Regent Street. Tony the owner clattered about as DJ Steve Wright blared from a tinny transistor. "Here's 'Ghost Town,' the brand new forty-five from The Specials," said Wright. "Middle of June and they've already got their Hallowe'en single out. Blimey, that's what I call getting ahead of yourself."

The music was eerie and downbeat as the singer crooned about how his once vibrant home town had become empty and forgotten. It was very different to the fixed smile pop Radio One normally force fed the nation and Anna considered "Ghost Town" far more representative of Britain than the New Romantics. The single pulsed with brooding threat, similar to the feeling on London's streets. Anna sensed the capital was preparing to burn again and the city jittered with negative potential. The Specials sang of how bands didn't play any more and fighting on the dance floor.

Forget "Ice Age," this is the real *soundtrack of 1981*, she thought.

The Specials faded away as reverb swamped singers repeated the title and became ghostly themselves. Then it was business as usual on Radio One as a falsetto Smokey Robinson told the listener the only important thing in his life was 'being with you'.

"There she is!" boomed a familiar voice. Anna didn't quite recognise the woman it came from.

"What do you think?" Mary Price shook her hair and did a little twirl. Price's shoulder length white-blonde style had become a pitch black Sally Bowles bob.

"You dyed your hair?"

"No, it went black overnight through shock. Of course I dyed my hair. Well, the hairdresser did. What do you think? Be honest, but not too honest, there's a dear."

"Well, it's very now."

"That's what I thought. The young people have all gone a bit Weimar Republic, which as you know, is my favourite pre-dictatorship era, so I thought I'd join them."

"Well, it's a bit of a shock, but I like it. I do. Honest, I do."

"Tch, you sound like you're trying to persuade yourself. I just fancied being someone else for a bit, you know, compare and contrast. *Do* blondes have more fun? Or will I be enticed by the dark side? I intend to find out."

Tony the owner brought in a cup of tea for Mary and she sat down.

"Right, you first. What have you been up to since we last met? That was April, wasn't it?" She lightly slapped Anna's wrist. "Too long, dear, far too long. So tell me everything. Work, love, life, everything."

Anna decided to tell Mary about Robin's death first. Price was appalled and upset for her friend, "But you never should have been with him in the first place," was her eventual conclusion. Mary offered some advice from her own life and they moved on to current affairs, work and gossip.

Eventually Leeding talked Price through her suspicion that a run of recent deaths and suicides may have been murders.

Once Anna finished, Mary looked very pleased with herself. "Well, what I've found will be of very great interest, I think."

"Really? How?"

"I'll let someone else explain that."

Anna laid out photographs of the blue charcoaled words and Mary flicked through them. "Well, as I say, these mean nothing to me, not my area. But that's why I showed them to a few others. No joy there, either. Then I remembered Helen Thompson, who was very high up at the Royal College Of Art a few years back, still lectures around the country. I thought if anyone could recognise the artist behind these, it's Helen."

"I don't mean to be rude, but couldn't you just give me the artist's name? Why does, er, Helen, have to come here in person?"

"Because in light of your suspicions, what she has to say is now *very* interesting and much better from the horse's mouth, as it were. Can we order a sandwich or something? I'm starving."

*

Helen Thompson arrived at one thirty. She was in her seventies and instantly identifiable as somebody with an "arty" side. Long grey hair tumbled about her shoulders and she wore a rainbow patterned muumuu.

"Mary, darling!" she shouted. "Goodness, look at your *hair*. It looks wonderful. I wish I had the bravery to do something like that but I fear I am far too long in the tooth, or short in the tooth, since mine are false."

"Helen! Lovely to see some colour in an otherwise dull world. This is my friend Anna who's interested in the provenance of the art I sent you."

Helen took a seat and a few pleasantries were exchanged. Price and Thompson gossiped for a while then got to business.

"I met Helen at a gallery opening back in 1975, I think it was. Hit it off immediately."

"Difficult not to hit it off with Mary isn't it?"

Anna had to agree on that score. Eventually, Helen looked down at the photographs on the table. "So you want to know who's responsible for these? I won't ask why, Mary said mum's the word and all that, but I'll tell you what I *do* know."

"Do you mind if I take notes?" Anna asked.

"Of course not. I'm rather used to people taking notes when I speak, it comes with the territory. Now I can't guarantee the person I'm going to tell you about is the same artist responsible for these, but it's possible. So, this happened back in the early or mid sixties, I can't be sure of the exact date. I was at the Royal College Of Art and we had open days for potential students to look around. We held loads of them, which is why the dry old brain can't quite pinpoint this particular one, sorry about that. But I remember the day very well, because Professor Birch was so beastly."

Anna looked up from her notes in shock. "Professor Birch? *Paul Birch?*"

"Yes, he died recently, didn't he? What was it, a fall? Can't say I'm surprised. I know one shouldn't speak ill of the dead but he was a lush and, I'm sorry to say, a very unlikeable man; pompous, condescending, an arse, if you'll excuse my Middle English. Oh, he was an expert in his field, I'll give him that, and his Picasso biography was exceptionally well done but my goodness, he knew it. Are you all right, dear? You look a little pale."

Anna waved a hand over her face. "It's a little hot."

"It is. Shall I get you a water?"

"No, it's fine. Please, go on." Anna looked at the art work that had hung over Birch's body, **GO**. She flashed back to the scene and pictured his twisted corpse. "You were talking about an open day."

"Yes. Paul had been drinking, as was his wont. Anyway, this girl came in, quite shy, a little dowdy as I remember. Glasses. It's a bit hazy, as you can imagine. We are talking about fifteen years ago, maybe more. So she showed us her work and well, Paul was in one of his regular patronising moods so just completely wiped the floor with her, poor lass, totally deconstructed the work. Again, I can't recall the details but I do remember feeling just *awful* for her. I tried to find positives but Paul was having none of it. I can picture the look on her face, she looked utterly destroyed. But what I *do* remember in detail was her work, all blue charcoal. Some of it was expressionist, some still life, landscapes, all in this monochrome blue. But she also had lots of works that were just single words in the middle of paper, like these."

Oh dear God, thought Anna. *I feel sick.*

Helen picked up the photos of the framed works from West and Birch's homes, **FACE** and **GO**.

"So when Mary sent them over I immediately thought back to that day. It never left me, Birch's withering appraisal of the girl and all that blue, all those words. Now I can't obviously say for certain these are by the same person, but I haven't seen anything like them before or since. It is a very distinct style."

"How old was she?"

"Oh, again, time hasn't been kind, but she could have been anything from, say, sixteen, seventeen, to her mid twenties. I can't be clearer than that. She wore a hat but her hair was bright blonde, similar colour to yours, actually."

"Did you have a name, or an address?"

"No addresses, it was just an open day, nothing too formal. But I remember her name, well, her *Christian* name. I remember because it was so ironic. There was Birch, throwing insults at her from his high horse and the poor girl had the most inappropriate name for the occasion."

"What was it?"

"Gaye, she was called Gaye." Helen pulled a small, sad smile. "And her appointment was anything but."

Anna wrote GAYE? then stared at her notes for a while. "Did you see her again?"

"Never."

"Do you know if Paul Birch ever saw her again?"

"No, but I can't imagine she'd ever want to see him or indeed he'd want to see her."

Anna pushed the **GO** picture toward Helen. "This was hanging in Professor Birch's house."

It was Thompson's turn to be shocked. "*What?*"

"That's why I asked if Birch had ever seen her again, because this implies he had. *If* this Gaye is the same artist."

"I knew Paul well, but only professionally, of course. I rarely spent any personal time in his company but I promise that is not his taste *at all*. He *hated* art like that, his reaction to it on the open day was proof enough of how little he tolerated works like this. He would never, *never* have hung that in his home. Hold on. Wait."

Anna saw the cogs in Helen's mind working.

"Where was this picture hanging exactly?"

"At his Southampton Row home, in the hallway, just to the left of the front door."

"No. No, no, no." She waved her hands to dispel the very thought of it. "I went to that place a few times. In fact, I was there in February this year, to pick him up for a viewing. He *never* hung art in that spot, that was where he hung a mirror. Paul was extremely vain, would always look at himself just before he left the house. I saw him do it. There was no art work there, just a mirror, and as I say, even if he'd taken the mirror down, he'd have never hung *that* in its place."

Birch insults a girl because of her art work, thought Anna. *Years later, a piece which resembles that same art is hanging above his body. A framed piece where a mirror normally hung.*

She looked down at her notes again.

So who are you, Gaye? Who are *you exactly? And what does GO mean?*

43 / 10th July 1981, London.

Joseph Wiseman slumped in front of the TV, bottle of cheap whiskey at his side. He hadn't moved from his living room since earlier this evening and had no intention of going out. Since the start of July Britain had descended into collective madness and there was a horrible sense of déjà vu on the nightly news; crowds surged down streets, outnumbered police failed to hold their lines, cars blazed and windows shattered.

So Joseph bunkered down alone in his detached house with only whiskey and television for company. He'd watched skinheads and Asians as they fought pitched battles in Southall, seen Toxteth ignite, chaos in Liverpool, Coventry, even apparently genteel High Wycombe, for God's sake. The streets of Wood Green had been taken, then Manchester demanded a riot of its own when over one thousand people besieged a police station in Moss Side. Every night Joseph grumbled then eventually shouted at his TV screen, outraged, emasculated, drunk and unable to stop his country going up in flames.

Everybody blamed everyone else. Leader of the Labour party Michael Foot cited mass unemployment as the cause and held the Conservatives responsible. Prime Minister Margaret Thatcher obviously relished the prospect of a fight so threatened the use of water cannon and armoured vehicles against the rioters. There was a civil war going on just outside Joseph's curtains and he was firmly on the side of order, so rejoiced every time a truncheon was brought down into the fray, clenched his fists with excitement when police rushed at the *rabble*. He'd worked hard all his life and to see these *layabout scum* tear down his beloved Britain was too much to bear. He ached for the return of conscription, or even better, hard labour, and applauded whenever another IRA hunger striker died.

The BBC kept a stiff upper lip, so tonight they'd broadcast yet another repeat of the 1972 situation comedy "Dad's Army" in which a well meaning but inept Home Guard tried to defend Britain's shores, "with hilarious consequences." Joseph wondered if Auntie Beeb was trying to make a point. That was followed by another comedy repeat, "The Good Life," where a cheery suburban couple cut themselves off from the rat race and went self sufficient. Again, Joseph thought there may be a subtext to that choice of programme.

Some fluffy entertainment and a drama followed, then The Nine O'Clock News. Newsreader Kenneth Kendall sat ashen faced and hosted yet another instalment of The Britain's Burning Show. That particular production had a different cast every night but it was the same exhausted faces of the police, the same exhilarated faces of the rioters.

So Joseph sat and watched alone.

He'd been alone for a long time now. His first wife had died of a stroke so he'd moved home and found himself another woman. She'd keeled over from a heart attack four years earlier and now Joseph was too old and lazy to find a third.

He didn't care, since all his relationships had been functional rather than emotional. Wives number one and two weren't much different to the mass-produced art he hung on his walls or the Ercol sofa on which he sat. They were part of the general accoutrements that made up Joseph's ideal life, which was; one must have a respected career (he was an accountant), own a decent sized house, an expensive car, attend the right social gatherings, have a dress suit, wife and a child.

In that order.

Sadly, his own daughter had been a disappointment. From an early age she'd been wilful, self centred and unable to respect her elders. She'd demonstrated an embarrassing tendency toward art rather than science, failed to gain good passes in her exams and felt like a lodger he couldn't evict. Joseph had no emotional connection with his daughter but then again, barely any attachment with his wives either. They were accessories, nothing more.

His daughter had managed to get a low level bank job, which was *something* but hardly a position Joseph could crow about. Wife number two had understandably taken an instant dislike to his daughter, since the girl was unlikeable, sullen and had a deeply unattractive air of superiority. Thank heavens she'd moved jobs and moved out. She hadn't given him an address, he hadn't cared and was, in fact, overjoyed they had no interaction any more.

He'd received a few letters but they were more like employment reports. She'd finally given him an address in Nottingham, where she talked of her new accountancy job, of bland hobbies, bland friends, of nights out and meals in. Joseph often had a slightly disgusted curl on his lips as he read them. She'd related her "news" as emotionlessly as Kenneth Kendall related his. He'd sent a couple of equally noncommittal replies but that was the sum total of their communication and *good riddance to her*.

He'd recently started to scan the faces of rioters in case she was among them. Joseph imagined his daughter was exactly the kind of deviant who would cavort among disorder, so fantasised seeing her throw a brick then receive a truncheon in the head for good measure. Joseph liked that mental image very much, but never saw his daughter in the crowds and hadn't seen her for years now. That was just fine.

He heard sirens scream in the distance. The riots were too close and so Joseph always kept his door locked.

The Nine O'Clock News ended and a dreadful American drama called "Knots Landing" began. It offended Joseph as much as the disturbances but he watched anyway, if only to shout more abuse at the screen. That was followed by a regional catch up of news, obviously broadcast from an alternative Britain where no cars burned. Jolly presenters compared their fuchsias, an awful band called The Wurzels unleashed a racket, two shouting Northerners debated nothing in particular and a Geordie blathered on interminably about the weather, with not one mention of anarchy. This on screen Britain was made of cricket on the village green, foaming ale in the snug and aimed at an audience who were as deaf, dumb and blind as the three wise monkeys. A recap of the news followed, then Joseph realised his whiskey bottle was empty. That was the cue to stumble upstairs and escape it all for another night.

Within half an hour he was asleep.

*

"Wake up. Wake *u*-up, Daddy dear."

Joseph mumbled and waved one hand to make the annoyance go away.

"Wake *u*-up," a voice singsonged at the edge of his drunken sleep. He managed to open his eyes and took a moment to focus, but surely he was dreaming because his daughter sat on the edge of the bed with a knife at his throat.

As if the girl knew exactly what he was thinking, she put a finger to her lips. "No, you're awake. You're awake and I am real and although nobody can hear you, I really do suggest you keep nice and quiet."

"Gaye? What?" He managed.

"The one and the same," she smiled. "I tried to find a dress like I used to wear when I was young so you'd recognise me quicker, but then I thought, well, he never paid any attention to me then, so the effort would be *rather* wasted."

He tried to sit up, but she pushed him back into the pillow. "It's been a long time, but then again, I'm guessing you never wanted to see me and I certainly never wanted to see you, so," she waved the knife around like a wand, "as if by magic, I appear. Like the shopkeeper, hm?"

"What do you want?" he croaked, "where have you been? How did you get in?"

She frowned and counted on her fingers. "That was, one, two, three questions in one sentence. Oh, too many, Daddy, too many. In fact, I'm flattered, 'cos that may have been the most you've said to me in years. But take it slow, daddy-o, we have all night. Well, maybe not all night. Right, let's go through them one by one. What do I want? I'll get to that. Where have I been? Well, not too far geographically, mentally, however, that's a whole other story."

She sighed and waved her hands around again. "I've been here, there and everywhere, mentally, that is. Between you and me..." She leaned forward and whispered. "I believe that I am irreparably insane but I think I may have been born that way. Or did you make me so? A question for doctors and psychologists to answer, I fear. But where have I been physically? Did you get my letters?"

"Yes," he said, eyes wide, terrified. "I wrote back. What is this? Please put the knife down."

"*Naaaaah*, think I'll keep it handy. Well, *if* you wrote back, which I doubt, the address I gave is a derelict building in Nottingham so your letters are probably stagnating in a post office somewhere, or thrown away."

"Why give a fake address?"

"I wrote those letters for you, not me. Part of my..." she raised her arm and pretended to put a cape over her lower face, "...my clever, villainous plan. I sent those letters in case anyone should ask. If I'd just disappeared then people would go looking for me and I didn't want that, so I covered my tracks. It wasn't the most sophisticated scheme but it didn't have to be. What did you write? Did you ask me to come home, enquire after my health, happiness or safety? Did you put kisses at the bottom?"

Joseph continued to stare at the knife.

"Hm, didn't think so. *Plus ça change* and all that. Now, what was the other question on your list? No, don't tell me... how did I get in? Well, you silly, silly Daddy, you've lived in this house since I was here. I took a chance that you'd never changed the locks because, ta dah!" She held up a bunch of keys. "I still have my old set. Oh, good bit of advice for you, never get rid of old keys, they could always come in handy."

"What do you want?"

"Mm, as I said, I'll defer that question for a while."

She stood, walked around and picked up little nicknacks dotted about the bedroom. A sad little drummer boy particularly amused her. "I remember this one. He looked like I felt, banging away, nobody listening. You don't actually like any of this stuff, do you? It's all just for show. You pick things up, show them off then hide them away or get rid when they are of no further use. Mum dying of a stroke was the best thing that happened to you, me disappearing out of your life was second best, I'd imagine."

"If you're here to just insult me and the memory of your mother, then..."

"Oh, do fuck off. If I was here to insult you, I'd have come years ago. No, *nooooooo,* this is unfinished business. Have I changed much?"

Joseph looked his daughter up and down. "Not really. Why, are you here for flattery?"

"I don't need it, Father. But this isn't how I normally look. Oh, you should see my *other self* and I think you might be quite proud of my new career. I got out of banking years ago, swapped it for something far more exciting. But I'm not here to give you my *curriculum vitae.* Did you *ever* notice me as a child, as a teenager?"

"Of course I did. What is this about? I don't see you for years and then you break in with a *knife?*"

"Be quiet or I'll slice your tongue out," she said, low and slow. "I'll ask again. Did. You. Ever. Notice. Me?"

"Yes."

"Yes, you noticed me just fine when I didn't conform to your ideal of a daughter, when I let you down, or couldn't, wouldn't, rise to an occasion. When I simply existed, most of the time. My existence was enough to anger you, wasn't it? I couldn't talk about anything, ever. You and Mother were like those Easter Island heads, lips pressed together, staring, silent. So I'm going to ask you a question and you'd better tell me the truth or I will throw *such a tantrum*. Are you going to tell the truth?"

Joseph stared up his daughter, then nodded.

"Two words. I'm going to say two words and watch your reaction. Uncle John."

Joseph said nothing, but his Adam's apple moved as he swallowed. His daughter put a hand to her mouth and backed away.

"You *knew*? You knew what he did when he babysat me and you let him?"

"No, no, we, I, didn't know anything. Only later, when you left home and he was arrested for something similar. I suspected then. But he was let off, no charges, no evidence, see? And then it was too late to do anything."

"*Too late*? Too late? It's never too late, as you are currently finding out. *Too late*," she sneered. "How convenient, 'It was a long time ago,' isn't that what the Nazis said?"

"I'm sorry, I'm so sorry, I didn't know, not for sure. I hoped he hadn't but I didn't know."

"It must've been so shameful for you, so embarrassing. You wouldn't want anyone to know would you? It was easier not to say a word, lock it away, brush it under the carpet, like everything else you did. God forbid anyone should find out your daughter had *that* happen. Better to keep up appearances, yes? Same as always, yes? Oh dear God, you *knew*. Have you any idea what those nights did to me? Ah, from the expression on your face perhaps you finally do. Just look what they did to me, *Daddy*. I'm here with a knife because of Uncle John and everything that happened after."

"Gaye, I'm sorry, I didn't know."

"Don't you dare use that name. I hate that name."

Gaye sat down and her shoulders jittered as she breathed heavily. "You named me after a stupid rhyme but now I'm using that rhyme to make everything better. I can't make them *all* pay their debts, there are too many, but at least my name gave me a method, Daddy dear. You gave me a method to choose but you were always on my list. Oh, I killed Uncle John, by the way."

"What? Oh my God, oh my God. Who are you? What *are* you?"

"Don't invoke a deity you don't believe in and don't pretend to be surprised. He became a reverend. A reverend! I ran him down like a dog. You should have seen the look on his face when he recognised me. So Uncle John, or rather *Reverend* John Martin as he reinvented himself, is in Heaven now, or Hell. *Or*, as I believe, he's become nothing, just dust, gone, scattered to the four winds. *Poooof.*" She blew on her fingers as if they were a dandelion. "Fuck him. Now here I am and I want to show you something. I'll show it to you, then I'll go, OK? I promise, I'll show you, then I'll leave."

"You're not going to...kill me?"

"No. You're my Daddy, I couldn't kill you. I promise when I leave you will be alive, intact and unharmed."

"You promise?"

She gave a little salute. "Girl Guides' honour. Come on, Daddy. Come and take a look, then I'll go and you'll never see me again."

He shook as she led him downstairs. "Cold," his teeth chattered.

She put an arm round his shoulder and he shivered even more. "Let's see what we can do about that."

*

She led her father to the basement door. "I spent a lot of time down here, not that you ever noticed. You could scream your heart out and no-one would ever know. I did, on quite a few occasions."

She saw him glance at the knife and recognised the look in his eyes. "Ah-ah, no. You're thinking about grabbing this aren't you? That would be a very silly move. I'm stronger and faster than you ever were. This would be in your heart before you got near, so please don't make me do something I don't want to."

She opened the door to the basement. "Go on, take a look. Then I promise I'll leave."

Joseph froze at the top of the basement stairs. "I don't want to. I'm scared."

"Scared is good, it focusses the mind wonderfully. Go on, it'll only take a second."

A light switch was on the wall by the door. She switched it on and he looked down. "It's empty."

"Mm, I moved a lot of the stuff out while you were sleeping. It was your workshop, wasn't it? Not that you did much work down there, as I remember. But go on, there's something you need to see."

He reluctantly took a few steps downward, then she closed the door behind him and switched off the light.

Joseph gasped in the dark, turned and rattled the handle but it didn't move.

She leant against the door. "I never realised just how thick this is. Can you even hear me?"

"Open the door!" he screamed. "What are you doing?"

"So, here's how this will work," she shouted. "I *do* hope you can hear. I moved anything out of the basement that might help you get out, so apart from your fingernails there are no other tools. I had a little tinker with the lock, too." She could hear him shout from behind the door but ignored the noise.

"Ah-ah, no point yelling. You loved your locks didn't you? So when they finally find your body they'll surmise the door shut behind you and, *oh dear*, the faulty latch engaged. The poor man just got locked in his own basement and no-one could hear him shout. He died in the dark. What a tragedy."

"Stop this! Let me out!" He bellowed but the sound was muffled and faint.

"Shut up," she shouted back. "I had to really work on this one, quite hard, actually. It's poetic. Don't you see? You kept me isolated, ignored, unheard and in the dark for years. It's only right you should end your days in the same way, just to have an idea of how it felt, you know?"

There was more noise from behind the door, bangs, shrieks, wails.

"You really should have got to know the neighbours better, because nobody will even notice you've disappeared. That's what happens when you're a sad, bitter misanthrope. When this is over, I will have reduced you to one word and it isn't *Daddy*." She leaned back into the door and cupped a hand round her mouth. "One word to sum you up. You gave me my name, I give you yours. Tit for tat."

She stepped back, smiled and listened for a little while.

"I'm *ig-nor-ing* you," she roared. "And…it…feels…wonderful."

*

Gaye Wiseman waited a week, then went back under cover of night to finish the job.

44 / 18th July 1981, London, 10:45 a.m.

Inspector Walker stepped out of his Rover. Some houses appear to smile but the one in front of him scowled. It didn't look shabby, in fact, quite the opposite; the paintwork was bright, a bronze door knocker shone and the porch was flanked by two baskets full of colourful flowers. Walker felt one and realised it was plastic. Somehow, he wasn't surprised.

This place looked like any other well kept detached house except for the ambulance which idled outside.

Walker spotted a poster stuck in a front window, the famous engagement photo of Prince Charles and Lady Diana. Diana wore a striking royal blue outfit and held up a hand to show off the ring. Charles looked like a jolly plain clothes officer who'd collared a *very* upper class shoplifter. Above the happy couple, swirling gold Copperplate read; "Prince Charles & Lady Diana Spencer, Royal Wedding July 29th, 1981."

Walker couldn't work out what was off kilter about this place, but then it hit him.

It looks like someone's idea *of what a house should be. Everything is neat and tidy but almost too carefully placed, like a show home. It's trying very hard to fit in, right down to the poster of Charles & Di in the window. But every single curtain is shut. No-one's welcome here. I can feel it.*

David looked up and down the road. He thought all the houses looked similar, but others felt more vivid. Red, white and blue bunting hung in preparation for the big day, Union Jacks fluttered from windows and even from here Walker could see more pictures of the Lady and her Prince.

Yes, whoever-you-are, you've taken your poster from a newspaper and stuck it there to fit in. But that's the extent of your engagement with the Royal Wedding, isn't it? Or, I should say, was.

Even though the door was ajar, the inspector knocked and a sergeant answered.

"Oh, sir, yes. Come in."

"I got a call to attend a domestic accident. Fatality, yes?"

"Yes, sir. We wanted a senior officer to take a look."

Another sergeant waited inside and Walker stepped into the house. A wide staircase dominated an equally grand hall but despite the expanse, the view was dark and murky. Sickly light from a chandelier fought a losing battle against closed curtains, which denied entry to the bright fine day outside.

Reproductions of popular art works lined the walls with no sense of aesthetics. The Laughing Cavalier, Constable's Hay Wain, The Mona Lisa, The Birth Of Venus...all the usual suspects were present and correct.

Art for people who don't really like art, observed Walker. Trinkets and nicknacks stood on shelves; little porcelain children, busts of philosophers, carved wooden soldiers. *I'm getting a headache just looking at it all. Ah, I see it now. This is a house* play acting *at being a home. It feels like I could pull back the walls and see it's just a film set.*

"So what's what, then?"

"Right," said the sergeant and pulled out his notebook. "A neighbour called Great Portland Street, said they were concerned the owner of this place hadn't been seen for a week or so. Said he rarely went out or went on holiday, so..."

"Right, which neighbour? Did they leave a name or an address?"

"Nope."

Walker sighed. "Handy. Go on."

"So we attended, got no answer, couldn't see anything obviously, what with the curtains being shut. Since the owner hasn't been seen for a while we were concerned about protection of life, so affected an entry."

"Good. Go on." The inspector glanced into the living room, which was just as pristine and soulless as the hall. Mops and cleaning items were arranged with military precision in a small cupboard under the stairs. At the rear of the house the kitchen was equally busy, yet anonymous.

*OK, so the owner of this house is...*Walker tried to think like Anna again. *Twinset and pearls. Widow. Belonged to the local Conservative Club. Prissy busybody, had coffee mornings, was a terrible gossip.*

"Right, sir. The owner's name is, was, Joseph Wiseman."

Damn. Wrong on all counts.

"So, we entered and there was no sign of him."

"Any indications of forced entry anywhere in the property?"

"No. Doors were all locked, windows shut, none broken. Obviously haven't carried out a detailed look yet, but nothing to raise suspicions."

"OK. So why am I here?" he asked, aware Anna had framed the same question on Professor Birch's doorstep.

"Well, it's an unusual accident. So we wanted to err on the side of caution and ask for a senior officer."

"You're certain it's an accident?"

"Pretty much. This way."

The sergeant led David to a door behind the stairway. "This was the last place we looked, sir. We were starting to think the owner had gone on holiday and the Met were going to have to pay to repair the front door."

The sergeant indicated the lock. "Look here, sir. The latch appears to be faulty, see? It engages whenever the door is shut. You can turn the handle and open it from this side, but not from the other."

Oh dear, I see where this is going, thought David.

The sergeant turned the handle. "It's not pretty, sir."

The back of the door was covered in scratches and gouges, many of which were bloodied. The inspector walked downwards, where Joseph Wiseman waited for him.

"What we know so far from a quick chat with a neighbour is that he's lived here for a long time. The neighbour had been away for a few days, but it wasn't them that called us. Wiseman was married, his wife died four or five years ago. He's an accountant, semi retired, so often worked from home. We think he's in his mid sixties or thereabouts. Obviously we'll get more detail as soon as we can."

The basement was a mess. Shelves lined the walls but most of the contents were on the floor; books, manuals, Betamax tapes and more. There were boxes upturned in corners labelled with dates. David looked down at the detritus that spread from them; files, accounts and paperwork.

Wiseman sat with his back against a workbench at the far end of the basement. His head was tilted back and he looked up at the light fitting. Joseph's expression looked strangely beatific, like someone who'd just seen Christ appear through clouds. His mouth was open as if in awe but the sense of religious peace was undermined by his broken nails and fingertips, which were a mass of blackened and ripped flesh.

Walker looked back up at the door, covered in Wiseman's last desperate graffiti of scores and gashes.

"So we *think* he'd come down here for whatever reason then the door shut behind him. The latch clicked into position and at that point he may as well have been locked in solitary at Pentonville. No windows, no way out, the poor man probably died in the last couple of days or so. There's no water supply down here, which wouldn't have helped."

"Hold on, sergeant. Was the light on when you found him?"

"No sir, the only working light switch is on the wall outside, at the top of the stairs. There was another one down here, but it doesn't work." The sergeant pointed to a switch which had been unscrewed from the wall.

"Oh, Jesus, so he was alone in the dark for all that time?"

"Seems so. We haven't found a torch."

Walker tried to imagine what this man's last few days had been like.

No wonder it's such a mess down here. Wiseman had probably staggered about in the pitch black trying to find something, anything *that might help him break through the door. He would have desperately felt his way around, arms flailing like a blind man. How many times did he fall? How long was it before his voice gave out from the screaming? How desperate was he before resorting to his own fingernails, torn at the thick wood knowing it would never yield? That was an awful, awful death,* he looked down pitifully at the corpse. *Days of abject panic and terror, all because of a faulty lock.*

He'd seen equally tragic, pathetic deaths but something about this one was particularly sad. Over the last few months, IRA hunger strikers had *chosen* to starve themselves but this man had simply walked into his basement one day and never come up again.

Walker looked back at Wiseman's body frozen against his work table. A12 WORKBENCH was written along the facing edge.

No more working for you, not ever. When did you give up, I wonder? How long was it before you just collapsed there and decided that was where you'd stay, forever and always?

David gazed around the room one more time.

You're missing something.

He took in the mess scattered about the floor.

This is your work room. You have a work bench. So where are your tools? Where are the only things that could have got you out of this?

"The tools," said Walker. "Where are his tools?"

"Oh," said the sergeant, "oh yes. Didn't really think about that." He looked about the basement as if they might suddenly appear. "That is odd, sir, yes, very odd."

Inspector Walker strode back up the stairs and quickly found what he was looking for in a back room. Two tool boxes stood on a table with an electric drill, circular saw, torch and jigsaw next to them. Inside the boxes were hammers, screwdrivers, pliers, spanners... everything a man could want to fix and create with.

...And get through a locked door, thought David. *Everything you would need if you were trapped in a dark basement. Perhaps he was moving all this stuff up* here *when he got stuck down* there. *How unlucky could one man be? He moves the exact things he needs moments* before *he needs them.*

But Walker hadn't convinced himself. He went back down to the basement with fresh eyes in case there was anything else he may have missed.

Then he saw it.

Joseph Wiseman sat on the floor against the table. The back of his head was where the word A12 WORKBENCH was stencilled. But the angle of Wiseman's head obscured most of the word.

All David could see was A12 WORK....

But as Walker got nearer, he saw WORK had been carefully written over in blue charcoal.

45 / 18th July 1981 London, 13:00 p.m.

Anna sat at her desk and tried to climb the mountain of papers, reports, and general police housework that always built up. Every time the desk was clear and she stepped away, Anna returned to find several new stacks of paper had taken up residence.

She looked up at the clock. Five more hours on a Saturday shift, but at least she wasn't missing good weather. So far July had been unseasonably cool and overcast but that was par for the course in 1981, when everything seemed topsy turvy.

I'm thinking about the bloody weather, she admonished herself. *How very British of me.* Anything *but think about this small paper city that's risen here. Any minute, I'll collar someone and say,* "Ha, call this *British* Summertime? *Ha!"*

She tried to work out a plan of attack. Everything had to be looked at *now*, filed *now*, started *now*, finished *now*.

Robin's face kept appearing in her mind so she tried to hang on to a life lesson Father once taught her; "you can only control two things in this world; your thoughts and your hands. Absolutely nothing else will do as it's told."

Robin's decisions had been carried out by *his* thoughts and *his* hands but part of her mind hissed, *your actions didn't help either, did they?*

Alongside thoughts of her ex-boyfriend she was also aware of one particular file which still waited to be deciphered. *That* file contained reports of suicides (apparent and confirmed), domestic accidents and a hit & run. There were photos of odd little 'messages' that all *happened* to be written in blue charcoal, letters from a mysterious "Sarah," and forensics that still implied…*absolutely nothing suspicious.*

That file was a brick wall which Anna hit a long time ago. But she just kept on reversing and running into it over and over again.

If I could just work out who "Sarah" is, she thought for the umpteenth time, *if I could discover the identity of "Gaye" then surely I could shut that file up for good. But I'm lost down a dead end with no way out and I can't leave it. If "Sarah" and "Gaye" are the* same person*, then that would be something concrete. But how to prove it?*

At that moment, her phone rang. Grateful of the distraction, she answered.

"Leeding."

"Anna, it's me, it's Daniel. Daniel Moore."

She smiled. Dan always sounded like a particularly keen cub scout.

"I only know one Daniel, er, Daniel. So you don't need to give me the full introduction. How are you? What can I do for you?"

"Oh, I'm OK, fine. Weather's a bit shabby though, isn't it? For July?"

Don't say it, Anna. But she did. "And they call this *British Summertime.*"

"Yes, ha. Joke, isn't it? Look, I hope you don't mind me calling. It's probably nothing. I can phone back if you're in the middle of something."

She scowled at the never ending paperwork. *Ah, sod you, papers.* "No, it's fine, nothing that can't wait. How can I help?"

"Well, are you still looking into, you know, our little Indian restaurant game? The blue chalk thing?"

Anna went a little cold. "Well, officially, no. In fact, there was never any *officially* about it. It's still an interesting set of weird coincidences but nothing I can fit together, not really."

"Right, right. So you're no nearer to finding out whoever wrote those fan letters to Jeanette West? Was it Sarah? Was that her name?"

"Sarah, yes, whoever she is."

Down the line, she could feel him weigh up whether to continue but then he took a breath and ploughed on. "Right, this may be something, may be nothing, you've probably thought of it already, anyway, so if that's that case, I'm sorry to waste your time…"

"Daniel, just tell me. What is it?"

"I was filing some negatives here at my studio, just tidying up, really, putting stuff in date order. I randomly picked up one of the negs from the Jeanette West scene. It was of that art on her wall which said, FACE, right?"

"FACE, yes."

"And then I saw the FOG marking and a few others. They were all in capital letters, yes?"

"Caps, yes." *Where is this going?* Anna wondered.

"*That's* what got me thinking. Correct me if I'm wrong but didn't the letters from "Sarah" have words in capitals, too? I didn't really think about it when I saw them at the restaurant, because "Sarah's" letters are written in Copperplate and the markings, art, or whatever they are, they're written in standard capitals."

As he spoke, Anna pulled the file from her drawer, found the fan letters from "Sarah" and looked through them.

Daniel was right. Both the letters and markings contained single words, capitalised. Leeding picked out some from "Sarah"'s text;

'FUNNY' 'SOUL' 'YOU' 'ME' 'SAD' 'PLEASE'

"That's why I didn't put it together until now," Daniel continued at the end of the line. "The Copperplate distracted me. But what do you think? Capitals in both? Is that a connection?"

Leeding looked through all three of "Sarah's" letters. They featured more capitalised words like, 'HATE' 'LIKE' 'MAKE' and 'LAUGH'.

"So what do you think?"

"It's a possibility," she conceded.

"Uh, right." Daniel sounded very slightly disappointed.

"No, it's a good thought, certainly a connection of sorts. Thanks Daniel, I appreciate the call, I really do."

"Well, I hope it's of some help."

"So do I. We should all go out again, shouldn't we? The last time was really nice."

Until you got home and Robin called, Anna's mind spoke up. *Then everything turned to hell.*

"Yes, we should. Hey, perhaps we could have an *anti* Royal Wedding do. Get away from all the bunting and forelock tugging. It would be a blast."

Leeding laughed. "That sounds like a very good idea, let's work out a good time. Thanks for your thought about the capitals. I'll digest it. Bye, Daniel."

"Thanks for indulging me. Bye, Anna."

She put down her phone then looked back over the file. Across the way WPC Fisher watched her.

*

At one thirty p.m. Inspector Walker returned to the station. He headed straight over to Anna with an intense expression on his face.

"Blimey," she looked up at him. "Bad morning?"

He leaned down closer. "*Blue charcoal* morning."

"What? You're kidding."

Walker explained Joseph Wiseman's strange and pitiful death, of no forced entry nor way out of the basement. David talked of how Wiseman's tools were conveniently stacked upstairs, "Or *inconveniently*, depending on which side of the basement door you were." Then he finally described how the word WORK of WORKBENCH was traced over with blue charcoal.

Anna sighed. "But like all the others, I'll put money on forensics and pathology concluding nothing except a terrible accident."

"I agree. But I am coming round to your way of thinking."

She snapped round and stared. "No! You? Mr Cynical? What's changed your mind?"

He thought for a while. "OK, we were alerted to a problem because one of Wiseman's neighbours called us this morning, said they hadn't seen him for over a week but didn't leave their name or address. Here's the thing though; I doorstepped all the neighbours in that street except a couple of families who are away on holiday, and *not one of them* said they phoned us. They have no reason to lie so that rather begs the question; who called? And if that caller wasn't a neighbour, how did they know Wiseman was missing? How?"

The question was rhetorical, but Anna answered anyway. "Unless the caller already knew he was down there."

"*Exactly.* I spoke to Officer Newton, who took the call. All he could tell me was the person at the other end sounded like a fairly young female."

*

Across the way, WPC Fisher watched this latest development with interest.

What are you talking about? She wondered. *And what's the deal between you two, exactly? He marches in, doesn't look left nor right, goes straight over and you're into a little huddle again. Walker's like a kid who waits while teacher marks his homework, trying to impress them. So why are you trying to impress Anna, David? What's your motive here? And what's yours, Anna? Have I got this all wrong? Am I out on a limb?*

She noted how Walker said something that made Leeding's eyes widen.

Well, well. Is there something I should know?

*

"I'm going to do some digging," Anna said.

"Digging? What kind?"

"I just want a bit of background on Joseph Wiseman. Might lead nowhere, might go somewhere."

"Why, what are you thinking?"

"He's easily the oldest of, for want of a better phrase, *the potential victims*. That might be important."

"Why?"

"It's just a thought. I'll let you know if I find anything worth reporting. See you later."

"OK."

As Anna Leeding watched Walker go, so did WPC Fisher, each interested in different ways.

46 / 18th July 1981, 5:45 p.m.

Anna approached David Walker's desk. "Fire me, tell the bosses, call the commissioner, I don't care. It's Saturday, I need a pint and I'm knocking off early. What time do you finish?"

"Six. Are you OK?"

"Not really, as I say, I need pint or five and I think you will, too. I've done some digging." She ran her hands through her hair. "Jesus, it's insane. I'm going to the Yorkshire Grey, please join me."

"I will. What's happened?"

Leeding held up a sheath of papers. "I connected a lot of dots. Now I have an appointment with a Carlsberg, or quite a few."

"Sounds good, I'll see you there."

As Anna was about to leave the station, she turned back to WPC Fisher.

"Officer, what time do you finish?"

"Six, ma'am."

"Excellent. Come and join me at the Yorkshire Grey. I know officially you'll be off duty but that's an order."

Fisher gave a little salute and smiled. "Order acknowledged, ma'am."

Despite herself, Anna returned the salute and chuckled. "I have news."

"Blue charcoal news?"

"Afraid so."

"OK, Mine's a pint, please. Lager, not bitter, thanks."

"Done."

*

Walker was first to arrive and found Anna in the snug. She looked up and scowled. "You know, even when not in uniform you still appear to be. What *is* that you're wearing exactly?"

He'd swapped his starched shirt for a bright orange top with a green crocodile logo. "It's a Lacoste."

"It's a horror. And how much did your *Lacoste cost?*"

"Sixty quid."

"Sixty quid? It looks like something golfers wear. Honestly, *sixty quid*? They saw you coming, mate."

"It's smart casual."

"It's neither smart nor casual. I prefer you in uniform. That way, you can't go wrong."

"Are you just going to spend the evening having a go at my fashion choices?"

"I like the way you used the word 'fashion,' that's very positive." She waved a hand at a pint on the table. "I'm teasing. That's yours."

"Thanks, Coco Chanel."

Fisher turned up ten minutes later.

"Now, David, *that's* how to dress outside of work. Officer, would you give us a twirl?"

Lisa laughed and did as asked. She'd changed into pleated trousers and a blouse that asymmetrically buttoned up toward the shoulder.

"You look like a pop star," grumbled Walker.

"Well, thank you, sir. One tries. I'm auditioning for The Human League tomorrow. They love my love action."

"I have no idea what you're talking about."

"Well, with respect, sir, that's because you're the kind of person who wears a Lacoste shirt."

"Yeah, I've already pulled him up on that," Anna giggled.

"I *am* your superior officer," grumbled Walker.

"Yes, but not in the fashion stakes, David," Leeding waggled a finger in his direction, "*not* in the fashion stakes."

A few more pleasantries were exchanged before Anna got serious.

"Right. I've spent the afternoon digging, made a lot of calls, pulled in a few favours, and...Jesus. Joseph Wiseman's death was the Rosetta Stone." She tapped a pile of papers which were covered in scribbles, arrows, exclamation marks and names.

"The Rosetta Stone to what?" asked Fisher.

"Blue charcoal." Anna took a big gulp of her pint and riffled through the papers. "Where do I start? All right, we have two names connected to...whatever *this* is; "Sarah" and "Gaye." "Sarah" wrote those odd fan letters to Jeanette and someone called "Gaye" made similar works of art to ones we found at West's and Birch's place. Are Sarah and Gaye the same person? I still don't know. But here's what I do..."

She shook her head and sighed. "So I started with Joseph Wiseman, because his age got my attention, sixty-one. I wondered why Wiseman was so much older than the rest, how he possibly fitted in. Unlike the others he had a child, to be precise, a daughter."

She paused to make sure she had Fisher and Walker's full attention. "Joseph Wiseman's daughter is called Gaye Wiseman."

Fisher's mouth dropped open and Walker's eyes widened.

"Yeah, *bit* of a coincidence, don't you think? Gaye's an unusual name and Wiseman just *happens* to have a daughter with it. Gaye was born in October 1947, so she'd be thirty-three now. But whether Gaye's currently *claiming* to be that age is open to debate, as will become obvious." Anna consulted the notes and scratched her head. "I found Joseph's previous address and looked up the nearest school. Bingo. A Gaye Wiseman attended King Edmund grammar in Clerkenwell. Now hang on to your hats, everyone. Guess who was in the same year?"

She saw Fisher do the arithmetic.

"Jeanette West?"

Leeding clapped her hands. "Ten bonus points to the officer. Yep, Jeanette West. Were they friends? Enemies? Strangers? Don't know. The school secretary couldn't say. This April the seemingly happy and successful West kills herself and FACE is written in a frame above her body. Gaye Wiseman pretty much failed her exams, left school and went to work at a bank in Dalston, but I'm getting ahead of myself. Let's move on to the Reverend John Martin. I poked around his past and…bloody hell."

"Do I need another drink?" asked Fisher. "Something stronger?"

"Probably. OK, here we go. Back in the fifties John Martin lived on *the same road* as this Gaye Wiseman. Four doors up, in fact. He had an "interesting" history, shall we say. In 1964, he was interviewed in connection with "impropriety with minors" but no charges were brought, no convincing evidence put forward and it all went away. By 1973 he was based in Primrose Hill and there he died, victim of an apparent hit and run with FOG daubed near his body. What might that suggest?"

"'*Impropriety with minors*'?" mused Walker. "So he was a nonce."

"Possibly, but no charges, remember."

"But if we allow ourselves a little supposition, maybe Martin was, er, busy with Gaye Wiseman."

"Maybe. A very big 'maybe,' yes, but it's on the table." Anna scanned through her papers and found the next dot to connect. "Nicholas Atkey, poor, WOE IS ME Nick Atkey was next. He was

paralysed from the waist down after a drunken fall at a party, and...
ready? He worked *at the same bank* as a Gaye Wiseman in Dalston."

"Fuck *off*," whistled Walker, "with respect, obviously."

"Respect recognised. I thought the same thing. Was she at the
party? I don't know, but they worked at the same bank. All right,
moving on. Are we all keeping up?"

Both Fisher and Walker nodded.

"I'm glad, because I'm not. So, I spoke to a manager at that bank
and Gaye Wiseman left there in 1966. He thought she was moving
away but couldn't be certain of any details. Next, Professor Paul
Birch. During an open day at the Royal College Of Art, Birch totally
demolishes work by a girl named Gaye. Same Gaye? Possibly, but
there's no hard evidence for it. All we have are words written in blue
charcoal capitals which match apparently similar art works by this girl
Gaye. The bank manager described her as pretty, petite and blonde.
But Helen Thompson the art lecturer described the "Gaye" she met as
being *dowdy* and blonde. I don't have any photographs so I can't ask
Thompson for an ID. But I'm treading carefully. To reiterate, Gaye's
an unusual name but not unique, and there are plenty of pretty blondes
about."

Walker smiled and went to say something, then shut up and
reddened with embarrassment.

"Now at that point, Gaye Wiseman disappears off the face of the
earth, well, as far as I can see, and remember, I've only spent a couple
of hours on this. So next we come to *officially* a nonce, pizza man
Damon Whitehall, who apparently drowns in his pool with LOVING
charcoaled on a nearby wall. I got a bit stuck with that one for a while,
but does anyone know how he lost his eye?"

Fisher shrugged, Walker shook his head.

"An ex-girlfriend stuck a lit cigarette in it."

"Ow," moaned Fisher,"why?"

"Damon didn't know. Well, that's what he told the police. He said
they'd split up then a few months later, he's lying in his restaurant
with a fag stubbed out in his eye. So he reported her to the police,
obviously. Ready everybody? Whitehill was blinded by a girl called
Joy Smart."

Anna waited for her colleagues to make the connection.

"Joy Smart...Gaye Wiseman?" said Fisher. "It's not concrete, but
bloody hell, it's close enough for jazz."

"He described her as pretty and blonde. So the police go to her address and guess what? Joy Smart has vanished into thin air. Again, it's an unusual name, but that's where I draw a blank. Is Joy Smart Gaye Wiseman? Whoever she was, Joy becomes a non person. Her flat's empty even though she'd paid the next few months rent up front and gave no notice of leaving. Joy Smart clears up her entire life, goes to visit her ex and blinds him. Years later, Damon Whitehill drowns and blue charcoal tells us he's LOVING. Sarcastic? Who knows? And today Joseph Wiseman, Gaye Wiseman's father, is found dead, locked in his own basement, with the word WORK highlighted in blue charcoal."

"Fucking hell," whispered Fisher.

"Fucking hell sums it up. So what do we have? Connections between Gaye Wiseman and *five* of the deaths involving blue charcoal. A possibility that Joy Smart is the same person, but only a possibility, mind. And we have blue ink letters from "Sarah" to Jeanette West, with words capitalised. Those letters have prints that *might* match partials on West's windowsill. So the real question is this; are Gaye, Joy and Sarah the same person?"

"I definitely need another drink," said Fisher. "Anyone else?"

"I think that's a yes all round," said Anna.

Lisa went to the bar and David Walker looked through Leeding's notes. "This is astonishing. We still don't have any *real* evidence that the deaths are murders but the connections between Gaye Wiseman and these six people are persuasive."

"Persuasive is the word, David. Not written in stone, not anything we could hold up as solid evidence but a through line.So what next?"

Fisher returned with the three pints, holding them together and walking like someone on an egg race. "Have I missed anything?"

"Nope, just wondering what we do next. Thoughts?"

"Well," Fisher took a drink."God, that's nice. Well, all we really have is "Sarah," same as we had from the beginning. If Gaye Wiseman has reinvented herself as Joy, Sarah or *whoever*, then the letters are our only physical piece of evidence, even though they're not threats. We can possibly place "Sarah" at West's house but only *possibly*. I think Gaye Wiseman is no longer using that name, *if* she's behind this, which is still up in the air."

"Agreed. I hate to suppose, but my mind has been wandering this afternoon. So let's pretend, just for a moment. Try this; Gaye Wiseman is murdering people who have potentially crossed her but how many are there and when will she stop? How does she choose her "victims"? Is it random, or is there a plan? Because if this is a killing spree then I'm scared it'll just go on and on."

"And here's something else, we've talked about it before. I think Daniel brought it up," said Fisher. "Why write words at the scenes in blue charcoal? Without them, the deaths *are* suicides and accidents. We only suspect they're deliberate because of the charcoal, so why?"

"Well, as I've said, the charcoal is for the *killer*, not us. The words are part of the plan. If we can work out a method we might know who's next, but first, we've got to track down "Sarah." Does anybody have the faintest clue where to start with that?"

Fisher and Walker both picked up their pints and drank.

"That's a no, then," sighed Anna.

*

That night Anna lay in bed, fuzzy with alcohol. Her head span but not through lager. Despite many connections between Gaye Wiseman and the deaths, they were still no closer to solid evidence of her current identity and involvement. The many pints of beer hadn't helped and her two colleagues (*friends,* Anna qualified, *friends*) had eventually strayed off the topic and wandered into royal weddings, hunger strikes and riots. Anna's throat was dry from cigarettes, lager and conversation.

She shut her eyes and willed sleep to come but it remained elusive, so switched on the bedside lamp and reached for a book to fog her mind. Leeding picked up the treasure hunt, "Masquerade."

For the first time, she really studied the cover. It depicted a young boy who held a hare mask and skipped around a tree trunk. A slightly disapproving moon stared down from amongst branches festooned with giant acorns and bright pink flowers.

That's weird. I've been so busy pouring over the paintings inside *I never thought any clues could be on the cover.*

She took in every detail. A quaint English village stood in the distance, the boy wore tights covered in constellations, and some of the leaves were serrated, blood red at the tips. But Anna's gaze kept returning to the giant flowers.

Flowers. Should I put flowers on Robin's grave? Yes, I should. That would be the right thing to do. Yes, flowers. I should do that, at least. He wasn't bad, just sick.

Her head tick-tocked and she blinked five times exactly. Anna sat up, turned out of bed then walked naked into her living room where the "blue charcoal" file sat on her table. She flicked through the contents and came to the letter from "Sarah," dated December 1980.

Flowers.

Anna scanned the note and found what she was looking for in the very last line.

"I sent you some more flowers, your favourite, roses. Did you get them?"

"I sent you some more flowers," she whispered out loud.

Yes, when somebody dies, you lay flowers. That's the thing to do. So have you, Sarah? Have you laid flowers?

47 / 19th July 1981, London.

"It's three minutes past midday and look who's number one in the charts! Watch out, here come The Specials and their spooky, kooky "Gho-*o*-o-*oooo*-st Town" on 275-285, National Radio One!" Clanking and moaning filled the airwaves as DJ Adrian Juste added his own sound effects to The Specials' downbeat hit.

Fisher and Leeding headed east through deserted London streets. Pubs were only just opening but very few people were around to take advantage. Sunday trading was illegal so the capital was effectively closed. You might find an opportunist chemist or corner shop but generally, as The Specials pointed out, the city was a ghost town. With nothing to lure them in, people stayed away.

The mainly empty pubs would shut again at two thirty then reopen from seven. Finding somewhere to drink was very difficult on the Sabbath but Leeding and Fisher had no desire for beer. For starters, they both felt fragile from their previous night and more importantly, were on duty.

"How's your head?" asked Anna.

"It feels like the floor of a pub, ma'am, a bit sticky."

"Same here. Where does everybody go? London Sundays never fail to surprise me. Like that film "Day Of The Triffids," remember that?"

"The walking plants?"

"Yeah, I half expect to see a Triffid waiting at a zebra crossing. I tell you, if Hitler really wanted to invade he should have come on a Sunday, there would have been nobody about."

Virtually the only vehicle on the road, their Rover joined the Westway, slid past Euston, St Pancras and King's Cross Stations, caked with soot and equally deserted. Bunting and flags hung limply from buildings and it seemed Lady Diana was in every other window.

"Lots of Di," noted Lisa. "Not so many of Charles, I see. I'd be pretty miffed if I was him."

"Well, she looks like a film star, he looks like a cinema manager. And who'd want to stare at *that* all day?"

"She does, clearly."

"Well, there's no accounting for taste, is there?"

"No ma'am and for that we should all be thankful."

Whenever they were on duty, it was always "ma'am" and "officer" which Anna found both odd and completely proper. Once they carried warrant cards the idea of using each other's Christian names was ludicrous.

"Oh, here's a tip. You get a lot of the faithful double parking on Sundays, Fisher. One to watch out for. They're sneaky, those Christians. Pious all week but on Sundays, watch them totally ignore parking restrictions."

"Hardly holy, is it ma'am?"

"No, it is not."

"Now we're heading to the ballet!" shouted Adrian Juste from the radio. "The *Spandau* Ballet, I should say, and they really don't need all that pressure on, do they?" The sound of a popping ballon burst from the speakers. "I said *not too much pressure*! Here it is, "*Chant Number One*" on national *Radio* One!"

Fisher sang along quietly as the car travelled through Tower Hamlets then Stratford. The East End was just as quiet as the West End.

"If we find "Sarah," do we arrest her?"

Anna turned to the WPC and pulled an exaggeratedly shocked face. "I do hope that was just badly thought out musing and not a genuine suggestion."

"Well, I was wondering…"

"Bloody hell, officer, I think you need to go back to Hendon for a refresher course. Can you tell me what is wrong with the phrase, '*do we arrest her?*'"

Lisa thought for a while as they headed into West Ham. Then she smiled. "Oh, yes. Sorry, of course. We don't have any reason to arrest her do we?"

"And why is that?"

"Well, the fan letters are odd but contain no overt threats. The fingerprints on them *might* match partials at Jeanette West's house, but not to any degree that a half decent defence couldn't tear to pieces."

"Correct, so if we *can* find "Sarah," we're just going to talk to her, see what she can offer, find out just how connected she is. As I've always said, I just want to eliminate her from this, that's all. I certainly don't want to speed into her driveway, roll over my bonnet and shout 'you're nicked, sunshine,' through a loud hailer."

"Might be fun, though."

"Yes, it might. Of course, there's no guarantee we'll even track her down, so let's take things one step at a time."

Soon enough they arrived at the City Of London Cemetery & Crematorium where Jeanette West was buried. The vehicle passed through an impressive stone arch then stopped in a relatively empty car park.

"West would have to be bloody buried here," muttered Anna.

"Sorry, ma'am?"

"Nothing." Leeding looked around the grounds. The CLCC is the second biggest municipal graveyard in Britain but Anna immediately strode in one direction and Fisher had to walk double time to keep up. "So ma'am, you already know where West is buried?"

"I phoned ahead. Always planning, officer, always planning. One of Jack The Ripper's victims is buried here, did you know that?"

"No, ma'am."

"And John Merrick, the elephant man. He's here too."

"Oh don't. I saw that film last year, cried my eyes out."

"Nothing changes, Fisher. People just find different freaks to point at these days. We can all be a freak show without even trying."

As they walked deeper into the grounds Anna never deviated from her course. "You know this place well, ma'am," puffed the WPC.

"I do. Jeanette West is there."

They stopped in front of a plain marble headstone, which read, "JEANETTE WEST, October 14th 1947 - April 4th 1981. My only love, one day I shall fly with you, until then, R.I.P."

Leeding and Fisher stood quietly for a little while. Eventually Anna broke the silence. "We don't know she died on April the 4th do we? But it seems likely and what are they going to do, put a question mark next to the date?"

Many flowers were laid about the headstone. "As you can see, celebrity death has a gravitational pull on flora and fauna, Fisher. Come on, let's see what we can see."

Anna started to work through the tributes. Many had no cards attached, but she recognised famous names on others; Kate O'Mara, Nicholas Parsons, Paul Nicholas, Martin Shaw…There were framed, faded pictures of West in her 1960s glory, teddy bears and items of jewellery.

"Roses," said Anna.

"Roses?"

"Uh huh. In her 1980 letter, "Sarah" talked about sending Jeanette roses, said they were her favourite. Let's start with the roses."

Fisher started at one side of the pile and Anna went through the other. Older, faded and rotting sprays were hidden beneath fresher blooms. There were single red roses, bunches of different colours, giant bundles wrapped in paper.

Reverentially, Leeding placed them to one side then stopped. Almost at the bottom were the remains of roses in a heart shape. Their petals had virtually disappeared but tucked inside the construction was a small card, protected from the elements by the other wreaths which had been placed on top.

In swirling blue Copperplate, a message read;

I miss you and I love you, Sarah x

The likelihood of any surviving fingerprints was low but Anna still pulled the tweezers from her Swiss army knife and picked up the card. WPC Fisher looked over her superior's shoulder and whistled. "Bloody hell. It's *her*. You were right, ma'am. But what do we do now? How can we find her from that?"

Anna smiled and turned the card over. On the flip side was a name and address; *"The Enchanted Florist, 14, Holles Street, London W1. 01 6248055"*.

"Better than nothing, don't you think? First thing tomorrow, we pay a visit to The Enchanted Florist."

"Why not now?"

Anna waved her hands around the cemetery. "It's still Sunday, remember?"

"Oh, in all the excitement I forgot."

Leeding carefully picked up the crumbling garland.

"Ma'am? You're *taking* it? With respect, it's a wreath."

"With respect, officer, it's evidence. Come on."

They made their way back to the car and Anna gently placed the heart shaped spray on the back seat. Leeding was about to get in when she stopped.

"Officer, would you mind if I just had ten minutes?"

"Er, of course, ma'am."

Anna nodded, then walked into the cemetery without looking back. When she returned ten minutes later the WPC noticed Leeding's eyes were wet.

"OK," Anna slid in next to Lisa. "OK, good. Right. Thank you. We've achieved something today I think. Good. Let's go. OK, back to Great Portland Street."

"Yes ma'am."

"Put the radio on, would you?"

Lisa switched on Radio One, where DJ Jimmy Saville introduced, "An oldie but a goodie from Freddie and his esteemed Dreamers, how's about that? It's "You Were Made For Me"!"

Anna shut her eyes.

"Turn it off, please. I don't like this man."

They both went silent and stayed that way back to Central London.

48 / Monday 20th July 1981, London.

D.I. Leeding and WPC Fisher walked down Holles Street in West One. It was still too early for shoppers in any real numbers so they had the pavement to themselves.

Leeding approached The Enchanted Florist then walked straight past. Fisher stopped in front of the shop, confused. "Er, ma'am, it's here."

"I know. But I want to show you something first."

Anna walked to the end of the road and waited for her friend to catch up.

"Look where we are."

Fisher took in the surroundings. It was a circular park, flanked by red and white bricked buildings. "Ah, yes, ma'am, Cavendish Square." She pointed at a conurbation to their left. "Jeanette West lived over there."

"Yes, she did."

"Is that relevant?"

"It may be. Worth knowing though, huh? Geography is sometimes as important as psychology or motive. That's lesson…what lesson are we up to?"

"Six, I think."

"Our proximity to things affects our compatibility with them."

Fisher whistled."I need a moment to take that in."

"You have approximately twenty-five yards. Let's go to the flower shop."

*

A little bell tinkled as Leeding and Fisher walked into The Enchanted Florist, which had really gone to town with the upcoming Royal Wedding. Lady Diana smiled from walls, windows, even a T-shirt on the middle aged woman behind the counter. "TRUE LOVE" read the legend above a photo of the happy couple's heads (one on each breast) followed by "29th JULY 1981. A ROYAL ROMANCE."

Anna took in the T shirt and whispered, "If I *ever* get married, I hope the entire congregation wears one of those. It has a quiet dignity."

Fisher managed to stifle a giggle.

The shopkeeper looked up from a spray of carnations and her mouth dropped open when she saw the WPC's uniform. "Oh. Oh. *Oooh*. How can I help you?"

Anna produced her warrant card. "D.I. Leeding, WPC Fisher, Great Portland Street."

The woman looked between the two of them. "Not often you see two ladies on the beat, as it were? That's what you say, isn't it? Like in Dixon Of Dock Green, on the beat?"

"Well, this is more of an enquiry, on the beat is a foot patrol," said Fisher.

"Ooh. Well, this is an exciting way to start a Monday morning. Is it about the riots? Are you expecting more? Terrible, isn't it? Would you like a cup of tea?"

"No thank you," said Leeding. "It's really just a quick enquiry. I hope you can help with a couple of things."

The woman stuck out her hand. "Julie Fletcher. I'm the owner, well, part owner." She shook their hands, did a curious little curtsey and looked Fisher up and down. "You're like Juliet Bravo, aren't you?" Lisa smiled thinly. "I do love that programme. Is it like the real thing?"

"Well, sort of," she shrugged, "but we don't tend to wrap up our cases in one hour, though."

"What? Oh, ha! Yes, one hour," she waggled a finger at Fisher, "that's funny. So, are you supposed to do that thing on me now? You know, *don't say anything, because if you say something in court that you rely on in court then you shouldn't have said it should you?*"

"No," laughed Anna. "We're not charging you with anything. *Should* we be charging you with anything, Julie?"

"Guilty of great excitement about these two!" she pointed at her T shirt and once again the D.I. and WPC found themselves staring at Charles and Diana's faces hideously stretched out over a pair of K cups. "Oh yes, lock me up for that one. Guilty as charged!"

"Well, you and everyone else," replied Anna, diplomatically. She reached into her bag and pulled out the collapsed heart shaped wreath from Jeanette West's grave. "OK, I need some information on this, if you can help. It had your card attached." Leeding handed over the shop's business card.

"That's us, yes, but Mum handles those kinds of jobs, she's out the back. Mum. Mum? *Mum?*"

Julie turned and pulled a conciliatory face. "She's quite old and very deaf. I may have to drag her out so can I trust you two in the shop alone?"

"I think we can resist making off with the lupins, yes."

"MUM!" Julie bellowed. "The police are here for you."

There was a squawk from somewhere inside and a flustered looking woman in her late seventies scuttled into view. Leeding wasn't surprised to see Mrs Fletcher senior was a baggier, more lined version of her daughter complete with another Royal Wedding T-shirt which struggled to keep her in. The older Mrs Fletcher's design had the two faces superimposed over wedding bells, which strained against her equally ample chest.

"The police?" she looked from Detective Inspector to WPC and back again through comically thick glasses. "What do they want? What do they want, Julie? We've had no trouble here, have we?"

Anna held up the crumbling wreath. "It's about this, Mrs Fletcher. We're trying to track down who ordered it. Your daughter said you were responsible."

The older Fletcher stepped forward and examined the arrangement like a dog would consider a treat. She squinted then smiled. "Blimey, yes, I remember this one. Months ago, it must have been..." She thought for a while. "Late April? Maybe a bit earlier? You see, the heart shape is quite small. Most people opt for a larger design, more striking, but I remember this one because it's so petit. Ours is not to question why, though, is it Julie? *The customer pays, the customer says,* that's our motto."

"Do you have a record of the customer involved?"

Mother Fletcher held up one bony finger and wandered to a set of drawers. "Keep my receipts in one, Julie's in the other. That way we can play the game, you know, who's done the most jobs."

She began to riffle through the paperwork. "Why are you interested, if you don't mind me asking?"

"Missing person, in a roundabout way," said Anna. "Can't say much more, you understand, Mrs Fletcher. Police work."

"Of course, of course."

"The wreath was ordered by someone called Sarah, if that helps."

She held up a finger again, to say *shut up, wait, I'm working on it.*

"Sarah...heart wreath...Sarah...heart wreath...Aha, here we are."

The older woman triumphantly held up a piece of paper. "Here you are. Rose heart wreath, for Sarah, ordered the fourteenth April, 1981.

Paid cash up front, £4.99. It's all there." She handed the invoice to Anna whose shoulders slumped as she studied it. "You don't have a phone number, or address?"

"No, she came in, ordered, collected, paid up front. Why would I need any contact details?

"She came in?"

"That's what I said."

"Mrs Fletcher, what did this Sarah look like?"

The older woman frowned. "Well, it was a while back but she was blonde, like you. About your height, too. Wore dark glasses, yes, but then people who order wreaths are generally upset, so a lot of them turn up in dark glasses."

Damn, thought Anna. *Damn, damn, damn. Think.*

"There's no time on this invoice. Can you remember when she came in?"

"Oh yes.It was lunchtime. I remember because I was starving hungry and had my sandwiches laid out with a cup of tea and a slice of Battenberg, then the bloody bell went. My stomach was rumbling like Kilimanjaro, I can tell you."

"Lunchtime. Can you be any more specific?"

Fletcher The Elder cocked her head at Julie. "Blimey, it's like they're after Ronnie Biggs, isn't it? Must have been about one o'clock if I was about to start me sarnies."

"Just a couple more questions then we'll leave you to it."

Mrs Fletcher waved her hand imperiously, like a queen who has given her subject permission to speak.

"Had you seen her before?"

"Not to my recollection."

"OK. Can you remember what she was wearing?"

The older woman puffed out her cheeks. "Well, she was dressed for work in some kind of tabard. But I don't pay *that* much attention, I'm afraid. I'm not Juliet Bravo, or Columbo."

Anna looked around the shop, then back out of the window. She scribbled down a number and handed it to Julie. "If you think of something, *anything* else, any details at all, no matter how small, then please call me, I'm D.I. Leeding. Thanks for your help."

"I'm not sure I was much help at all, but if you say so."

Julie escorted the officers back to the door and whispered, "It's not a missing person is it?"

Anna smiled sympathetically. "I can't say. But if your mother thinks of anything else please call us as quick as you can, is that OK?"

Julie nodded solemnly and shut the door behind them.

*

"What do we do now?" asked Fisher, "it's a dead end, isn't it?"

"Not quite, follow me." Leeding marched south down Holles Street and into Oxford Street. She reached into her jacket for a packet of Benson & Hedges. "I know I shouldn't," Anna shrugged, "but I bloody need one. And don't get any ideas, *you're* in uniform. *I* could work in John Lewis."

Fisher waited while her boss looked up and down the road. Leeding rubbed her temples, puffed on the cigarette and Lisa knew this was the moment to stay quiet. Eventually, Anna's head tick-tocked, she blinked five times exactly, started to pace on the spot then circled like a cat trying to get comfy.

"OK, OK. "Sarah" left no address or number, paid up front in cash. So?" She turned to Fisher and waved a hand in her direction. Lisa tried to keep up.

"She didn't want to leave any clues? Sarah deliberately kept it vague?"

Leeding waggled an impatient finger. "No, no. How many times have you bought flowers?"

"God, not many. Two or three times?"

"Right. Flowers are a luxury item. You either order them over the phone, you know, by Interflora, or pick them up. If you order by phone then the shop delivers the flowers, if a pick up, you deliver them yourself. Agreed?"

Fisher took a moment to process the thought."Agreed."

"So last time you bought flowers, did you order by phone or pick them up?"

"I picked them up. They were a birthday present."

"Right, think back. How long was your commute to get to the flower shop?"

"The commute? I didn't *commute*, it was local, just round the corner. Who *commutes* to get...oh, wait. I see. " Some of the pieces clicked into place. "Who commutes to get flowers?"

"Uh huh. Nobody does." Anna looked around Oxford Street. "So what does *that* suggest?"

"Sarah works near the flower shop."

"Exactly. Let's work the clues." Leeding smiled like a teacher to pupil. "What time did Sarah buy the wreath?"

"Lunchtime, wasn't it?" Anna nodded and waited for Fisher to put it together."Oh.It was *lunchtime*."

"And when you only have an hour to eat, get out, socialise, whatever, you don't travel far, do you? Realistically, how far have you ever gone on your lunch?"

"No more than a mile."

"Right, look about you."

Lisa followed Anna's gaze up and down London's busiest street. Even from here she could see literally hundreds of windows, multitudes of shop fronts, side roads and alleyways. "I've never really looked at the city like this before," she sighed, "it's endless. How can we possibly know where Sarah could be?"

"It's not endless, officer. You just have to know how to shut down the possibilities."

Leeding saw the WPC was floundering. "Take my arm."

"Sorry, ma'am?"

"Take my arm. Let's pretend we're Sarah. We want to buy flowers." She guided Fisher to the centre of the pavement at the crossing between Holles and Oxford Street. "We're on our lunch break so we don't have much time. How many flower shops can you see from here?"

Lisa gazed about. "One, The Enchanted Florist. That's a *really* good name isn't it?"

"It is. Concentrate."

"You already know, don't you?"

"I think so. But I'd like you to work it out, go on."

Fisher frowned and started to focus on each shop. "They said Sarah was wearing a tabard. That eliminates quite a few of these places. Tabards aren't very up market, are they?"

"No, not very John Lewis. Think back. Can you remember Sarah's fan letter? The one from last December?"

Lisa shut her eyes and tried to recall the details of that blue Copperplate stream of consciousness. "Not really."

"Sarah mentioned she'd got a job. Remember?"

Fisher pictured the letter in her mind's eye and tried to pick out the relevant section. "Oh, wait, yes. Something to do with fashion?"

Anna clicked her fingers, pleased. "There are a lot of clothes shops round here. We could visit them all but let's not be silly. So, Sarah got a job in "fashion," any specifics?"

Lisa tried to focus on details, but the words whirled and blurred. Leeding saw confusion settle on the officer's face, so stepped in. "Remember, Sarah wrote about how she'd got a job in fashion and said, *'if you can count uniforms and work blouses as fashion.'* Uniforms and work blouses. Sarah wore a tabard so we're not talking about some high end, hoity-toity, chi-chi kind of shop."

Fisher looked around again and mentally scrubbed out possibilities. One by one shop fronts disappeared from her vision.

"C&A" the WPC said, eventually. "The assistants wear tabards. They sell uniforms, school uniforms, blouses, functional clothing. C and bloody A."

C&A was a high street clothing chain that focussed on cheap, utilitarian, production line fashion. It had outlets in most British cities and one stood just a few streets away. "Child & Adult," whispered Fisher. "She works at Child & Adult."

Anna clapped her hands, delighted. "Close enough. It's only British people who think it means, 'Child and Adult.' It actually stands for Clemens and August, the brothers who set it up. Common misconception, but I'm proud of you. Good work. So let's go shopping."

*

Anna left Fisher at the department store door to avoid any undue attention and took an escalator up to C&A's school uniform department. She casually flicked through some sensible pleated skirts and studied the assistants, but none fitted the description until one emerged from the changing rooms, a petit, blonde, mid-twenties girl who jittered between the racks like a bird searching for food. The assistant moved as if she'd been edited with every other frame removed, a staccato flickering of nervous energy. Her blue eyes fluttered in a pale, pretty face with lips pursed as if in constant disapproval. The girl spotted Anna looking her way, glanced around as if there was someone else in the field of vision, then reluctantly came over.

"Can I help you, madam?"

Leeding took in the tabard, hair, agitated expression and name badge which read, "SARAH".

"Hello. I do hope so, Sarah." She held out her warrant card. "Detective Inspector Anna Leeding, I don't want you to be worried or scared, I'd just like your help."

Anna steeled herself for the prospect that Sarah might make a break for it, but the girl had frozen.

"Can I speak with you about Jeanette West?"

Sarah's face twitched and she put a shaky hand to her mouth. "I didn't *do* anything." She looked around for help which wasn't there. "I loved her. I did. I only loved her."

49 / 20th July 1981, London.

She gave her name as Sarah Nicholls, aged twenty-three and who lived at home with her mother in Clerkenwell, to the east of Central London.

Slightly dazed, she attended the interview voluntarily but even though Anna had nothing to charge her with, Leeding ensured a solicitor was present. Anna briefed the solicitor and he, in turn, talked to Sarah before the interview formally began.

The girl was both painfully shy and painfully thin. *She can't weigh much more than seven stones,* thought Anna. *But look at those translucent blue eyes. Her skin is clear, her blonde hair shines. Except I'd bet money she's never had a boyfriend. I'd also put a hefty wager she's never killed anything bigger than a fly. Possibly not even a fly.*

Sarah repeatedly looked around the interview room as if seeing it for the first time. She had a peculiar habit of tapping her front teeth with long, immaculately polished nails. *She really could be a model,* wondered Anna. *But she'd never look at any camera with anything less than a startled, shocked expression.*

At that moment it hit her. *She could be West's younger sister. Good God, They might have come from the same family.*

"Would you like a drink, Sarah? A cup of tea?"

"No thank you," she replied, in a voice so quiet it was hardly there at all. Anna got the legal preliminaries out of the way then attempted to look Sarah in the eyes. It was difficult as the girl kept her gaze focussed downward.

"Sarah, I just want to remind you that you're not in any trouble. We have a problem and we're really hoping you can help us with it. So do you understand, I'm not here to trick or trap you, but I'd just like you to answer my questions truthfully and then you can be on your way. Understand?"

"Yes," she whispered, blue eyes fixed on the table.

"I know this feels intimidating and a bit scary, but you're here to help us. Just like at C&A, you know, think of us as the customers, you're the assistant and we need your expertise, right?"

Sarah managed a little giggle which tinkled like bells. "*Expertise,*" she sniffed. "Yeah, it takes a lot of expertise to sell cotton blouses."

"Well, forget blouses, I'm hoping you can apply yourself to our problem. But first I'm going to give you some dates and times and I'd really like you think about where you were on them."

"I thought you said I'm not in any trouble. That sounds like I am." She crossed her arms like a petulant child. "That sounds like I am *a lot.*"

"No, it's just for us, OK?"

Sarah nodded, warily. Anna went through the dates of Reverend Martin, Nicholas Atkey, Paul Birch, Damon Whitehill and Joseph Wiseman's deaths. As Leeding mentioned Wiseman's name, she studied Sarah carefully but as with the other dates, she answered calmly and unemotionally. Anna deliberately didn't mention the date of Jeanette West's "suicide." She needed to tackle that particular area very carefully indeed. Once Sarah had given all her answers, Leeding nodded at Fisher, who'd taken detailed notes. Lisa nodded back, stood and left the room to start making enquiries, collate and cross reference.

Here we go, then, thought Anna. *Softly, softly, very softly now.*

"Sarah, now I have to ask more personal kinds of questions. Is that OK?"

"I suppose so. I don't really have much of a choice, do I?"

"You do," said the solicitor. "Just say."

"Sarah, what was your relationship with Jeanette West?"

The girl stopped moving and it was like someone had just switched her off at the mains. Her eyes fixed on a point behind Anna's head, her lips parted and stayed that way.

"Sarah?"

"I loved her," she said from far away. Her mouth barely moved.

"Tell me about her. When did you first see Jeanette, how did you fall in love with her?"

She smiled, but it was an empty kind of smile, more like a reflex action. "I saw her on television. It was May the thirteenth, 1975. A Tuesday. The Bay City Rollers used to have a show called Shang-A-Lang. Do you remember it?"

"I was a little too old for the Rollers. I'm more of a Beatles' girl."

"The Beatles are good," she agreed, wistfully. "I only watched because Marc Bolan was on. I liked him. Such a shame about the car crash."

"It was." Anna let Sarah ramble. There was no hurry.

"So I put it on and I didn't really like The Rollers anyway, all that stupid tartan. But then *she* was on. Jeanette. She was appearing in "Jesus Christ Superstar" as Mary Magdalene. She sang "I Don't Know How To Love Him" and I was transfixed. She was *so* beautiful. She talked to the Rollers afterward and I remember thinking, *we are connected, I know we are, I can feel it.* Have you ever had that? When you just click with someone and you know they are another part of you?"

Anna had to internally admit she hadn't, but nodded anyway.

"So I spoke to the TV. I said, 'If you know I am here, Jeanette, and you know we are connected touch your ear.' And at that moment she reached up and touched her ear. She turned and looked straight down the camera at me. *At me.* And then I knew. I never had many friends, not real friends. They picked on me at school, pulled my hair, threw… things…at me. But I knew Jeanette was there for me. I'm not pretty, I never have been. Mum told me not to worry about it."

Oh, I'm seeing it now, thought Anna. *Mum wants to keep you all to herself. Mum has grown this insecurity, this shyness, so her daughter won't ever leave. The only person Sarah trusts is Mum, and Mum won't let her be with anyone. So she creates a relationship Mum can't ever touch. But Sarah, you* are *beautiful and have no idea.*

"But you know what Jeanette said? She *knew* I wasn't pretty, but Woody asked her a question about getting into modelling and she looked down the camera again and said, 'There are models just like me out there, models just like *you,'* and pointed at me. At *me.* I felt like my head was going to explode, I was so happy, I jumped from the sofa and danced around the room. I had someone who *knew* me and *loved* me and *saw* me for what I am inside."

She smiled again, lost in the folds of her memory.

"So did you contact Jeanette to tell her?"

"I didn't want to assume too much so eventually I just wrote to her fan club, told her how huge an admirer I was and asked for an autograph. You don't know who reads these things, so I had to be careful. I put a few clever codes in there that I knew Jeanette would understand and I used some of her favourite words. I wrote some in capital letters, dotted throughout. If you put them together, it said I LOVE YOU AND IF YOU LOVE ME PUT THREE KISSES ON THE PICTURE. Clever, wasn't it?"

"That was very clever, yes."

"I didn't always use the capital letter code. Sometimes I just used to put words in capitals to let her know how I was really feeling, you know, like SAD or HAPPY. She understood. Well, she sent me a photograph and guess what? There were three kisses on the bottom! She understood the code! And there was a message on the back, too! It said, "My VERY best wishes!" VERY in capitals! From that moment, I knew we were together."

"Wow," Anna said, encouragingly and humoured her. "I'd like to see that picture one day."

"Would you? Would you really? I'll show you, I'll bring it to you. She looks lovely. Would you?"

"Er, yes, please. Did you ever meet Jeanette?"

The question seemed to distress Sarah and she waved her hands at Leeding. "No! No! It would have been terribly dangerous. She was married, living this lie. If people knew we were in love, then…well you know what people are like. They detest anybody different. They loathe men who love men and women who love women, they despise anyone who doesn't fit in." She sneered and her pretty face twisted into one of pure hate. "So the only way she could communicate with me was through interviews in magazines and on the TV. I could understand the code you see. She'd use certain words and I have a notebook of what they *really* meant, you see? So if she said, 'happy' then that was code for 'Sarah' and if she mentioned 'modelling' that was code for 'I love you.' It was very clever. Nobody ever knew. She could never write back or people would know. Sometimes I admit I was angry that she couldn't just send one note, but I understood, of course. It was too risky. I knew she was just waiting for the right time, and then…and then she…why did she? Why?"

Her eyes brimmed over with tears and she furiously tapped her front teeth. Sarah bit her lip so hard it drew a little blood and then she took back control.

My God, you have constructed an entire universe and lived in it for years, thought Anna, sadly. *And now Jeanette is gone you have no direction any more. You poor, poor girl, you're utterly lost and have no-one to guide you out of this maze of self delusion you've put yourself in.*

"May I smoke?" she asked.

"Of course."

Sarah lit up and the action seemed to calm her yet further.

Your degree of emotional control is exceptional. That's how you've survived, avoided anyone's unwelcome attention. You've been quietly drowning and no-one has ever seen. You're gasping for air but nobody spotted how you slipped beneath the waters. Now I must slow down even further. We are in uncharted territory.

"Sarah, I need to ask. Did you ever find out where Jeanette lived?"

She brightened again, put a hand to her mouth and laughed, wrangled her emotions again. Anna was astonished. *I can hardly imagine you were weeping just twenty seconds ago.*

"I couldn't believe it. I was on my lunch break and suddenly there she was on the street, walking along for real. I just froze. She looked around and for a moment our eyes met, she smiled and I knew. I knew she was saying, 'come, follow me, let me show you where I go.' I knew she had a place in London for when she was working and this was the moment! Obviously I followed at a discreet distance and she went to Selly Mews. This was in February."

"Did you ever send anything there directly?"

"Do you think I'm mad? Who knows who might have found my letters first? The cleaners? Her so-called *husband* ? No, we had our way of communicating and I stuck to it. She just wanted to let me into that part of her life."

OK, here we go.

"Sarah, did you visit Selly Mews on the night of the fourth of April?"

"I didn't do anything."

"I know. But did you?"

She sighed, long and loud. "There's a back gate. You get to it by a little alley."

"I know it."

"Now that back gate was always closed but on that night it was open. She'd left it open for me, I think. I still wonder why. So I crept in. Jeanette was there with a woman. I stood very still at the back of the garden in the dark."

Anna had prepared for this. She picked up a copy of "Smash Hits" and laid it on the table. "Sarah, would you take a look through this magazine and see if you can find the woman you saw?"

Sarah frowned, confused, but leafed through the pages anyway. She stopped at a poster of Sam Bizarre, AKA Nigel Blundell.

"I think that's her. Sam Bizarre? Is she a pop star? That makes sense. Jeanette had lots of famous friends."

Leeding didn't want to get into the whole gender bending craze so simply agreed. "Yes, she's called Sam Bizarre. And what were they doing?"

"Isn't this spying though? Are you going to arrest me for spying?"

"No, no, it's fine. Just carry on. What were they doing?"

"Well, at first they were drinking. I just watched. I was hypnotised, I couldn't believe she was there, *right there* in front of me. But I couldn't say or do anything. The woman she was with couldn't know about us, could she?"

"No."

"No. But then they went down the hallway and the woman started shouting. I couldn't really hear what was happening but they were having an argument. Perhaps Jeanette had told her about me. That's what I think. Jeanette had told her and she was threatening to go to the papers or whatnot and that's why Jeanette…"

She nearly broke but clenched her fist and carried on. "That's why Jeanette did what she did. But this woman, er, Sam Bizarre, she stormed off. I wanted to console Jeanette but I couldn't in case the woman came back. And we'd agreed not to ever meet until she was ready. Jeanette drank some more, put a few records on. I watched. She danced a little, I danced too, at the back, in the dark, out of sight. She went to the front of the house. I was desperate for a cigarette so I quickly had one, but had to put it out, because that's when the other person came in."

Anna had been taking notes but her hand froze above the paper. As calmly as she could, she asked, "*Other* person? Did you say another person?"

"I don't know if it was a man or a woman. You can see from Jeanette's kitchen to her hallway, but it was dark, so I couldn't see much detail. I suppose they, he, *she*, was quite petit, though. A bit like me, or you."

Jesus. JesusJesusJesusJesus.

"How sure? What did they look like?"

"I guess about your height. They might have been blonde or maybe brown, I couldn't tell with the light. But Jeanette was pleased to see them. She was very drunk, though. She gave them a big hug but could barely stand. This person had to put down their bag and hold her up. I did feel sorry for her. I didn't like seeing Jeanette like that but this person was helping."

"You said a bag, what kind of bag?"

"A weird bag."

"Weird in what way?"

"Well, you couldn't keep much in it. The bag was really big and flat, with a handle on top, like if you took a briefcase and ran it over with a steamroller. All big and very flat."

Anna thought for a moment, then drew something on the paper in front of her.

"Did it look like this?"

Sarah glanced at the drawing.

"Yes, that kind of thing."

It's an art portfolio. Whoever visited Jeanette had a fucking art portfolio *with them. Oh my God. It was Gaye. Gaye Wiseman, I have you at Jeanette's. I have you.*

Leeding's heart rate leapt but she kept her voice even. "OK, then what happened?"

"The person helped Jeanette up the stairs. I really wanted to see what happened next, so I was naughty."

"Naughty?"

You climbed up the drain pipe, didn't you, Sarah? You weigh next to nothing, you're obsessed, you want to see. It would have been easy for you.

"I climbed up the drain pipe."

Bingo.

"I got right to the top and put my fingers on the windowsill, but I just couldn't hold on. So I slid back down again, made a bit of a noise. Made quite a lot of noise, actually. So I got scared and I ran for it, in case I got caught. Then...*then* happened."

She burst into racking sobs. Anna reached for Sarah's hands and she didn't draw away. "It's OK, it's OK."

"It's not OK, is it? It'll never be OK again. She's gone, she's gone and we never kissed. We never kissed, not once."

She hung her head and tears fell onto Sam Bizarre's pouting face.

Anna watched her, powerless. *I thought you were a suspect Sarah, but you're just a little girl with no-where to go. You were no suspect. You were a* witness.

*

The following day WPC Fisher approached Anna's desk with a sheath of papers. "Here it is. I got there in the end."

"Ah, is this Sarah Nicholls' whereabouts?"

"What I have so far. It all checks out but I'd like to shore up a couple of things to be double sure. These are my notes but I thought you'd like to hear before I typed it all up formally."

"Good. So what did you find?"

"She's Sarah Nicholls. No *nom de plume*, no stage names, certainly no Gaye Wiseman. She's twenty-three, which is easily ten years younger than we *think* Gaye is right now. She lives in Amwell Street, Clerkenwell, with her Mum. She left school with a few exams, got a job in Woolworths then in December last year, moved up, down, sidewards, however you want to call it, to C&A. She is not Gaye Wiseman."

"I knew that as soon as I saw her."

"Same here. Right, we know where she was on the night West died. She doesn't drive and her Mum has her at home when Rev. Martin met his maker. Naturally, I'd like some other corroboration than a relative, which I'm sure I'll find, somehow. She was on holiday in Wales with Mother for the whole of bank holiday week, I checked with the hotel and they have her there for those dates. Therefore she was nowhere near Nicholas Atkey. We think Prof. Birch died somewhere between the ninth to eleventh of May. She was working all day on the ninth and eleventh. She spent Sunday with her mother. Again, I'm looking for any extra corroboration."

"Good. Belt and braces."

"We believe Damon Whitehill "drowned" on the fifteenth of June. Sarah was at C&A all day, then at a birthday party in the evening. The manager of her department had turned fifty and all the staff were invited. It wasn't like she was a preferential guest or anything. They were at The Iron Duke in Mayfair with *loads* of witnesses. She's there, then gets a taxi home to Clerkenwell, which also checks out one hundred percent."

"She's clear."

"Yep. Joseph Wiseman could have died any time from, say, the tenth to eighteenth of July. She's at work Monday to Saturday in that time but other than that, I can't *not* say she wasn't there."

"Double negative. No, in fact, that was a triple negative. That takes some going."

"Sorry. But on balance, I think I can safely say Sarah Nicholls' only crime was entering Jeanette West's back garden without permission."

"So she's out of the picture. That leaves us with just one name."

"Yes, Gaye Wiseman, who is almost certainly *not* going by that name any more."

"So our only question now is; what *is* she calling herself these days?"

Fisher and Leeding went silent for a while.

"I'll tell you something though," Anna stretched, "I could *murder* a drink."

50 / 28th July, 1981, London

Five months of febrile expectation were nearly over. Eager royalists had started to camp out on the parade route to St Paul's Cathedral, hoping to get a glimpse of the happy couple. Experts made predictions about Diana's dress, which had been kept an Enigma code level secret. On streets up and down the UK anyone who *hadn't* covered their home with red, white and blue was considered slightly seditious.

The Specials' grim musical commentary "Ghost Town" had been replaced at the top of the charts with "Green Door" by the denim encrusted Shakin' Stevens. But even that song's upbeat honky-tonk was strangely appropriate, since the singer was excluded from a shindig by the titular green door and the Royal Wedding was a party to which substantial amounts of British people weren't invited. But everyone gritted their teeth and bunkered down ready to have *fun*, come what may.

Anna sat at her desk and wondered where to start because the production line of cases never stopped. They reminded her of the conveyor belt from the BBC's "Generation Game" where endless prizes slid past the contestants. As she looked at the piles of files, Leeding heard host Bruce Forsyth say, "…Vehicular Manslaughter… Teasmaid…Cheque Fraud…Cuddly Toy…Murder…"

And then there was blue charcoal.

Gaye Wiseman disappeared in 1965. If "Joy Smart" was the same person, she came from nowhere in 1966, put out a cigarette in her ex-boyfriend's eye then also pulled a Lord Lucan. At that point the trail didn't just go cold, but froze over. Whoever Gaye Wiseman was now, she stalked London invisibly and other than blue charcoal, she'd left nothing of herself behind.

Riots and revenge, thought Anna, *but nobody out there cares. They just want princesses and parties. And why not? The world is listing badly, so we just grab whatever we can and hold on.*

Since Joseph Wiseman was discovered there'd been no further signs of Gaye's handiwork but that didn't mean anything.

Since she'd designed her murders to look like something else, how many others are out there somewhere, with a blue charcoaled message that hasn't *been spotted?* But Anna didn't think there were any others. She wasn't sure why that hunch felt right, but the six deaths so far seemed like a deliberate, self contained pattern. *I wish I knew how,* she thought, and not for the first time.

Leeding looked up and saw WPC Fisher stood at her desk. Lisa seemed a little nervous.

"Yes, officer?"

"Ma'am, I have a couple of things I'd like to discuss with you."

"Sounds ominous. What things?"

"Something professional, something else."

"Something else? Can you give me any clues?"

"I was wondering if we could have a chat later, you know, over a pint."

"Well, that's always guaranteed to work as an invitation. But have you *seen* it out there? Pubs will be mobbed, I think everyone wants to watch Charles and Diana's wedding through a hangover. Give people a day off and just watch the cells fill with drunks."

"Well, we'll just head for the pubs with the fewest flags outside. They should be safe."

"Excellent observation. You'll be a detective yet. OK, I finish at six."

"Same. And rather brilliantly, ma'am, I have tomorrow off so I can drink with no guilt."

"I'm in for nine, so I'm jealous. Oh, if this is work related, should we ask Inspector Walker?"

Fisher looked over at Walker, who'd been watching the two women, but quickly glanced away. "Er, no, not for this I don't think, is that all right?"

What is this about? Wondered Anna. *She's not usually so sheepish.*

"Of course. Shall we say the Yorkshire Grey? Quarter past six?"

"Wonderful."

The WPC walked away and as Leeding watched her go, she felt slightly unsettled.

*

Anna was first at the Yorkshire Grey, just a couple of minutes walk from the station. There were some perfunctory flags stuck in flower pots outside but certainly not the rabid red white and blues that covered The Crown & Sceptre over the road.

Ok, this'll do, she thought, *at least it doesn't look like a National Front Clubhouse.*

For once, Anna had changed out of her work blouse and grabbed a light, strappy white summer top from her locker. Leeding lined up a couple of pints in the snug and waited for Fisher, intrigued. Lisa arrived a few minutes later. The WPC had added a touch more make up, her black bob was teased out and she wore an electric blue all in one.

"Blimey Fisher, are you going to a party later?"

"No, but sometimes I just want to completely remove all traces of the day job and be me."

"Well, it's a striking outfit."

Anna noticed some of the customers appreciatively look Lisa's way. The two women got on with the ritual of wandering around a conversation. They never quite settled on one subject but meandered about, took side roads and went off the beaten path, completely at ease. The first pints were quickly consumed and another two were purchased.

"So you have something to discuss?"

Fisher wiped foam from her top lip. "Yes, er, a few things, actually. I thought it would be better out of the station."

"Why?"

"I'll get to that."

She really does look nervous, thought Anna. *Why? We get on fine, what could she possibly be worried about?*

"Right. I can't stop thinking about the blue charcoal. I lie awake at night going over it in my head."

"You and me both."

"Mm, and it seems to me if we can work out Gaye Wiseman's pattern then we'll have more of a clue to what she'll do next, maybe even an idea who she really is these days." Fisher shrugged. "But that's a lot of maybes, isn't it?"

"Agreed, but we've been going round and round in circles with this for weeks. Whatever those words mean, they're for Gaye, not for us. She derives context and meaning from them."

"Exactly. So I've tried to look at every angle. Do the victims' birthdates match, or are they in consecutive order? Nope. What about days of the week? Were they murdered on, you know, Sunday, then Monday, Tuesday etc? Nope. West died on a Saturday, Martin, Atkey, Whitehill probably all on a Monday, we don't know exactly when Birch and Joseph Wiseman died, so that was a dead end. The places they were found don't form any pattern on the map, you get the idea. I've been going mad with it."

"I know the feeling."

"So I went to the library and looked up the blue words, to see if there is any connection. OK, so which is the odd one out?"

"The odd…?"

"You always test me, I'm testing you. Which of the six "messages" is the odd one out?"

Anna thought. FACE and GO had been framed. FOG and LOVING were written on the surrounding area. One had been stencilled over the word WORK and WOE IS ME was placed upright on Nick Atkey's table.

"Oh. I never thought about it before," Leeding was surprised she'd missed something so obvious. "WOE IS ME, yes, all the others are single words, that's three. How did I not see that?"

"Well, we were looking at them as a group rather than individually. I wondered if that was important, so I went looking for the phrase WOE IS ME to see if there was any relevance beyond Nick Atkey's job at a charity phone company."

She reached into her shoulder bag and pulled out a piece of paper covered in notes. "The librarian was very helpful, thought she remembered *"woe is me"* from the Bible and she was right. Now, Job is one of the oldest books in the Old Testament. *Job 10:15: If I be wicked,* woe unto me*; and if I be righteous, yet will I not lift up my head. I am full of confusion; therefore see thou mine affliction.*"

Fisher let it hang for a while. "It's not quite WOE IS ME, but *"woe unto me"* is pretty close and it talks about righteousness, *"yet I will not lift up my head."* Gaye Wiseman doesn't lift her head, either, right? She's faceless, we can't see her. *"I am full of confusion; therefore see thou mine affliction."* I'd imagine that was a pretty good description of a killer's mind."

Anna nodded. "Impressive, Fisher, very impressive. So we might be looking for someone who knows their Bible."

"Maybe, but as you always say, 'beware coincidence.' It might be something or I'm seeing things that aren't there."

"Good. You're learning."

"So I tried a different angle. I wanted to find that *precise* phrase, "woe is me". Not "woe *unto* me" but "woe *is* me". Now, there are a few other uses in the Bible…" She consulted her notes, "…in Psalms,

Isiah and Jeremiah. But it depends on which translation you're reading, so I wasn't convinced."

Leeding took a long drink from her pint. *You have come on in leaps and bounds, Fisher. You're a natural at this.*

"So that's when I thought I'd better stick to English uses of the phrase, where I'd have no problems with deviance in translations. The librarian came through again and guess who uses it first in English?"

Anna shrugged. "Tell me."

"Shakespeare, of course. "Hamlet". Act Three, Scene One. You know "Hamlet"?"

"Did it at school but it's a bit of a blur."

"Yeah, same here. But this is what Ophelia says," Fisher started to read, but her face changed and she *became* the words. "Oh, what a noble mind is here o'erthrown! The courtier's, soldier's, scholar's, eye, tongue, sword; th' expectancy and rose of the fair state, The glass of fashion and the mold of form, th' observed of all observers, quite, quite down! And I, of ladies most deject and wretched that sucked the honey of his music vows, now see that noble and most sovereign reason like sweet bells jangled out of tune and harsh, that unmatched form and feature of blown youth blasted with ecstasy. Oh, *woe is me* t'have seen what I have seen, see what I see!'"

Anna watched Fisher read, astonished. She didn't simply recite the words but lived them, gave a performance at a corner table in a tiny Central London pub. "If you weren't an officer, you could have been an actress."

"Ugh, no thanks. But what do you think? Ophelia mentions how noble minds are overthrown, of *scholars*. Professor Birch? She says an *eye, singular*. Damon Whitehall had one eye. She speaks of 'fashion and the mold of form,' Jeanette West, anyone? And 'tongue,' the Reverend was an orator. 'th' observed of all observers, quite, quite down!' Nick Atkey was an observer of life. He sat, watched, listened, as people told him about their lives and in the end, he was *down* there on the floor."

"It sounds persuasive, but you're joining a lot of dots that might not even be there."

"I know, but then Ophelia talks about, 'I of ladies most deject and wretched…blown youth blasted by ecstasy…oh woe is me t'have seen what I have seen, what I see!' Ophelia was one of Shakespeare's great, mad, tragic heroines. She drowned, driven insane by grief."

Anna sat, drank and thought for a while whilst Fisher looked on, expectant. "All right, we know Gaye was, maybe still is, pretty. We know she tried to be an artist but was rejected by Birch. That she went to school with West, worked with Atkey, lived on Martin's road. We know she disappeared in 1965, know her father died locked in his own basement. But Lisa, that's *all* we know."

The WPC looked disappointed. "I'm not saying this isn't thorough, intriguing, brilliant work, it really is." Fisher brightened a little. "And it may help. Let me think about it, there's a lot to take in."

A little light went on in Anna's head. *Hold on. What did Lisa say? Not about The Bible or Shakespeare, something else.* That light wouldn't stop blinking on and off. *What did she say? I think it was relevant, I need to consider it further.*

"Can I take your notes?" Leeding asked.

"Of course," Fisher replied, flattered, and handed them over. "All part of the service *ma'am*." She gave a little salute and a smile, which Anna returned. "But there is something else."

"About WOE IS ME?"

"No, about Joseph Wiseman. So, think back, we got an anonymous call from a neighbour saying Wiseman hadn't been seen for a few days. But when Inspector Walker talked to the neighbours, *not one* of them said they'd called the police."

"Yes, Lisa, we discussed that. We thought possibly the caller knew Wiseman hadn't been seen because *they* locked the poor bastard in his basement and wanted us to find him."

"Exactly. They wanted us to find him."

Anna frowned. "Lisa, we've already talked about this, but got nowhere."

"Mm, but we weren't thinking about it in the right way."

Leeding didn't like Fisher's tone of voice. She sounded a little scared. "Go on."

"We weren't looking at the bigger picture. We've just fixated on that phrase, 'they wanted us to find him'. She repeated the phrase with dark emphasis "*They wanted* us *to find him*."

Anna shook her head, lost.

"Us, Anna, *us*."

"You're going to have to spell it out."

"That anonymous caller didn't dial 999, did they? When someone's concerned about a person's safety, most people call 999. But the "neighbour" didn't, they called us directly. Great Portland Street."

Fisher's meaning began to dawn on Leeding.

"Anna, they called the one station in London, in Britain, that suspects the deaths are linked by blue charcoal. The only station that has an open file on it. I know you warn against coincidence but don't you think that's a very, very long shot? That caller knows. They know we're looking for them, which means they know who *we* are. And if they know who we are, then how? I'm scared, because what might they intend to do about it?"

Anna took another long drink. Her mouth had suddenly become very dry.

51 / 28th July, 1981, London.

Fisher and Leeding sat in the Yorkshire Grey and turned over the ramifications of Lisa's idea. It was *possible* the person responsible for blue charcoal had realised Great Portland Street's suspicions, but highly unlikely. There'd been no stories in the papers, since Anna had nothing but theories and supposition. Fisher postulated that perhaps they'd been watched from the very first day. "Maybe *someone* waited to see who found Jeanette West, saw us, then took it from there."

"Perhaps, but, ah, I feel like Alice through the looking glass," Anna threw up her hands in surrender. "Everything is topsy turvy. You look at something solid from one angle, but change your perspective and it blows away like fog. I think I've grasped rope but it turns out to be straw."

"I have an idea. For our own sanity we need to move on, both conversationally and geographically," Fisher said a little too loudly. The beer was having its desired effect. She stood and offered Anna a hand. "How do you fancy a pub crawl?"

"Oh, Jesus, I'm working tomorrow."

"Well, it's not like Charles and Diana are going to get married again, is it? We might as well go and take a look. Think of it as an anthropological study to go and see the British in their natural habitat."

Leeding laughed. "As long as we don't get too close. As we know, the British can bite."

They stepped out into a golden July evening. A crowd sang inside The Crown And Sceptre on the corner of Great Litchfield Street. To the tune of "Daisy Bell" they bellowed, *"Di-ana, Di-ana, give me your answer do, I'd be a span-ner, not to say yes to you."*

Anna winced, but Fisher winked. "Come on, you only live once."

They stepped into the pub and were confronted with a rolling mass who shouted, laughed and danced. Many wore plastic Union Jack bowler hats, quite a few waved flags. Anna and Lisa stood at the doorway and took it all in.

"Remember that film, "The Wicker Man"?" asked Leeding. "That's what this is like. It feels as if we've stepped into some kind of weird pagan ritual."

"I think we'd better find somewhere else before they wheel out a giant wooden wedding cake, stuff us inside and set light to the icing."

"I agree. There are some things you really don't need to experience, plus there are no tables and we'd take an hour to get served."

"Excellent decision."

They tactfully retreated and Anna led Fisher to The Horse And Groom on Great Portland Street,where they took a decision *not* to talk of blue charcoal and Gaye Wiseman. Instead the women retreated into the safety of generalities, histories, recommendations, relations, TV, music, and fashion, but not work. Tonight work was off limits.

After a couple more drinks they weaved, arm in arm, to The Cock Tavern, where both ordered gin and tonics.

"This…" Anna waved her drink at Fisher accusingly, "…this is going to be a very bad idea."

Lisa waggled her own drink back. "Or a very good one. Come on, ma'am, we need to let our hair down, it's been a *fucking* weird few months, excuse my French."

"Excused. Just don't let me catch you using such profanity in uniform. That would get a *fucking* warning."

"Understood."

As with all conversations held from the bottom of a glass, the chat quickly jumped between subjects but never stayed on anything long enough to stick. By nine p.m. both women were in a bubble. If anyone else had joined them, they'd have thought Fisher and Leeding to be drunk, slurring company, but here in their bubble they made complete sense to each other.

"I once asked you something," Lisa lit up yet another cigarette,"and you never answered."

"What something did you ask? When?"

"That first day at Jeanette West's place, ah, *after* her place, actually. I drove you back to the station and asked why you'd got into the force. You said your Dad and then changed the subject. Do you mind if I ask you again? I'm interested."

Anna's head tick-tocked and as she blinked five times. Fisher watched, transfixed. Leeding zoned out for a moment then her eyes refocused. "Ah, shit. I did the thing, didn't I?"

"The thing?"

"Come on, I saw your face. I can always tell when people notice, they become embarrassed, yet fascinated. I call it "the thing," but it's a tic, an involuntary movement, a twitch, a spasm…none of them are very nice words, are they? So I just call it "the thing." It usually doesn't happen if I've had a drink, don't know why, but most of the time "the thing" comes along when I'm focussed, stressed, or thinking about something in particular."

"Oh, OK."

Anna sighed. "Did you notice what brought it on just then?"

Lisa thought for a moment. "I mentioned your Dad."

"Uh huh."

"I'm so sorry. Honestly, let's change the subject, we're having a nice night, I'm sorry, I shouldn't have pried, it's personal."

Leeding took a large gulp of G&T. "No, I think you should know. It's why I've fixated on Jeanette West, why we've ended up with blue charcoal and Gaye Wiseman, and why I joined the police in the first place. Inspector Walker knows, so you should, too."

"I feel terrible," Fisher slurred. "I shouldn't have said *one*. *Single*. *Word*. I don't want to know, it's not my business."

"It has a bearing on all this, so it is your business."

Lisa waited while Anna reached into herself, defiantly set her jaw, took control and started to talk about the past.

*

Fisher sat quietly and thought, *hold on tight, Lisa, because I think this is going to be a horrible, bumpy ride.*

Anna quietly began.

"I was born in the Royal London Hospital in Whitechapel, January 1943. Before you ask, I don't remember the war or my Dad's absence when I was little. I think kids accept whatever is in front of them. I just thought all children had a Mummy at home and Daddies were *somewhere else*. Let's face it, that was the case for most of us, but I was only two and a half when Dad got back from France. I had an older friend who was born in 1938, so she grew up not really knowing her Dad *at all*. When he came home she was seven and told me she hid behind the curtains, couldn't relate to him at all. But when you're two and a bit you just accept what Mum tells you."

Anna didn't seem to notice the crowd who bustled around the pub. She lit a cigarette and continued to channel her past.

"So he was a bit older than other dads and after he war, he reasoned people would want to relax and let off steam, so got into the pub trade. Did you know, pubs never shut during the war unless they were bombed or ran out of stock, of course. To keep morale up, alcohol wasn't rationed, although it did get weaker and more expensive even after the war ended, but Dad was right about people wanting to have fun again. So he became landlord of a boozer called The Flying Scud in Hackney, much bigger than our old place. I never questioned why Mum and Dad had people round *every night,* it just happened. Then we moved to a bigger premises in Whitechapel, the George & Dragon. I would have been about eight and it had this big wooden carving of a dragon behind the bar, I loved it, especially at Christmas. Can you imagine being a kid and *every single day* running up to Christmas is a party? Beautiful decorations everywhere, snow falling outside, fires lit in the hearths, it was magic. Of course, I never saw just how hard Mum and Dad worked. When you're in the pub trade, it does *not* stop. You go to bed later then everyone else, without even the benefit of having a night out, then it's up first thing for the drayman, cleaning, doing the books, and running your family. There was only the three of us, but it's still a hefty load to deal with."

She stopped and coughed a little. "Lisa, would you mind getting me another G&T? A large would be lovely." Anna grabbed her purse and picked out a few pound notes, but Fisher dismissed them. "No, it's my turn. Honest, you don't have to tell me this."

Leeding shook her head, vehemently. "Don't be offended, but I'm telling this for *me.* I can count on one hand the amount of times I've said it out loud, perhaps I should talk about it more. So please don't apologise or feel guilty, just listen. I need this."

Lisa nodded, went to the bar and when she looked back over her shoulder, saw Anna motionlessly staring at the wall.

I've opened a box I really shouldn't have, Fisher thought, *and now who knows what's going to fly out?*

Leeding gratefully took the drink and carried on. "I won't say it was idyllic, but life was certainly better for me than some of the other children I knew. So, to, er, 1954."

She paused, shut her eyes for a moment and then took a longer drink. "It was an evening in July 1954 and Mum and Dad had an argument, which was unusual, but not unique. If you run a pub there's never a day off. You get Sunday morning and afternoon but it's not like other jobs, because the workers are in each other's pockets twenty-four hours a day. When do you ever see pubs with a sign up saying, CLOSED, ON HOLIDAY?"

Fisher smiled. "You know, I never thought about it before, but no, I've never seen one."

"Right. If a landlord really wants a break the brewery hire a temporary manager, but generally, gaffers are reluctant to hand over their family home and business to someone else just in case they do it better. Mum and Dad were running to stand still so tempers frayed occasionally. Anyway, this particular evening, Friday, the second… Friday the second…of…July…"

Fisher took Anna's hand. "Look, I think you should do this when we're not so drunk, certainly not in a pub the night before a public holiday."

"Do I look like I can stop?" Anna hissed and threw Lisa's hand off. She looked down at the table then back to Fisher, pale faced. "I'm sorry, I'm so sorry. The train's running and I can't get off now, got to ride it all the way."

"I understand." *I thought I was on a night out with my boss, no, my friend. Now I'm somewhere very different. It looks like a pub, sounds like a pub, but I'm in Anna's life now.*

"So they had an argument. To this day I have no idea what it was about. I was upstairs and heard the regulars cheer, so Mum had obviously said something cutting to Dad and the customers were showing their appreciation, you know, like men do when *the good lady wife* stands up to the old man. I looked out of my bedroom window and saw her striding off. It was about nine."

There was a very long pause. Anna looked around the pub as if seeing it for the first time.

"They found her body behind bushes in Weaver's Fields. She'd been raped and murdered, strangled. I didn't know that at the time, of course, not the details. I still don't know, really, I prefer not to. The words "raped and murdered" are enough, aren't they? But she was dead. The last time I saw her, she was marching off into the distance, blonde hair catching the last of the evening light. She never looked back."

Oh my God. Oh God, Anna, no. Fisher looked down, away from Leeding's haunted eyes.

"Jesus, Anna, I'm so sorry."

"Thank you. The funeral was unreal. That's the best description I can give. Me and Dad went through all the rituals you're supposed to, but it was like acting. We were playing our parts but never really thought we were on anything but a stage. We couldn't, wouldn't accept it. Dad was understandably consumed with anger, vengeance. The pub shut for a while, which was the first time I'd ever known when our living room wasn't full of friends and strangers. I used to walk about the place and see it with new eyes, empty of people, empty of Mum. Our home wasn't really our home anymore, I realised it was no different from Woolworths or the Co-Op, just another business where customers went for a service."

"Did they…?"

Anna knew what Fisher was trying to say. "No, they never caught him, it was 1954, things weren't as sophisticated." She laughed then, a dry, bitter chuckle. "Mind you, look at us here in 1981, not much better. So whoever he was, he could still be out there. How old was he then? Twenty? Thirty? Forty?"

She looked around the pub and her eyes thinned as she took in the men's faces. "Nowadays, he might only be in his early fifties. Maybe even younger than that, might even be dead, but I hope not. I want to find that fucker, find him and kill him."

Anna fell silent.

"I'm so sorry."

What do I say to that? What can I say to that? Lisa wondered. *Some things are so beyond our experience that silence becomes our only viable response.*

"It's a lot to take in but I wanted you to know, Lisa, because that's how it started."

"That's how it *started?*"

"Mm, me and Dad, we just muddled on at the pub. He didn't want to leave, wanted to be close to her memory. I now know that people go one of two ways after that kind of trauma. You either face up to reality or run away, hide and build a wall around the past. Dad took the latter road, which was the wrong decision. He grinned and bore it, hired a barman and a cleaner then got on with serving beer to the good pissheads of Whitechapel. He was a good Dad."

Fisher smiled along with her boss.

"But it was another act, I know that now. The trips to Southend Pier, Regent's Park Zoo, Christmas and birthday presents, parties, pretty dresses and help with homework…It was all just wallpaper, you know? It looks nice but has no depth. I didn't know that at the time, I thought we were just coping. Not moving on, no, that would have been terrible, but rather shifting our view a little, adjusting to the fact we had Mum and then we didn't, but still had us. Then I turned sixteen."

Please, I hope this isn't going where I think it might be, Anna. I think I want you to stop, right now, Lisa pleaded internally. *Pull the emergency cord on that train and bring it to a halt. I want to get off.*

"I'd just finished school. Did well in my exams, actually. Dad held a party for me at the pub, naturally. All the regulars were there. Dad's sister, my old Gran, friends from my class...he was so proud. He'd hand made a banner and I remember looking at him as he did a little speech. He wasn't one for speeches, so that was different, and he was beaming, overjoyed. But that's how it works, apparently; a sudden euphoria, a lifting of the dark, sun coming through clouds, all the clichés. Again, I just thought he was proud and having fun."

She went silent again and stared at the ceiling. Anna lit up another cigarette to add to the butts that had already congregated in the ashtray.

"I went to bed about eleven. There were some late stragglers, Dad always had a few regulars staying after the bell but then it went quiet, as it always did eventually. Well, not *quite* quiet. I could hear him downstairs, singing "It Doesn't Matter Any More" by Buddy Holly. Ha. Then I drifted off. I was asleep for an hour or so and he must have looked in on me, because my door was open when it had been shut. I wonder how long he stood there?"

Anna's eyes began to water but she pursed her lips, took another drag and carried on. "Then I was woken up by a bang from downstairs. I called for Dad, but there was no answer, so I crept down and..." She shut her eyes. "I couldn't take it in. You know when something happens and you think it's happening to someone else, because it's just too alien? That's what this was like. My Dad was flying, he was *hovering* in front of the bar, mid air, arms by his sides, looking down at something on the floor. And I put my hands to my mouth, because it was magic, look! My Dad could fly, hover like a humming bird! And then I saw the rope around his neck which kept him up there. He'd fixed it to one of the beams, stood on the bar, flew, and there he was, in the air. I couldn't say anything, just stood there with my hands to my mouth and then felt this...*sound*...coming from me, no, maybe coming from somewhere far away, making its way to my mouth. It was a scream, but not just me, it was like the whole universe screaming *through* me. I unbolted the door and just ran through Whitechapel, screaming, screaming. I don't remember who found me or where I ended up, but I still dream of that night, running from my Dad hanging up there, running away because maybe the further I got the less real it would be."

Fisher felt tears on her cheeks. The mouths of the other customers moved and their faces pulled expressions of laughter and happiness but suddenly there was no sound anymore. Just Lisa, Anna and the past, here at this tiny table.

Fisher took Anna's hand again. "I'm so sorry," was all she could say.

Leeding nodded. "They buried him in the City Of London Cemetery, next to Mum, which is why I know it so well. I went to live with my Auntie and that's when "the thing" started. Doctors put it down to shock, stress, trauma…They didn't really know. I think a bit of my mind is replaying it over and over, like when you pause a video tape and it…stutters. Part of me will always be standing in the bar, trying to make sense of what I'm seeing. I blink and twitch but can never understand it." She shook her head. "They shut the pub soon after that and I've never gone back. It's offices now, which is fine by me. He never left a note nor gave any hints, but Dad waited until I'd left school to do it. I sometimes wonder if he believed I was finally an adult at that point, so I could cope with what he planned to do. I didn't, of course. First Mum then Dad, both taken violently away, one by their own hand, the other by person or persons unknown, but the result was the same, I needed direction, couldn't find it for a while, but then I joined the force. I didn't know why at the time, but if I'm going to analyse myself like a bad amateur psychologist it may have been a need for *literal* law and order. I nearly quit in 1964 after a bad experience. Someone died because of my actions, but I kept going."

You're still looking for reasons, thought Fisher. *One day you hope to find your Mum's killer and also discover why your Dad jumped.*

Perhaps Lisa's thoughts were transparent because Anna smiled, sadly. "I don't think it's because I want vengeance or answers, not really. But maybe it *is* as simple as a need for order. It's why I became fixated with Jeanette West's suicide. Her death seemed cut and dried but I just knew it demanded more answers, she deserved that, at least. But you know what nearly broke me?"

Lisa shook her head.

"I told my ex, Robin, everything I just told you and he *hung himself*. He knew what my past had done to me and still chose that way out. It was no coincidence, he wanted me to suffer, throw me back, make me watch my Dad hover there in front of the bar again. I know Robin was sick, I know he needed help but that was just evil. His final act on this earth was evil, designed to destroy himself but hopefully take me with him as collateral. For a while he nearly did, but I wasn't going to let him have the satisfaction. I never went to his funeral, you know. People thought that was weird but they didn't know his suicide was an act of violence against me, a petulant, foot stamping terminal tantrum. I've tried to find genuine pity for Robin, but I can't."

She hung her head, spent. "So there you are. It took a bloody pub crawl and who knows how many drinks, but that's why I do what I do."

"Thank you for telling me. I can't begin to imagine what it took."

Anna lit up another cigarette and stared at the burning end. "I just thought it was important for you to know who I really am."

You could leave it there. Thought Fisher. *You could get another couple of drinks, slowly change the subject then end the evening laughing again, eventually. You could go home and keep things as they are.*

Lisa lit a cigarette of her own and Leeding smiled wanly at her.

But you can't do that, can you? You may never get this opportunity again, never be this drunk, or uninhibited. Anna might not ever want to be this honest again. You have to do it now.

Fisher took another drink, then looked Leeding in the eye. She could see Anna sense the change in atmosphere and stiffen up a little.

"Lisa? Are you OK?"

"You said it was important for me to know who you really are," she said softly, slowly, carefully. "But Anna, I've known for some time. I know *exactly* who you are."

52 / Gaye

Later that same night, Gaye Wiseman stood back and proudly studied her achievement. It had been literally years in the planning and months in the execution, but finally her life's work was nearly done.

There was just one more to take care of.

She looked up at the walls with a wide smile.

"Yes," she said quietly, "*yesyesyes*, that's it."

Gaye took a few steps back to see everything in a wider context. From here she could see the subtlety of it all, admire how everything fitted together *just so*. Wiseman allowed herself a moment of vainglory, since she deserved it.

Fuck you, Birch, she thought. *You knew nothing. Shame you're not around to appreciate this. Mind you,* professor, *you couldn't even see what was right in front of your face.*

She thought back to Birch's *hilarious* shock as he'd tumbled backwards, and at the professor's pathetic pleading expression when she'd grabbed his head and *twwwwwisssssted*. Gaye giggled like a schoolgirl.

Wiseman walked over to a table and cocked her head at what was on it.

Ooh, you little beauty, she thought. *You may be an ugly little fucker but to me, you're gorgeous. I'll never have children, but you'll do, you'll do just fine. Make me proud, huh?*

Gaye stretched her arms out and span on the spot like Julie Andrews at the top of a mountain. Wiseman span faster and faster until she lost her balance and tumbled to the floor.

She looked up and around the room then laughed until tears spilled down her cheeks. After a while, Gaye wasn't sure if she was laughing or screaming.

53 / July 29th 1981, London.

Beep beep. T-Bom-Bom. Tikitatikatatikatatikata. Ki-Bom-Bom.

Anna Leeding's clock radio sounded at 7:15 a.m. BBC Radio One DJ Mike Read was on the air. "A brand new sound from a brand new band!Climbing the chart, it's Soft Cell with "Tainted Love" on 275/285, National Radio One."

"Please God, no," Anna moaned. Soft Cell, whoever the hell *they* were, bleeped on relentlessly.

Beep beep. T-Bom-Bom. Tikitatikatatikatatikata. Ki-Bom-Bom.

Oh. Oh, here I am, she managed to think. *Good God. My head feels like it's full of lighter fluid.*

She opened her eyes and stared at the ceiling.

She let the music *ki-bom-bom* to its conclusion, too drained to care.

"I think that could be a future number one, what about you? But there's no "Tainted Love" today, that's for sure, ha! Today's a celebration and Kool And The Gang have just the song! Is it too early for a party? No!"

Yes, for the love of God, it is. I don't want Kool or any of his gang now.

Anna slammed down the OFF button.

Oh. Last night. Oh, a lot was said, wasn't it? Too much? No. Yes.

She willed memories to come back through the white light of her hangover.

Fisher knows. Fisher knows, but more to the point, Fisher doesn't care.

Lisa Fisher.

She pictured the WPC's face and smiled.

Thank God for Lisa Fisher.

She swung out of bed, gingerly looked in her wardrobe mirror, inspected the wreckage that had been a blonde bob then ran her fingers through it. The bob fell into place as required and Anna managed to creak to her feet.

*

Leeding had a brief wrestling match with a dressing gown before she managed to pull it into submission, then padded out into the hallway.

A scrap of paper with a smudged phone number sat on her hallway table. Anna looked at the number thoughtfully then gave a little smile.

Unexpected, but very welcome. Coffee. My head needs coffee. My life *needs coffee.*

She walked into her tiny kitchen and flicked on the kettle. While it boiled, she dragged herself next door into the living room. The television screen regarded her blankly. Just as impassively, she stared right back and thought about last night.

*

"I know exactly who you are," Fisher said slowly.

"Sorry, what? What do you mean, '*you know exactly who I am*?'"

"It's OK. You've been truthful with me but I'm not sure you've been altogether truthful with yourself."

"I don't know what you're talking about." Anna felt her face redden as the pub seemed to have become smaller and hotter.

"Please, Anna, just hear me out."

"I don't like people telling me who and what I am. I know who I am."

Lisa didn't break eye contact. "I'm so grateful you opened up to me about your parents, I really am. That must have taken such a lot. But you just need to take one more step, don't you?"

"One more…? I'm not in the mood for riddles." Deep down, Leeding thought she knew where her colleague and friend was heading. She felt herself become flustered.

"I think we'd better finish up now. Thanks for listening to me, I've had a lovely night and I appreciate your patience and company, but I've had a lot to drink and need some fresh air."

"Please." Fisher took Leeding's hand and Anna didn't resist. "Just a few more minutes. Please, it's important, *really* important."

Leeding lit another cigarette and wasn't surprised to see her hand shook.

"I lied to you," said Fisher.

"Lied? What about? When?"

"After Robin did what he did. Last month we went out for a drink, you told me about him and I told you about my boyfriend. How he'd killed himself, too."

"You lied about that? Jesus, why would you lie about something like that?"

Anna went to stand, but Fisher kept hold of her hand. "No, I didn't lie about it. Please. Killed themselves, jumped out of the window, that was the truth. Everything I said was the truth. Well, not quite everything."

Leeding sat back in her chair, took another drink and then realised both her pack of cigarettes and glass were empty. "Should we get another one?"

"Yes, I think so."

Fisher disappeared to the bar and Anna thought, *I'm going to need this, aren't I?*

She watched Lisa work her way back through the mainly male crowd. Quite a few heads turned and appraising eyes slid down her body. Fisher sat down with two more glasses.

"Her name was Janice."

"Her name? Who?"

"My boyfriend wasn't a boyfriend. Her name was Janice. My first girlfriend."

"Oh." Anna felt her heart rate leap a few notches. "I see."

"You see what? You see why I lied? You see why I'm telling you now? You see why she jumped?" There was no vitriol in Fisher's voice, just a gentle sadness. "Janice jumped because..." Lisa bit her lip, "...although she taught me who I was, she never really accepted who *she* was. Her parents disowned her, she got forced, well, bullied out of her job when they found out, had to take a lesser one and tell nobody. Not being allowed to be who you are, it's a prison. It killed her, quite literally. This world..." she looked around the pub, "...it wasn't made for Janice, or for me. Look around at everyone, square pegs fitting neatly into their square holes. No squares in round holes, or if there are, they keep it well hidden. You have to hide to survive. Everyone's celebrating Charles and Diana, but that's not the only story, is it? Here we are in a new decade but it's the same old world. Janice saw the future but couldn't see any part in it for her. She freed me, then freed herself. I loved her, *and* I hated her for it."

Lisa made no attempt to wipe away or hide her tears. She seemed proud of them. "So I reinvented myself, learned how to live under the radar, if you like. That's what Janice called it. 'Under the radar,' I liked that. 'They can't stop you if they can't see you,' she'd say. One day in the future people might have seen and accepted her but that's not today, is it? I couldn't think of a more drastic inversion than joining the force. Punk rock to police officer, quite a flip, wouldn't you agree? Under the radar, but in full view."

"I see. I understand."

"Yes, you do see and you *do* understand, don't you? Remember that first day we met, at Jeanette West's house? I opened the door and recognised you immediately."

"Recognised?' Wondered Anna. "But you'd only just been transferred, I hadn't even seen you until that day."

"But I saw *you*, wearing a black wig, dressed totally different to anything I've ever seen you in, but you can't hide that face. You're beautiful, Anna, surely you know that?"

Leeding's head spun.

She knows. Oh God, she knows. Thank God she knows.

"It was back in February, at the Ivygreen."

"I see." Anna realised she'd said those two words a few times now. They were noncommittal and nothing else seemed appropriate. The Ivygreen was a pub in Earl's Court. Casual visitors may have noticed the clientele was made up of more women than usual, but other than that, The Ivygreen, like its customers, also kept itself under the radar.

"Do you remember that night?"

Anna nodded.

"I was there with a couple of girlfriends. Not *girlfriend*, girlfriends, you know what I mean. You walked in and I won't say the pub stopped, it wasn't like those Westerns where everyone turns to the saloon doors and the piano player freezes mid song, but enough people looked. I remember thinking you looked like a Bond girl. Black hair, bolero jacket, short skirt, little suede boots. Actually now I think about it, you looked like a pop star, but you left Sam Bizarre in the shade."

"He's a man!" Anna laughed. It was the first laugh she'd had for a while tonight.

"Well, Debbie Harry, then, or Kim Wilde. I spotted you were in disguise straight away. To some extent, I suppose everyone at The Ivygreen is in some kind of disguise but you weren't quite comfortable in the outfit, which is a bit of a giveaway. But even so, you looked amazing."

"Thank you."

"You went straight to a corner and there was a woman sitting there. She was blonde, too, attractive. Who was that?"

"My friend Mary Price, the pathologist I told you about, she's been helping me out with you-know-who."

"Well, that's the problem, we don't know who, do we? Sorry to be so forward, but are you and Mary...?"

"No, no. We had a very brief thing a few years back but realised we made better friends than girlfriends." Although Fisher already knew her truth, Anna realised she'd just confirmed it. She pressed on. "Mary spotted who I was years ago. But like you, like me, she was never open about it. She hated me having boyfriends, thought I was being unfair to them and to myself. I suppose I was."

With every word, Anna felt freer. There'd been so much she'd kept in and now it was coming out, in a poky Central London pub.

Funny how massive moments in your life can appear with no fanfare, in the strangest of places, she thought.

Fisher shook her head. "What was it John Lennon said, bless him? "Whatever Gets You Through The Night"? None of us can judge anyone else, whatever gets us through the night."

"It *was* unfair to them, though."

"Did you think you might have been straight? Tried to convince yourself, go through the motions?"

"There was an element of that. But it was mostly fear, no, it was terror. I didn't want to be found out, so yes, I did whatever it took. I wish I hadn't."

"No, don't ever say that. You did what you had to, we all do, so when I saw you at West's house, it was hard not to just stare with my mouth wide open. At The Ivygreen there was this vision, and then here she was, a detective inspector, my superior. That was weird. I'm afraid I did some digging, sorry."

"Digging?"

"Well, I wanted to be sure. You get some women at The Ivygreen who, well, they're just women, you know? Straight women who feel more comfortable, safer in there. Your file had no next of kin mentioned, no husband, boyfriend, not anyone."

"Wait, you looked in my file?"

"Just a quick peek. And I asked around, you know, on the scene. I described you and eventually found a couple of girls who'd spent the night with you."

Anna didn't know whether to be offended or amused. "Jesus, Lisa. I thought you could make a great detective and now I'm sure. That, or a blackmailer." That made Leeding think for a moment. "You're not going to tell anyone, are you? Please don't, I've worked so hard, I…"

"Anna, please. Who do you think I am? We're on the same side, we've fought the same battles, mainly against ourselves, if we're honest. I just wanted you to know you're not alone. You don't have to do this by yourself, OK? We are…" She searched for the word, "…in camouflage. Because we have to be, there's no choice in the matter. I hate skulking about, I hate having to go to a "special" pub, I hate pretending to be flattered when some bloke pinches my arse. But what else can we do? If you take off your camouflage, you become a target. But you have me, now, you're not alone and that's the most important thing in the world, because loneliness is unbearable."

They sat silently while the rest of the pub went about its business, oblivious.

"Why didn't you say something sooner?" Anna asked.

"Because I didn't know you sooner, did I? And that's not exactly a conversation you can have with a stranger, or a superior officer."

"Thank you," said Leeding. "Thank you for being true. There's not enough truth in the world."

"Shall I tell you another truth?"

"Go on."

"I am cataclysmically pissed."

They clinked their glasses and laughed.

Leeding and Fisher talked for a while longer of shared experiences and histories, of the profane and the banal. But eventually Anna shook her head and held up her hands. "I really do have to go now. I'm at work first thing and I don't know if I'll even hear the alarm."

Fisher stood and held out her hand. "Well, you can't say it wasn't a memorable night."

"Hm, after this much gin, I'm not sure how much I'll remember of it."

Arm in arm, they slowly weaved up a deserted Great Portland Street. Lisa turned to Leeding, rummaged through her bag, found eyeliner and some paper, then wrote her number on it. "I know you could get this from work." She handed it over, laughed and bowed, formally. "But I always think it's better when somebody gives it of their own volition."

"You used the word, "volition" this late. That's impressive."

"Well, I try. You're in Tottenham Court Road, aren't you?"

Anna waved airily to her left. "Uh huh, five minutes. Well, ten, since my legs seem to be insisting on walking diagonally."

"I'm in Ladbroke Grove, so I'll be attempting to get on a tube without falling onto the tracks."

"Good luck. Enjoy your day off."

"Enjoy your day on."

"Thank you, WPC Fisher."

"Thank *you*, D.I. Leeding."

Before Anna could register it, Fisher leaned forward, kissed her on the lips, saluted, then turned and headed for Oxford Circus station. Leeding watched her go and smiled.

*

Hungover, Anna sat on her sofa and watched Britain prepare for a Royal Wedding. She thought of riots, Romantics, rippers and royals, considered blue charcoal and a vengeful fury named Gaye Wiseman. Then with a pounding head but a skipping, lighter heart, she went to work.

And died.

54 / Wednesday 29th July 1981, London.

By nine thirty, Anna sat at her desk and tried to concentrate on the mountain of paperwork that needed to be done. Most of the station was on crowd duty today, including Walker, so the place was comparatively empty. Her hangover hadn't shifted and several cups of coffee had only made her jittery rather than focussed.

I should have taken the day off, she thought. *Gone to Ladbroke Grove, sat with Fisher and compared notes on Lady Di's dress. That seems like a brilliant idea.*

She stared at the pile of information which needed to be processed but couldn't focus on one single thing. Her mind returned to Lisa instead.

I've never spoken to anyone like that, not even Mary. So what does last night mean? Does it mean we're something, *now? No, but do you* want *it to be? Ah, I don't know. But I have a friend, a friend who understands, understands the world, understands me. I feel free. I might not be, but inside that's how I feel. Last night may have been the first hours of the rest of my life. That's a lot to take in.*

She sighed and pulled out the blue charcoal file. It was nebulous enough to give her something else to think about but not too specific to spike the hangover. The same photos, notes, interviews, photocopies…Still nothing leapt out, so it remained a crazed map full of roads that all led nowhere.

Anna remembered Fisher's notes and pulled them from her bag. Lisa's chaotic handwriting covered the pages with no sense of order. There were quotes from The Bible, Shakespeare and more. Seemingly random dates and names worked their way up the margins and question marks were dotted about the text.

Jesus, Lisa, you'll make a great detective one day, but you have the handwriting of a doctor.

Leeding looked over the pages and tried to find an idea to develop. Fisher's biblical interpretation of "Woe is me" was interesting but needed a lot of assumptions to make it work and like many conspiracy theories, it seemed plausible until held up to the light. Then there was her Ophelia angle, which Lisa had bent and twisted to make fit the facts but couldn't stand up on its own. Anna didn't know what half the shorthand notes meant and then there were dates and days of the week, which Fisher had tried to connect in myriad ways but failed. Leeding could see where a frustrated Lisa had pushed so hard with the pen it had gone through the paper.

But there's something here, she thought. *I remember last night, one part of Fisher's theories had stuck. What was it? Days of the week. She mentioned days of the week and a little light went on. Why was that?*

Anna grabbed a 1981 desk calendar and flicked through. The dates had notable birthdays and events from history.

Saturday, April fourth was the death of Jeanette West. On that day in 1964, The Beatles had the entire American top five. Martin was killed in a hit and run on Monday, thirteenth of April and on that day in history Guy Fawkes was born. Woeful Nick Atkey probably died on Monday, twenty-first of April and on the same date in 1918 the Red Baron is shot down. Woe is me, indeed, thought Anna. *This is pointless, meaningless. The only person who knows the pattern is Gaye Wiseman and she isn't going to make it easy for us.*

Fisher had written WOE IS ME across the top of one sheet.

There's something about that phrase which got Lisa's attention, but it's not a biblical or Shakespearean context.

Leeding tapped her fingers on the notes and thought.

She was flipping between days, dates and those words. Fisher obviously thought there was some connection between them, but what? WOE IS ME. It's so archaic. Nobody says, "woe" any more. You only find it in old texts, yet Gaye Wiseman specifically chose that word, and the rest. It has weight, it's important. She could have written I'M SO SAD, or I CAN'T LIVE, but used WOE IS ME. Where did she hear it?

Anna's head tick-tocked and she blinked five times exactly.

No, no, not where did Gaye *hear it, where have* I *heard it before? Forget Gaye, think about your own experience.*

Leeding closed her eyes, searched her memory and went looking for where she may have heard the word "woe." She imagined it as a key and tried to find the right lock.

Woe. Woe. Woe. Woe.

The word stopped having any meaning and simply became a sound in Anna's head which rolled round and round, over and over,

Woe and days of the week. days of the week and woe. Think back, back to when you were very young.

Her eyes snapped open.

Oh Jesus Christ, that's it.

That is it.

Gaye Wiseman, you weren't thinking about Shakespeare or The Bible, this wasn't some allusion to classical literature. You were thinking about nursery school.

55 / 29th July 1981, London.

Anna arranged the SOC photos on her desk in chronological order from Jeanette West to Joseph Wiseman.

How did I miss this? It's staring me in the face and always has been. But solutions are only easy once you've found them.

A radio blared somewhere in the station. Until the wedding parade began there was nothing left to say about the occasion, but the DJ was saying it anyway. Anna tuned it all out and stared down at the photographs.

She saw Jeanette West in bed, head beatifically tilted back as if awaiting Jesus to float down on a sunbeam. Her open wrists lay either side and blood soaked into the sheets. The word FACE was framed in blue charcoal above her.

Jeanette had been to school with Gaye.

Right in front of me. Anna shook her head. *Right there.*

The Reverend Martin lay broken on a pavement in Primrose Hill. Leeding thought back to that frost kissed night. A car had mounted the pavement, struck him, and she'd found the word FOG just behind his body.

Martin had lived in Gaye's road.

Nicholas Atkey hung from a bar in his kitchen as if knelt in prayer. Anna winced at that, since the noose was a trigger, but forced herself to look. Propped up on his kitchen table was a note, WOE IS ME.

Nick had worked with Gaye Wiseman at a bank.

Professor Birch was twisted into impossible angles at the bottom of his stairs in Southampton Row, eyes open, head bent round further than nature intended. Framed on the wall above him, the word GO.

He'd smashed Gaye's dreams of attending art college.

Anna saw Damon Whitehill, the pizza baron and paedophile, face down in his pool, arms outstretched like he'd been given a water crucifixion. On the wall, in blue charcoal; LOVING. He had no direct connection with Gaye Wiseman but Anna was pretty sure that Joy Smart, the woman who'd put out Damon's eye with a lit cigarette, was the same person.

Full circle.

Nearly.

Leeding looked at Joseph Wiseman, fingernails bloodied, slumped against his workbench in the home his daughter Gaye had once shared. He'd died in the dark and the word WORK had been picked out behind him in charcoal.

Patricide, Gaye. So what did he do to you? Or was it a case of what didn't he do for you?

WOE IS ME had been the key. That strange old English word, WOE blinking like a beacon, waiting to be spotted.

Put together with Gaye's name and all the other words, the killer's pattern jumped into focus.

Model Jeanette West was FAIR OF **FACE**.

Reverend Martin was FULL OF GRACE, **F.O.G. FOG.**

Charity phone Samaritan Nick Atkey was FULL OF **WOE**.

Globe trotting Professor Birch always had FAR TO **GO**.

Cheating pervert Damon Whitehill was, surely sarcastically, **LOVING** AND GIVING.

And Daddy Wiseman clearly had no time for his only daughter when she was growing up. He'd **WORK**ED HARD FOR A LIVING.

A child's nursery rhyme. Gaye Wiseman, you bitch, you're choosing your victims through the rhyme, "Monday's Child." Their lives fitted the words.

She thought back to the last line of that particular verse.

"And the child that is born on the Sabbath day is bonny and blithe, and good and gay." Although Anna also remembered another version which said, *"And the child that is born on the Sabbath day is fair and wise and good and gay."*

Wise.

Oh, you spelled it right out, didn't you, Gaye Wiseman? But what does that last line mean? Who's the final victim? What's your definition of "gay"? Does "gay" mean happy? Or are you referring to being gay? Or is it a pun on your name, in which case, do you intend to finish this with your own death?

Anna put her head in her hands because along with the hangover, it felt like her brain was being boiled in there.

So I have the pattern but still don't know why she's leaving the words. What function do they have? As Daniel pointed out, without the blue charcoal she could have killed without alerting any suspicions, so what is their point?

Leeding didn't know, but reached into her pocket and found Fisher's number written in eyeliner. Anna picked up her phone and went to dial.

Oh Lisa, you were so close, you just had the pieces in the wrong order.

At that moment, a WPC appeared at her desk. "Ma'am, there's someone out front to see you. She says her name is Sarah Nicholls and that you asked her to come in."

"Sarah Nicholls?"

Jeanette's number one fan and imaginary lover. What's she doing here?

"Ah, I never asked her to come in."

"I thought that, because her name wasn't on the appointments list. But she insists you asked. Something about a photo."

Anna shakily stood then reluctantly followed the WPC to the station entrance. Sarah Nicholls sat on a bench, a sensible bag primly clutched in her hands. She stared straight ahead and was clearly in her best outfit, a curiously formal buttoned up blouse, bright green cardigan, A-line skirt and black court shoes. Her blonde hair was tied into a ponytail and Sarah wore the barest hint of eyeliner and blusher. The whole appearance made her look like an extra from 1970s retro comedy, "Happy Days," waiting to be given stage directions. Leeding wondered just how lost she was.

"Sarah?"

Sarah looked up and fashioned a smile. "Detective Inspector Leeding. It's an exciting day, isn't it?"

You have no idea, thought Anna.

"I don't normally leave the house on my day off but I bought a camera, look."

She had a little Olympus round her neck. "I'm going to the Mall. I'd imagine around St Paul's will be extremely busy. I don't like crowds, but I'll do my best today."

"Well, enjoy yourself. But I'm a little confused because I didn't ask you to come in. You've been very helpful and I do hope you're coming to terms with your loss, but…"

"Oh, I don't think so, " she said quietly. "But we do what we can, don't we? But you *did* ask me to come in. You specifically did."

Anna sat next to her on the bench.

Now is not the time, Sarah. But I'll listen then send you to meet Charles and Diana.

"Do you remember? I told you about the first autographed picture Jeanette sent me, and I asked if you'd like to see it." She shut her eyes and spoke in an eerily accurate impression of Anna's voice, "You said, *'wow, I'd like to see that picture one day'*. And then I asked if you really did and you said, *'Yes please.'* See?"

Oh, God. She's picked up on a throwaway line and homed in on it. This is how delusion and obsession start."Oh, yes I did, didn't I?"

Sarah reached into her bag and proudly pulled out a black and white fan club shot of Jeanette West. The picture must have been taken around 1977, judging by the fashion and haircut. West sat on a wall and smiled widely at the camera. She wore an "Annie Hall" waistcoat and tie, which was briefly popular with women in those days. "See?" Sarah pointed at three Xs along the bottom. "I asked her to put three kisses and she did. She knew."

I really don't want to have to do this again now, Anna thought as her head began to pound again. She took the photograph, feigned interest and turned it over. On the back was an ink stamp of the photographic company responsible, CLICKSNAPZOOM PHOTOGRAPHY, and in West's handwriting, the words, "My VERY best wishes!"

"See? She used capitals, so I knew Jeanette understood my code."

Anna turned the photo over again and handed it back. "Well, thanks for bringing it in. I can see it means a lot to you."

"It does."

Leeding stood to usher Sarah back out into the world but Nicholls didn't move. "Oh, there was another thing."

"Another?"

"When I was leaving last time you said if I thought of anything else, anything at all, I should let you know. Well, I have, detective inspector, I racked and racked my brains going over it and I remembered something else."

Anna sat back down again. "Go on."

"You know I said that person came along? The one with the big flat bag."

That woman who I'm almost certain was Gaye Wiseman? "Yes."

"Well, as you know, as I said, it was quite dark but I think they got something out of that large flat bag and showed it to Jeanette. I couldn't see what, but it wasn't big. She was very drunk and leaned down at whatever-it-was, then nearly fell over. The person held her steady and Jeanette looked at...something. That's when they helped her upstairs and left the flat bag up against the wall."

Anna considered this development. "You can't say what it was?"

"No, sorry. But Jeanette seemed interested, the way she leaned down to look. Although that might have been because she was so tipsy, you know how people squint when they've had a few? Something small, maybe not much bigger than..." She thought for a moment, then held up the autographed picture of West. "Not much bigger than this, maybe. Is that helpful?"

"It might well be, yes. Thank you Sarah, thank you for coming in."

"Well, it's good to help the authorities in these trying times."

Her old fashioned formality was amusingly sweet. *You're an anachronism*, thought Anna. *A beautiful, confused, astray anachronism.*

"Well, take care, Sarah."

"You take care, detective inspector. I think you need to take a lot more care than me, in your line of work."

Leeding walked her to the door and she held up her camera again. "Wish me luck! I hope they kiss. I'd love to get a photo of them kissing."

"Well, I hope you do."

Sarah gave a little wave and disappeared into London. Anna leaned against the door frame, watched her go and thought.

*

She returned to her desk and went over what Nicholls said. Anna shut her eyes and tried to picture the scene at West's house, to play it again from a few angles, like how a film director would choose their shots.

Jeanette West has a blazing, drunken row with Sam Bizarre, who dramatically exits, slamming the door behind him. According to Sarah, West drinks some more, puts on some music and dances around. But then, ten, fifteen minutes later, someone knocks at the door. West stumbles up the hall and then lets whoever-she-is into her home. Even if you're drunk, you don't invite a stranger in.

Anna mentally walked into the hall along with the mysterious visitor, who was possibly Gaye Wiseman. She looked at drunk Jeanette, who swayed and leaned on the wall to stay up.

West went to school with Gaye Wiseman, Did she recognise her? Did Jeanette and Gaye stay friends after school? No, no. For whatever reason, Gaye hated *West, despised her enough to kill. So Jeanette only knew Gaye as* somebody else. *Gaye had taken on yet another role, like "Joy Smart." But who?*

Anna tried to look through Jeanette's eyes. *Who did she see? Or rather, who did she* think *she saw? It's someone you know, someone you trust, maybe even somebody you're glad to see, a friendly face. There's a knock at the door, it's late. You were supposed to be spending the whole night with Sam Bizarre but that all went wrong. So you wouldn't have arranged to see anyone else that evening, would you?*

Mentally, Leeding walked around West's hallway. She looked up the stairs lined with photographs, then through to the kitchen where music played and empty wine bottles stood.

No, you had your night all planned out. So this was a surprise caller, wasn't it? But someone you knew well enough or at least trusted *enough to invite in. Who? What? A special delivery? Surely not on a Saturday night, though I suppose it's possible. A neighbour? Friend? Police officer? Work colleague? Who?*

Anna saw West smile at her unexpected guest, drunkenly pull them in, maybe even give them a hug. *"Boy, am I glad to see you." Does the visitor say they were "just passing"? What reason did they give to come knocking? They had a big, flat, art portfolio bag, just like an artist would use, an artist like Gaye Wiseman.*

Leeding watched as the visitor smiled and said they had something West needed to see. The portfolio bag was unzipped and the caller held something up. But Jeanette could barely stand, and mentally, Anna walked around her as she leaned down and squinted at what was being offered.

And what is being offered?

Leeding tried to peer over West's shoulder, but she was in the way.

Is it the blue charcoal artwork that reads FACE?

Anna watched as the visitor held up the FACE frame for Jeanette, but West grimaced then waved her hands at it like a bad smell.

No, no. Clive St. Austenne said his wife wasn't keen on modern art. She wouldn't have been impressed with that kind of thing. So what did *Jeanette like? What was enough to let somebody in to her home late at night, drunk, after a screaming argument?*

Anna left the model and her visitor in the hallway then walked back through to the kitchen. In her mind's eye, she saw Sarah Nicholls silently watch from the shadows at the end of the garden. Leeding nodded and Sarah nodded back.

If anyone at Great Portland Street had been paying attention, they would have seen D.I. Leeding's eyes were shut, her expression blank and chest barely moved. But inside her head she examined West's house one more time.

The woman held something small. Something as small as…

Leeding imagined Sarah in the garden. Nicholls held up a camera round her neck with one hand and the autographed photo of Jeanette in the other.

A photograph. *What else do you keep in portfolio cases? Photographs. The whole of West's home was covered in her image, it was the only thing she really cared about. In her current identity, Gaye Wiseman had gone along to show Jeanette the one thing that she admired above all.* Herself. *It was a photograph of West. Jeanette knew and trusted her killer, because they* photographed *her.*

Anna's eyes snapped open, she stared down at the photos on her desk and saw them for what they were.

Now I know why the WOE IS ME note was propped up on Nick Atkey's table facing a wall, *not the door. Because that's the best angle, the best* composition.

Leeding looked through Gaye's eyes at her victims, saw them *in situ* as the killer figured out where the nursery rhyme's words should go.

That's why Gaye left the blue charcoal and why the scenes were staged, because she's taking photographs of her crimes. These murders aren't just figurative *works of art, they're literal. Gaye is curating a photo gallery she can admire and relive over and over. The blue words are the* titles *of these art works, taken from a nursery rhyme. Jesus.*

Leeding pulled out West's wooden box of memories, photos and clippings from where it had sat under her desk for months. She studied every photograph and checked for any credits. Some were stamped with the names of newspapers, others had phone numbers, a few featured company and individual photographers' names and yet more were blank. There were easily dozens, with so many leads to follow.

I could be here for days and I don't think I have the time. Gaye is building to the centre piece of her gallery and it's going to be completed sooner rather than later. But who? Who is the next subject?

Anna forced herself to slow down.

Work it carefully. Think. Maybe the visitor had a photograph to show West, so it can't have been something she'd already seen. It must have been new, a shiny bright thing to capture her attention, win her trust.

Leeding focussed on the leather book marked "DIARY" which was a record of work and appointments rather than somewhere West wrote her innermost thoughts.

OK, Jeanette, did you have a photo shoot in the weeks leading up to your death? Some pictures the visitor recently developed to show you? She opened the book and started at January 1981. There were parties and lunch dates, times and addresses but nothing concrete. February was the same, full of scribbles and shorthand.

But then, on March eleventh, she found it. "CLICKSNAP PHOTO SESSION" read the entry. "2 PM".

Clicksnap? thought Anna. *Where have I seen that before?* Then she remembered Sarah Nicholl's autographed photo of Jeanette had an ink stamp on the back; CLICKSNAPZOOM PHOTOGRAPHY.

So, CLICKSNAPZOOM, did you develop your March eleventh photo of West then drop it off the night she died? Is it you, Gaye Wiseman?

Leeding went back to Jeanette's photographs and began to re-check for any credits. There was a black and white of West, topless, with one hand over her chest, chewing her lip. On the reverse, PAUL JOHNSON PHOTOGRAPHY, HAMMERSMITH.

Jeanette at a party talking with Princess Margaret, dated 12/3/71, credited to GDJ and a number.

Some simply had a date and stamp which read © THE SUN or ©THE DAILY MIRROR.

She came to a photo of West and Roger Daltrey at the Leicester Square film premier of "Tommy."Anna flipped the pic. *Bingo.* CLICKSNAPZOOM PHOTOGRAPHY read one stamp, © THE SUN 1975 read another.

A few minutes later, there was Jeanette in hot pants and a T shirt which read "HAPPY NEW YEAR 76". CLICKSNAPZOOM's stamp was on the back with ©THE SUN JAN 76.

From the pile, Anna methodically separated out nine pictures by the same company or photographer. The earliest was from 1971 but there were none later than March 1976, which meant Sarah Nicholl's autographed picture was the latest.

The latest until Jeanette had a session with CLICKSNAPZOOM in March this year, she thought. Leeding fetched a copy of The Yellow Pages and flicked to "Photographic Services" but there was no company of that name listed. *So what happened? The business shut up shop until this year and then resurfaced for just one more session?*

Anna called directory enquiries on 192 and they had no contact listed under that name either. In a flash of inspiration she asked for The Sun newspaper's number, called, then asked to be put through to the paper's photographic department.

At the end of the line, an unfeasibly croaky East End accent answered, "William Benson."

Anna gave her name, rank and station, then asked William to call her back at Great Portland Street, extension 242, to verify her identity. One minute later her phone rang. "D.I. Leeding?"

"Hello Mr Benson, thanks for calling back."

"I thought every copper in Britain was on wedding drill today. What did you do wrong? Or right?" He laughed.

"Well, not all of us have the privilege."

"So how can I be of help to the Met? And is there a 'you scratch my back, I scratch yours' kind of deal going on?"

"If there's something I can legally offer, I will."

"I'll hold you to that. I have your name and extension number now."

"That you do. Mr Benson, please humour me. How long have you been at The Sun?"

"Since we went tabloid, 1969. "Horse Dope Sensation" was our first headline, you know."

"That sounds exceptionally Sun-like."

"It is. Why do you ask?"

"I'm trying to track down a number or address for a freelance photographic company. I've got copies of some of their photos here and a few have your paper's copyright stamp on the back."

"OK, what's the name of the company? We use hundreds of them, as well as our own snappers of course. Basically, if you take a brilliant picture, as far as we're concerned, you're a freelance, even if it's the only photo you take in your entire life. But we've used loads of people over the years so I can't promise anything."

"They're called Clicksnapzoom. From what I can gather, you bought pictures from them, approximately 1973 to 1976. I don't know how many, I only have a few here."

"Clicksnapzoom? That's a mouthful. All right, give me a moment, I need to go over to the filing system. Well, I say, "filing system," it's a cupboard in the corner I haven't opened since Lady Di was still at school. Bear with me."

Anna heard a *clump* of the phone being put down and waited. "Righty ho. You still there?"

"Still here, Mr Benson."

"The files are in a proper state. I found a couple of mentions, some payments…No phone number but I do have an address. Whether the company are still there is another matter, because the last job I could find from them was 1976, which suggests they are no longer with us."

"Well, that's very helpful, thank you."

"Got a pen?"

"Always."

"So the address I have for Clicksnapzoom in 1976 was 4A, Scala Street. I don't know that one myself."

"I do, it's near where I live, just by Goodge Street tube station. 4A, you say?"

"That's what I have."

She wrote it down.

"Mind me asking what this is about? Anything juicy?"

"Well, all I can tell you is that it's something going back quite a few years and the moment I can say anything else then I'll be phoning William Benson, OK?"

"Thanks. Are you going to get a chance to enjoy the day?"

I hope so, thought Anna.

"Oh I'm sure. Thank you, Mr Benson."

"Pleasure, Detective Leeding."

He hung up.

Anna puffed out her cheeks and looked at the paperwork now scattered across her desk. Earlier this morning she only had a hangover. Now she had something to get her teeth into. Bursting with excitement and expectation, she called Fisher and told her the latest developments.

"I don't have a number for Clicksnapzoom, but it's literally five minutes away. I'm going to go and check it out. I doubt anyone will be around…"

"I know, " drawled Fisher from the other end, "I heard there was a wedding on, or something."

"Mm, apparently. But I'd like to find out if Mr or Mrs Clicksnapzoom was at Jeanette's on the night she died and if so, what happened. If they *were*, I'm rather keen to know why they haven't come forward to tell us."

"That's the million dollar question, isn't it? Can I come and meet you after?"

"It's nowhere near lunch."

"I know but let's face it, today is the Chaz and Di show, you're hardly going to be snowed under, and I really could do with coffee and company."

Anna couldn't say no. The thought of meeting Fisher so soon made her tingle. "This company is possibly still at Scala Street, number 4A, just by Goodge Street station. Want to meet me there in, say, forty-five minutes? We could go for a late breakfast or early lunch."

"Brilliant. The further I can be from a TV today, the better."

"Same here. Bye, officer."

"Bye, *ma'am*." Anna heard Fisher giggle before the line went silent. She stood, stretched, felt her head protest again, but then the photographs on the desk gave her another idea. Anna fetched another file, found a phone number and dialled. The bell rang for around thirty seconds and Leeding nearly hung up before it was answered.

"Hello, Daniel Moore."

"Daniel? It's me, it's Anna."

"Oh, hello, Anna. I was just getting ready to go out. Believe it or not, I'm actually going to the wedding."

"Really?"

"I feel it's my civic duty to mingle with the great unwashed. Plus if I don't, my mum will be very upset. She loves Diana and has threatened me with excommunication if I don't join her, which puts me in a bit of a rock and hard place situation."

She laughed. "Don't let me stop you, then. It's just a quick enquiry. I'm at work and something's come up so I wondered if I could quickly ask you something."

"If I can help, I will."

"Ah, it's about blue charcoal."

"Bloody hell. What's happened? Have you got something new? A breakthrough?"

"Possibly. I'm looking into a photographic company called Clicksnapzoom. There's a chance someone from it went to Jeanette West's house the night she died, so obviously I'm rather keen to establish whether that's correct. I know it's a long shot and not your area but I wondered if you'd ever come across them in your line of work. They're Central London based."

"Did you say *Clicksnapzoom*? That rings a bell from a few years back. Wait, yeah, I'm pretty sure they were that all female photo company."

Anna felt a chill descend over her. "*Female* photo company?"

"Yeah, it was quite a good idea, actually. Let me think, yes, early, mid seventies kind of time. A few female photographers got together, pooled their resources. As far as I remember, the name "Clicksnapzoom," was made up of their initials, you know, Caroline, Sarah, Zara, C, S, Z; "ClickSnapZoom"."

"Why all female?"

"Why not? Also having a girl taking their photos instead of some sweaty old pervert meant the models were more at ease, you know. I suppose Jeanette West would have used Clicksnapzoom for exactly that reason. I don't think they operate any more but as you say, it's not really my area. But as far as I remember they did glamour work, showbusiness, film premiers, celebrities, in fact, they were all quite attractive, so got a lot of attention themselves. I think they even appeared in "Playboy," or one of those magazines, but not as photographers, as models. Nice work if you can get it."

"What happened to them?"

"Now you're asking. I think they must have folded a few years back but I can't swear to that, sorry."

"Can you remember anything else?"

The line went silent for a while. "You seriously think they might be involved?"

"As I say, it's a possibility I want to take further or eliminate. Their address is just round the corner, I don't have a number, so I'm going to take a look."

"Right. Oh, *Rock Follies,*" Daniel said, out of nowhere.

"Sorry, what?"

"Remember that TV series a few years back? *Rock Follies*? Three girls in a band?"

"Oh, yes."

"They were a blonde, a redhead and one with black hair. That's what the press called them, "The Rock Follies Of Photography," because the three Clicksnapzoom birds were the same."

"One was blonde?"

"I think so, pretty good looking if she's the one I'm thinking of but I wouldn't want to give you any duff information. Tell you what, Anna, let me phone around a few of my mates. I know some blokes who are in that same line of work, you know, snapping famous people, publicity shots, party doorstepping. Let me ask about, see what else I can dig up, then get back as soon as I can. To be honest, any excuse to avoid Mum and the wedding hysteria for a little longer. How does that sound?"

That sounds great, thought the hungover majority of Anna's head. *I can save myself a walk, meet Lisa, drink coffee and recover.*

"That's very kind of you. Would you mind?"

"Not at all. Wait, weren't we supposed to be having an *anti-wedding* drink today?"

"We were, but I don't think I could touch another drop for a year or two."

"That bad, huh?"

"That bad."

"All right, I'll make some calls, you sit tight and I'll phone back as soon as I have anything."

"Thanks Daniel, I really appreciate it."

"No problem at all, give me half an hour or so."

He ended the call and Anna sat back, relieved. But while the alcohol blurred half of her brain prepared to switch off, the professional part still whirred, intrigued.

She stood.

It's only five minutes walk and almost certainly going to be an empty building or some other business by now, but it's still a viable excuse to get out of this stuffy office and clear my head. I'm just taking a look, anyway, see if Clicksnapzoom's even still there. I can go back later with someone else.

If Anna's head hadn't been quite so fogged with the remains of last night's alcohol she would have taken a fellow officer along to Scala Street. Her failure to do so would prove to be a disastrous mistake.

56 / 29th July 1981, London.

Anna took the short walk to Scala Street, near Goodge Street station. Her flat off Tottenham Court Road was only a couple of minutes away. *Why don't I just go home*, she thought, *lock the door, pull the curtains, shut out wedding fever and blue charcoal for the rest of the day? That sounds like a very attractive proposition.*

It was a public holiday, which meant Central London was almost completely shut, so Anna had the pavements to herself. She knew millions of people were crammed along the procession route, The Strand, Fleet Street and especially St Paul's, but here, just a few tube stops away from the expectant masses, it was eerily deserted and silent. The sound of Leeding's heels echoed off the walls and a multitude of windows reflected her solitary journey.

July had been uncommonly overcast but as if aware of the day's importance, the sun had made a welcome reappearance. Scala Street, however, remained shadowed and cool. It was made up of dirty terraced Georgian homes and shuttered businesses, all of which seemed to watch suspiciously as she checked their door numbers. Anna realised 4A was up some external metal stairs and part of what appeared to be a Victorian building, sliced up over the years into separate and more profitable spaces.

As Leeding climbed, her shoes clanked against the rusted risers and their sound reverberated around the street. At the top was a green door, its paint flaked and faded like the dead skin of a snake. A rusted sign was screwed into the wall with a large piece of black gaffa tape across it, also curled at the edges, reptilian. Written along the tape in Tipp-Ex was one word, CLOSED. Anna pulled at one edge of the gaffa to reveal CLICKSNAPZOOM etched into the metal.

Hm, as Daniel said, it's long gone. I'll have to try Companies House.

Relieved, Anna began to descend the stairs but at that moment, there was a muffled sound from behind the door like something heavy had been dropped, so Leeding slowly turned back.In the distance was a muffled *dee-daw-dee-daw* as a police car sped to one emergency or other, but Scala Street remained hushed. Normally Anna equated silence with tranquility, but this stillness was oppressive. She put a hand on the doorknob, internally debated for a couple of seconds, then committed. The knob creaked, turned, and the door opened.

"Hello?" she said, quieter than intended. Anna realised the hairs on the back of her neck had risen, but had no idea why. "Anyone around?" Leeding almost whispered, aware she didn't actually want a response.

Stop being stupid, she commanded herself but a large part of her mind pleaded, *go and get someone else.*

She pushed at the door and that jittering area of her brain laughed hysterically. *It's a green door. Of* course *it's a green door and what's behind it? Shaky, where are you when I need you?*

Anna stepped into 4A, Scala Street.

To her left was another door, in front, a tiny reception desk with another entrance to its side. This little room was shabby and uncared for, the walls, once white, were yellowed like the fingers of a habitual smoker and the tired floorboards complained under her feet. There were hooks dotted about the rear wall, which suggested it had once been covered with framed pictures, but square shadows on the jaundiced paint were their only markers. A phone sat on the otherwise empty desk, still connected to a box on the wall. She picked it up and heard a dial tone.

Why is the door open and phone connected if this place has shut down? she wondered, *because it's* not *shut down,* the other part of her mind answered, *and what does that mean, Anna, what does* that *mean?*

Leeding backed away. There were two doors in this unwelcoming reception, left and right. She didn't want to choose either, every part of her screamed to pick the entrance and *run*, as a manic internal gameshow host chuckled, *what's it going to be? Door one, two or three? Big prize or booby prize? It's time to play, time to choose, time to win or time to lose!*

Anna chose the door to her right.

It was a dark store cupboard. She reached up and scrabbled against the wall, found a light switch and discovered the room was lined with shelves stacked with cameras, tripods, lenses, boxes of film, lights, a rucksack, and myriad pieces of photographic equipment.

Right, this place is not *closed, no, not by a long shot. Somebody wants the world to think it is, but that's just camouflage. And who do I know that's a master of camouflage? Jesus, God, Jesus, no. The door is open because* she *is here. I have made a terrible mistake. I have walked straight into her world. I am about to meet Gaye Wiseman.*

"Oh, Anna," said a girlish voice from behind her, "what *are* you doing here?"

Then everything went black.

*

Lisa Fisher padded about her little flat in Holborn with a cigarette in her mouth and a hangover in her head. Last night had been enjoyable, upsetting and liberating in equal measure. *If I hadn't been so plastered I wouldn't have said a thing,* she thought. *But good old Dutch Courage paid off. Anna opened up and stopped hiding. Well, from me, at least.*

Lisa knew exactly what hiding could do to a person after her first love had soared from a high rise. *You can't lie low forever,* she thought. *Because then you're in a constant state of anxiety. But if people like us can stop hiding from ourselves then that is a start. That is a very* good *start.*

She'd kissed Anna on the lips as they'd parted, which in itself was a dangerous, stupid, wonderful risk. Although London was mostly empty at that time, the wrong sort of witness could have meant disaster. In her job Lisa was horribly aware that gay people were beaten up for much less.

But I wanted to, she smiled to herself. *And I think she wanted it, too. Anna didn't recoil, she leaned into me. It felt right, I felt good, accepted and alive. I think we freed part of each other last night, in Great Portland Street of all places.* She laughed out loud. *In a pub called the* Cock Inn *of all names.*

Fisher opened her tiny wardrobe and looked over the few sartorial choices. They were only going for a lunchtime coffee so there was no need to go too crazy, but this also felt like *more.*

Uh huh, it feels like a date, doesn't it? She pulled out skirts and tops then held them up against herself. *Yep, it really does. Up until now, we've just been going out for drinks but now we know who we are, this is a date, so give it some respect.*

Fisher chose a denim skirt and red satin blouse. She clipped up her hair and applied a little more make up than a Wednesday lunchtime warranted. Lisa looked over her shoulder at the wall clock. *Oh, get a move on, girl, you don't want to leave your boss stood on the corner of Scala Street feeling like a lemon.*

She turned and admired herself in the mirror. *But being a little bit late, just a few minutes, turns up the anticipation. For both of us.*

Fisher smiled at her reflection and was pleased to see the grin on her mirror image was big, joyful and *real*.

*

As Anna opened her eyes and tried to focus, blackness bleached into blinding white, accompanied by sheets of pain which folded across her temples. She slammed her eyelids shut and moaned. After a few moments of rolling nausea Leeding looked again then realised she was propped against a wall with her right hand handcuffed to a pipe. Her shoes lay discarded on dirty wooden floorboards a few feet away. She'd obviously been knocked clean out of them. Through the seasick swaying of the room, Anna raised her gaze and saw a clothes rack, which was hung with many different outfits and uniforms.

I am handcuffed and I hurt, were her first thoughts. *I walked into a deserted photographic studio which...wasn't deserted at all, was it?* She experienced a rush of agony from the back of her skull, reached up, then wasn't surprised to see her fingertips were stained red.

The red stuff is supposed to be inside. I've been coshed. For the first time in my life, I've been coshed. I've never had to use a truncheon, always wondered what it felt like to be on the receiving end and now I know. It's horrific.

Anna turned back to the room, her eyes widened and she took a deep, shocked gulp of air.

Across the far wall were six huge framed colour photographs.

Jeanette West was arranged like a martyr on her bloodstained bed as a picture on the wall mocked her FACE.

Reverend Martin, photographed from almost pavement level, posed like a broken doll. Blue charcoal spelled out an acronym of FULL OF GRACE; FOG.

Nicolas Atkey, taken from one corner of his kitchen. Anna could now see why WOE IS ME had been placed upright on the table. It made the "best" composition, and led the eye to Atkey's body bent downwards as if in supplication.

There was Professor Birch, photographed flat on, contorted in his physically absurd position, head twisted never to GO anywhere again.

Wiseman had snapped Damon Whitehill from a low angle, which captured the top of his floating body while her charcoal derisively named him as LOVING.

Then there was Gaye's father Joseph, dead in his basement.

Anna realised the six pictures had a symmetry. Arranged like this, she saw how Jeanette's pose at one end was mirrored by Joseph's at the other. Both were propped up, bloodied hands to their sides, with a word behind them. In Joseph's case, it was WORK.

Martin and Whitehill's pictures also reflected each others in composition, low angled with the words just above their heads. Nick Atkey and Professor Birch's corpses were in the background and foreground respectively, arranged as counterpoints to each other. Anna slowly took in the other studio walls. They were covered with prints of the murders, taken from different positions and angles as Wiseman had obviously tried to find the perfect structure for her "installation". The six largest frames were clearly the culmination of a long and thoughtful process. If Leeding hadn't known they were real people, she would have recognised and perhaps even admired the artistic intent.

Murder as art. Gaye became the artist she always wanted to be and took the models from her broken life.

Anna pulled at her handcuffed hand but the pipe was iron and bolted firmly to the wall in several places.

"Ah, the sleeper awakes!" trilled a happy voice from one corner of the room. She turned and a figure walked slowly into her field of vision.

Languidly, Gaye Wiseman sauntered into the middle of the floor like a catwalk model then stopped, flanked by her art. This short walk had a knowing, amused theatricality about it, as if she was hitting a mark on stage for a captive audience of one.

Anna stared open mouthed, astonished to finally see Gaye in reality. Short blonde tousled hair framed a face with wide, appraising, clear blue eyes and her high cheekbones pointed down toward full, painted red lips. Gaye wore a short black jacket, high collared white blouse and a black knee length skirt. Black heels completed the two tone outfit.

"Gaye," was all Anna could say. Wiseman gave a little curtsey.

"The same." She twirled on the spot. "Am I what you imagined? I'm extremely shocked to see you, by the way. Didn't expect that, no, no, no. Sorry about the old…" She mimed bringing a cosh down on someone's head, went cross eyed and stuck out her tongue like a Looney Tunes cartoon character. "I didn't want to have to do that, but you rather forced my hand, you naughty girl."

She tick-tocked her index finger at Anna as a teacher would admonish a pupil. "Now, the absence of a horde of patrol cars and flashing lights outside makes me come to the conclusion you've acted alone and this is just a chance poke around. Would I be correct in that? Don't lie. As the Mistress Of Deceit, I am really *rather* good at spotting porkies."

Gaye pulled out a flick knife which she sprung open with relish. "If I even suspect there's back up on the way, I will cut you. Sorry, but that's my line of work. So, are you alone?"

"Yes," Anna whispered.

"Thought so. I foolishly left the door unlocked. That was a bit stupid but I think I may have got a trifle arrogant in my relative old age. I've got away with murder quite a few times, as you know. That tends to make one a little over confident."

As Gaye twirled the knife in her hand, Leeding looked closer at her adversary. Wiseman seemed very familiar, like someone Anna already knew, but in disguise.

Who are you? She thought. *I know you, don't I, but not like this. How do I know you?*

"But I like to see a silver lining in every dark and dripping cloud, so you being here is a positive. You can be my *independent witness* to verify what I have achieved. What do you think of my work, by the way? Even though I say it myself, they are somewhat on the magnificent side, don't you think?" She gestured up at her photographs like magician's assistant Debbie McGee, then did a little moue. "I know you're not an art critic but you've got to give the photographer her dues. I put these together in very difficult and stressful circumstances, like a war correspondent in many ways."

"Gaye, you need help."

Who are you? Why do I know that face?

"Oh, Anna, please. I've needed help since the day I was born. Help I never received, not from my so-called *parents, friends, colleagues* or, ha, *lovers*. You'd think I'd have eager patrons hanging off me, I mean, look."

She did another twirl. "But for some reason, I psychically repelled everyone I came into contact with. Not at first, but they all turned eventually. As I've discovered many times, beauty is not what it's cracked up to be, so don't give me your half baked Freud. Stick to detecting, it's obviously what you're good at, because you've found me. Although you never really found *me*."

Gaye became thoughtful for a moment. "Do you know what all this has been, Anna? A pantomime. And what do the audience shout about the villain, hm?" She spread out her arms and bellowed. *"They're beeeeehind you!"* Wiseman squealed and slapped her thigh like Dick Whittington. "I've been the Principal Boy all along. You know, the girl who plays Dick, Jack, Aladdin, Peter Pan. But *beeeee-hind yoo-ooooou!"*

"Gaye, I don't understand…"

"Oh yes you do-ooo!" Wiseman shouted like Widow Twankey. *"Oh* yes you dooo-oooo! Remember, I told you to sit tight and wait for me to call back. I gave you a chance to keep out of all this but you had to poke about anyway and now look at the detective, handcuffed to a pipe with a knife pointing at her face."

"You told me to wait until you…called back?" Wiseman's statement made no sense to Anna. As she tried to process it, Gaye's voice changed, became deeper, more East End. "Let me phone around some mates in the business, call back as soon as I can, you sit tight."

Anna looked at Wiseman again and suddenly realised who she was reminded of. Gaye resembled Daniel Moore's pretty sister.

No, more than that, you are *Daniel Moore's pretty sister,* she thought.

"Wait, are you related to Daniel Moore?"

"Keep up, darling. I just said I'd call you back this afternoon."

Leeding took in Gaye once again, disbelieving.

"You're Daniel? Oh my God, you're *Daniel*?"

"No, dear. I'm Gaye. I've always been Gaye. Daniel Moore was just another character I invented to escape myself, get done what I needed to. The Principal Boy, if you will."

She looked down at her painted fingernails. "Outwardly, gender is just a bunch of signs and signifiers anyway. I've become a master at it over the years, just to survive. I tried on lots of different personas, as I believe you have too, Anna. But they were all female and as we both know, the world is not kind to us girls. Look about the planet. In every single race, creed, colour, political or religious system, who's at the bottom of the heap? Us, second class citizens everywhere on account of our chromosomes. So I became a man to complete my purpose. People saw what they wanted to, what I intended them to. A bit of padding here, bit of restricting there. Five 'o' clock shadow, wig, contact lenses, make up to highlight masculinity, recede femininity. I couldn't hide it all, obviously, and I'm aware that people referred to Daniel as "David Cassidy" but as long as they thought I was male, then that did the trick. David Cassidy is a very pretty boy, but still a *boy*, yes?"

She's enjoying this, thought Anna.

"Becoming someone else is more than just surface appearances, though. It's a whole host of subtle pointers that led people to my desired assumption; attitudes, mannerisms, history, opinions, how I walked, especially how I talked. Funnily enough, the hardest part was talking."

She dropped back into "Daniel's" voice. "*Keeping it pitched right down there* was exhausting. But even though I say it myself, a *fabulous* act, don't you think?"

"You wanted to be a man? Gaye, please, there are people, doctors who can help, *I* can help, you just need to…"

"Do be quiet. I don't want to be a man, I just *appeared* to be one to get things done. Who'd want to be a man for God's sake? Blondes have more fun, as they say, but it's so much easier when you're a bloke. I was getting nowhere as a girl, you must know what that's like, so Daniel was born." She became strangely wistful. "Do you know why I chose that name? Well, back at school, I was in "The King And I" with the class heartthrob, a lad called Danny. I truly believed he was attracted to me but it was all just a spiteful, selfish act. I have concede he was quite brilliant. Such total character immersion, such focus, such *consistency*! So in hindsight I suppose he was responsible for first showing me the kind of performance that can be achieved if one wants something badly enough. Danny was killed in a car crash a few months later, nothing to do with me by the way, so I never got the chance to add him to my gallery. Therefore in *homage* I named *Daniel* for Danny. Now *Daniel's* gone, too and here we are, nearly at the end." Gaye threw a little salute Anna's way. "Thank heavens for D.I. Leeding, my star witness. You can tell the world what they did to me."

She curtseyed and waved away imaginary cheers from a fictitious audience. "No, no, please, boys and girls, it's nothing. So are you sitting comfortably? No? Shame. Then I'll begin."

*

Lisa Fisher stepped out of her flat in Holborn. Just a few roads south she could hear the rumble and cheers of millions of people who filled The Strand and Fleet Street, but at this spot it was almost empty.

A tale of two cities, she thought. *Here it's like a Sunday morning, but not ten minutes walk away, the streets are packed as if it were the end of World War Two.*

She stopped for a moment and looked up and down the road. There were no cars in sight, just a solitary Routemaster bus headed toward Tottenham Court Road. *Damn, just missed it.*

Fisher had a choice. She could take the tube, one stop from Holborn to TCR then walk to Scala Street, a journey of about six or seven minutes, or could opt for a thirty minute walk. Lisa started toward the station, but then thought better of it. *I hate that bloody place,* she grimaced. *Bloody lifts and steps, like going down into hell. Ah it's a nice day for a change. I'll only be a* teensy *bit late.*

Lisa walked on and swung her bag like she didn't have a care in the world.

And at that point, she hadn't.

*

Gaye Wiseman held up an A4 sized envelope. "I'm going to post copies of the photos and a letter explaining my actions to The Sun when I leave here, so people will know. By Monday, when all this is done and dusted, the papers will have the whole truth but you coming here today is a bonus. In fact, I even sent a little communiqué to you at Great Portland Street. A *letter* to the press is all very well but a personal account from a detective inspector, wow, you're going to be world famous, Anna, how about that? So pay attention, remember everything I'm going to tell you. I can see the headlines now, "MY HUNT FOR GAYE WISEMAN, BY THE DETECTIVE WHO FOUND HER." I just want everyone to know. That's what this has been about, you see. There's been hundreds of people who have abused me over the years, so many slights, attacks, bullying, degrading…Ah, I've lost count. I couldn't make them all pay but they will, in a roundabout way. They'll all know what they've done to me by the end of today."

"Gaye, please, stop now. What you've done doesn't change anything. The past is over, surely this can't make you feel better. In fact, it makes you just as bad as those people. You're smarter, better than that."

"Nice try, Gandhi. Non violence is all very well, but I found watching their reactions when they realised who'd killed them extremely satisfying. You see..." she said wistfully, "...I've always known I was insane. I found my way of looking at the world comforting, my ability to change and occupy whole other characters was like, well, I suppose it was like armour. It made me strong, fuck, it made me impregnable."

She stared at her photographs proudly. "Do you know how I picked these six?"

"The nursery rhyme."

Wiseman's red lips formed an "O" of shock and she gave a slow handclap. "Oh, bravo, *bravo*, Anna. How *did* you guess?"

"I didn't guess, I put it together. Lisa Fisher thought there was something about the word 'woe' and I took it from there. So you're not as clever or obscure as you'd like to think."

"Oh, I am and you know it. Pretty, isn't she, Lisa Fisher? I think she had a bit of a thing for me that night at the Gaylord, when I was Daniel."

"Daniel Moore wasn't her type."

"Oooooh, the plot thickens, how *very* interesting. So cute old Dan wasn't her type of man, or wasn't her type at all?"

"You have to stop this now."

"Says the woman handcuffed to a pipe. No, this is going all the way, so let's get back on track, I don't have all day. My Mum and Dad named me after that stupid rhyme because I was born on a Sunday. That made me bonny and blithe, happy and gay, so Gaye I became. Oh, how I hated that name, but I think it has a certain ironic *je ne sais quoi* these days. I couldn't make up my mind who was getting the chop and the rhyme stepped in to give me some much needed structure. It also gave me the titles for my art works, as you can see." She gestured up to the framed photographs. "Becoming a photographer was all part of the plan."

Gaye went over to a pile of photographs on a filing cabinet, riffled through and held one up. "This is one of the very rare photos of me as a kid. Pretty little thing, wasn't I? I'm not going to give you my whole life story, you'd need a big bag of popcorn and a maxi sized Kia-Ora for that, but let's just say, '*the hand that rocks the cradle,*' and leave it there. You wouldn't have thought anyone could be beastly to such a cute little button, could you, but no."

Wiseman gestured to the photo of dead Reverend Martin, laid out on a frosted pavement.

"I won't go into the details of what he did, but, 'babysitting' isn't the description I'd use. I found out he'd been questioned about similar...*proclivities* but nothing came of it. No matter, I was the avenging angel, waiting in the wings. Stole a car, ka-boom. Honest, the look on his face when I told him my name, it was worth the price of admission just for that."

"You can't hand out your own justice."

"Oh how high and mighty of you. But the law never handed out any other justice, did it? So what's a girl supposed to do?"

Gaye stood in front of the picture of Nicholas Atkey kneeling on his linoleum, held in place by a noose.

"Nick Atkey raped me at a party. I shoved him down the stairs afterward and oh, that felt good, but finding out he was paralysed felt even better. He was always going to feature in my gallery because a rapist is a rapist is a rapist, you know, like becoming a doctor, the title is for life. I paid him a visit as a WPC. I have my own fancy dress shop right here, built up over years." She pointed over at the clothes rack. "Just a walk on part, I didn't need much of a character for that one, the uniform does most of the work. I thought he should have been racked with guilt over what he did, so I gave him an enforced suicide."

Anna could still barely look at the noose around Atkey's neck. She glanced around the room to see if there was something, *anything* she could use, but cuffed to the radiator rather limited her options.

"Professor Birch came along next in my life, what a pompous scumbag. I wanted to be an artist, he stopped me and so I stopped him, eventually."

"I know. I found out your name after Birch died. Helen Thompson remembered you, and your art."

"You *have* been busy. She did?" Gaye seemed pleased. "Well, that's flattering. Maybe if Helen had been in charge I would have got my place at the Royal Academy and all this would have been a fever dream. Maybe not, though, I believe I was always on this course. You know, old Birchy...I particularly enjoyed that one." She looked at broken Birch almost fondly. "I knew he discreetly had *lady friends* at his place in Southampton Row, so it wasn't difficult to become a journalist and blag my way in, knowing he wouldn't tell anyone, the dirty old man. I played him like a fucking piano, pushed him down the stairs and still the oily git wouldn't die. I'm stronger than I look, which is worth bearing in mind, Anna. I do hope you're paying close attention. The papers will want to know *all* the details."

Fisher, thought Anna. *Fisher knows I'm here. Oh God, Lisa, be careful, please be careful.*

"I never made it to Art College, as I think you know. I went back to banking, yawn, yawn, but found myself a new name, address and identity."

"Joy Smart. Very clever, it took me about two seconds to work that one out."

"Ooooh, ain't *you* smart? So you know what I did, then."

"Blinded Damon Whitehill. So what crime did he commit against you?"

"Please don't say you're on his side. Whitehill was scum then, and he got worse. He liked the younger ones so I gave him fifty percent less of a chance to look, but he carried on looking and worse. You have to admit, I did the world a favour when I drowned him. I do love this picture." She gazed at Damon face down in his pool. "It took a while to get the framing right since he kept bobbing about, the cheeky lad. But it came good in the end. Well, after the fag-meets-eye incident I'd rather made Joy Smart a difficult persona to keep up, what with the police looking for her. Time to remake, remodel, but who to become next and what to do with my life whilst I put this together?"

Gaye walked back to the photograph of Jeanette West on red stained sheets, arms by her sides.

"That bitch made my life hell at school. Jeanette and her coven of pretty, petty witches. Day in, day out, they ruined my future, I failed exams, became a wreck. Was it jealousy or just evil in their DNA? Bit of both, I think. I killed her rabbit but that wasn't enough. And then look what happened, she only became one of the biggest models in the world. Well, you can imagine what *that* did to me. But she was my inspiration to become Daniel Moore, photographer."

She waved her arms about the studio. "My greatest creation. I suppose I owe Daniel a lot but even he had to die in the end. I became a man, you know why?"

"You're insane?"

"Touché, but do remember you're talking to a woman with a knife and much as I like you, it wouldn't take much to ruin that pretty face of yours. No, I became a man, and specifically a photographer because of that old phrase, 'Keep your friends close and your enemies closer.' I trained up and started a freelance photography company, Clicksnapzoom, which you obviously know, although I doubt you knew it was me behind it. All that stuff I told you on the phone earlier about it being an all female company, 'Rock Follies,' blah, blah, blah, all that was bullshit I made up on the spot, because I was trying to misdirect you. Not well enough as it turned out, but hey-ho. Daniel Moore did pretty well for himself, good looking lad, the models loved him, of course they did, he was one of them, they just didn't know. Daniel did all right as a freelancer but I was just using him to get close to my old *friends*."

She went back to the pile of photographs and picked them up. "Nobody spots the photographers you see, but it's a great way to go poking about, keep an eye on people. So over the years I was able to get reacquainted with some blasts from my past and that included Jeanette West. I'm guessing that's how you tracked this place down, from photo credits."

"Partly."

"Partly? Oh, you must tell me more but I'll finish my tale first. Back in 1971 I did a few shots with Jeanette, got to know her in a professional capacity. As you can imagine, that was weird, looking through Daniel's eyes at a woman I literally hated to death and her looking back, seeing nothing. She even flirted with me but let's face it, Daniel was a catch. If I were a lesbian, I'd have had a field day as Mr Moore." She deepened her voice again. *"I 'ad the birds 'anging off me.* So I shut down Clicksnapzoom then retrained in SOC photography. I needed to have a way into the police so once I started all this…" She waved her hands at the murder photographs, "…I could keep tabs on what anyone knew, to an extent. It was also great training on how to cover my tracks, which is why I settled on what looked like accidents and suicides. It was Jeanette West that started the whole ball rolling back in April, you know."

"How? Why her?"

"Ah, 'Dallas,' of all the bloody things, fucking J.R and his posse. I heard Jeanette had landed a job in the show, which meant in all likelihood she'd relocate to America and I'd lose any chance of making her pay. So I brought everything forward, not by much, you understand, but Jeanette could not have been allowed to escape Britain alive. I got in touch, congratulated her, wondered if I could take a few shots for old times' sake. West agreed immediately, as I knew she would, her being such a rampant narcissist."

"And you used those pictures to gain entry that night in April, when you killed her."

Gaye clicked her fingers and pointed at Anna."Bingo,baby. Obviously I thought everything was off when that stupid girly pop star Sam Bizarre was there, but they had a steaming row and he flounced out, which was great for me, it really helped give Jeanette a "motive" for topping herself. I claimed to be passing with the prints and West was *so* pissed, she never even questioned it. Jeanette made my first act so easy. You know, I was prepared to knock her out using ether, which wouldn't have been ideal by a long way but as a photographer, I can get it without any questions asked. Photographers used ether in Victorian times so that would have given me an excuse I never had to use. But she was almost paralytic, so I helped her upstairs, gave her a few more drinks then told her my real name. She tried to get away, but couldn't even stand up. Soon enough, lovely Jeanette passed out. Then I got busy."

"You were seen. By Sarah, the fan who wrote the letters, she was in the back garden."

"I *thought* I heard something!" Gaye clapped her hands together in delight. "I assumed it was a cat. Well, I never. Of course, I could not *believe* it when I was called to Jeanette's place to take the photos. It was all I could do not to burst into hysterical giggles. I mean, I'd only been there opening her wrists a couple of days before and there I was, back again, pretending to be professional and compassionate as Daniel Moore. I wrote "her" suicide note, of course. It's how *I* feel, not Jeanette."

Anna laughed to herself.

"Something funny you want to share with the class?"

"So that's why "Daniel Moore" was so helpful. You kept pointing me toward *Sarah*, didn't you, away from the real killer. It was like those fake Yorkshire Ripper letters and tapes, drawing the police away from where they should have been looking."

Gaye shrugged, spun, laughed. "Guilty as charged, but isn't it delicious? How many murderers get to suggest clues to their own investigators? I think I must have brought myself a good few weeks, even months taking you down that dead end. *Daniel* even pointed you to Jeanette's FACE picture, do you remember? I wanted to play the game, see how good you were and it turns out you're pretty...

fucking…good." Gaye reverted to Daniel's deep voice again. "You know what, Anna, *my friend*, I think Sarah should be your priority, she's your best link to Jeanette. And, oh! Guess what, I just spotted Sarah uses capital letters like the blue charcoal writing! Aren't I clever? Oh, and I helpfully went back to photograph Reverend Martin's crime scene, do take a look at the prints." Wiseman flicked back to her own light, fluttering, East End accent. "I enjoyed our drink at the Ten Bells by the way. I like you, Anna, so I hope I won't have to do anything you might regret. And now we're all up to date. Well, nearly."

"Nearly?"

"Of course. The rhyme has seven subjects, does it not? And there are only six photographs. The final photograph, alas, will be taken by somebody else, in fact, quite a few others. I do hope they make a good job of it."

"Gaye, what are you doing?"

"The final rhyme, the one that gave me my name. Today is all about the final rhyme, Anna, surely you worked that out already?"

She walked back toward the door. "Don't go anywhere, now. I have something to show you which I'm rather proud of. It's only small, but it'll make history."

57 / Wednesday 29th July 1981, London.

Inspector David Walker returned to Great Portland Street from a vehicle patrol with a sergeant. He knew Anna was also on duty so had steeled himself to ask her out for a drink and to hell with the consequences. He'd pussyfooted around for a long time and had to know one way or another if his feelings were reciprocated.

David believed they were. She'd always looked at him fondly and he'd caught her glance his way across the station on many occasions. Of course there was a chance he was being optimistic and, if wrong, the atmosphere at work could get awkward. But he was confident enough to imagine a situation where he'd tell her how he felt, she'd laugh, blush, and say, "Thank God! I just didn't know how to tell you that's how I feel, too!"

It made for a very good daydream.

Today was the perfect time to ask. Love was on everyone's minds, Charles and Diana were obviously a match made in heaven and conversation would surely move from them to more personal emotions. He rationalised that they shared so much common ground, so much *life,* there couldn't possibly be another man on earth more suited to be with her.

The negatives and positives had whirled around David's head for a long time and he couldn't keep them in any more. The inspector walked into the station with his head high and practiced a smile which faded when he saw Anna's desk was unoccupied.

"Where's D.I. Leeding?" Walker asked a nearby WPC, then realised he'd sounded more irate than intended.

"She left a little while back," the officer replied.

"Where to?"

"Didn't say, sir."

"Alone? Did she take a walkie?"

The WPC looked around at where the portable communications sets were kept. "No sir."

Walker's shoulders slumped, he wandered over to Anna's desk and was surprised to see she'd pulled out the blue charcoal file. He flicked through the papers, saw the SOC photographs and a still, sharp fear descended over him.

What's she been looking at? Or looking for*? What got her attention so much that she left without telling anyone?*

There were also publicity shots and candid photographs of Jeanette West on the desk. Walker examined them but saw nothing that gave him any clues.

She's onto something, I feel it. She's spotted a lead somewhere in this lot, but what and where?

There was a pile of nine photos to one side, all of West.

She specifically separated these out. Why?

Jeanette in hot pants, Jeanette at a film premier, laughing at a party, staring down the lens, sitting on a bike. There was nothing in their content that obviously connected them. David turned the pictures over and saw each had a credit; some an ink stamp, others handwritten, but all from the same company, CLICKSNAPZOOM.

CLICKSNAPZOOM? What has that got to do with anything?

He looked back over her desk and found a small note written in pencil, "CSZ, 4A Scala Street."

You got up in a hurry and left without a radio or telling anyone, then went to 4A Scala Street. But who did you think was there?

Walker realised he was frightened but had no idea why. David called over to the sergeant he'd just patrolled with, "Manning, don't get comfy, we're going back out."

"Sir?"

"Just get the car keys, quick as you can, son."

*

Gaye Wiseman walked out of her studio singing, "Making Your Mind Up." Anna knew she only had a few moments to do something, *anything* to take control of the situation but was trapped, handcuffed to the wall. Leeding rattled the cuffs again but clearly the pipe had been there since Queen Victoria's day and had no intention of going anywhere.

Stop panicking, clear your mind and think, she ordered herself. *You can get out of this, be calm, be clear, you have the answer. You have just forgotten it.*

Anna's head tick-tocked left to right and she blinked five times exactly.

Jeanette West's home. What happened, what did you do?

Images flickered through her mind at lightning speed.

Fisher met me at the door, I went upstairs, looked around the bathroom and the back bedroom, found the Duffy portrait…no, no, no, too early. Go further forward. You went into West's front bedroom, saw the corpse, her "suicide" note, then picked it up…

…No, you didn't just pick it up, you used…

Tweezers.

Anna reached into her jacket breast pocket. The little Swiss Army knife was there, as it had been for years, so much part of her daily furniture she'd forgotten about it amidst all the confusion.

Outside, Gaye Wiseman had gone silent but surely it was only a matter of seconds before she returned. With her left hand, Anna pulled out the knife and managed to extricate its tiny tweezers. Handcuffs are not sophisticated methods of restraint, which is why Houdini always used them. The public saw the thick chain and solid clasps and thought them inescapable but the actual lock system was a primitive square peg, turned by an equally simple key. The tweezers would perform the same function if used carefully. Leeding unconsciously stuck out her tongue and manipulated the lock peg, aware that her hand shook.

"Missing me?" shouted Gaye from outside, which made Anna jump and drop the tweezers. "Won't be a moment!" she laughed. "But I have to be rather careful!"

They were perched precariously on the edge of a floorboard. If Leeding made a wrong move, the tool would fall between the boards. She shut her eyes for a moment, concentrated and used her long nails to delicately retrieve it. Anna brought the tweezers back up to the lock, inserted them and turned the mechanism.

With a tiny click, the cuff around her wrist unlocked.

She pulled out her right hand, then unfolded a small knife from the body of the tool. It wasn't much, but had to do. Anna placed the open knife in her left jacket pocket, put her hand back up against the pipe and turned her wrist to mask that the cuffs had been unlocked. She hoped that Gaye wouldn't look too hard.

I have one chance at this and there's no cavalry coming to save me. The thought made her nauseous.

Wiseman walked back into the studio with a large rucksack, the same one Anna had seen in the store cupboard. Gaye gingerly placed it on the floor and stood back. "It's amazing what you can achieve when you really put your mind to it," she said. "Bonny and blithe, happy and gay, that's me."

*

Lisa Fisher came to the end of New Oxford Street at the junction with Tottenham Court Road.

I could get used to this. She looked around the almost empty crossroads. *I like vacant London. If only things were always this way, it would make my job so much easier. The city is fine, people are the problem.*

She checked her watch.

Bugger, I'm five minutes late. Is that fashionably late, or just rude?

Fisher picked up her pace.

*

"I have no intention of going to prison, you must know that," said Gaye. "My life has been building to this moment. I've become so many other people, I don't know who I really am anymore, but just want to leave all this behind." She sighed and it sounded like the last ever wave crashing on the last ever shore."Aaaah, 'The beauty of the world, The paragon of animals. And yet to me, what is this quintessence of dust? Man delights not me; no, nor Woman neither; though by your smiling you seem to say so.' This is my final act, the closing of the circle, one last glorious hurrah. You see, Anna, I couldn't enact my reckoning on every single person who helped destroy me. I would have been stopped a long time before I could ever complete it, I'd need a lifetime, many lifetimes and still not finish so this…" she looked proudly down at the rucksack, "…this is how all of them will know they are responsible. When you and The Sun tell my story, every single one of those *scum* will read my name and know they have contributed to my last act." Gaye turned to look at her photographs. "They will realise there is blood on their hands, so much blood. They'll be eternally haunted by their responsibility. This is my gift to them. It is all they deserve."

"Gaye, what are you doing?" Anna felt the weight of the open knife in her pocket and judged the distance between her and Wiseman.

Too far. Come closer, Gaye, come closer.

"It's a very primitive bomb," she said plaintively. "And won't win any trophies at the annual bomb makers awards. Do you have any idea how difficult it is to find any information on how to make one? They were dropped all over the world forty years ago, but is there an instruction book? The hell there is. But I had time and more importantly I had motive, so this will do just fine. There are millions of people just down the road, all crammed onto tiny pavements to get a glimpse of the *happy couple*. I just have to stand close enough and… poof." She blew on her hand and opened it like a flower. "How many will I take with me, do you think? Does it even matter? The deed is enough, the action is plenty and all of those who ruined me will never sleep soundly again, knowing they helped start my bomb ticking. So goodbye, Anna, it's been a pleasure knowing you, it really has. I like you a lot, you're one of the good people. Tell my story, and tell it well."

She carefully picked up the rucksack and went to leave.

"You forgot something," Anna whispered.

Gaye turned back. "What?"

"You forgot something," Leeding muttered. "Something very important."

"Don't get clever."

"I'm not. But if you have forgotten this one thing, what else is there?"

Wiseman put the rucksack down and walked over to Anna, but kept her distance and pulled out the flick knife again. "Talk, talk and be quick."

For the first time, Leeding faked her twitch, tick-tocked her head left to right and blinked five times exactly. It was enough to confuse Wiseman, just for a second. Gaye tilted her head to one side and tried to work out what she was seeing. "What are you doing?"

"I call it my *thing,* it happens when I'm concentrating very hard. I can't help it."

"Concentrating? Concentrating on what?"

"Look at your bomb. You've forgotten something."

Gaye turned round to check the rucksack. "What? Tell me what?"

It was all Anna needed. She leaped forward and plunged her pocket knife straight into the large femoral artery in Gaye's upper thigh.Wiseman fell to the floor but lashed out wildly with her own blade and caught Anna in the throat. Leeding grasped at the wound, aware that blood had already started to flow. Gaye's knife was wickedly sharp.

With her artery and tendons cut, Wiseman couldn't stand but continued to slash out. Anna fell and backed away from the woman who'd become a spitting, seething animal.

"You fucking bitch," she squealed. "You fucking *bitch*, what have you done? What have you done?" Gaye wailed and looked up at her photographs. "You've ruined everything. Can't you see what they did to me? Can't you understand? You're going to let them get away with it?"

"It's over, Gaye," said Anna, who held her throat and tried to staunch the blood. Wiseman began to cry. "I hurt so much," she wailed and Leeding didn't know if she was talking about the wound or her life. "I've hurt *forever* and you do this to me? You of all people should know. I know what you are, I always suspected, so you should be on *my* side. They destroyed me. Ah, fuck. *Fuck*." She began to pull herself toward the rucksack and left a trail of thick, bright blood behind her. "You stupid bitch," she panted. "Looks like it's just you and me."

Anna began to drag herself away from Wiseman.

*

Lisa Fisher stood in Scala Street and looked for Leeding. *Anna can't still be busy at wherever it was, can she? Maybe she's gone back to the station.*

Fisher tried to remember the address. *What was it called? Click click something?* She stared about the quiet street. *Was it number 3? 4?* Her gaze fell on a metal staircase and she followed the risers up to a green door. Next to it was a sign and a peeled piece of gaffa tape revealed the word CLICKSNAPZ…

CLICKSNAPZOOM, that's the place. Can't hurt to look.

Fisher began to climb the steps and at that moment, Inspector Walker's Rover turned into the far end of Scala Street.

*

In agony, crying and screaming, Gaye crawled towards the rucksack. She blocked Anna's path to the door and still held her knife. Leeding looked around for somewhere to go but the room was almost empty.

Almost.

To the left stood a filing cabinet and Anna staggered towards it with one hand on her neck and blood seeping through her fingers

"You fucking bitch," Wiseman howled on repeat. "Goodnight and thank you, you fucking *biiiiiiiitch.*"

Using the last of her strength, Leeding managed to push the filing cabinet to the floor. Photographs and papers flew into the air, and then, as the cabinet smashed into the ground, time stood still.

Fisher stood in the doorway, hands to her mouth, unable to process the scene. Lisa glanced about the room and saw Anna with blood running down her throat and a screeching female stranger who grappled with a rucksack on the ground. The injured woman looked up and smiled. "Two for one!" she laughed. "It's the WPC! Everything must go!"

"Run!" Anna yelled, but Fisher hesitated for a second. "*Run!*" Lisa backed out of the doorway, Anna threw herself behind the fallen filing cabinet and the world became brighter than a thousand suns.

58 / 29th July 1981, London.

Inspector David Walker watched with horror as Lisa Fisher flew from the metal staircase and landed on the roof of a car. At the same time, there was a bass boom as smoke and debris billowed out from the building. Walker jumped from his vehicle even before the sergeant had brought it to a full stop.

The WPC's arm was at an obscene angle to her body but she moaned and her eyes flickered.

She's alive, thought the inspector. *Damaged, but alive.*

"Take care of Fisher," he shouted at the sergeant. "Be careful, she's injured, check before you move her."

David looked up at the once green door. Smoke continued to dance out of it and papers slowly fell through the air like fluttering birds. He ran up the stairs and found himself in a scene from hell. As Walker tenderly lifted the prone body of D.I Leeding he didn't dwell on the blood and other matter that speckled the walls and ceiling. Anna was blackened, bloody and hung from his arms like a broken doll.

While the sergeant radioed for an ambulance to take care of Lisa Fisher and crowds cheered not a quarter of a mile away, Walker rushed his friend to the Portland Street hospital.

And it was there on the operating table that Anna Leeding died.

59/ ...

Darkness. Silence. *Nothing*.

60 / 3rd September 1981, London.

"Four whole minutes?" Anna whispered. "I still can't believe it was four minutes."

She sat up in bed as machines chattered and whispered around her. Leeding's face was a chaotic map of cuts and bruises, and her throat was wrapped in thick bandages. Fisher sat at Anna's side and held her hand.

"Uh huh. You're the only dead person I've ever talked to."

Leeding managed a tiny laugh then winced. Lisa's left arm was plastered and held up by a sling. Her face was equally damaged and she had two black eyes. "What does having your heart stop for four minutes feel like?"

"How am I supposed to know? The first thing I heard about it was when I came round. Dead, I suppose, I would have felt dead."

Lisa squeezed her hand and smiled. "Please don't die again, I couldn't stand it."

"I'll try not to. It's not on my list of things to do in the rest of 1981."

Fisher tut-tutted. "1981, God, I *hate* 1981. I can't wait for it to fuck off and become 1982." She held up a copy of The Daily Mirror. "But there is good news, of a kind. The papers have put two and two together to make twenty-five and are saying the explosion which has rather ruined our joint chances of becoming Miss World was possibly the result of an IRA bomb factory where one of the devices went off ahead of schedule."

"What's the Met's official line?"

"We're keeping it vague and saying, 'investigations are ongoing,' which is true, I suppose."

"So for now, Gaye Wiseman's intention of the world knowing her name and past has been shut down."

"Yes, for now. All the evidence was destroyed in the blast, her photos, equipment, files, the lot. So as far as the papers are concerned, it was as if she never existed. There wasn't much of a body to find because she was disintegrated in the explosion, lying on top of the bomb when it went off, I guess. She took most of the force, which did you a favour, I suppose. Oh, the building was registered to Daniel Moore and he's disappeared off the face of the earth. Dead ends everywhere you look. Nobody else has connected West and the rest of Gaye's victims but I'm frustrated by that, because you saved a lot of lives and nobody even knows."

"Believe me, I wouldn't want my face on the front pages again. Once was enough and I prefer to work without a spotlight on me."

"I understand."

Anna looked out of the window at the blue September sky. "Part of me pitied her, you know."

"Really?"

"Mm, Gaye never had a chance, so consumed by attacks, real and imagined, she never saw her own potential. In another universe she would have been a genius, feted, adored, but it seemed like everything conspired to send her on a different path. I often wonder what she might have been, what Gaye could have done if she'd applied that intellect and drive to something positive. You should have seen her, Lisa, she was beautiful, hypnotic, even."

"I saw enough of her in the last moments, thanks."

There was a light tap at the door and Inspector Walker entered in full uniform with flowers and a paper bag of grapes.

Fisher giggled. "Forgive me for being forward sir, but flowers and grapes? That is very cute."

"Thank you. Yes, yes." He leaned over and kissed Anna on the forehead. "You can't believe how happy I am to see you."

"Same here."Anna smiled up at him.

Lisa stood. "I'm going to ask the nurse for some tea. I'd make it myself, but…" She shrugged her shoulder and moved the broken arm up and down. "I am slightly indisposed." Fisher sighed. "All that extensive, invaluable tea making experience at the station, *wasted*." Lisa left the room and David watched her go.

"I really like her," he said. "I'm glad she's our friend. That girl is going places."

"Yes, she is."

Walker stared at Anna for a little while as a tiny smile played across his lips.

"You look like you have something to say, David."

"Well, yes. No, not really."

"Vague. I like it."

"I was just wondering if you'd allow me to take you for a meal. Once you're out of here, obviously."

"Really? I thought you meant right now."

He laughed."But not as professionals or colleagues, as, well, let's see. I don't want to talk about work."

Anna registered how uncomfortable he'd become. *I think I know what you're trying to say*, she thought, *but I can never be the person you're hoping I am.*

"OK, as *friends*," she said with emphasis. "Because that's what we are, right? What we've always been, always will be, friends."

She saw how he fought off the disappointment and her heart cracked a little for him. *But this is the kindest way and it would only make things worse if I went along with this.*

"But we could try, couldn't we?" He asked, quietly. "We've known each other for so long and there's more to us than just friends, you *know* there is. You feel it too, I know. Why can't we just try?"

Do I really have to spell it out? But if I don't say this now, will I ever? I've hidden from myself for too long, so I won't hide from you. You don't deserve it.

"Listen, this is important. I need to say something and I trust you, David. I think I trust you more than anyone else in the world."

"So trust me now. I really think we could be something together."

Anna shut her eyes and took a deep breath.

"I trust you, which is why I'm telling you this. It's something very, very few people know and very few people *should* know. So the fact I'm saying it now should prove exactly what my feelings are for you."

She could see the mix of confusion and hope on his face but pushed on.

"You and I, we could never be together the way you want. Do you understand?"

"Anna, you just don't know me, not really. You just haven't seen that side of me. And if there's something I can change, I will. Can't we just give it a go?"

Fisher appeared in the doorway and immediately tuned into the atmosphere. She went to back away, but Anna glanced over and nodded, *stay*.

Walker looked round, spotted the silent exchange and frowned.

"There are some things you can't change, David." She sighed and fixed her gaze on his. "There are some things you just are. Your eyes are green."

"My eyes?" he asked and looked around at Fisher again. "I don't understand."

"You *could* wear those coloured contact lenses, but underneath, your eyes would still be green. You'll never change them, they're you. What I am," she struggled, since saying it out loud again remained difficult, "isn't the kind of woman who should have been with any of my exes, any of those *men*. Do you see? Do you see what I'm trying to say, who I am?"

She turned to Fisher and Walker did the same. Lisa smiled. Anna watched as his expression cycled through realisation, confusion, stoicism, before settling on determination. "I think, yes. This is…I didn't know, didn't expect…You can't change? Even try?"

Anna reached out and took his hand. He didn't resist. "Green eyes, David. There are some things you can't change or would even want to."

He squeezed her hand and she spotted those green eyes had grown wet. Walker hung his head for a little while, then looked up again. "Yes, I see. I see now. Yes. Thank you," he said.

"Thank you?"

"For trusting me, telling me the truth. Thank you. It can't be easy."

Leeding smiled at Fisher, "It's getting a little easier."

Walker acknowledged the inference, looked between the two women and also smiled. "I see. Yes, it's getting easier. That's good. That's very good."

A nurse squeezed past Fisher carrying three cups and a tiny transistor radio. "Thought you might like some music or something," she said cheerily and switched on the radio.

Beep beep. T-Bom-Bom. Tikitatikatatikatatikata. Ki-Bom-Bom.

"Oh, good," said Anna."Happy memories. Listen David, I know this was…sudden, unexpected. But when I get out you *can* take me for a meal, as friends, as very best friends, and I'll tell you everything I should have years ago but was just too scared."

"Don't mind me," the nurse tactfully placed the tray down and busied herself with checking drips and IV lines.

Equally tactfully, David changed the subject and reached into his jacket pocket. "Oh, this arrived at the station for you a couple of days ago. I pocketed it because you were, er, you weren't doing well."

"That's an understatement."

He handed over a little envelope. Typed on the front was "DETECTIVE INSPECTOR ANNA LEEDING, GREAT PORTLAND POLICE STATION, GREAT PORTLAND STREET, LONDON W1." The stamp was also postmarked West One and dated

29th July. Inside was a single sheet of paper, which Leeding unfolded. Written in blue charcoal was, "I'M HAPPY AND GAY NOW, G.W."

"What is it?" asked Fisher. "Who's it from?"

Anna crumpled up the page and threw it into a bin at the side of her bed.

"Nobody," she said. "It's nobody."

The End

"Ice Age" by Grey Velvet, first released in March 17th 1981, has been rereleased by Vivid Records along with the band's album *"4FOGv,"* which was originally released September 7th, 1981.

You can hear this new, remastered version of *"Ice Age"* by looking for "Grey Velvet Ice Age" in your preferred search engine or following this link; https://www.youtube.com/watch?v=mPNzptimWRM

Anna Leeding will return for her next case in 1985, alongside Live Aid, the Miner's strike, Kate Bush, and the Sinclair C5 in *Don't You (Forget About Me).*

CULTURE IN 1981; SELECTED READING

Sweet Dreams; The Story Of The New Romantics by Dylan Jones. *(Faber & Faber)* Detailed, funny and insightful oral history of the movement that came to define the 1980s.

New Romantics; The Look by Dave Rimmer (*Omnibus Press*). Full colour breakdown of the Cult With No Name and a companion piece to Rimmer's important contemporary look at the scene, *Like Punk Never Happened* (*Faber & Faber*)

We Could Be Heroes: Punks, Blitz Kids & New Romantics 77-84 by Graham Smith & Chris Sullivan *(Unbound)*
Indispensable visual history of London nightlife with contributions from all the major players.

Future Sounds: The Story Of Electronic Music From Stockhausen To Skrillex by David Stubbs (*Faber& Faber*) Does what it says on the tin, brilliantly.

Rip It Up And Start Again by Simon Reynolds *(Faber & Faber)* This whole section is not a puff piece for Faber & Faber, despite how it looks. Fantastic look back at post-punk and beyond.

Masquerade by Kit Williams (*Jonathan Cape*) now out of print but can be found online. Beautiful, enigmatic, and you'll instantly see why Anna Leeding became fascinated by it.

ALSO BY RICHARD EASTER; THE SNOW TRILOGY

The *Snow Trilogy* is three self contained stories; *The Gentle Art Of Forgetting, The General Theory Of Haunting,* and *The Littel* Tale Of Delivering (The Sleigh).*

Although the stories can be read independently and in any order, they are connected. The 22nd of December is a crucial date across the trilogy. They all feature a mysterious box that is the key to secrets and events from hundreds of years ago impact on every work.

Love, loss, memory, and of course, *snow* weave around all three. Snow is as important a character as the individuals you will meet.

In *The General Theory Of Haunting,* snow has a sinister purpose. In *The Little Tale Of Delivering (The Sleigh)* snow is an agent of change, and in *The Gentle Art Of Forgetting,* it is well, you'll need to find out for yourself.

* Yes, it is "Littel".

THE GENERAL THEORY OF HAUNTING

Six work colleagues have battled their way through dense snowfall to reach a New Year's Eve party at a remote mansion in Dorset. Isolated with no phone signal or internet the guests' secrets and personal demons begin to surface.

But the Hall itself also has a secret built into its walls. A grand and terrible purpose, kept hidden for over two hundred years. One by one the party-goers begin to experience "events," that may or may not be other visitors.

In the following excerpt one of the guests, Anne Barker, is first to suspect *others* have been invited and they've waited a long time for the festivities to begin...

*

Anne Barker sat on the edge of the bed and watched as the snow pushed and jittered against the window. Her eyes flicked to a bag on the floor. It contained her pills.

No, she managed to think distantly. *No, too early. You just had them. You had the pills when you were supposed to have them and you're not taking them again until eleven. You know that.*

But the pills were such a welcome exit. The medication kept her blurred rather than focused and acted as an antibiotic against herself.

She stood, as she should, and tried to do what was expected of her. But what was that? To join her colleagues downstairs and pretend?

Anne walked slowly over to the desk and mirror, where she stared at an emptiness that stared back at her. She tried a smile and it looked real enough. Anne picked up a brush and pulled it through her hair, as if corralling those stray strands would bring order elsewhere.

She took a small bottle of perfume, sprayed it into the air, then watched as the droplets flew and disappeared. They were another nonexistent layer to hide behind.

But then as Anne sat back on the bed, a small creak came from behind her and the mattress shifted downward, just a little more.

It felt as if someone or *something* had also sat down. Someone or something that wanted to join her this evening.

Anne didn't move.

There was no one else here. She'd seen Dan leave but the bed had *creaked* and the mattress had *rolled* and she'd felt that movement so many times. It was a simple tilting that said, "You are not the only one sitting here. I am behind you. Look around, see, *I am here.*"

A sharp aroma came from that place. Another fragrance joined Anne in that room, similar to her own perfume, feminine, but not the same. Similar, yes, but filtered of its gentle bouquet, harder, harsher. If it were music, the scent would be *discordant.*

Anne closed her eyes. She'd had moments like this before, 'events' she'd never told Dan about in case he tried to take the pills away. That could not happen. Anne needed the pills but occasionally they magicked up these little 'performances', where reality wobbled for a moment.

Moments, seconds, yes, but never like this.

The mattress shifted again behind her as if that somebody or *something* had changed position.

Anne knew she should just look round and see for herself that her room was empty, that nothing and no one stared at her back, at her vulnerable long white neck, nobody wanted Anne to sit awhile with them and *see what happened.*

But Anne couldn't. She was frozen. Her chest rose and fell imperceptibly and she kept her eyes shut. The room was silent, save for her breath and the tiny taps of the snow as it flittered and jumped against the window.

If Anne had opened her eyes and turned her head a little, she could have seen the desk. If she saw the desk, she could see the mirror and, it followed, the reflection of whatever sat behind her. But Anne's mind was more fragile than even she knew and if something *were* reflected there, it would shatter her.

Slowly Anne opened her eyes, but couldn't turn her head. It had been fixed in place by fear. She simply stared ahead at the bathroom door. Anne breathed like her lungs were made of paper, would rip if she gulped air down like a drowner. So she inhaled softly in case the sound made whatever was sat there shuffle forward to investigate.

Don't breathe, she told herself, but simultaneously thought, *this is not real. This is the pills, this is the pills made real, nothing more. I must not look round because if I look round and there is someone sitting there, grinning, I will never come back. I will be lost, my mind will tear and I will never return. If I look round and there is a shape*

under the sheets, a shape that reaches out, I will stop. I will stop being
Anne Barker. I will stop being of this place. Just breathe. Be calm.
Breathe.

Quiet and shallow, Anne took in the barest oxygen she needed and
continued to stare at the bathroom door. She prayed her peripheral
vision wouldn't register movement in the mirror. If something moved
there, Anne suspected she'd simply sit paralysed as whatever it was
reached for her.

Anne breathed then realised she was not the only one who did so
here.

Yes, she heard it. Faraway, soft, yes, but she heard it. Something that
had no need of oxygen behind her inhaled, exhaled. The breaths
became deeper but rolled, almost mechanical, like a respirator in an
operating theatre. Human but inhuman, like the other perfume that had
filled the air, not quite right somehow, not quite of *here*.

"Oh," she managed to vocalise but it was a sound with no emotion,
it simply escaped like air, dumb in meaning.

No, no, no, she thought from afar. *I am broken. The pills have*
broken me.

The breath behind her changed. The mechanical in-out-in-out
fluttered and shifted like a broadcast picked up by a dying transistor
radio. This new sound weaved and bent but was recognisable,
nonetheless.

No, no that cannot be, Anne thought. *It is the sound of crying. Who*
is crying behind me?

A tiny part of her took control, the ancient centre of her brain
responsible for survival.

Anne Barker slowly stood, put one foot in front of the other and
walked toward the bedroom door.

If she could reach the door and turn the handle like an ordinary,
normal person, the *world* would return to ordinary and normal, too.

Such a simple thing, to open a door.

Not far, now. This 'event' was the pills. The pills that helped her
now damned her. The pills had become real.

Anne reached for the handle but stopped.

She had to look, to know this was just her mind in the throes of a
short circuit. That alone was a terrible enough idea but preferable to
the thought that something impossible waited there, just a foot behind
her back.

She closed her eyes. She would turn, face the bed, open them and there would be nothing apart from what the pills had dreamed up.

Decision taken, Anne turned with her eyes still clamped shut.

Then, from two feet in front but a billion miles away, from the other side of the universe, but here in the room a voice suddenly whispered, harshly, "You are *nothing*."

Anne tried to keep her eyes shut but couldn't.

She backed up against the door in terror and looked in the direction of that rasped, hateful statement. "Do it," that accusing voice grated like metal on metal and went silent.

The bed was empty.

She staggered a little and put her hand out to the wall.

I am lost, she thought and felt faint. She fell against the door, which was still mockingly solid. *I am hearing voices now. I am lost.*

Anne Barker, already buffeted by a storm within her, had become untethered.

THE GENTLE ART OF FORGETTING

A thirty year old woman named Jane Dawn wakes up in a hut, deep in a snow covered forest.

She has no memory of who she was, where she is and how she got there.

She is not alone.

To uncover Jane's truth and why she's in this strange new frozen place, you must jump and slide about time and space. Piece by piece, the jigsaw of her life will be revealed .

This is a tale of true love, great loss and how the tiniest decisions can have the greatest consequences. Here is part of the first chapter, where both you and Jane are thrown into the very deep end of the story.

*

Listen.

For a moment, there was something that sounded like an old fashioned kettle boiling.

Then Jane Dawn woke.

She came to, blinked and slowly her eyes focussed.

It took an effort for her to see as everything seemed blurred and white. Then she realised everything *was* blurred and white, because her vision was filled with thick snow.

Her mind was blurred too. Thought itself was an effort.

Distantly, Jane knew she was now *somewhere different*. She faced a window, *somewhere else*, and eventually managed to think, *now where am I?* But putting those words together in the correct order proved difficult.

Wherever she now found herself, it was completely silent. No background rumble of traffic nor aircraft droned overhead. No ticking of clocks or conversation in another room. Just Jane, this wood framed window, and the deepest of silences. Against it even her shallow breathing seemed a cacophony.

She looked through the window and saw a dense line of trees in the distance. Their branches drooped under a thick layer of snow.

There was an empty clearing between wherever she sat and the tree-line. No green shoots, saplings or rocks peeked from that smooth, frozen landscape.

Jane was drawn to the snow that fell outside. She couldn't pull her eyes from it.

In the sky above this frozen clearing, a green Aurora performed aerial origami, folded into shapes; a wave, a sand dune, a sheet drying in a brisk wind. Then it dispersed like ink in water. The Aurora diluted, faded and was gone.

She never saw it.

But with every flake that fell past her eyes she felt strangely comforted, as if the snow hadn't just erased the ground, but *her* too, like chalk from a blackboard ready for the next lesson.

Jane was inexplicably calm, because other than her name, she couldn't remember anything. Her memory, like the ground outside, had whited out, become smooth and featureless.

So she watched as both the snow and her mind drifted.

She had no desire to look away from this window. Jane knew there was something she should think but it was just out of reach, a lifebelt that floated one way while the drowner chose to flail in the other.

*What should I. Be thinking? I don't. Know. I am…*and then, oh so slowly, words came with difficulty fetched from part of her mind she no longer knew.

I am numb. Dumb. I am. Strung. Out. Inert. Yes.

She reached up and placed her hand flat on the window.

It was solid.

Aha, oh, take note. This is. Solid.

That was important. The window was solid. The window was real. So it followed that all this was real, too.

Outside, the Snow chased its shadows to ground, thicker and thicker.

Part of her inside, only a small part, a tiny sensible aware Jane, many hundreds of miles away, shouted, ran in circles and tried to attract her attention.

Listen! What's happening? This tiny Jane deep in her mind screamed. *What is happening to you? What is happening? What is happening Jane? What is happening you were not here you were somewhere else not here* before*, ask yourself what is happening?* Ask ask *ask.*

Oh be quiet, she thought, still oddly tranquil, in emotional slow motion. *I'm just Watching The Snow.*

And even as Jane thought that phrase she realised the words had capitals, like a heading in an instruction manual. *I am Watching The*

Snow, she thought again and there they were, the capitals, **W.T.S.** Watching The Snow, in bold, capitalised in her mind. Curious.

*You don't give a capital to a word...*she tried to remember. *Oh no, you do NOT give capitals to words...unless...the beginning...sentence of a noun...proper noun?* She stopped, confused, and stared back at the flakes.

"I think that's enough, Jane," someone spoke from behind her and she felt a rough, dry hand gently touch her face and pull it softly away from the window.

COVER STORIES
8 Classic Songs Remixed And Covered As Short Stories

Richard Easter's short story collection, "Cover Stories" offers a *literal* remix of some of the world's greatest pop songs.

The tales answer such questions as; did The Rolling Stones' "Devil" really deserve sympathy? Who was Jimi Hendrix's "Joe" and why did he really shoot his woman down? And where did The Beatles' "Prudence" go out to play? It's a compilation album on paper rather than vinyl, a chance to *read* songs rather than *hear* them.

Here's an excerpt from Richard's literary 'cover' of David Bowie's "Space Oddity," which fills in all the details of Major Tom's tragic life; who the major was, how he became an astronaut and why he became lost in space.

In this part of the story, we join David Jones, nickname, *Major Tom,* shortly before take off...

8th January 1947, Heathrow Space Dock

This was it. Showtime. And what a show it was going to be, courtesy of the world's greatest circus. The audience were ready, the drumroll had begun, and the spotlight was on him and him alone as he waited higher than any trapeze act.

No-one could stop the show now. He'd been checked and rechecked, taken protein pills and given cardiograms. He'd put his helmet on, ready to be waved off. David Jones had prepared for this moment forever, it felt, but now Major Tom was ready. Ready for what, though, he still didn't know.

8th January 1947, B.S.N. Ground Control, Brixton.

The children filed into Observation Room Six. There were thirty of them in all, aged between six and fifteen.

O.R.6 resembled a large white classroom, complete with rows of chairs. Painted across the back wall was the logo of the British Space

Navy, a stylised rocket with a Union Jack nosecone. Underneath, three italicised letters, *B.S.N.*

A man in his mid thirties wearing a tweed suit, stood at the front. He bounced on the spot, excited, eager to begin.

"That's it, children. Welcome! Chop chop, find a desk, quick as you can. Twenty-five minutes until launch!" He clapped his hands together impatiently, looked through a window behind him and gestured at a room below.

"Down there, children, are the people about to put the first ever human being in space. This is Brixton, Ground Control, today is 8th January, 1947 and you know your job. You are here as witnesses to history."

The children had been specially picked as part of Britain's "Future Legend" programme, that ensured major events within the British Empire were witnessed by the very young who would then pass on those experiences over their many decades to come. Since the thirties, British children had been invited to watch most of the Empire's epoch defining events, to mythologise them into legends for the future.

They watched Ground Control intently. Most of the people down there sat behind ugly control panels comprising equally unwieldy dials and switches. It was *very* British. Dials were politely turned, switches carefully thrown, the occasional cup of tea sipped and biscuits nibbled.

"Busy, isn't it?" asked the man. "But I'm getting ahead of myself. I haven't even told you my name. I am Terence Jones. Terry. I am the brother of David Jones, soon to be the first man in space."

He knew that would get their attention. There were a few gasps and a couple of uncontrolled whoops of excitement. Hands shot up to ask questions.

"Yes, a few miles west at Heathrow Space Dock 1, my brother is sitting on a Jupiter 8 rocket ready to be the first person in history to leave this planet."

Terry had just jumped several hundred places in the children's estimation. One young boy couldn't help himself. He jittered in his seat and his hand fluttered for attention like a trapped bird.

"Your brother, sir? He is your brother? He is Major David Jones? So why does everyone call him Major *Tom*?"

Terry took a moment.

"Ah yes. Major Tom is the nickname my brother had since...a while back. You see, there is a character called Tom Jones, from a book by an author called *The History Of Tom Jones, A Foundling.* In his younger days my brother, David Jones, reminded people of this character. He was, er popular with women. So instead of Major David Jones, they started calling him Major *Tom* Jones, you see?"

Terry looked down at Ground Control and thought; *please take care of my brother. Because I don't think he can take care of himself.*

Heathrow Space Dock, 8th January, 1947.

David Jones, "Major Tom", sat in his capsule, alone.

He could only see two small circles of sky through the windows of his capsule. *If something were to go wrong,* he thought, *this would be my last ever view of Planet Earth. Just blue. No trees, no seas, no people. Just this endless blue. Maybe when I get up there I'll see what eternity looks like.*

Jesus, David, calm it down. You don't suit pretentious.

He shook his head. Those kinds of odd thoughts wouldn't do. He often drifted like this, away from the moment into other realities. He didn't know why. It puzzled him.

It's almost as if there is another David Jones somewhere and we meet in our dreams. David thought. *In other universes, maybe many different versions of me exist. Perhaps,somewhere, I am a leader of men, or, in another reality I'm just a simple singer. Or maybe elsewhere I'm just a clown. Perhaps. Probably not. If there are other versions of me, I hope* they *are happy.*

"Twenty minutes until launch," said a voice in his headset. It was Pitt, flight director at Brixton Ground Control. "Everything is across the board here. Slight drop in air pressure, nothing in red range. Ah, as you know, your wife is here."

David silently carried on with his checklist.

His headset went dead for a moment. There was a crackling noise and angry squeal of feedback before Pitt's voice came back on line.

"We were on public comms, David. I've switched to private but I can't do it for long. Just talk to your wife. You agreed. Talk to Angela."

"You know I have nothing to say to her." David grunted.

"It's a British Space Navy order, as you know. She's on in ten seconds. Going back to public comms now."

David sighed. It was showtime. The world was listening and he had no choice but to give this performance.

"*Darling*," she said breathlessly. Even now she sounded like she was flirting. David knew she was, with the entire planet.

"Hello, *darling*," he answered equally aware of the millions of strangers listening.

"I just wanted to say God speed and how everyone is proud of you. None prouder than me."

"I just hope I live up to everyone's hopes."

"You will."

"Remember, David, this may be one small flight for you but it is a giant leap for all mankind."

Oh, bravo, David tried not to wince. *That'll be Angie, staking her claim on the history books. She must have sat up late for nights on end thinking of that. I need to do better.*

"I am just one man," he improvised, wildly. "But through me, Man*kind* will fly. To the stars! Farewell for now, my darling!"

A tiny light on the camera above him blinked twice and went out. The camera was blind.

A crackling in his ear told David the radio frequency had changed. Now the rest of the world was deaf for thirty seconds.

David waited for his wife to speak again. He was in no rush. Let the seconds tick away then the world come back into his capsule.

"Oh, well done, David, good line." Her voice was suddenly tinny and small in the headphones. For a moment, his heart fell away from him, aching, beating for what could have been.

He watched the clock count down.

"Where are you watching from?"

"I won't be watching. David. You know that. I still have no wish to see you die."

"Really? That surprises me."

He knew that now was not the time, but couldn't help himself. Successful mission or not, this was it. Goodbye, in thirty seconds.

He had too much to say and had tried to say it for some time. But it had never come out right.

"Enjoy your life, Angie."

"I will. Whatever happens, you know I will."

"You always did."

"I tried, David."

"You tried for you, Angie. You always did everything for *you*."

She sighed, a long, whooshing sound, a lonely wave crashing on a distant shore.

"Ashley would be proud."

"Goodbye Angie."

"David…"

The comms line crackled again and there was a brief hum before Pitt returned to David's ear.

"Jupiter 8, we're back on public comms, *public* comms, Jupiter 8. We're starting main pumps. Please engage."

David Jones, Major Tom, sat in his tin can and prepared for blast off. He felt more alone than ever. *I'm about to be the first man in space, but I feel like the last man on earth.*